Queen Mother, Ms. Thang, Sista-Girl . . .

"Each of these dimensions is in all of us. The demand is to determine which dimension should be called upon in answer to the daily situations life confronts us with. The next demand is to strike a balance, an inner harmony among the dimensions, so there is not one that is continually subordinated or superior. Ironically, it is once this inner accord is acquired that we are our strongest and most dynamic. . . .

Life is frightening, yes. But if we, Sista-Girls, Ms. Thangs, and Queen Mothers, are to serve on the thrones that are rightfully ours, we must rise to the occasion and look life straight in the eye, going toe to toe and head to head. You're frightened? Fine, be afraid, but don't let that stop you."

—Max Elliott in *Ms. Thang, Real Knights Don't Show Up at 3 in the Morning*

For orders other than by individual consumers, Pocket Books grants a discount on the purchase of **10 or more** copies of single titles for special markets or premium use. For further details, please write to the Vice President of Special Markets, Pocket Books, 1230 Avenue of the Americas, 9th Floor, New York, NY 10020-1586.

For information on how individual consumers can place orders, please write to Mail Order Department, Simon & Schuster Inc., 200 Old Tappan Road, Old Tappan, NJ 07675.

MS. THANG,

REAL KNIGHTS DON'T SHOW UP AT 3 IN THE MORNING

WHAT EVERY BLACK WOMAN NEEDS TO KNOW ABOUT LOVE, INTIMACY, AND RELATIONSHIPS

MAX ELLIOTT

POCKET BOOKS
New York London Toronto Sydney Tokyo Singapore

Names and other identifying characteristrics of certain people mentioned in this book have been changed to preserve their anonymity.

An *Original* Publication of POCKET BOOKS

POCKET BOOKS, a division of Simon & Schuster Inc.
1230 Avenue of the Americas, New York, NY 10020

Elliott, Max.
Ms. Thang, real knights don't show up at 3 in the morning : what every black woman needs to know about love, intimacy, and relationships / Max Elliott.
p. cm.
Includes bibliographical references
ISBN 0-671-00235-X (pbk.)
1. Man–woman relationships—United States. 2. Afro-American women—Psychology. 3. Afro-American women—Sexual behavior. I. Title.
HQ801.E397 1997
306.7—dc21 96-48421
CIP

First Pocket Books trade paperback printing February 1997

10 9 8 7 6 5 4 3

Cover design by Lisa Litwack
Front cover illustration by Elisa Cohen
Back cover author photo by Arthur Coleman

Printed in the U.S.A.

dedicated to Queen Mothers Lady,
Reenie, and Ginger

I wouldn't be without
your love and wisdom

Acknowledgments

first and foremost, to the One and Only, I will always be a most grateful and humble servant.

to my husband, the strongest, craziest, beautifulest, blackest man I know; a fellow trekkie, nihilist, and info hound, I'll love you forever for bringing me home.

to my sister, stephanie, whom I can always count on to keep me grounded, I finally found the words to describe our most special relationship (you know where they are) and ya better know you're my numero uno sista-girl!

mom and dad, thank you for providing me with the symmetry of poetry and mathematics.

miss addie, that first phone call couldn't have been made without you—here's to good Karma! and pocket books sista-girls joan and pam, your support was invaluable—I hope I continue being worthy.

to the rest of my strong, supportive, large, and extended but, oh, so close family, just keep on being the positive examples you have always been, and Spirit will see to the rest.

my friends, ms. thangs, sista-girls, queen mothers, brotha-men, and mr. men all, your faith was unwavering and ya know i'm gonna always be there for you, too! let's keep riding the wave! and a special lovebug hug to my girl, ms. v. smith—time to partyyy!

to my agents, ling and ed, your direction, ability to laugh with me, and tolerance of my anxious faxing and worrisome phone calls has made this a blast! ya know I got the fever now, so I won't stop till my fingers fall off!

for the editorial team julie, leslie, amy, and penny—all of my hats off to you, and may God bless you for letting me speak.

to those who lent me their voices and visions for this work, as keepers of the wisdom, I pray you keep spreading the knowledge, and I thank you for all of us.

big daddy, gran-gran, paw-paw, uncle bob, aunt donnie, and ms. thang, david—you will forever be in my heart and forever a part of everything I do. and lil' mama, I'll always do my best to take care of him.

peace and love always,
ms. max

to love others, one must love first
and foremost thyself

Contents

PART 2: UNDERSTANDING OUR SEXUALITY

PART 3: LOVING OUR MATES

A Note to the Reader

I discuss many personal experiences in this book, and when first drafted, I used the term "mate," not wanting to alienate those of you who are heterosexual because of a sexual bias you may have, nor wanting to alienate those of you who are homosexual because of a similar but opposite bias you may possess. Since then, I have wed and am proud to acknowledge that fact, so please don't hold my sexual orientation against me. I love you both and have something to say I want you both to hear.

Black people have lost a lot due to our forced ignorance. Sometimes not knowing compels you to look further and, consequently, gain more.

I witness the pain
experience the suffering
hear the pleas . . .

Introduction

While talking the other day with some friends, a brother commented that in no other time in history have so many women rejected or, even worse, taken the lives of their children for apparently self-seeking motives. I tend to agree.

In the streets of my hometown, Chicago, like in the streets of most major cities . . . when a two-dollar high is more important than the child who comes from your womb, when the man you sleep with becomes more important than the life you have brought forth from your loins, when the love of self is beaten down into disgust for that from which you were born and that which you bear, enough is enough. Something needs to be done; something needs to be said. So, in one of the few ways I know how, I answer the call.

It's the call that rings in my head when mother and child are gunned down because of a drug war; its ringing is telling me to explain to my sisters that the luxuries purchased with drug money and the expedient way in which it brings about a lavish lifestyle are time bombs (and you never know who else is going to be with you when the explosion occurs). It's the call that rings in my ear when sisters talk about trading in their three-year-old automobiles for a new car; its ringing is telling me to advise them to finish paying for the car they have and set their sights on purchasing something that will *appreciate* in value, like a home, perhaps. It's the call that rings in my ear when I hear sisters disparage each other because of cosmetic and/or lifestyle differences that may exist between them; its ringing is telling me to inform them that cosmetics and lifestyles are choices not to be judged by anyone except those wearing or living them. It's the call I get when I hear brothers say, "Sisters need to be more patient and understanding" and when I hear sisters exclaim, "Brothers need to get about the business of taking care of business"; its ringing is telling me to bring brothers and sisters face-to-face because there is a most apparent need for sincere, loving, and constructive dialogue.

It's the call ringing for me to help ease the peer pressure many of my brothers and sisters are feeling, ringing for me to take some friends across the tracks and make even more friends, ringing for me to inform my sisters about the two faces of sexual activity, ringing for me to warn all whom I encounter about the dangers of things with two faces. Yes, Lord, it's a mighty big call. But somebody's got to answer the phone. I just can't leave y'all hangin', right?

Karen had the biggest, brownest eyes with the longest, thickest lashes I had ever seen. We met some years ago while in beauty school, two Ms. Thangs out to conquer the beauty industry and the world! The first two months of hangin' were too much fun! Karen, always perky and bubbly, knew how to party! We drank, laughed, and danced north, south, and west (Chicago's "East side" is Lake Michigan). But as I recall now, we did close out one night of partying on the lakefront, too, watching a brilliant orange sun rise over cool, breezy, sobering waters. We dumped our empty bottle of Grand Marnier, grabbed some burgers, fries, water, a "Happy Meal," and picked up her three-year-old daughter, Aisha. Then we drove to The Point, where the three of us sat, strolled, and waded.

Little Aisha loved playing in the water. Her tiny toes and fingertips were beet red by the time Mommy could cajole her away, using a small chocolate milk shake and fresh salty-greasy-smelling French fries. Smiling, the toddler took a potato sliver and sipped on the shake for a few seconds. She then giggled and ran back into the water. Karen gave up trying to keep the child from the water, so she and I just sat talking and watching this small creature enjoy the lake. We discussed my owning a salon and her finding a good daddy for Aisha and finally, as of the night before, her being able to dump her no-good, drug-dealing, abusive ex-boyfriend.

On another occasion, Brenda, also from beauty school, invited us to a party. We arrived the following Saturday evening at a beautiful town house, oozing with beautiful people and offering a more than generous bar. Brenda asked us if we would like to join her and her friends in a limousine parked out front for champagne and caviar. Out the door we went, into the cushiony, backseat of a white, stretch limousine with personalized license plates. Not only was there caviar and champagne but there were also pink hearts, Ts and blues, marijuana, and a *Scarface*-like mountain of cocaine. I don't remember much about that night except suffering from extreme paranoia.

From then on, our duo turned into a trio. The three of us went out almost nightly for about two weeks, and then I had to chill. My body, my mind, and my spirit, not to mention my studies (yes, cosmetology requires reading and writing), needed severe attention. But Karen kept going. One afternoon I let Karen and Brenda persuade me to go with them after school to a party at the home of a friend of Brenda's. It turned out there was no actual party, and Brenda just wanted to trade me (sexual intercourse with me, that is) for narcotics. She and Karen wanted some blow but couldn't afford it. So they decided to visit a friend who Brenda knew would have some and would share it if they brought the right kind of female along. Karen apparently didn't know this was the deal and didn't appreciate the gesture; I didn't like it at all and decided to leave Brenda and her parties alone for good. But Karen didn't.

A couple of weeks later rumors began: sexual threesomes involving Karen, Brenda, and different guys; Karen's no-good ex-boyfriend coming back on the scene and giving her hell, once again; and other nasty stories that I paid little attention to. Karen had a daughter and knew what she was doing. At least I thought so until a friend from school phoned me one Sunday afternoon. A drug deal had gone sour, and, somehow, Karen was involved and had been gunned down in a telephone booth. "Where is Brenda?!" I screamed into the phone.

Nobody knew. It seemed she had just stepped on the gas and sped off, leaving Karen cold, bleeding, and alone to die.

Before she died, Karen's last month at school had been a bad one, too. She'd missed several days and was always complaining about being tired. Well, now she's resting, no longer having to face the seemingly difficult choices peer pressure provides. Even young women in their twenties (especially those in search of self) have peers they emulate or want to emulate. Unfortunately, Karen's emulation was fatal.

And I am compelled to answer the call. . . .

Adrienne was the sharpest Ms. Thang I'd ever met. Of all the friends I went out with, I just knew, as did Adrienne, she would get what she wanted out of life, first and foremost. After all, she had traveled and lived abroad in her teens, had acted on and off for several years, and all the guys loved her whenever we went out. She always appeared to be the most savvy and the most sophisticated.

Yes, she insisted, she would not settle for anything less than the best. You could tell she meant it, too. Tall, immaculately groomed, brown, stunning, with high cheekbones, flawless skin, the best of human-hair weaves, Adrienne dated only affluent white men, and when we socialized, it was at the most popular places, where only the to-be-seen people would meet. She lived in the Near North area of town called the Gold Coast. At the time, it was the hottest, most convenient neighborhood in Chicago, and Ms. Thang insisted on taking a taxi or walking wherever she needed to go, claiming that if she couldn't take a taxi or walk to where she was going, it wasn't worth her time and energy.

She suffered from what a lot of my brothers and sisters suffer from in Chi-town, *across-the-tracks-itis. Across-the-tracks-itis* is a kind of discrimination that prevents many folks from venturing outside of their residential neighborhoods. Blacks on the South Side feel brothers and sisters living north or Near North are trying to be white, while many blacks living north or Near North wouldn't be caught dead on the South Side. So whereas Adrienne could probably get a taxi to take her south, it wasn't worth the effort, time, or money to her. *She felt nobody who was anybody lived south.*

Her most famous suitor, Joel, a very nice white guy who owned a chain of small businesses, took care of all of her needs, buying her furs, fine jewelry, and taking her out to the finest dining establishments. And while Ms. Adrienne toured Europe for six months (an all-expenses-paid tour sponsored by Joel), he made sure her superbly decorated flat, along with her Persian cat, was waiting for her when she returned.

One afternoon while we were out having lunch, Adrienne arranged for me to visit the condominium he promised to buy for them. I was, of course, impressed.

A few weeks after viewing the condo I asked her when they were going to be closing on the deal and if they needed any help moving. She told me she wasn't moving anywhere and, in fact, she wasn't seeing Joel anymore. I was flabbergasted. What had happened?—they seemed so happy. She said he kept procrastinating about marriage and she was getting bored, anyway. The relationship was going nowhere; he wasn't ready for a commitment; so she broke up with him.

Funny thing, though, a few weeks later I dropped in to give my sister, Stephanie, a quick hello at her job at a very posh restaurant on Chicago's Magnificent Mile, and I saw Joel. I didn't go over to speak to him because he was sitting very cozily with an absolutely gorgeous blonde woman. I asked my sister if she knew what was going on at that particular table—hostesses always know the scoop on clientele. She said the couple had just returned from their honeymoon in Bermuda and was still celebrating. I asked her if she was sure, and she said she was positive, showing me the notes by their reservation reminding the hostess of the celebration and to give them a complimentary bottle of champagne: *Mr. and Mrs. Joel Levine.*

And I am compelled to answer the call. . . .

When a friend, William, first introduced me to Tina, I was somewhat taken aback. Eighteen years old with drawn sallow skin, fingernails bitten down to nubs, red glazed-over eyes, and slurring speech, she looked and sounded as if she had just finished off a pint of gin. As a favor to her mother, whom he worked with, William was tutoring Tina for the GED examination. She had dropped out of school to have a baby and found it difficult to get a decent job without a high school diploma.

"Isn't she getting any help from the baby's father?" I asked.

"She's not quite sure who the baby's father is," I was told.

"Does she have a boyfriend?"

"Yes, there's this one guy who's crazy about her and the baby, but she doesn't really like him because he doesn't [perform well in bed], and he doesn't like to get high."

"Oh."

While talking weeks later, William asked me, "What would you think if you and your man—whom you've been sleeping with for a couple of years and who says he is in love with you—were engaged in foreplay, and for the sake of exploration, you tried to go where most heterosexual men don't want anybody going, but you were successful, and, furthermore, he responded like he enjoyed it, and you then [we'll say, expanded the horizons] and he went wild and [climaxed]?"

"I would be pissed off because this man is obviously bisexual [most heterosexual brothers are not so comfortable with their sexuality that they'd allow for the pleasure of something being inserted into their anuses] and has been deceiving me throughout the duration of our relationship."

"That's what I thought."

"Now, who's this about?"

"Tina."

"Did you ask her how she felt about her man being bisexual and supposedly in love with her?"

"Yeah, and she said that it didn't really matter because he was so well hung and had fire weed."

"She needs help."

"Yeah, especially since her mom threw her out, *again.*"

Sometime later, as we were shootin' the breeze over soda and pizza one day, I asked William how Tina was, hoping he would tell me she was in therapy.

"She just got out of the hospital."

"What happened?"

"She decided to leave the bisexual boyfriend alone and deal with the brother who really cares about her. He makes a lot more money than the bisexual, which means when he's not around, she can always buy weed with the money he gives her, instead of taking money from her mother's purse, like she used to do. She softened him up by telling him that she loved him and that he was the only one she was seeing from this point on. But then the bisexual guy comes by one day, and he and Tina smoke a bag of weed. They end up in bed, and he's still in her bed when the other guy she's sworn her love to stops by to visit her and the baby. Her mother comes downstairs to get her, finds ol' boy in her bed, and goes upstairs and tells this other guy that she's downstairs . . ."

"Her mother, I thought her mother threw her out?"

"She did, but her mom has a soft heart for the baby and Tina promised to get her act together. Anyway, when the other guy gets into the basement, he sees Tina in bed with ol' boy but says nothing, just turns around and leaves. They evidently didn't even hear him come down. But turns out that he's not really gone. He waits for the bisexual guy to leave and for her mother to leave for work. Then Tina is walking to the store and he commences to beatin' her ass all up and down the street with the butt of his forty-five until some brothers finally grab him and somebody calls the police."

"Shit."

A few weeks later William and I were gabbin' again, and he asked me, "If your period is usually regular, but you haven't had one for six months now; you've been experiencing chronic, sharp pains in your stomach; and your vaginal discharge has become yellowish and bloody for a couple of months, would you think that something is wrong?"

I looked at my friend squarely in the face and said, "Let's not talk about Tina anymore, okay?"

And I am compelled to answer the call. . . .

* * *

I miss David, sorely sometimes. He was my nail tech, confidant, and wine-tasting pal. Although he wasn't very attractive when we first met, you could see that at one time David was a strikingly handsome man. Remnants of his beauty were still visible—thick, black curly hair; deep-set, hypnotic green eyes; a chiseled jawline, a prominent nose, full luscious lips; and some definite muscle on a slender five-foot-eight frame.

And, oh, the tales he could tell. About his Creole grandmother and that crazy Irishman she married; about his most recent conquest, a famous stylist who had just bought a condo in Jamaica and paid in cash; about his most recent ex, a leather-boy from the West Coast. Oh, and did we chuckle but good when he called my honey a *baby doll.*

David was badly beaten once, a victim of gay bashing. The cuts and scrapes on his knuckles and knees made me hate hate-filled people. But when he continued on about how he fought off four guys by himself with a broken beer bottle and his combat boots, and how they looked much worse than he, I joined him in a celebratory, snap, snap, high-five.

I loved visiting with David, not only to be serviced, but often to just sit and gossip and people watch. His station was in front of a huge picture window overlooking State Street.

Occasionally, we would go to a wine bar and try various vintages until it sounded as though his tongue had swollen to fill the entire cavity of his mouth. And poor me, things kept doubling right before my very eyes. So he would walk me home, both of us laughing hysterically at nothing and everything.

Once I went for my regular appointment and he had called in sick. When I saw him the next week, I felt immeasurable relief.

You see, David had AIDS. I knew it the first time he serviced me. His cuticles were rotten; his teeth were a dull ivory and decaying; his body often racked with chills, after which he would hold his chin just a tad bit higher. Sometimes when we laughed hard, it would turn into a coughing fit for him. I simply made sure he had enough water and passed him a tissue.

I tried getting to know more about David—where he lived, his home telephone number—but he was a proud man and wouldn't let me in on his tragedy.

Then, one Saturday I popped in to say hello and no one had heard from nor spoken with David for days. Days eventually turned into weeks, and weeks into months. Eventually I found out David was gone for good.

And I am compelled to answer the call. . . .

Through blessings, hard work, and perseverance I have endured as a relatively successful black woman. Now it is time for recompense. Here, my sister, are the keys, wisdom, and experiences that have helped me develop and continually enjoy relationships of all kinds, even in this color-sex-gender-religion-youth-struck American society. And having meaningful, productive relationships is one of the primary determinants of success in life.

However, before I begin, let me say to all of you, when it comes to having loved and lost, you're not alone. When it comes to friendships that didn't deserve to be referred to as friendships, as the individuals didn't deserve to be called friends, you're not alone. When it comes to goin' through all the gyrations of lovin' black folks and tryin' to get some lovin' back—even if it's just a little bit—you're not alone.

I've cried over guys who I eventually learned weren't worth crying over, and then I got pissed. Being too immature to understand looks aren't everything, I've walked away from men who promised me (and had the wherewithal to deliver) the ocean, the moon, the stars, and everything in between, and then, once I matured and it was too late, I *really* got pissed. I've also caught lovers cheating on me, and then, of course, I got even.

Individuals posing as do-gooders have used me for their own gains, and when I stopped letting them use me as an area rug, they tried defaming me and even tried hurting me through hurting my loved ones. I've lost friends and relatives to terminal illnesses and instantaneous tragedies, seen beautiful black women turned inside out by destructive relationships, and watched the hope of having good lives ripped away from little black babies because their parents were uneducated in the ways of positive parenting.

There were days when I stayed in bed because I found no reason to rise; holidays when I stayed at home, alone, because I could see no reason for joy; moments when I questioned my reason for questioning my reason for being. But I always managed to get up eventually. Either I prayed and cried until I was so tired of prayin' and cryin' that I found my two feet again, or there was someone who loved me enough to show me the way out of that particular funk.

Who am I? I am you, your sister, your daughter, your mother, your grandmother, your best friend. I am a black woman telling you that if I found my way through and out of cow dung, and believe me I've been in it up to my eyeballs, you can, too. You must. We must. Our future, the future of our children is depending on it.

In this book I try to return our attention to where it should be—to nurturing ourselves and each other. I delve into the three-dimensional soul we sisters seem to have and explore finding the balance between those dimensions: Queen Mother, who brings us wisdom and stillness; Ms. Thang, who provides us with confidence and sophistication; and Sista-Girl, who equips us with strength and humility. Allowing for the mature development of these three personae permits the love we need to find its way to us naturally and stabilizes our efforts, so we are not so exhausted and give up, so that instead we have natural and Divine energy and vision, boundless in quantity and scope.

African-American women are strong, magnificent, human beings when working positively and constructively. When Sista-Girls, Ms. Thangs, and Queen Mothers come together, no obstacle is too large and no detail is too minute. We are creators and our community depends on us.

Yes, African-American men, our men, have been the recipients of devastating blows, and when the black man is attacked, it is an attack on the black community. But are we to underscore the attack by turning our backs on them? Are we to deliver one more blow to them and our people by giving up on life completely because the fathers of our children can't be with us, for whatever reason? Are we to act as cowardly accomplices by shutting our eyes, our ears, and our hearts and by hiding in our private cul-de-sacs, hoping we can always depend on being perceived as being *different* from *the other* African-Americans? Or are we to rise up, as Sista-Girls, Ms. Thangs, and Queen Mothers, holding out our hands, our love, our energy, and our wisdom so that the weak in our communities (be they men, women, or children) can become strong?

On October 16, 1995, legions of beautiful black brothers traveled to Washington, D.C., to stand up and acknowledge the love, respect, and responsibilities they felt for their families and communities. Enough is enough they said. I agree.

Now it is time for black women also to rise again and show our brothers they are not alone. Sisters have been standing for a long time, even carrying the weight, but it's time for us to get moving—forward.

To help us along the way, in this book you will find insights and experiences from mothers, grandmothers, brothers, and sisters whom I conversed with. My purpose is to show black folks the need to return to some traditional thought—*our* traditional thought—if we are to move forward, and to explain that we, indeed, want to unify. Despite how it might appear, brothers want to be closer to sisters. For this to happen, it's just going to take a lot of EFFORT from both sides. And through the love and energy I bring to you, I hope you can find the way to join me in relating to one another, sister to sister, sister to brother, human being to human being, through honesty and thoughtfulness and positive emotion, so we can complete the task that was set before us so long ago and that we've digressed so far away from. So we can create a forward moving, unified, glorious people.

I pray daily for everyone in this confused, technology-driven, socially-depraved world because although one individual can make a difference, the entire conscience of humankind needs to be elevated and only Spirit can oversee this particular commission.

When I talk about Spirit in this book, I am referring to God, Buddha, Allah, Jehovah, Yahweh, whatever you want to call It. As I discuss the Universe, I mean God's world, not just this ol' planet, galaxy, and universe. I discuss It more here than I ever do publicly because the relationship between me, God, and the Universe consumes my heart and everything else in my small world, so I need not profess. Moreover, I do not hold one spiritual ideology over another; I am no preacher, nor am I omniscient. I am aware, however, that ultimately only through our connection with the Creator can we achieve harmony and peace in ourselves, with each other, and within our communities. So it is paramount to discuss keeping that connection with Spirit alive and open on all channels.

And I quietly and humbly try to answer the call. . . .

Perhaps you have noticed that even in the very lightest breeze you can hear the voice of the cottonwood tree; this we understand is its prayer to the Great Spirit, for not only men, but all things and all beings pray to Him continually in differing ways.

For the Great Spirit is everywhere; he hears whatever is in our minds and hearts, and it is not necessary to speak to Him in a loud voice.

—Black Elk, holy man of the Ogala division of the Teton Sioux[1]

Our Kingdom

As I often mention throughout this book and discussed briefly in the Introduction, we are born into this world as Queen Mothers, Ms. Thangs, and Sista-Girls. These colloquial terms may seem derisive to some, but they were conceived by individuals recognizing the spiritual wisdom, beauty, and strength African-American women possess. I use these terms frequently to remind us of our greatness, of the kingdom in which we not only reside but also preside over. References to Queen Mothers, Ms. Thangs, and Sista-Girls are acknowledgments and celebrations of the truth that black women are the first women—warriors and rulers and mothers to all.

dimension one: the throne

Our compassion and nurturing reach beyond our families and friends, often to complete strangers. When problems or concerns are found within the family or within the community, our wise matriarchs are sought out for advice and solutions. When we are frightened by confrontational circumstances, Queen Mothers simply gather their armor of wisdom and sabers of truth while marching to the forefront.

Like Queen Mother Rosa Parks, who decided she was too tired after a hard day's work to get up and go to the back of the bus, and refused to relinquish her seat to a white passenger when the bus driver told her to. She went to jail for breaking that Jim Crow law, but African-Americans can sit anywhere we please now.

Like Queen Mother Harriet Jacobs, born a slave and the mother of two children. She attempted to escape to freedom once, only to relegate herself to a crawl space for seven years to avoid capture and severe punishment. Queen Mother Jacobs successfully escaped later and traveled to Europe with the employer who purchased her freedom (what a strange phrase, "purchase freedom"). Years later she returned to the United States and worked for abolition before the war between the states, and during the war she was employed as a nurse for black soldiers.

And take Queen Mother Sojourner Truth, for example. Also born a slave and eventually freed—she traveled on foot from New York to Massachusetts to Washington, D.C., spreading the gospel, meeting with dignitaries such as Frederick Douglass and President Abraham Lincoln and lecturing as an outspoken suffragist. In addition to supporting the rights of women, she understood the responsibilities of women in raising children properly. In 1853 Sojourner Truth told the Fourth National Women's Rights Convention, "Sons and daughters ought to behave themselves before their mothers, but they do not. I can see them a-laughin' and pointin' at their mothers up here on the stage. They hiss when an aged woman comes forth. If they'd been brought up proper, they'd have known better than hissing like snakes and geese."[2] And although she never learned to read or write, from 1843 through 1878, she traveled extensively to revivals, conventions, and camp meetings across more than twenty states. This Queen Mother stayed on the march quite a bit!

Don't you find every now and then, regardless of your own age, that you still feel the need to speak with a woman possessing a higher wisdom, a woman who has already marched admirably the trails you are braving? I know I occasionally need my mother and grandmother to let me know that everything is okay; that regardless of what I am feeling at the moment, it is only temporary; and that the road may be stony and jagged, but it's the correct one to take. They, along with all my other matriarchal sages, assure me that in the grand scheme of things, circumstances always work out for the best. So when I see an old Queen Mother sitting in the park or crossing the street with her plastic bags and dusty brown stockings, I have a need to say something or do something for her because I know what she can give me I won't be able to get anywhere else—*Queen Mother wisdom.* I'll share a little of it with you now.

When you're very young and something traumatic happens to you, you feel as if the world is ending and you will never recover; but you do. When you become a little less young and something unnerving happens, you know the world isn't going to end; however, you worry because you believe your life will be transformed forever, irreparably, by this one event and you still don't think you will ever recover; but you do. Once you become mature and something disturbing occurs, you don't care about the world, you just wonder when will you be able to recover; it takes a little too long for you, perhaps; but eventually you do recuperate. And as you become a Queen Mother and experience something shocking, there's no need for you to get over it because you were somehow expecting it, *and you spend your time telling others to get over it.*

Now, don't misunderstand me and think you've got to

wait until you're in your sixties or seventies to be a Queen Mother. You don't. I have women friends in their thirties and forties who qualify. But you must realize the experiences that accompany age are the tools black women use to construct the Queen Mother's throne. And this is not just a throne for us to sit on and dictate from. It is a lap for our children and our children's children to rest in. It is a haven for our companions and mates. It is a beacon in the darkness for all those lost spirits we encounter who are in need of sustenance and warmth.

Remember the last time you stood before a child. There you were, hovering at least two or three feet over this little being. The ability to harm it, ignore it, or nurture it lay squarely on your shoulders. And you fed the child with a loving embrace. This was your *Queen Mother in action.*

What about the last time someone needed to talk to you about something important? They sought your advice, but you really didn't give any. You just responded occasionally with a "How do you feel about that?" or something rhetorical, letting them find their way to the answers and solutions you innately knew would work best for them. You were using that *Queen Mother silence.*

Queen Motherhood is the dimension of our soul that helps us attain the balance and harmonious essence required for happy and successful living and a joyous and thriving, posterity too. Queen Mothers don't concern themselves with the shortage of good black males because for them there is no shortage. How many grandmothers do you see pining because they don't have boyfriends? Or because their grandchild, the doctor, was born out of wedlock? Mama told me there is always another bus coming, and another one after that and another one after that. Queen Mothers use their time efficiently, caring for the children already here, loving the people who love them, feeding the hungry, healing the sick, and teaching the uneducated in the ways not only of the world but of the Universe. When the Queen Mother inside you says,

"Honey, don't worry about men. They come and they go, but you are here only for the undetermined amount of time God gave you. What are you going to do?" *What are you going to do?*

dimension two: the crown

Men come and go—that's the attitude Ms. Thangs generally have regarding the opposite sex, too. Have you ever been at a party when a sister enters through the door and a hush moves over the crowd, not for long, but just long enough for everyone to notice her. She's perfectly coifed, perfectly shaped, perfectly made up, perfectly manicured, perfectly fragranced, perfectly dressed, just making you perfectly ill. But you had to give the sister her props. While all the women were hissing, all the men were clambering for a dance, her phone number, something, anything, *from her*. And all you could say was, "I want to be like her when I grow up." Or maybe you've seen Girlfriend walking down the street, without a care in the world, wearing a cute little smirk or a dazzling smile because someone has just said something nice or funny to her. She had that energetic bounce to her stride while the sun glistened in her hair.

"Who does she think she is?" we sometimes ask. Well, she'll be more than happy to tell you. *Beauty* is her first name, *Confidence* is her middle name, and *Attitude* is her last name. Those of us who know her intimately call her *Ms. Thang*. Haven't you yourself ever felt that way before, even once? I hope so. I have. When you knew you had all the answers, and even if you didn't, you could fake it till you make it? And you did. Well, go on, Ms. Thang. Yes, you just go, girl!

Personally, I love to see black women like this because just looking at them gives me a little pick-me-up. It makes me want to exercise more regularly or buy that trendy new lipstick or drink champagne in the afternoon. Sometimes it even makes me envious. Sure, why not be a little covetous? It keeps me on my toes. And when my act is pulled together and I stroll along Madison Avenue like I own the world, they can be envious of me, too. Being Ms. Thang lets us see just how beautiful we really are, not only to ourselves but to the rest of the world. These African-American wonder women receive daily confirmations on how gorgeous their skin is, how sharp their clothes are, how truly fine they are. And there's nothing wrong with that. Compliments make people feel good, and when you feel good—believe me, it's true—you look good. It's a delicious circle. So the next time you feel Ms. Thang trying to burst her way through, just let her. You are in need of her services. You are in need of journeying through that second dimension of black-sister soul.

dimension three: the scepter

Sista-Girls are usually too busy *trying to do everything* to take the time necessary to command anything. We signify, cuss, and cry with each other. We share the most intimate details about our relationships. We hold each other's hands in hours that are dark and frightening. We comfort each other when the time is confusing and strength is waning. We drink wine until our speech is slurred and then in the morning sun we pour each other coffee and pass the vitamins. The misgivings between us are more painful than anything else in this world, but with time we find our way back to each other again and embrace and say, "I love you." We may not hold the same philosophies toward mates, entertainment, fashion, or literature, but that doesn't prevent us from becoming best friends.

I can tell you everything, even negative feelings I have toward you. I won't lie to you because I don't want you to lie to me. I won't hide things from you, and I know how straightforward you are. I want you to be direct with me and correct me if I am wrong. I will treat you with the respect I insist on from myself and others. You won't forget that you are black—I won't let you—and don't you dare allow me to perpetrate for the sake of societal dictates. I do love you. We are like the sun, the soil, the water, and the wind—forever interdependent. I am and always will be your Sista-Girl.

Let me ask, are you ever so blue that the only person whom you can talk to, because you know she's been through it too, is your sister? Perhaps she's related, perhaps not, but she's still your sister, your *Sista-Girl.* She may not have all the answers, but she knows just what to say and how to say it. Sometimes she lights a fire under your rear, and sometimes she shares a bottle of vino. But whatever it is, she is there for you. Girlfriend doesn't always look like a beauty queen; her gym shoes are sometimes grungy and her sweats funky; she's usually on the move, but every once in a while you'll phone her, and she'll be just veggin' in front of the boob tube. She's comfortable with who she is, her strengths and weaknesses. She knows she's not perfect but she's willing to try *for you.* Her scepter is always there for you to lean on or grab ahold of if you feel yourself falling. Don't you know someone like that? Someone with a solid strength who loves hard and plays hard but still has her feet planted firmly on the ground. That is until she needs you, because, like I said, she doesn't have all of the answers. She's just your Sista-Girl.

She is the other dynamic found so prevalently among strong, beautiful black women. She's someone whom we all need to be sometimes. She may live next door or down the hall; she may catch the same bus or train that you travel on every morning going to work, grumbling because she woke up late and hasn't had that first cup of coffee yet. But she's someone you know and should get to know better, especially since she's inside of you.

This is the kind of sister who will find that needle in the haystack all of us other sisters search for day and night (and may very well decide she's not interested in it). She's just that strong. She's that dimension of black-sister soul able to stand alone but is never lonely.

The three ladies discussed here, Queen Mother, Ms. Thang, and Sista-Girl, embody what African-American women can be. They personify that three-dimensional black-sister soul: the throne of Queen Mother, likened to the Universe we work within and the sanctuary we can provide; the crown of Ms. Thang, likened to the way we wear our beauty and our heritage, confident and proud; and the scepter of Sista-Girl, likened to our shoulders and spines, wielding strength and healthy doses of reality. Sometimes we find ourselves acting more a Queen Mother than a Ms. Thang. Sometimes all we can be are just Sista-Girls.

Yes, some of us phase through each of these personae, perhaps being "all that" as Ms. Thang first; then, as friends and lovers our roles change, and we become stronger and more companionate as Sista-Girls; and still, as our roles diversify even more, becoming mothers, community leaders, corporate executives, and family heads, we must locate and provide wisdom and guidance we were unaware we possessed, finally becoming Queen Mothers. But, you will learn, sincere and unaffected self-love is derived by striking a balance between all three, knowing when to let one lady out and when to silence the others. *Through our cultivation of each, we grow into human beings who love each other and, most significantly, love ourselves.*

dimension four: the oath

Tragically, some sisters are so far removed from their potential, from love of self, that getting a warm, home-cooked meal and a bath are major accomplishments. We see these sisters dressed in layers of rags, roaming the streets with their shopping carts. Their faces soiled and dingy and lined with deep, pain-filled, crevices. Occasionally they'll stop at a garbage can, picking through it for anything they think can be of some use to them. Sometimes they just rest on the curb, ever mindful of their cart because it is their only possession. A discarded morning paper may keep the rain from their head, at least momentarily, or provide a few seconds of kindling for a warm fire on a cold night in the alleys where they sleep. These sisters rarely ask us for anything because they're too proud, too tired, and/or too embarrassed. So we walk by them, sometimes thanking God for sparing us, or sometimes, those of us who are more generous, praying to God to grant them some kind of mercy.

There are sisters so blinded they sell their bodies for hard, crystal pieces of death found in putrid little glass vials. We see them at night. They walk the streets brazenly when they're high, looking to score one more trick for the next high. When they're coming down, they're peeking out from corners and vestibules of abandoned buildings or transient hotels. During the day, we rarely see these tragic sisters, and if we do, they're usually crouched in doorways next to some supermarket, cash station, or drugstore. The morning caught them with no money for their fix, and they are desperate. So they tremble and scratch and compete with the homeless who are standing near them, trying to sell their *Streetwise* newspapers. Sometimes we give them change, sometimes we don't, sometimes we say a prayer for them, and sometimes again we thank God for the beneficence we are blessed with (for the time being).

At one point I thought about asking one sister, whom I saw almost every day, if she'd like to come home with me and my boyfriend for dinner and a bath, but he asked me, "Honey, what if she has lice or something?" So I gave her a couple of dollars, as usual, appealed to Spirit for her, but still felt bad.

We also have girlfriends who work for the weekend party, hoping and praying the sixty-dollar coif and the fifty-dollar nail work they sat for hours for in the beauty salon will pay off—attracting that knight in shining armor. They pull out the slinkiest outfit and the spikiest heels. These Ms. Thangs got the girl or guy behind the cosmetic counter to show them how to make their face up to look like a movie star. The lips are pouty and the attitude is on, and they are out the door to sit at the bar or in a booth to wait for Sir Galahad. They are convinced that these cosmetic treatments they have spent all of this time, money, and effort on will attract a mate who will take care of them, love them, and devote himself entirely to their needs. They might as well be waiting for that comet that won't be back around the earth for another fourteen million years.

It is for these sisters our oath is beholden. Each of them needs our help, be it a gentle word of guidance and prayer or a few dollars for a hot meal and an old woolen coat for warmth. And each of us who is able must take the vow and reach into our heart to give. In the heart is where we will find spare change and the helping hand to extend to others, is where the strength can be found to pry that lady from the vise those fatal pieces of momentary heaven have imprisoned her in. In the depths of our hearts we must reach for the compassion and audacity needed to party with our sisters while simultaneously explaining why we must leave at midnight instead of three or four in the morning, why we don't party every weekend, and why we need no knight in shining armor. We must be bold enough to tell our Ms. Thangs why real knights don't show up at three or four in the morning, anyway, and that while partying like this may be fun at times, there are other celebrations of life that are more enjoyable and rewarding.

We must set examples for our sisters, using our hearts and our brains, showing them, instead of telling them, that all is possible and all they truly need can be found internally, not externally. In our hearts and souls, we must pledge allegiance to each other, to nurture, love, protect, understand, and accept those sisters who may not share our views, our tastes, or our blessings, but share the indisputable milliliter of blood that binds us together forever in sisterhood.

We must construct paths for them to follow, bridges for them to cross. Taking it day by day, little by little, an inch at a time, or a half-inch if necessary. We may have to think and rethink and rethink again. Because, although I'm ashamed to admit it, sisters don't follow other sisters easily unless you can prove to them that it's worth it. So we must talk to the women who have made it—our mothers and grandmothers. Listen to the women who have contributed and learn from them. Take our own experiences—good and bad—and make tar for the pavement. Use all the skills we've acquired, all the knowledge and wisdom we've accumulated and been blessed with, and get sisters like those just mentioned onto Queen Mother Boulevard. We may be required to drag them onto the road as they kick and scream; we may be required to wait patiently for them as they decide to join us. But once they step on that trail, we can help them discover all is never lost permanently. *Liberation is just a Sista-Girl away, and all we need do is empathize, embrace, and walk with them.*

PART 1

LOVING OURSELVES

The subject of sex is so prominent in our culture and, yet, so taboo. Perhaps it is this paradox that is largely responsible for the erosion of traditional relationships and female self-esteem. How can we fight a society that overtly favors women who are surgically enhanced for the sake of appealing to the momentary fancies of men? How can sisters feel good about their inner being when almost all of the top black female models are insultingly thin, wearing weaves to the top of their heinies, and have naturally light-colored eyes or wear colored contact lenses? What chance does a coffee-eyed, short-haired, pear-shaped sister have for romance in this society with the messages we are continually bombarded with? What chance does any woman have? Must she agree to spread her legs whenever given the opportunity for fear she may not get another?

Maybe my "old" age has elevated my objectivity concerning relationships and my experiences (good and bad) have broadened my perspective so that I can understand the dynamics of human relating a little more than some others. Maybe it's a combination of any or all of the above. Maybe I just don't have a whole helluva a lot to do, so I do a lot of people watching. Whatever the reason, I have noticed black females, especially those of us in the "thirty-something" group and younger, are finding ourselves in far too many situations ("relationships" hardly seems an accurate term) that are disastrous, distasteful, and disparaging.

We're letting ourselves get dissed all over the damn place. Why? Because we don't know our value as human beings, and society is most definitely not helping.

We've got young mothers with misplaced priorities engaging in sexual relations with their birthing stitches barely healed while not quite sure where the next meals for their babies and themselves are coming from.

Young women are confused because the men they slept with during the first few dates are not giving them enough attention. "The relationship is only a couple of months old; what's wrong with him?" they ask.

There are women who, when their self-esteem is at its lowest ebb, become victims of extreme religious orders (I was one once), absolving themselves of all responsibility, including for themselves and their children. Why? Because *God is responsible and will take care of everything.*

My first husband was gone often, literally for hours, even after working late. He refused to account for this time, and he was also a vicious, abusive man-child. But I looked to God to heal all. I went to temple at least four times weekly, sometimes more; prostrated myself five times daily; quoted scriptures regularly; and tried to behave like a good helpmate. However, that didn't stop the abuse, even when I was pregnant.

Eventually I miscarried, and a couple of weeks later while I was sulking at home, my grandmother paid me a visit. She hadn't been able to be at the hospital with me because she was also very ill. She heard through that infamous family grapevine I still wasn't quite myself, and decided to interrupt her convalescing to come see me. So we sat on the edge of the bed (in the bedroom I rarely shared with the man I married), and she asked me what was wrong. I complained about all of the weight I had gained, about how my husband never came home now, about how I just felt kind of useless, about how I wanted to give her a grandchild before she passed away. She turned toward me and gave me one of those huge, soft, warm, and strong grandmama hugs, raised up my chin, and firmly said, "Get up and get goin', girl. Keep on pushin', and leave that little boy alone. You're a grown woman, and you need a grown man. This one's not ready yet, so leave him alone. You're too pretty and too smart to be caught up in all this nonsense. You have a family who loves you and cares about you."

It was at that point that the abuse stopped. It took a Queen Mother telling me I didn't have to take this nonsense. Telling me I had married a boy, not a man. Telling me that my husband should have been by my side at the hospital when I miscarried, not my aunt. Asking me, if I was hanging on to him because I needed somebody to love me, why was she here holding my hand as I cried into her bosom while he was out Lord knows where. Explaining to me that the Lord helps those who help themselves, and it was time I started doing just that. Making me realize that if I didn't like the fact I was thirty pounds overweight, God wasn't going to do the exercising for me. Saying to me that if I didn't like the fact I cooked a meal every night and my mate was rarely home to eat it, God wasn't going to sit down and keep me company—He had more important work to do for the truly hungry.

"God knows you love Him, that He's in your heart," she assured me. "You ain't gotta go nowhere to prove that to Him or anybody else. Now, you listen to me. You have me, your Gran-Gran, for as long as I am breathin' air, and I am never gonna let anybody hurt you. Thank God for that, and let Him get about His other work."

And I did. I helped myself and left.

Yet, for a long time afterward, I suffered from very low self-esteem and even what I now realize was a nervous breakdown. Why would a man treat me like that? Was I not good enough? Was I not pretty enough? What was wrong with me? I was ambitious. I was intelligent. I tried to be a good wife—cooking, cleaning, and so forth. What was I lacking? It took years for me to reconstruct a *genuine* self-confidence. Years for my grandmother's words to make real sense to me. Years of wrong relationships and wrong turns. But looking back, I wouldn't change a thing because of where I am now. Doing anything differently back then, even the mistakes, might have changed something now. And I'll always remember that talk with my grandmother, sitting on the edge of the bed. It's a foundation for me now. As is much of the wisdom and advice brought to me by all the beautiful black women I have come to cherish.

Yes, indeed, we need to know we are loved and that above all others, we should love ourselves. African-American women need to know why we are so priceless, and the answers cannot be found in fashion magazines, on television, or in the beds of lovers. The answers can only be found in all the Queen Mothers that have come before us and in the depths of our own beings.

1

Fiction and Fact

I'm every woman, it's all in me
anything you want done, baby,
I'll do it naturally. . . .
I'm every woman, it's all in me
I can read your thoughts right now,
every one from A to Z. . . .
I can cast a spell, secrets you can't tell,
mix a special brew, put fire inside of you,
and anytime you feel danger or fear,
send for me, I will appear,
cause I'm every woman, it's all in me. . . .

—"I'm Every Woman"
Chaka Khan and Rufus[3]

I remember my young, militant years like a dream that might have been a dream or a nightmare—you aren't quite sure. Some parts are happy, vivid, and colorful; then others are frightening, vague, and gray. *The bright orange triangles of Daddy's dashiki and his wispy, curly Afro. The fuzzy white-and-black television pictures of Martin's funeral procession and the hushed faces watching; it was cold and gloomy that day. "Say it loud, I'm black and I'm proud."*

In the sixties, not even ready for my training bra, I was too young to join in the protests. When the seventies hit, the protests were over and my menses began; so still too young to engage in any kind of radical politicking, I did what everyone else did—acted proactively by trying to sport an Afro (my hair would always flop down in the middle though); took black history courses as my high school electives; studied the black female militants of that era, Angela Davis, Nikki Giovanni, and Carla, who lived down the street; and wrote poetry and prose about racism. I did, however, get to participate in one demonstration.

The neighborhood around my high school was impoverished and gangs there thrived. One evening after practice, some of the guys on our track team were mugged, and this wasn't the first time it had happened. They brought it to the attention of the principal and faculty, but nothing was done. In retaliation, one day the following week, the entire student body walked out, refusing to come back unless security was beefed up. The next day we had extra security. That was pretty cool.

In addition to the facts about my blackness learned through family life and school, there were the wonderful, profound bits and pieces of knowledge I discovered through reading the works of Nikki G., Maya Angelou, and others. I could also feel the beauty of my blackness while grooving to the earthy, rhythmic tones of Chaka Khan and Gladys Knight. My peers and I understood the necessity of the arrogance behind "I'm Every woman" and the "uranium bowels" of Nikki Giovanni's "Ego-Tripping." We (like Nikki and Chaka) knew if we didn't express the fact we were beautiful and, despite what anyone else said, were princesses growing up to be queens, nobody would. Then, we would weaken and eventually lie at the feet of the opposition, conceding to a fictional conspiracy that made blonde hair, pink skin, and blue eyes the epitome of beauty and womanhood.

No, we would be strong and triumphant, shouting our truths from the rooftops with fists clenched and raised high in the air, if we had to. (I think one time we actually did.) Letting everybody know our colors and textures—rich, deep, glowing, and sensual—were the undeniable, universal properties of real beauty. Nikki, Maya, Chaka, and Mama said so.

Learning and living as a black militant teen was sometimes a dreamy, romantic escape. Still, realistic victory was ours. The fact remains that bronze, butter, caramel, copper, cream, gold, mahogany, and sand are just as beautiful as pink and blue.

I continue to read the writings of my sisters for strength, guidance, and reaffirmation when things get too noisy. And I still believe now, as I did so many years ago, that we cannot be denied, and neither should we be dismissed nor debased. Our birthright is that of Queen Mother, Ms. Thang, and Sista-Girl. National leaders, world caretakers, and universal stars. We were not born to be harlots, slaves, or whimsical playthings. The fact is we were not born to serve the needs of others for the sake of their laziness, greed, and ignorance, regardless of the fiction the white forefathers of this country may have taught their descendants.

For a long time, understanding the true relevance of our history, black history, escaped me. It's not surprising, given that for ages our predecessors had the idea literally beaten into them that anything other than white was bad. In fact even the significance of my Native American ancestry was hidden from me until my grandparents one day were discussing their loved ones and how their friends used to have to enter certain towns in downstate Illinois from the back of town, often known as Squaw Alley, because of the *Indian* blood that ran through their veins. I remember the long, silver ponytail my great-great-grandmother, who was Choctaw, would sit on while rocking slowly in her chair and staring out of the window. Her face was often very still, as if she were somewhere else thinking about some other time in her life.

I have a photograph of her when she was much younger,

standing by a Duesenberg. Her hair was shiny black back then, and she was wearing a more forceful look, almost indignant. This picture was taken shortly after she and my grandmother moved to Chicago from Louisville. They were poor and alone, but that's nothing when you have the determination of more than five hundred years of survival in your ancestry. The Choctaw were the last to leave during the Native American uprisings against the soldiers in the South. They were usually a peaceful people but fiercely adamant about their homes and land.

Now, looking at our young women, I realize that they, unfortunately, are not privy to the pride of our history as it was brought to myself, my peers, and our parents and grandparents. The fact that they are unaware of the significance of this history and of the pride that is a giant part of our history is more evident to me than ever. Our young women must know that they are a product of nobility, and not just nobility of blood-kin and material wealth but nobility of Spirit. They must be able to envision the greatness from which they were born in order to see the greatness that lies ahead, waiting for them. Young black women should be made aware that there were not just one, two, or three great black women throughout history. But, that there were hundreds and thousands of black women who endured, achieved, and accomplished wondrous things, leaving a legacy they oblige all black women to carry on.

Like ninety-three-year-old Queen Mother Aunt Francis, who prepared meals for anyone she knew was ill, who still attends church almost every Sunday (unless her arthritis is painin' her), who regularly has dinner company for whom she cooks full-course meals, and who came to Chicago from Georgia with her family, graduated from Roosevelt University, married a dentist, and is responsible for two generations of black college graduates.

Like Queen Mother Ginger, passed now, but who was a single parent in the forties and ensured her child had tailor-made clothes until he was twenty-one years old, saw to his parochial school education, assisted with his new family as he pursued his college degree while working full-time, and literally worked until a month before she died at the age of sixty-four.

Like Queen Mother Reenie, who gave her AIDS-stricken son refuge and love in her home until he succumbed. She cooked his meals, washed his clothes, made his bed, bought his medicine, and held his hand until the very end.

Young black women should learn our history, not just what's in the textbooks, but the history that's all around them. Everywhere Queen Mothers are standing tall and proud providing us with glorious examples of love and strength. Yes, they should learn the history, not only the facts, but the glory and the honor that accompanies it. They should celebrate it and contribute to it.

Like Queen Mother Paine, who, as a single parent, worked full-time, made sure the family dinner was hot and ready on time, and always kept the house clean and orderly. She also served as a Camp Fire Leader for her daughter's Camp Fire Group and as a den mother for her son's Boy Scout troop. A very serious woman regarding her children's education, she tolerated nothing less than As and Bs from either, and screened all of their calls to ensure such grades. This no-nonsense woman now has a doctor in the family to show for her nurturing.

Like Queen Mother Li'l Mama, who stood a good six feet and kept her wily, young ten-year-old grandson out of trouble by making him work from sunup to sundown: cleaning chandeliers, checking the boiler and the furnace, sweeping and vacuuming the foyer, helping the old man down the street who fixed cars, helping her prepare meals, doing the laundry, and double-checking his homework. "If I've got to get up with the dawn every morning to start workin', so does everybody else," she proclaimed. Eventually her grandson would graduate with a degree in mathematics and gain successful employment in the world of finance.

Like young Queen Mother Debbie Swain, who became a surrogate daughter for a dying woman I knew, caring for her, cooking for her, comforting her, compassionately easing her transition on a daily basis, organizing and orchestrating the woman's daughter's wedding activities and ceremony, and, of course, standing by the family when it was time to say a final farewell; who also accompanied to the south another good friend who was in mourning over the loss of a loved one, lending the same kind of quiet, empathetic, strength. At the age of thirty-something, this magnificent young woman has already earned her halo and wings.

We should all learn from those beautiful black women whose efforts, sacrifices, and diligence ensured that their progeny had all the tools required to succeed in today's world—good health, a good education, a good work ethic, mountains of love, and superior role models—and learn as well as from those African-American women whose love and gentility brought a peaceful stillness to those saying good-bye to this world.

beauty and respect

We are some of the most desired women in the world and often the most intimidating. A female makeup artist who happened to be white told me about the time she was doing a fashion show and the black models sneered at her. One of them spoke up saying, "Don't come over here with that white powder like you know what you're doing!" The others chimed in with affirmations. At that point, she told me, these tall, gorgeous, black divas had thoroughly terrified her. I replied, "Yes, we can be something when we know we're beautiful." But I also told her she had no reason to be afraid and that her confidence in her work should be stronger.

Like our *brown-haired, brown-skinned, brown-eyed sister, Cleopatra,* black women satisfy all needs for beauty and strength, both physical and mental (real or imagined). Those who turn away from us in disgust and reject us as big, ugly, and dark are premising their opinions on fictional, media-perpetuated stereotypes or experiences with those of us who have yet to find our true selves. I cannot deny that fewer of us than should be are realizing our potential, but I will not allow this to overshadow the fact that there are just as many of us struggling to be everything our ancestry calls for and more.

However, this struggle is difficult to discern when the public (primarily white society) and certain members of the media whitewash your efforts, when for some strange reason, most often, the only blacks subjected to the scrutiny of the television cameras are those who fit the "ghetto black" stereotype. How often do we see poor whites subjected to this subliminal ridicule? Not very. So we must add to our struggle competition against the memory of individuals who dismiss us because they recall, and unjustly categorize many of us with, the inarticulate, bandanna-wearing, semitoothless, hype-scratching, dirty sister telling the reporter her version of the shooting, rather than the intelligent, eloquent, female, African-American, journalist herself.

It is little wonder then that those of us who are reaching our potential at times strike out in almost embarrassing fervor to attain and keep our due. Once we are in the light, few shine brighter, thus, we are forever guarding against being pulled out of the light. Forever guarding against those who don't want the stereotypes destroyed, who profit from the negative, fictional portrayal of our people.

But we will not be concealed. Our physical beauty is astonishing at times, truly awesome. However, because of the strength that lies behind that beauty and our comprehension of this strength, we also struggle continually against the panic in others. This fear-driven panic or intimidation by the black woman's beauty is likened to the male black widow spider's apprehension of the female black widow spider: he finds her absolutely irresistible, and once he has fed upon her beauty he discovers how absolutely undesirable and unnecessary he has become. He then scrambles around uselessly in mortal fear, knowing he's about to be destroyed. This is what frightens people about black women. Our strengths combined with our beauty are weapons and shields both irresistible and unbeatable.

Yet, what is even stranger is people don't comprehend the fact that because we recognize that our beauty lies within ourselves—within our spiritual grasp of the Universe—and not within our cosmetic bags, fear is unnecessary. Most of us will not use our beauty for selfish, greedy, malevolent, godforsaken purposes. The fact is our spiritual beauty will not allow us to intentionally "do unto others" the wrongs they have done unto us. Not that we believe in continuously "turning the other cheek." It is simply beneath most African-American women to use beauty solely for materialistic gains. We're too intelligent and too wise.

This wisdom also teaches us something else we must pass on to our younger sisters: outside beauty and material wealth can only go so far. Gran and I talked about this once when she reminded me about the time she took me shopping one Christmas. We walked into one of the big department stores for ladies on State Street. I was five years old and could barely see over the countertops, but, she said, when I saw the many pretty women standing behind the cosmetic counters, I proclaimed that when I grew up, I was going to be just like those ladies and work in a store like this.

And at twenty-something when I decided working in a retail store, even behind illustrious cosmetic counters, wasn't all it was cracked up to be (unless one owned the store), Gran reminded me of the reason why she and my mother wanted me to take typing in high school instead of French. Clerk-typists made at the least five thousand dollars a year more than I did in retail. So I left the beauty world behind and locked myself in my bedroom with a rented typewriter and my mother's old high-school typing book to get myself up to speed. It wasn't too bad. The job I interviewed for only required typing forty five words per minute, and I could already type ten. So Gran didn't see me that entire weekend except during bathroom and meal breaks. I got the job, and she told me she was proud—I had finally learned to use my brains. "What's between your ears is always going to give you the key to unlock any door. Dependin' on your looks is like dependin' on the weather. A pretty eye shadow ain't gonna do squat for you when it's stormin' outside. And remember, money can't buy happiness," she told me as I shampooed her hair. Which is why I eventually left the corporate world, along with the daily, fifteen-minute ritual of cosmetic application.

One can be young only for so long. Then one can use only so much cream and powder. Then one can get only so much surgery. If a sister finds herself unable to go a day barefaced—that is, without any makeup on—it's time for a reality check and for her to do like all the rest of us—GET REAL. Fact is that it's not the cosmetics on the face that make the woman, nor the silicone in her breasts, but the expert use of her mind. I've yet to hear anyone say, "Yeah, I really respect that lipstick."

But real, honest-to-goodness black women are usually guaranteed respect, sisters who move easily from silks to sweats, from a sweaty face to an evening face, from sweet praise and empathy to candid and fierce opposition. These women not only demand respect but command it. Because these women have paid their dues, so to speak.

I can promise you it is a rare black woman who radiates from anything other than inner strength and spirit obtained through trials upon trials upon trials. She's probably been through relationships both intimate and familial, jobs and/or careers, and self-inflicted struggles—been through what you and I have gone through, are going through, and will go through—and has come out a champion. What's the new phrase now? She's *been there, done that.* And who cannot respect a woman who can make so many transitions with such seeming ease except those who do not understand and must, by human nature's design, fear her? Fear her because things that we do not comprehend we fear, and I dare say not enough Caucasians on this planet understand us enough not to fear us.

tuning in

It is imperative that our young sisters see that with their beauty and strength cultivated from inside, the outside world (even with all of its complexities) can be conquered. When working from the inside, we have intuition, insight, and knowledge of the Universe at our beck and call. So-called intellectual people often laugh at and ridicule the woman of color's relationship with the Universe, that is, until she and Spirit turn fiction into fact and prove themselves a formidable team.

Our young women must see the wonders that would lie at their feet if they would only work with the Universe and listen to Spirit, the Creator. Whatever others may say or others may feel, no one is as in tune with the Universe and the One like sisters. As women we are blessed with "women's intuition," and as women of color, we are intimately connected beyond the realm of intuition. Perhaps this connection exists because for hundreds of years in this country, black folk had little else to look for to guide them properly. We didn't—and often couldn't—trust white folks to show us the way, and we couldn't ask each other, that would have resulted in "the blind leading the blind."

So we looked to Spirit. We looked, asked, and prayed every day and every night—not always aloud, not always in groups, but with our hearts and minds. If we asked for something, it was understood we were asking the One and Only, whether we were asking Farmer Brown for a couple of chickens on credit or Mrs. Green for some extra work to pay that debt. Whatever we asked for, we understood the true source of all our answers would be God.

And for some of us, it is so innate, it is now just becoming understood. When I asked for this book to be published, there was only one entity I was actually directing my question and energy to. When I told my mother about the good news, she knew what to ask me, "Well, did you get down on your hands and knees yet? 'Cause you know it's all the work of the Creator." *It's all God's work; it's God's Universe. We've known that for a long, long time.*

That primordial knowledge of the Universe, combined with intuition and the way it can guide, help, strengthen, and shield us, is what got some of us through the genocidal middle passage of the original journey to this land (our Dark Continent); it's what got some of us through the homicidal hanging frenzy in the evil south; it's what's now gettin' us through crack, crime, and chaos. Often, it is all we can depend on, all we have. So we've made the connection as strong as possible. And Queen Mothers don't do anything until they can hear that whisper of intuition.

How often have you listened to your "first mind" to be completely satisfied and free of all doubt? You know, the first mind is that feeling in your gut telling you what to do or what not to do; it's that seldom heard tiny voice way back behind that seldom used brain matter; and sometimes it's as loud as a train signaling for you to get off the tracks (which, unfortunately, is usually when SistaGirls are doggedly determined to stay put).

Then, how often have you ignored this utterance only to be left feeling like the biggest damned fool in the world?

If this happens more often than not, you must find more quiet time around you and within you—a place of tranquility in or near your home and within your mind where you can go when you're puzzled, frustrated, anxious, or just questioning something. A place where you won't be disturbed, where you can block out all the external and internal noises for a few minutes—that's all Spirit needs. Close your eyes, open your mind, stretch out your limbs, feel the pressure in your chest from your heartbeat, breathe deeply until you can sense the energy pulsating in your fingertips and toes. And when there is stillness, you will be provided with the proper feedback. Call it prayer, call it meditation, call it whatever you like, but it's what sisters throughout the ages have perfected—our own direct line to the Universe. As a matter of fact, all we have to do is call.

2

Light and Dark

In this day and age, it is unforgivable that sisters of color can be pitted against each other because one sister's skin is light brown and the other sister's skin is dark brown, that variations on the theme of racism play not only outside the black community but inside as well.

My own sister and I share this difference, she being the darker sister and I being the lighter, but that difference has never and will never be an issue for discussion. When asked what my sister looks like, I tell people she is a darker, taller version of myself, and that is the end of discourse with respect to physical characteristics. I refuse to become involved in any conversation that harps on the physical differences between human beings. Concentrating on differences is divisive and demeaning.

Still, there are hordes of black people who believe the lighter a black person is (what an ambiguous turn of phrase) the more attractive they are. Hogwash! This type of thinking dates so far back in our past it's disheartening to know it still exists. But it does, finding its root in the false standard for beauty I mentioned earlier, only Caucasian features: pale skin, light-colored eyes, and thin, straight hair. One of my Queen Mothers told me about a couple of sororities established for young black women at the turn of the century. To qualify for pledging in one, you couldn't be any darker than the color of a paper bag and to apply to another, people would have to be able to see the blue trails your veins made through your skin. Talk about pledging criteria!

In the last three decades, the fact that blacks have been brainwashed into believing our features are unattractive has been well documented. One study demonstrated numerous instances where black children were given the choice of playing with a pink doll with straight, blond hair or with a brown doll with curly, black hair.[4] Most of the children always chose to play with the pink, blond-haired doll. One child even decided that since all of the pink dolls had been taken, it was better to play with no doll than to play with the brown one. When the children were asked why they felt this way, they said because the pink doll was prettier than the brown doll. And when asked what made the pink doll prettier, the children responded quite frankly by listing physical characteristics such as the light skin, the straight hair, the yellow hair. Walk into any large drugstore and you can find several brands of bleaching creams located in the black-products section.

And although it's getting a little better now, when it comes to advertising, let us contemplate for a moment what we see regarding beauty and who is wearing it. For a while, one of the top fashion models was a beautiful, dark-skinned woman with a short natural. But, unfortunately, as of late, top black models are sporting straight hair (unless the designer calls for something different), straight noses, and waiflike bodies. Most of the models we see in advertisements are white, and the black ones are so cosmetically altered, it's hard to tell if they are of African-American descent.

Now, Ms. Thangs, don't misinterpret me here, because it is not the fault of the models. These young women are fully aware of what is going on, and some aren't very happy about it. But they are models, and they have to do what their profession tells them to. Just as you and I have to do what is necessary in order to succeed in our lines of work—even when we don't like it or are temporarily uncomfortable.

However, we must be sure to compensate for this gaunt standard of beauty by noting all the other beautiful black women we see and whom our children may be exposed to and making sure our children understand that a slender, turned-up nose is not the only beautiful nose there is, that thick, curly, dark brown hair is just as beautiful as straight and yellow hair, that brown skin is just as beautiful as pink skin. Sisters, point out the profit margins of the tanning booth businesses!

Do not allow our children to believe the one of the characteristics we cannot change, our skin color, is ugly. It is an explosive falsehood. Take the responsibility to point out that if our features were truly repulsive, master and mistress would not have found their way into our slave quarters in the late shadows of the night while everyone else was sleeping. If we were so unattractive, we would not have ancestors who are blood-related to the first presidents. There would be no light-skinned blacks were white slaveowners not attracted to their African slaves, to their wide noses, dark thick skins, luscious full lips, wonderfully round buttocks, strong thighs, and well-endowed genitalia.

Nevertheless, when you convince a person they are literally unattractive, you lower their self-esteem. Once a person's sense of self-worth has been devalued to the point where it means little or nothing to them, they can be manipulated and used to serve the will of others. They can be trained to obey like oxen or dogs, relying upon their masters for sustenance and shelter because they've been taught that they cannot be self-reliant. A person who feels worthless has no creative, industrious thought and, therefore, cannot take care of himself or herself properly. So they will accept whatever the master sees fit to dole out.

If we all would just take time to think and reason before we allow color lines to be drawn within our own community, we would be that much closer to fulfilling our destiny, creating a great unified people. Reasoning would tell us that the very skin, dark skin, they now continually imply is ugly, is actually appealing. Reasoning would teach us that hypocrisy runs rampant when one entity is trying to dominate another.

Let the hypocrisy not run in our families. Mothers, take care that you do not treat one child any better or any worse because of the lightness or darkness of their complexion. And if Grandmother or Grandfather displays this kind of favoritism, gently but emphatically, put a stop to such divisive behavior.

Favoring light over dark or dark over light is nonsensical for black people. It divides the family and by that divides the community. As Queen Mothers, Sista-Girls, and Ms. Thangs it is our irrevocable duty to keep the family and community together, making sure everybody realizes light, bright, and damn near white is no better than deep, dark, and far from parched. Likewise, we must see to the cessation of reverse color-struck thinking, too. Blackberry juice is not necessarily any sweeter than cream or honey.

I'll never forget my sister once telling me about a guy who was interested in dating me who approached her to find out what my "type" of man was. She thought about it and replied, "Male." She went on to explain to him I really had no type. She had seen me date black, white, Hispanic, Native American, and Asian; tall, short, and medium; thin, pudgy, and in-between; my age, older, younger; princes, paupers, and working-class dudes. I honestly had no category. However, I did remind her that in addition to being male, my men also had to be alive.

We are all of the same people, mixed beyond what the forefathers, all the forefathers, fathomed, but of the same people nonetheless. We owe it to each other to work with our hearts and minds to create, build, and unify. Leave the issue of light versus dark with the electric company, the only folks who should be concerned with such an issue.

3

Kinky and Straight

As unbelievable as favoritism over light and dark skin is, the issue of "good" hair (hair that is naturally wavy or straight) and "bad" hair (hair that is very curly, "nappy," or "kinky," if you will) is also ridiculous. It still relates to light versus dark, whereas fair-skinned blacks are usually considered to have "good" hair and darker-skinned blacks are often considered to have "bad" or "nappy" hair. Having been trained as a cosmetologist, I can tell you there is no such thing as "good" or "bad" hair. Thick and kinky hair is no worse nor any better than wiry and wavy or stringy and straight. Having wiry and wavy hair myself, I have cursed my sister many times for being blessed with thicker hair. Beautiful, thick, kinky hair can withstand almost anything; when relaxed, braided, or styled in whatever manner desired, it lies magnificently and remains so. Whereas wiry and wavy hair falls out with the use of chemicals that are too strong; when the wind blows, so the style goes; and if the humidity is above fifty percent, the only safe style to wear is none.

I am reminded of the time when "permanents" or "perms" (the process used by white people to get their straight hair curly like ours is naturally) became very popular, and then, how dumbstruck I was when products were being manufactured for black people so we could have "perms," too. Didn't we realize that getting a "perm," called a "curl" for us, was actually us imitating white people imitating us? That we were imitating ourselves? I was so disgusted with this concept that during the time I was a hair stylist, I refused to give anyone a "curl." Other stylists said I was missing out on making a great deal of money, but that was not my concern. I refused to wear blackface in this particular show.

Some of us are ostracized for "selling out" and getting our hair straightened or lightened. It hurts me when, I meet a beautiful black woman, and sometimes get snubbed because I am not black enough in her eyes. On the other hand, others of us are shunned for being so Afrocentric that communication with us is nearly impossible. Girlfriends can't relate or even try to understand the pride some of us feel while sporting short Afros, dreadlocks, braids, or being just plain with no cosmetics, no whipped up hair, no airbrushed nails, no cosmetic adornment whatsoever. Instead, we get disapproving glares and are looked down upon.

I'll never forget once when I was visiting a doctor's office and waiting in the reception area. A very attractive sister, dressed handsomely in her corporate attire, stared me down as I was updating my information form. I did as I usually do when meeting the eyes of brothers and sisters on the street, I smiled at her, acknowledging the presence of another Sista-Girl. But she looked at me from head-to-toe, frowned, and looked away. Okay, I had that naturally curly Afro-puff goin' on, wearin' my naturally knee-torn 'cause-they're-too-old-to-mention baggy jeans, my favorite oversized sweater, and a weather-beaten leather jacket—you know, the kind everybody wears, with all the zippers and snaps. Still, I don't think that warranted a frown. Do you? Some Ms. Thangs won't even take certain Sista-Girls seriously unless Sista-Girls are wearing the latest designer threads and the most current "do."

"So what's up for the weekend?" I'd ask a coworker.

"I'm going to the shop to get my hair and my nails done. Then I'm goin' out. Where do you get your hair done?"

"At home."

"Oh. *Hmm* . . . Well, I gotta go. See ya."

And no, I wasn't wearing the latest thing like Ms. Thang. My hair is too curly for finger-waves. I know that sounds strange, but you have to have relaxed hair or a grade that has a soft wave. The stuff on my head is too soft for relaxers—it falls out on the pillows—so waves ain't happenin'. Anyway, I guess I don't qualify for some of the sisters to converse with. Oh, well . . .

Sistas, sistas, sistas. This is all cosmetic. Cornrows, dooky braids, perms, weaves, ponytails, bobs, short Afros are all wonderful, beautiful testaments simply to what we can do with the concept of adornment—that's it, nothing more.

Every couple of years I spend Christmas in southern California with family. We have a very large extended one, and only at these family gatherings and in the subways of New York do I see at one time so many variations of style, shape, size, color, and texture of black folks' beauty. African-Americans come in so many varieties we should be readily accepting of all methods of beautification. Equating style with conscience is folly. I am no more or less aware of my origin because I choose to blow-dry and curl my hair than someone who chooses to wear a large braided crown. I am black where it counts—in my heart, my soul, and my brain. My hair, her hair, your hair has absolutely nothing to do with the degree of blackness or being a better person. "Good" hair, "bad" hair? Clean and trimmed hair is as good as any hair can get.

In her provocative book, *Sisters of the Yam: Black Women and Self-Recovery,* bell hooks reminds us of the days when hair grooming played an integral part in the bonding process between mother and child, and how, today, so many of us are petrified at the idea of letting someone else even touch our hair.

I remember sitting on the floor between my mother's legs as she would brush and comb my hair and how we would talk, love each other, and share things only mothers and daughters can share. I think about when my mate and I are loving each other and how he takes my hair and rubs it together, breathes into it, sweats into it, and how curly it gets as I begin to perspire and how excited that makes me. It's odd that people don't want to be touched. Have we become so afraid of the pure, physical and spiritual, exchange of love that we can no longer see the beauty in our naturalness? That we feel safer behind something purposefully manufactured for enticement? Is it not true that while adornment of our pates is important, what is more important is what lies *beneath* our hair follicles?

4

Black, Blue, Brown, Green, and Hazel

But, wait . . . we also have a tendency to trip a little on eye color.

Writing this is very awkward for me because the mere thought of me sitting here, at the computer, contemplating a discussion on eye color is almost laughable, especially since I'm not an opthamologist. Were this dialogue not necessary, due to the brainwashing that has been done, it would indeed be humorous. If we did not believe that having an eye color other than dark brown makes us more attractive, yes, I would be laughing. Yet, there are very successful black women who, at the beginning of their careers, were staring into audiences and boardrooms with rich, java brown eyes. Then someone told them that to become more accepted by the white community and possibly to reach more of the white market, perhaps they should change something, like their . . . eye color.

So today, we have those same talented, intelligent

women wearing light-brown- or hazel-green-colored contact lenses—not wearing them the way you would wear jewelry, changing from time-to-time and going without now and then, but wearing them as if they were a natural part of the body. And mind you, we're not talking prescription lenses here. It's bizarre, and very sad, that being "successful" can be so important that you let yourself be deluded into living a lie.

I once dated a man who, for the first three months of our relationship, wore colored contact lenses. He was so afraid I would not accept him with dark brown eyes that the charade continued until he began to develop an eye infection. He then was forced to "confess." Jay phoned me at work one day and said he had to see me immediately to tell me something in person, something that might make me not want to see him again; he said he desperately needed to see me right away. I was stunned and could imagine only the usual confession material—another woman, he was tired of me, another woman, and so on. Then he showed up and said, "What do you see different?"

I examined him, and for the life of me, I couldn't see anything different. "What is it?!" I exclaimed.

"Don't you see?"

"No, I don't."

"Look at my eyes."

"Yeah, and . . ."

"They're not the same color."

"Yeah, and . . . so what, you got colored contacts on or something?"

"No, I *had* colored lenses on. This is my real eye color—dark brown."

"Oh . . . Is this what you'd thought I'd be upset about? Give me a break, Jay. It's not that serious."

I felt so sorry for him because of his obvious lack of self-esteem. For someone, anyone, to risk their health trying to be something they are not is pitiful.

Sisters, eye color, like hair color and other parts of our anatomy (hair, nails, eyebrows, moles, etc.), is becoming an interchangeable cosmetic. Our hair length or color is likened to donning facial cosmetics—inevitably the real person should and is going to have to make a public appearance. I cannot imagine being emotionally and intimately involved with someone without them knowing that sometimes I get Samsonite luggage under my eyes because of sinus problems or lack of proper rest. That my ponytail turns into an interesting, geometric Afro-puff when I am intensely involved with a project or when I am exercising. That sometimes I look as if I don't care what I look like—and I don't sometimes. Wearing cosmetics full-time is like trying to hide the above things from a spouse or parent; it's virtually impossible, unless of course we are intent on hiding from ourselves as well.

Again, it's what lies behind the eyeballs, which is the same thing that lies beneath the hair follicles, that deserves our attention and focus. So let's keep this in mind when adorning ourselves.

5

The Big, The Beautiful, The Black Behind

Although many attempt to snub our birthright as Queen Mothers—refuting the black woman's command of Universal wisdom and knowledge, intelligence, creativity and industry—our most tangible birthright (also known fondly as the Black Woman's Heritage) is something no one can deny. And oddly enough, as often as we have been subjected to vicious comments regarding it, many nonblack women are now trying to attain it: everyone wants nice, big, round butts like ours. I find it ironic, how after so many years of the flat tush being "in," that the spherical, protruding shape of our backsides has now become one of the standards of physical beauty. History is repeating itself, echoing the late nineteenth century and the turn of this century, when bustles became the height of fashion after so many European explorers (usually male) returned from Africa marveling at the Hottentots, an African tribe made famous in Western civilization because of their gigantic, round, rear ends.

So, here we are, black women with nice, round behinds working out on the "butt blaster" machines so we can get nice, round, behinds. Sistas, sistas, sistas. The nice, round booty is already naturally ours. Butt blasters are futile—they only provide shape—something we already have. And for those of us who continually complain about how big it is—the fashion magazines say you should be a size six or eight instead of a ten or twelve—the booty isn't going anywhere.

If you're more than ten pounds overweight, any physician will tell you eating properly and exercising regularly will bring you down to your appropriate size. But, I repeat, *the booty ain't goin' nowhere.* Even Janet Jackson commented once in an interview that her nickname with her dance troupe is "The Booty," and she is reportedly five foot four and 110 pounds![5] At that size, if her butt is pronounced, believe me it is there to stay!

In one of her monologues, the black actress/comedienne Phyllis Yvonne Stickney discusses, "the power of the booty," and I love this piece every time I hear it. I'm reminded that we, black women, are powerful creatures and our power is found in every inch of us.

Sir Mix-A-Lot praises us righteously in his "Baby Got Back" rap:

> I like big butts and I cannot lie,
> You other brothers can't deny
> When a girl walks in with that itty bitty waist,
> and a round thing in your face . . .
> Even the jeans she's wearin',
> I'm hooked and I can't stop starin' . . .
> Oh, baby I wanna get witcha
> and take your picture . . .
> So Cosmo says you're fat

I ain't down with that,
36-24-36 . . . only if she's 5'3" . . ."[6]

Okay, I know homeboy is wild, his more recent thing being about "lungs" and all, but you get my drift. Listen to your brothers and sisters, girlfriends. "The power of the booty" is the power of the black woman as she takes her throne as Queen Mother, as she hobnobs and prances as Ms. Thang, and as she instructs, listens, and empathizes with others as Sista-Girl.

Queen Mother Lady once gave me some very good advice: "If it ain't broke, don't fix it." And sisters, there ain't a damn thing wrong with our big, beautiful, round, black, behinds.

The female body is a wondrous, precious thing. I wouldn't trade mine for anything in the world—cramps, PMS, bloating, dry skin, cellulite—no, not a single thing would I give up, having been blessed with this fabulous body. This is the body through which, if Spirit sees fit, lives will come forth and flourish. This is the body that allowed me to walk to the store for my ailing grandparents, whose bodies grew weak and immobile with grand age. This is the body that lets me concentrate on the peaceful tinkling of wind chimes, sending me to sleep during insomniac battles. This is the body through which I can smell rain coming and judge from the color of the sky when snow is about to fall; this is the body that embraces and comforts my Sista-Girls without my having to utter a single, solitary sound. No, this black woman's body is proud to be, and I wouldn't change a thing about it.

Extra Helpings and Waterloos

Self-perception, how we see ourselves, is critical when relating with others because how we view ourselves directly relates to the way we are treated, sexually and otherwise. Oftentimes, we blame others for our misfortunes in relationships. We say this person treated us unfairly, or that person disrespected us, excusing ourselves from all responsibility for this treatment. I cannot negate the fact that there are rude, disrespectful individuals in the world. But when people we care about—companions, spouses, relatives, friends—continually treat us in a way we find distressing, maybe we should be looking inside ourselves for the reason instead of outside at them.

How do we feel about ourselves? Do we feel we are unlovable, worthless, or undeserving? If so, this is how we are going to be treated. We are going to attract individuals incapable of love, kindness, and generosity, individuals who will abuse and mistreat us as we permit them to. If we believe we are "bad," this is the kind of person whom we will attract—someone who is "bad," someone who will bring nothing but negativity into our space.

On the other hand, if we feel we are loving, generous, good-natured individuals, this is the kind of person we will attract. These are the kinds of relationships we will become involved in. We will draw to ourselves people who will enrich our lives and make us feel whole.

That's all very easy to say, but the fact remains that many of us still harbor negative feelings about ourselves. Why is that?

Quite often, low self-esteem can be attributed to how we were raised as children. Parents and guardians did not necessarily have to be physically abusive to plant seeds of low self-worth within us. Some well-meaning parents believe praise, kind words, and generosity spoil children. Therefore, their children, after achieving some goal, are never given due credit and are only pushed further, implying to the children that their accomplishments were substandard. Think back. When you received high marks on your grade card, were you praised: "Honey, this is wonderful, I'm so proud of you." Or were you given a backhanded compliment: "Honey, this is good, but you received a C in science, you know that's your weakest point?" Were you sometimes called, "stupid," "brainless," or "lacking in common sense?" Were you favorably compared with other relatives or neighbors' children?

The relationships we are in now probably reflect the balances in our own childhoods.

Regarding compliments, do we pat ourselves on the back when we recognize we've done something exceptionally well, or do we wait for someone else's approval? Certainly the approval of a boss or colleague is important, but not as important as one's own approval of the self. I have a little saying I repeat when questioned about my self-praise: "If I don't pat myself on the back, no one else may do it." Bosses and colleagues may be more concerned with the "bottom line," not the steps required to get the "bottom line" they wanted. Thus, along the way we have to come to the rescue of our own consciences by giving ourselves pats on the back, not only for the completion of a task, but also for doing well in the steps required. It's called self-motivation. If you can't get motivational praise from anyone else, make sure you give it to yourself.

Continual chastisement stays with an individual longer than praise. When loved ones habitually treat us unkindly, this is sometimes what we will come to believe we deserve. We reach adulthood thinking we are unworthy of the beautiful love we see between our friends and their family members or the love portrayed (however seldom) on television or in the movies. Sadly, we sometimes grow to believe that this unkind, harsh treatment is the proper way to love someone. Even worse, we run away from relationships that could be rewarding and pleasurable because of psychological projections stemming from past relationships. Our view of loving relationships becomes unhealthy and distorted, bringing us never-ending unhappiness and anxiety until we break the cycle, which isn't easy but is possible.

By surrounding ourselves with positive people, we begin to see good within ourselves. Often it calls for another dose of that Sista-Girl courage, because we have to tell friends and family that we don't want to hear any more of their negative criticism. We've got to let folks know that telling us we don't need that extra helping of Thanksgiving dinner until we lose the weight we gained from our pregnancy does not help us lose those unwanted pounds any faster. Family members need to be informed that listening to us with glassy, inattentive eyes and then responding with "whatever" and "good luck" when we are discussing our hopes and dreams are not the most productive motivational techniques around. Just as womenfolk saying, "You ain't never gonna get a good man actin' [or lookin'] like that," isn't very healthy instruction on how to get a good man, either. They are our loved ones, and for that reason, we want to listen to them and heed their advice. But if it's hurting, you owe it to them, *and more important, to yourself,* to let them know, "Hey, what you just said [or didn't say or did or didn't do] hurt me."

And unfortunately, more often than not it will take a considerable amount of that Queen Mother faith to walk away from them when they don't stop. Sometimes loved ones just cannot see things the way you do, be it regarding a companion, your career, or your particular style of living. *However, what we must ask ourselves during these times of being torn between whom we love and who we are is the following:*

1. Whose life is it? (The answer to that should be obvious.)
2. Where do we want to go with this life of ours that will bring us the most joy and peace?
3. What is the most efficient, balanced, and constructive way of getting there?

I can virtually guarantee you that working with unnecessary negativity is not going to bring the most joy and peace, nor is it efficient and constructive.

So when loved ones approach you with or answer your ideas with pessimism, knowing this is unkind and causing you pain, simply say, "Thanks, but no thanks," and walk away. Don't be goaded into lengthy debates and empty discussions about what makes you feel good; these activities are draining to the spirit and therefore most counterproductive. Don't get involved, just walk away.

Once I decided to change careers and concentrate on writing, my business partner (whom I thought was my best friend at the time) and I had different perceptions about the way fundamental business operations should be handled. Additionally, I continually sensed a great deal of disharmony and agitation coming from her, not necessarily directed at me, but directed at life in general. So I decided to end the partnership, which also meant taking a break from the friendship, because with her they were inseparable. She was so angry and embittered at my decision and so distraught (because it was a very difficult business to go at alone), she contemplated revenge, not only on me but also on my husband.

Discovering her ploys, I became enraged. However, having learned from past experiences that it's sometimes best to let my anger cool overnight before making any decisions, I did just that. My husband was ready to proceed with a counterattack, but twenty-four hours later I told him I wanted to leave it alone, that we had neither the time nor the available energy to waste on the negativity that would be involved with seeking revenge on this child. Let her try to weave whatever she may. I had better things to do with my time. I once told her she needed to choose her battles more carefully. She evidently didn't listen; her revenge campaign was futile.

I want all you Sista-Girls out there to hear this: Battles of revenge are worthless because they are born out of malice. Whatever you broadcast into the Universe, you will undoubtedly become the recipient of later, receiving twice and even sometimes threefold as much. Fight for and with love, dignity, and truth; and when these return to you, you'll be two or three times the Sista-Girl you were at the beginning of the contest. As for all the other battles, just walk away.

This doesn't mean we should sever ties with our families or close friends because they don't provide us with the positive reinforcement we need. It means we have to look for certain kinds of support and strength elsewhere. And let me tell you, new friends, new experiences, and new beginnings are always right around the corner.

Irrespective of what we thought about others and how we viewed ourselves yesterday, we must ally ourselves with happy, radiant, individuals today. Learn to look at things through their eyes. We must change our perceptions for our sake and for the sake of our children, because *we really are worth it.*

7

Cronies and Cousins

The love shared between black men and women, especially those who are living together or married (which is specifically addressed in the chapter on marriage, entitled "From This Day Forward"), is as significant as the loving interactions of sisters, of kinfolk, of human beings.

Relationships between women are often strained for one reason or another. Yet, these are the very individuals with whom we have the most in common, who can understand and empathize with us more than anyone else. Too often we sisters allow petty grievances manifested through insecurities to create chasms between us. We literally argue and/or fight nonsensically over men, looks, personality differences, careers, mutual friends, and other issues. We talk about each other, reject each other because we think we're all that or we think they think they're all that. South Side sisters are compared to North Side sisters and East Side sisters are compared to West Side sisters. We feud all the time because we won't take the time to discover the things we have in common. Being negative and pointing out the obvious differences is much easier to do. I've had sisters actually tell me, "You don't need to waste your time with [that person or this person]," because the person in question didn't meet their socializing criteria. How time can be wasted on any human being is almost inconceivable to me.

The human experience is uniquely individual. Therefore, something can usually be learned from anybody you come across. No, we cannot be friends with everybody; this is impossible. But to disregard the value of another human being just because, for example, he or she does not have a college education or he or she is a single parent or he or she prefers partying on one side of town, while you prefer partying on the opposite side, is foolish. Discounting the personhood of another sister because she does not have an expansive, worldly vocabulary or because she does not speak using the rules of grammar and semantics as dictated by instructors of "the King's English" is sophomoric.

Thinking about this brings a particular incident to mind. When out at a club once, I was sitting at the bar discussing relationships with an attractive sister who I learned had recently separated from her husband. The place was (still is) one of those small clubs brothers and sisters frequent, on occasion, to step, kick back, listen to dusties, and talk about old school stuff. Where many sisters enter wearing three- and four-inch heels matching their three- and four-inch nails, completing the ensemble with dresses that appear to be painted on.

As I was saying, I was at the bar talking with this young woman. Through our conversation, I learned one of the reasons she and her husband were separated was she enjoyed going out occasionally and her husband didn't because he was Muslim. Actually, they both were, but she felt she could be a Muslim and still go out. Now, from studying Islam, I knew an orthodox Muslim wouldn't step one foot in a place like the one we were in, but perhaps this woman and her husband practiced a more relaxed version of the faith. She continued talking about how she could be happy by herself and so forth. Then, she went on to trash the barmaid.

Granted, it was obvious Ms. Thang behind the bar was interested in serving more than drinks. She had a Mae West figure and her outfit left virtually nothing to the imagination. She had been dipped into the leggings she wore, and one could suppose she decided to tie her blouse for effect because it certainly held nothing back. But, who was I to judge? Girlfriend was tending bar, pouring drinks very well, I might add, so she was obviously a grown woman making her own choices.

Well, Sista-Girl Muslim didn't care for the bartender's appearance at all, commenting that she looked like a slut, was embarrassing, and so forth. I offered that she wasn't embarrassing me because she and I were adult women doing nothing to each other but asking for and receiving legitimate service.

"Why would she dress like that?" the sister asked and answered her own question, "It must be for attention, but doesn't she know the kind of attention she's going to get?"

I replied by saying perhaps the kind of attention she got was the kind she wanted.

"But she looks like a hooker."

"Well, maybe she does have another business on the side. Who knows? Who cares? She's pouring my drinks fine and is not bothering anybody but you, and you're not drinking anything." I went to dance, tired of hearing one sister belittle another one without knowing anything about the woman's life circumstances, just offended by the way she dressed.

When I stepped off the dance floor, my Muslim sister decided to leave. She wasn't really having a good time because there were too many "bawdy" people at the club for her. That's understandable; gin joints aren't for everybody, especially those practicing intolerance.

Sisters, stay off of each other's cases. Some of us like fuchsia and some of us like taupe. Some of us are sluts and whores, and some of us are stone-cold bitches, and some of us are angels. All of us have something good to offer, but few of us want to take the few seconds required to go beneath a layer or two to get it. It takes all kinds to make a world, and unless someone is directing offense at you personally, there is no need to be offended. And if you ever decide to take the time to learn what's underneath another sister's clothes, what's underneath her skin—her heart, for example—instead of being irritated, you just might be pleasantly surprised.

African-Americans are not nearly strong enough as a group to start casting aside members of our community because of perceived differences; we can ill afford, as a people, to indulge in delusions of grandeur. And if we continue to behave as though we could—throwing the baby out with the bathwater, so to speak—we will always be a divided, angry, bitter, self-pitying people, instead of the majestic people our ancestors fought so hard and gallantly for. Let us not continue to bring shame upon ourselves and the beliefs of our ancestors by turning up our noses at our brethren. Instead, let us open dialogue and thereby widen the paths and reinforce the bridges that bring us closer together, closer toward the unified people we can be. And, sisters, *ain't no time like the present to start doin' so.*

Queen Mother Dr. Shirley, a corporate consultant and career counselor, and I were chatting one day on the phone about how we black women often mistreat and disrespect one another. Recalling one young sister who came to her office seeking advice on finding better employment, Dr. Shirley told me the young woman, like many she encountered, had a know-it-all attitude. She was an obtuse termagant. When this sister met Dr. Shirley for the first time, on a professional basis, she addressed the doctor by her first name. Dr. Shirley is a woman old enough to be her grandmother. Perturbed, but not surprised, the doctor told me most young sisters nowadays seemed to be lacking both respect for their elders and plain old common courtesy. "It almost seems as if they believe they are in competition with you," she remarked. "Imagine, being in competition with a woman old enough to be your grandmother! How ridiculous!" Ridiculous it is, yet I witness it all the time. We would rather believe what a man has to say, regardless of his motives, than listen to women who have undoubtedly seen, experienced and learned more than we have. We're always suspicious of our sisters, especially regarding relationships.

Because of the gravity of the love that can exist in intimate relationships, it may be difficult to refrain from irrational behavior when those relationships might be jeopardized by the threat of another human being, another sister. But if you have any respect for your relationship, your companion, and yourself, you will not allow yourself to be lured into acting irresponsibly. If a sister threatens your relationships, bring it to the attention of your mate and then call her bluff. Only one of two things can happen, and either will be for your betterment: in the end, either the strength of your relationship will be affirmed, or it will be sincerely questioned.

We have all been in ladies' rooms where sisters are primping and posturing. Any woman who is intimidated by the beauty of her sisters needs to take a good look in the mirror and review some family photographs, because we all came from the same place, ultimately. And though we may not possess the same physical characteristics, we are all beautiful children of the Universe, wondrous in our own individual ways.

I love to see beautiful black women walking along the boulevards, going to and from work, the health club, the grocery store, not even paying attention to the attention they receive because of their natural glory, just strolling along in their own Sista-Worlds.

The next time a sister looks at you while the two of you are primping in the mirror, smile and tell her how nice she looks. There has never been a time when I couldn't pick out at least one thing admirable in someone I encountered, be it sharp shoes, a sleek hairstyle, beautiful garments, a blindingly white smile, clear skin, well-manicured nails, or bright eyes. There is always something remarkable about us. Let's not squabble over it; let's rejoice in it.

Personalities clashing are unavoidable human occurrences. No one sees eye-to-eye all the time, and Sista-Girls and Ms. Thangs and even Queen Mothers are not spared from these experiences. However, we can prevent any severe damage by remembering we can always agree to disagree, amicably. My sister and I are, at times, as different as night and day when it comes to political and social views, but that doesn't stop us from discussing these subjects, debating them, arguing about them, and then concluding, "Okay, this isn't getting us anywhere. You're not going to change your mind, nor am I going to change mine. So I guess we'll just agree to disagree." Then we go on to talk about the sexiest new male screen actor, whereupon we get into another debate. But it's okay because we know we're different and we understand and accept and love the differences. They make our time together exciting and expand our perspectives. Don't let contrasting opinions prevent you from loving your Sista-Girl; so much more of the world is visible through the eyes of another, than through just the pair we have.

Likewise, sisters can learn a great deal from individual competitive sports. Track, gymnastics, and swimming athletes will tell you, only one individual gets to sit in first place. But although that is where the momentary glory lies, there is also a spirit of competition on and off the field that combines individual effort with friendship. Athletes help each other prepare mentally, work out together, and, once competing, push each other to do their absolute best. So the next time you meet a sister who has reached a level you are aspiring to—for example, in your career—don't backbite. Ask her how she did it. Talk to her. Gain insight. Learn. There are probably some things you still can help her with. Regardless of where we are on the learning curve, we should never stop learning, and smart Ms. Thangs never stop listening.

Not long ago, females were the last friends I thought I needed or wanted. Women were not to be trusted—they were back-stabbers, liars, cheaters, gold diggers, and God only knows what else. Relationships with sisters that had turned bitter on me resulted in my keeping a long arm's distance from most females I encountered. However, as I matured, I began to observe the support networks some black sisters had developed among themselves. When everything about them seemed weak and worthless, they had a group of sisters who gave them love, companionship, strength, and security. I watched how these Sista-Girls, Ms. Thangs, and Queen Mothers reached out to each other in good times as well as troubled times, in celebration and in mourning. And they all seemed to thrive and become more empowered from it. So I gave it a whirl—reaching out to my sisters instead of retreating, looking at their value instead of their expense, confiding in them about my failures instead of boasting of my triumphs. And now I am empowered by the relationships forged between me and some mighty strong Sista-Girls.

Beyond love between friends and between child and parent, there is the love between kinfolk. Numerous stories and anecdotes from older Queen Mothers are gathered in this work because these ladies are the kinfolk who have provided me and many other brothers and sisters the sage advice and support needed to move forward in the most frightening of times. The answers and guidance they impart when we're feeling cold, lonely, and scared are what we survive on, supplying us with the most enduring and incisive illuminations on our paths to destiny. Yet, far too often we neglect these saintly individuals.

In their aged and fragile years we visit irregularly, seek their counsel seldom, and love them even less. We let their beauty and honor fade, because in our youthful and foolish zest we can neither comprehend nor appreciate that which is not visibly bright, smooth, and speedy. We won't take a few minutes from our week to sit down and uncover the magnificence of generations gone by. Oh, we'll stop to drop off the grandkids or to pick up a pound cake, but we can't stop to share a smile and a hug.

I'll never forget, toward the end of an argument once, my late grandmother calmly saying, "You all are gonna miss me when I'm gone." She was right; we do miss her. Fortunately, there are other matriarchs still with us whom I can spend time with and talk to. So, as I have learned to, I am asking you sisters now, Will you please *slow down?* Some of the solutions you're so feverishly scurrying around to find are right there on your grandparents' porch. Just get on that old swing and listen, honey.

Grandfolk are just the tip of that wondrous kinship love. We all have aunts, uncles, cousins, nieces, and nephews who are deserving of our affection and attention. That annual family reunion is nice, but how about giving that crazy uncle in Tennessee a call this very moment, or writing your cousin who is serving in the military, or giving your niece a breather and baby-sitting for her?

In loving, accepting, and understanding ourselves, our sisters, and our kinfolk, we are able to provide those in need with the compassion and wisdom required to strengthen. We set good examples for all of the Universe's children to follow.

When we love ourselves and each other, we are committing our lives to setting noble goals, striving for perfection, and, simultaneously, accepting our humanity. We should search inward for talents and skills unique to us, seeking confirmation of these abilities from our brothers, our sisters, and Spirit. We then must go about sketching designs for our lives so we have focus and direction. And though the blueprints may change, with results not quite shaping up as we intended (life rarely does), we still have to continue forward, accepting and learning from both successes and failures. *Because self-love is planning and adapting.*

We must work diligently to be the best at all we undertake because although this excellence may not be expected of us from the outside world, in knowing who we really are—Sista-Girls, Ms. Thangs, and Queen Mothers—we dare not expect nor desire anything less from ourselves. We dare not disappoint our ancestry, our present relations, nor our future generations. We work arduously, sometimes tirelessly, and, at other times, are unaware of how we are able to continue. When our focus gets cloudy, we stop, we rest, we pray, and we go on. When the direction is tangled with dense obstacles and strange webs, we examine, we think, and we examine further, until we're able to prod our way through. We aspire toward perfection because nothing else is worth the price we have paid. *Because self-love is intelligent labor.*

Yet, throughout all of our endeavors, we must acknowledge our humanity—our interdependency on each other and our status as children of the Universe. We cannot afford to forsake anyone or judge anyone on the basis of any physical attribute or lack thereof because we didn't create any of this. We cannot afford to condescend because circumstances change within nanoseconds and that which is defined as *up* today may very well be referred to as *down* tomorrow. We cannot afford to backbite or seek vengeance because these activities drain and asphyxiate. Nor can we afford to be deluded by our strengths, believing we cannot err, and we can ill afford being misled by our weaknesses, believing we cannot succeed against whatever comes our way. All we can afford is faith in the Creator, in love, and in ourselves and in what can be accomplished within the sanctum of that energy. *Because self-love is nonjudgmental and realistic.*

So stand up, Sista-Girls, Ms. Thangs, and Queen Mothers. Let us place our arms around our very own bosoms and embrace ourselves. Then turn to the lady standing next to you and embrace her and the child next to her. *Because self-love is a reflection of true love—love you have for others and the love they have for you.*

PART 2

UNDERSTANDING OUR SEXUALITY

It's interesting that when I explain to individuals the necessity for providing sexual knowledge in the black community, they are amazed. "Isn't this basic knowledge?" I'm asked. "Don't people already know this stuff?"

Apparently not. Not when an informal survey among black college graduates of top universities reveals the fear of contracting AIDS through kissing. Not when pregnancy has still not decreased among young black teenagers. Not when incidences of AIDS is still rising in the heterosexual African-American community.

Not when I can ask a relatively intelligent and successful brother about practicing safe sex and he can tell me that he doesn't practice it one hundred percent: "I've been very bad about that over the years," my friend confesses.

"Well, what about contracting HIV?" I ask.

"It's a discipline problem, and it's an arrogance problem. It's like using a dental dam when you want to go down on a woman; what's the point? I want to be inside the woman not inside a piece of plastic or rubber."

"Rollin' the dice, huh," I comment.

"Yeah, I know," he responds.

Or another brother tells me, "I don't like the way they feel, and besides, as long as I have sex with women who aren't in the high-risk group, my chances of getting HIV are slim."

Yet some people *still* question our need. "The knowledge and information is out there, isn't it?" they continue to debate.

Yes, it is, but for some reason a lot of black folks still ain't gettin' it. So what do you do when important messages aren't being heeded? Well, in the case of sex today, you keep sending them, because it's a matter of life and death. In the case of the black family today, it's a matter of whole, good families versus dilapidating, broken homes. In the case of the future for African-America, it's a matter of an overwhelming underclass resulting from premature parenthood (not to mention an alarming number of premature infants), a lack of higher education, and indigence versus a burgeoning middle and upper class resulting from completed educations and successful careers and businesses.

When our young women still need to inquire about various forms of birth control, when they don't have proper information on devices and methods such as diaphragms, IUDs, Depo-Provera, and so on and are still refusing to take birth control pills because they are "afraid of the side effects." This is a clear indication that although the information may be out there, it still isn't getting through. When I was discussing contraceptive sponges with one Sista-Girl, she thought I was talking about the kind of sponge used to clean the bathtub. And this woman has two daughters! (Of course, I hipped her up.)

And you know, equally alarming are the conversations among young black women regarding the importance of having a sexual relationship, how these women place its significance above that of love, communication, education, self, and family welfare. "Once you're in a sexual relationship, you have it all," some of our girls think. Why do they believe this? Because they equate sex with love, apparently unaware that this kind of thinking is hazardous to one's health.

So, with the knowledge provided here, at least some of these girls may realize their thinking is wrong. Perhaps brothers will resign themselves to going "inside a piece of plastic or rubber" because sisters will give no other alternative to brothers desiring intercourse with women who are not members of the "high-risk group."

If we don't value and protect our own life, how can we expect anyone to share his or hers with us? If we don't know our body, how can we expect to share it properly with someone else and, more important, how can we entrust it to the desires and whims of another individual? If we are ignorant of aspects of sexual behavior other than the consequences of being involved with disease-carrying mates, how can we fully enjoy ourselves? If we don't comprehend the identities of sexual relationships and love relationships, how can we truly understand the relationships we partake in?

Knowledge, even if fundamental, is vital to participating in nondestructive, healthy sexual relationships, so, Sista-Girls, Ms. Thangs, and Queen Mothers, listen up!

8 A Sexual Preface

Our advancement—the successful progression of the black woman, individually and collectively—requires that we possess a clear understanding of ourselves. This evolution also entails having a crystal-clear awareness of our sexuality and the mental as well as physical role it plays in our lives and in the universe.

African-American women must acknowledge the fact that we are sexual entities and that this plays a definite part in who we are as human beings. When discussing the role of sexual activity, you will find that most people, because of the dense patriarchal fabric of American society, will hop on the "it is not the most important part of a relationship, in fact, it is the least important part of a relationship" bandwagon. We are so entrenched in this sort of morality, implying that sex is "bad" (although most of us participate in it as often as possible), we are more than willing to dismiss sex's relevance. Well, Ms. Thangs, the fact of the matter is that were it not for the important role sex plays in our lives as human beings, there would be no human beings.

celibacy, abstinence, and virginity

While chillin' and channel surfin' at home one Saturday evening, I stumbled across an old (1959) movie, *The Best of Everything,* about the scandalous lives of employees at a large New York publishing house.[7] Being a fan of the work of Joan Crawford, who was playing in the movie, I grabbed my bag of chips and diet soda, told my husband to go read a book if he didn't want to watch the movie with me, wrapped up in a throw, and gave the tube my undivided attention. At first I was delighted—the writing was interesting, the acting was superb, and the plot was engaging. However, by the time the credits began to roll at the end, I was extremely annoyed, to say the least.

The underlying theme of the movie was that no woman could be completely satisfied without being married, without having a man in her life. Having missed who wrote this fairy tale, I concluded it must have been a man—an ingratiating, chauvinistic, probably . . . Never mind. The leading characters in the movie were three young women, and Joan Crawford played a supporting character, Ms. Farrow.

It was obvious that one character, although she had "been around," was relatively mature and consciously decided to play the "casting couch" game for the sake of her acting career, like many actresses did then and unfortunately still do. But suddenly, during the second half of the movie, this beautiful, career-driven Ms. Thang becomes this untalented fatal attraction, accidentally killing herself because she is so distraught about not getting her man. *Message: "Bad girls" never fare well in the end.*

Another character decided to give her virginity to a guy

who swore he loved her and would most definitely marry a girl he loved even if she wasn't "pure." Of course, he pledges this while they are necking on the sofa in his flat. A little later, while driving her to get an abortion (without her knowledge—she thought they were driving to the church to get married), Boyfriend hands her a wedding band to wear and says that he has no intention of marrying her. Because she doesn't understand, he tells her where they are really going, and she jumps out the car while it's still in motion, determined not to get an abortion (talk about your subliminal messages!). Girlfriend ends up engaged to the handsome young doctor who treated her during her hospitalization—she miscarried after jumping from the car. *Message: Premarital sex is a no-no and so are abortions.*

Finally, the Sista-Girl who seemingly has it all together, who decides to concentrate on her career as an editor (which she had gone to college for) and leave romance to the birds and bees for a while, gets a telephone call from an ex-fiancé. Sista-Girl was in the middle of putting a nice finish on a lovely date with a colleague but nonetheless swooned when she received this phone call. Seems the ex-boyfriend will be in town and wants to get together for old times' sake. She agrees; exit handsome colleague.

She meets with her ex; he professes that he broke their engagement because he was young and very impressed by what the oil money of his wife's family could do. He also apologizes for being so immature; alas, she was the only girl he ever really loved. They begin seeing each other, and one day before he returns home to Texas, she inquires about how he is going to handle telling his wife about them, about getting a divorce. He is confounded; "What divorce?" Sista-Girl is now appalled that he would think that he could have her and his wife, too (permanently, that is; I suppose the weeks they spent together during this initial visit didn't count). Pictures of the mean old spinster Ms. Farrow start looming in her mind, and she leaves him for good after a soliloquy about "nice" girls versus "bad" girls. At the end it is implied she finds love with the colleague after deciding not to further her career. *Message: "Good/nice girls" don't become involved with married men and aren't career women.*

Ms. Farrow, the antagonistic older woman, was a senior editor at the publishing house and suffering in a relationship with a married man. It seems she decided on career instead of family, and now the young girls in the office who are getting married and leaving the company are reminding her of what could have been. She meets a guy, dumps the married man, gets married herself, and discovers she is too old to find true happiness as the housewife of a good, ordinary man, so all she can do is return to her career. *Message: Again, career women always end up lonely, unhappy, unfulfilled spinsters.*

"No wonder so many women were into baking cookies and husband-catching," I thought, "with this kind of stuff permeating entertainment." When the final credits began rolling, I reached for a barf bag. The end. (Now, you know I just had to find out who wrote this, this, uh . . . Anyway, as my luck would have it, the screenplay writers were a man and a woman, and it was based on a novel written by a woman. Go figure!)

As you read further, you'll notice that I continually underscore the fact that sex has nothing to do with emotions such as love, jealousy, and happiness. Nevertheless, please don't let the nonemotional connection diminish the significance of sex. The sex drive is one of the strongest instincts humans have, second only to that of self-preservation. Its importance, therefore, is obvious. Yet holding on to romantic ideals and archaic notions, like those of the movie characters described above, can be harmful to this vital facet of human life.

The sacrosanctity of sex in our time has demeaned it in such a manner that I am forced to sound contradictory and tell you that sex is not that serious. It is important, but it can wait, which is something disallowed by America's perpetual and childish struggle with the natural power of sex. For those of us continually riding the judgmental bus and the self-righteous train, celibacy has become a glorified pursuit. It is almost as if the Declaration of Independence should read, ". . . life, liberty, and the pursuit of celibacy," in the minds of some of our more conservative citizens. And for those of us aboard the freedom-fighter train, "sexual freedom" becomes just another cause to rally around.

Sisters, allow me: Neither sexual activity (in most of its forms) nor celibacy should be glorified or held in disdain. One is neither better nor worse than the other, and either can be harmful if engaged excessively. The example of religious personnel can be cited as an argument for celibacy or abstinence. However, they are a minority and an exception. So unless you are planning to devote your life to a religious tenet requiring you to abstain from sexual intercourse for the remainder of your days on earth (and most of us dare not), accept that sex is a natural, important part of your life as a human being.

Deciding one's sexual course is a personal matter that should not be held up for scrutiny by or the judgment of anyone outside the relationship, unless a psychological problem has been diagnosed by a physician. I will not justify or glorify personal decisions regarding very personal behavior. It would be like giving men who are genuinely faithful and devoted spouses medals of honor for their fidelity, which would be absurd.

premarital sex

I've always defended premarital sex on the grounds that sexual knowledge is important. If you are a virgin, marrying someone who is not, you may unknowingly be marrying a sexually dysfunctional person. Or, you could have a multitude of fantasies manifested from stories you've heard and romance novels you've read and be dreadfully disillusioned on your wedding night. Now, while sex is not the most important aspect of a relationship, I suppose it would be nice to know what you're getting yourself into, wouldn't it?

Anyway, being proud of virginity is like being proud of good posture. So what? You know how to stand and sit, but do you know how to communicate, how to forgive, how to love? These things are a tad bit more important than good posture *and virginity.* At the same time, flaunting the fact that you've had numerous sexual encounters is like flaunting the fact that you eat a lot. Do you exercise regularly to compensate for all of the calories, eat balanced and nutritional meals, drink plenty of water to keep your system hydrated and flushed? Eating properly is more important than eating plentifully *and sexual hyperbole.*

Ms. Thangs, premarital sex involving two mature, consenting, legally defined adults is nothing to be ashamed of and something that can prevent nervousness and paranoia on the wedding night. There's enough performance anxiety in the world.

sexual orientations

Comprehending and accepting that people are different should be a primary goal of future Queen Mothers. You or I may be heterosexual like perhaps ninety to ninety-five percent of the human population[8], but this does not mean that homosexuality or bisexuality is abnormal or wrong. Saying that people with nonheterosexual orientations are abnormal in analogous to saying a white rose stemming from a red rosebush should not be considered a rose. Well, it may be different because it's a white rose from a red rosebush, but it is still a flower, still a rose, carrying both alluring fragrance and irritating thorns.

Yet, there are individuals in our time insisting that homosexuality is wrong because if it were "normal" and morally correct, AIDS would not have annihilated such a great portion of the homosexual population. So, I suppose this means that the more than twenty-five million Europeans who were killed by the bubonic plague or the Black Death in the fourteenth century were all "abnormal," doing something wrong or immoral. Perhaps the earth really is flat, after all. GET REAL. It is time for our mores and ethics to move beyond the mythical and fabled beliefs of centuries gone by and catch up with the technology and intelligence we have developed in the twentieth and twenty-first centuries.

And for the record: One, the acronym of *A*cquired *I*mmuno*D*eficiency *S*yndrome is AIDS and should never be spelled or thought of as "Aids," *please. Aid* is "assistance" or "help," *AIDS* is the acronym for the disease; the terms are completely different in definition. Two, it is not a "gay disease." It is a disease that can be contracted in a number of ways, across sexual communities. As a matter of fact, the number of reported AIDS cases is rising in the *black heterosexual* community.

Sometimes I wonder if people actually realize what magnificent works and teachings would be missing from the human experience were it not for Plato, Leonardo da Vinci, Michelangelo, Tchaikovsky, Noel Coward, Ma Rainey, Bessie Smith, Collette, Gertrude Stein, Countee Cullen, Walt Whitman, James Baldwin, Jane Addams, Lorraine Hansberry, Ethel Waters, and Audre Lorde, all of whom were non-hetero.[9] Imagine, had AIDS been a plague of the fifteenth century, the Sistine Chapel might not have become the home of one of the world's most renowned and precious efforts of love and art. I shudder, holding back tears, when I think of the potential beauty and profundity that have most certainly been lost due to the toll

AIDS has already taken on the homosexual community, the human community.

Queen Mothers, I implore you to appreciate that we are all children of the Universe, no better no worse than anyone else. Different maybe, but this is what makes us interesting, what makes the world beautiful and provides us all with our own unique sanctuaries.

sexual impositions

As sexual human beings, we have to concede that our desires are not always the desires of our partners, nor do their desires always correspond with ours. Consideration and respect of our mate's limitations and feelings are a critical aspect of human relating. If you're tired, you want that to be respected, so "do unto others" and respect the needs of your partner. When your mate is exhausted from a hard day at work and just wants to go to sleep, try to remember the last time your body was tied up in knots of tension and how the cool sheets and downy pillows felt once your nerve-racked body lay down.

If you say no, mean no. Saying no but meaning yes is a cruel, frustrating sex game that immature adults play. Saying yes just to please your partner when you really don't feel like having sex can make it very awkward for you *both* if he or she senses your lack of enthusiasm; they may feel cheated or, worse, that you don't care about them when in fact you really do. This behavior has no business in mature relationships and results in bruised feelings and sometimes bruised bodies. Watch your body language, and make sure you don't send mixed signals. For some of the younger sisters, this is a little more difficult to do because it calls for knowing what you want and what you want to do before you do it—a mentality that frat parties and nightclubs discourage. For example, alcohol tends to loosen inhibitions, and if we aren't careful the next thing we know, we're flirting and making eyes at individuals whom we wouldn't normally flirt with under sober circumstances. So we must be careful. Don't play with other people's emotions. It's not funny, and it's unfair. *Sista-Girls say what they mean.*

There is absolutely no reason why you (or anyone else) have to participate in an activity you do not want to be a part of. Say no, walk away, and if a person imposes, communicate that the kind of behavior being displayed is something you will not tolerate and that if there is to be *any* kind of relationship between you, this behavior must stop. If the attempts to impose do not cease after that, be true to your word, Ms. Thang, and leave that individual alone. If you don't, be advised that you are playing with fire, possibly with dynamite, and placing your life and, perhaps, the lives of your loved ones in danger. Remember, my girlfriend Karen took her no-good, drug-dealing boyfriend back and ended up a casualty of the drug scene. *Ms. Thangs never accept threats or impositions.*

no excuses

Just as imposition is unacceptable in sexual relationships, so are the excuses used to rationalize sexual behavior. All of us Sista-girls, Ms. Thangs, and Queen Mothers have been blessed with our own brains. Using what your peers or friends do, or what they say they do, sexually (or in any other instance) as an excuse for your behavior is foolish. How often when we were children did Queen Mothers ask us, "If your best friend jumped off the top of a high-rise building, would you jump, too?" Yet, as young adults we ride in cars with friends knowing that everybody involved in the evening's party is inebriated and in no condition to drive. We talk about, poke fun at, and laugh at those less fortunate or less knowledgeable than we are because a friend happens to make their misfortune a topic of conversation in a misguided attempt at providing amusement.

Some comedians have a policy that goes something like this, "Nothing is sacred in comedy because it's just entertainment." And true, they joke about the disabled, criminals, drugs, poor folks, rich folks, religion, racism, marriage, celebrities, almost anything one could think to talk about. But I've never heard a comedian make fun of AIDS. So maybe we should take the hint and remember that everything is not funny, that some things, *like life,* are sacred. And just because your buddy's out having unprotected sex, doesn't mean that you should join in the Russian roulette game. Your Sista-Girlfriend's rhythm method may not necessarily work for you, so do you and your partner a favor and visit the local drugstore or clinic. (Condoms are free at the clinic.)

If you enjoy one-on-one sexual relationships, there is no reason to join in a multiple-partner sexual encounter simply because your friends are going to and want you to participate. If you're a virgin, the fact that many of your friends claim they are not (perhaps truthfully, perhaps not) is no reason for you to lose your virginity if you don't want to.

Likewise, if you feel you are ready for sexual relations and some of your friends are clinging to their virginity like a newborn to a mother, there is little reason for you to use them as a reason to hold on to yours.

If most in your peer group are heterosexual and you're experiencing sexual feelings, too, but toward someone of your own gender, don't feel pressured into heterosexual behavior. Talk to someone first (someone who is objective and nonbiased toward homosexuality), but don't give into acting in a way that you feel is unnatural for you.

Excuses are illogical and have little value in human relating. If they do anything, they only postpone the inevitable. And the inevitable consequences of not being true to ourselves are usually more devastating than the discomfort we sometimes feel by being truthful. Your excuse for making a play for your best friend was that you were drunk. And when she learns about you dating a lesbian, how is she going to feel? How are you going to convince her that she can trust you, that you respect her heterosexuality, that you are still her Sista-Girl?

Your excuse for not using a condom this time was that Boyfriend doesn't like the way condoms feel. What will it be next time, you couldn't take five or ten minutes to stop at the convenience store (one reason they're called "convenience")? And if your pregnancy test comes back positive, what will be your excuse then? Worse, what will be your excuse when you have to tell your parents that their daughter may die in a few years due to complications from AIDS? Leave excuses alone. Instead of encouraging and promoting positive solutions, they only exacerbate the problems.

Solicit advice wisely, make your own decisions without excuses, and take the credit or pay the consequences for your decisions. Be confident of the fact that one thing no one can take from you is that you acted on your own accord and are willing to be responsible for such action. Besides, the fewer excuses you use, the less dire the consequences will be. I think Queen Mothers call this behavior "being an adult."

the booty call

Sometimes single Sista-Girls, whatever their age, just *want to get some.* We simply want to have sex—no romance, no lovemaking, no mating ritual—just sex. We wake up in the middle of the night or, like me, can't go to sleep and don't feel like masturbating. So we reach for the telephone and make that call. Sometimes our buddies are telepathic and telephone us, but however it happens, we both get what we want and then the visiting party leaves.

This isn't anything to be ashamed of. For decades, sexually dynamic women sat by the telephone waiting and waiting for that ring signaling sexual gratification was a possibility that particular day or evening. We would sit on the end of a mental, sexual leash; we could answer the call, but could not make the call. Making the call was out of the question because it was deemed inappropriate behavior for any woman, young or old. Now, at the beginning of a new millennium, women are finally sexually empowered, not only with the ability to say yea or nay when propositioned, but with the ability to proposition others without stigma or novelty being attached to the act. So, if you don't have a steady, it's late at night, and the toy batteries are low, go ahead and make that call, Ms. Thang. It's your right.

I realize that this behavior is unthinkable to some women because, as I have said, for centuries women have been on the receiving end of the sexual zone. Women who pursued or solicited sexual activity for the sake of mere sexual fulfillment were looked upon as harlots or sluts. However, society approved men's pursuits, actually encouraged them. And black women, for fear of even hinting at the stereotype that surrounded us—nymphomaniacal, sexual dynamos—for too long played hard to get not only to give the pursuer a challenge but to disprove the stereotype. Additionally, brothers could love and leave us, but us loving and leaving them was not acceptable unless it was in answer to an even more ardent admirer. Even then we may still have had to brave the disapproving eyes of society, which decided to view us as unchaste women. Well, honey, IT'S ALL OVER. Thanks to a few hundred years and thousands of strugglin', fire-eatin', year-round flag-carryin', banner-wavin', corset-snatchin', bra-burnin' sisters who were willing to endure all the heat our male-dominated society wanted to mete out, WE ARE FREE.

Thanks to women like Queen Mother Francis Ellen Watkins Harper, born free in the slave state of Maryland in 1825, founder of the National Association of Colored Women and delegate to the Women's Rights Convention in 1866 frequently and who fervently addressed, among other issues, the importance of equal rights including what is now referred to as sexual freedom. The following excerpt from the poem "A Double Standard," written and published by Mrs. Watkins Harper[10], is testimony to one of several problems sisters as well as all women have been facing throughout the centuries. Let us praise and give thanks to this valiant lady and the legions of others before, during and after her time who have made our lives, as women, as sexual human beings whose relevance is just as significant as our male counterparts, just that much freer.

> ". . . Do you blame me that I loved him
> That my heart beat glad and free,
> When he told me in the sweetest tones
> He loved but only me?
> Can you blame me that I did not see
> Beneath his burning kiss
> The serpent's wiles, nor even hear
> The deadly adder hiss? . . .
> No golden weights can turn the scale
> Of justice in His sight;
> And what is wrong in woman's life
> In man's cannot be right."

Mama always said if you got an itch, scratch it. So, like I said, my sisters, go ahead, make that call. And if someone has the audacity to turn his or her nose up at you, tell this person that he or she must be smellin' the smoke from the flames you just put out.

Acknowledging our sexuality is the first step to understanding it. While celibacy, abstinence, and virginity all have their proper place during an individual's life, the absence of sexual activity in one person's life is not to be lauded, just as the abundance of sexual activity in another's life shouldn't be paraded. Both concern personal and private decisions, and neither are actions upon which judgment should be rendered.

If participated in by knowledgeable, mature, human beings, sexual intercourse is healthy and fun. The danger lies in turning away from those seeking our guidance and/or acceptance and understanding when they come to us regarding this subject. The danger lies in the fact that our turning away from them, from the truth, from understanding, turns us that much further away from understanding ourselves and our very own humanity.

It's Like Taking a Bath

It's hard for me to comprehend why several sisters I know refuse to believe sex is a purely physical act. I try explaining to them that there is no inherent link existing between sex and love, and they start rollin' their eyes, buckin' their necks, and wavin' those long forefingers. "What do you mean there is no relationship between sex and love? I have to love the person I have sex with, or it ain't goin' on," they insist. So let me try to clarify this once more, ladies.

Whatever other emotion is involved—love, jealousy, happiness—is due to one or both of the partners mentally projecting the emotion onto the act. The human body verifies this: sex evokes only the physiological, involuntary emotions of pain and pleasure. Immersing oneself in a tub of warm water can be pleasurable, or burning one's finger on a hot stove can be painful; both of these are also simply physiological responses. The water from the bath is soothing to the nerve endings of the skin, thereby sending signals to the brain, which decodes the signals as pleasure sensations. So we relax in the tub. The heat of the stove, when it touches the nerve endings of the finger, is so intense that a signal is immediately transmitted to the brain, which decodes this sensation as pain. So we instantly remove our finger. There is no intentional thought to respond physically in either case, as the events are purely involuntary and physiological.

The actual pleasure or pain derived from sexual intercourse is purely physiological. Nerve endings found in both male and female genitalia send signals to the brain, which, in turn, decodes them as either pain or pleasure. Love, the emotion, is in no way involved, and the person touching you is actually no more than an instrument prodding for physiological responses.

No, it's not very romantic, but Queen Mothers understand that incorrectly linking physical attraction and emotion can sometimes be disastrous. So let's keep everything in perspective, okay? It helps to keep us from getting burned.

10

It's a Hormone Thang

Because sex is primarily a nonemotional act, certain individuals can successfully participate in what is often called "casual" sex—intercourse where no emotion is involved nor evoked by either party—you know, booty calls. One participates merely for the sake of pleasure. People who find themselves in the throes of moral dictates also call this lustful sex (or sinful sex). Personally, because sex of this nature is the product of a hormonal drive, I tend to view it as "pure" sex. A primal necessity. Sometimes you read a book for knowledge; sometimes you read for pleasure; but, we all need to read.

Some of my sisters may be asking how I can consider sex in such a cavalier manner. Because, ladies, sex is so overrated. Inhibited, prudish, self-righteous, homophobic, AIDS-fearing individuals have placed the sex act in such a precarious position, its appeal is now found in its constricted societal nature, instead of its physiological nature, where it should be.

Sex is a pumping, grinding, sweating, clinching, pinching, squeezing, teasing, shouting, vibrating, gliding, rocking, swaying, sucking, licking, fingering, peaking, falling, action between two or more human beings. It can be wonderful. However, it is not, nor should it ever be, the beginning, defining, or ending of a human relationship. And, please pardon the expression (with no pun intended), this is where most of us fuck up.

There was a miniseries broadcast on public television while I was in the midst of this project. The title was "The Nature of Sex." Being the voyeur I am, and wanting more research for this book, I watched all six hours of it. I had seen humans "do it," birds "do it," dogs "do it," and fish "do it," but this Sista-Girl had never seen elephants, monkeys, or praying mantises "do it," and I must say it was one of the most fascinating programs I had seen in a long time. Not just because it temporarily satiated my voyeuristic need but because the theories behind sexual activity and behind man's own evolution with respect to sexual activity were intriguing.

In the animal kingdom, sex is driven by the need for procreation—one of the strongest instincts, second only to self-preservation. When many female animals are in "estrus" (the stage similar to ovulation in human females), their bodies secrete hormones that produce strong scents and unique physical characteristics to communicate to the males of their species that they are ready for copulation, at which point, eventually, a male comes along and has sex with her. (Humans term it being in heat. I often wonder if human females don't go through the same thing. You know, those times before your period when you're feelin' all funky and overweight and you're just attractin' all kinds of brothers?) Anyway, if this male possesses certain qualities she finds attractive, often he can remain with her until she becomes pregnant. Upon conception his role changes to that of provider or helpmate. However, this lasts only as long as the female needs the help. After the offspring is born, the father is no longer needed for sex or companionship. So fathers are rarely present among mothers and offspring in the animal kingdom.

Scientists have theorized that we, humans, attempted monogamy because of the very long period required for the maturation of human offspring. That maturation period is longer than that of any other animal on earth. Consequently, being together so long required another kind of commitment—beyond that of instinctual procreation—an agreement to provide, nurture, and protect offspring during this long time frame.

This brought human boyfriends and girlfriends closer together, and through time it became the socialized pattern that created families and the need and/or desire for monogamy. Polygamous human cultures have existed, and some still do. However, they are few and far between.

Yet, even in western culture, where monogamy is considered the norm, the primitive sexual conscience of human males is still a reality. Revealing itself in adolescence, college years, and sometimes throughout "serious" relationships, the instinct for males to "fertilize" as many females as possible is very prevalent. The Hite Report and Masters and Johnson studies, which questioned men and women about extramarital affairs and found a higher rate among men than women, also provide testimony to this theory. In most of these studies two thirds of men questioned have had extramarital affairs, whereas one third of the women questioned confessed to sexual infidelity.[11] Why? Because, some scientists suggest, males are more sexually driven than females due to the strong instinctual desire to procreate as much as possible. Therefore, monogamy is not a natural state. So what should Sista-Girls expect?

Well, I believe the monogamous socialization pattern

that existed for human females is slowly being altered. Because of economic factors requiring females to also become "hunter-gatherers," Sista-Girls today, in the first part of their lives, are deferring marriage and childbearing to secure a certain lifestyle for themselves and are therefore more inclined to be involved in "casual" relationships. Ms. Thangs are "hunting and gathering" what is needed prior to starting a family, much like laying a foundation prior to building the actual house. This also means they are dating two or more individuals simultaneously, unlike their mothers, who were basically monogamous, dating and marrying one man. And with the technological advances in birth control, sisters can safely enjoy more than one sexual relationship prior to marriage without worrying about increasing the population unnecessarily, sacrificing their careers, jeopardizing their health, or having to make difficult decisions regarding pregnancy termination. Therefore monogamy, while still an important facet of long-term relationships, does not carry the weight it did a few decades ago, nor does it appear in relationships as quickly as it once did.

The discussion here of the *Nature of Sex* program was to show how little we human animals differ from our relatives on the lower rungs of the animal kingdom ladder. It's a fact that instinct, which is hormonally driven, governs our sexual drives. In females, these hormones are estrogen and progesterone.

It is the level of these hormonal substances in the body that is responsible for the sexual drive. In certain instances, stress inhibits the production of these hormones and thereby diminishes sexual desire. If a Sista-Girl is emotionally stressed-out by a partner or a relationship, this can drive her into a vicious circle: stress inhibits sexual desire—a lack of sexual desire inhibits communication—a lack of communication leads to the erosion of the relationship, which in turn causes stress. This is the only way in which emotions play an actual part in sex. Likewise, if a sister is happy and content in her relationship, her hormones are being secreted normally and all else being equal, her sexual drive should be normal. What "normal" is will be discussed later (in Chapter 14, "Foreplay, Fetishes, Fantasies, and Faking It").

11

Sex Is Love . . . NOT!

Due to the funky (in the pejorative sense) viewpoint of sex-pervading Western "civilization," there are about as many myths surrounding sex as there are surrounding Creation.[12] Let Ms. Thang dispel some of them right now.

SEX IS ALWAYS WONDERFUL: FALSE. Sex is like everything else that can be controlled and manipulated by human beings—sex is whatever you make it. It can be wonderful or terrifying, depending on the circumstances. A ten-minute romp can be just as fulfilling or scary as an hour-long session, or an hour-long session can be just as insignificant as a ten-minute romp. Depends on who you're rompin' with and why. I once lived with a man who, one day after coming home from work, threw me on the bed boasting, "You know you want this." But I didn't. I was emotionally finished with the relationship and trying to determine how I was going to move out. I fought with him, begging him to leave me alone, but he didn't. Those were some of the longest, most agonizing minutes of my life. (The thought of this man and his arrogant, planetary-sized ego still makes me want to puke to this day.) But what was I supposed to do? I lived with him, and this was before a woman was allowed to say no to her husband or lover. *No ladies, sex ain't always all that.*

SEX ALWAYS RELIEVES TENSION: FALSE. Again, it depends on the circumstances. If a Sista-Girl is in the mood and needs to release tension, sex may be the answer. Sometimes if I am suffering from insomnia and I don't want to disturb my man's slumber, I'll masturbate, promptly falling asleep within fifteen minutes of bringing myself to orgasm. But, there are times when sex is the cause of the tension. For example, if there is a conflict in the relationship due to the frequency of sexual intercourse (or lack thereof), sex may cause a great deal of tension and anxiety as opposed to relieving it.

SEX SHOULD BE EXPERIENCED ONLY FOR THE PURPOSE OF PROCREATION: FALSE. If this were true, we would not be able to please ourselves alone (and I would be one cranky bitch from having chronic insomnia).

SEX IS HEALTHY: TRUE. Repressing sexual desires can be damaging to the human psyche, resulting in abnormal behavior.

One of the most recent compilations of research by the Kinsey Institute notes children who are reprimanded or punished for exploring their genitals are possibly being taught that sexual pleasure via masturbation is wrong, a message that could impede their ability to embrace mutually pleasurable sexual adult relationships.

SOMEONE WHO HAS A LOT OF SEX HAS A LOT OF SEXUAL KNOWLEDGE: FALSE. Unfortunately, far too many individuals believe that because they have had a multitude of sexual partners, they are sufficiently educated about sexual activity. STUPID! That's like saying since I drink a lot of coffee, I know a lot about coffee-beans and all. Wrong. This Sista-Girl has never worked at Starbucks.

ALL BLACK MEN HAVE HUGE PENISES: FALSE. Anyway, haven't you heard: "It's not the size of the boat, but the motion of the ocean."

ALL WHITE MEN HAVE SMALL PENISES: FALSE. See the above and check out some made-for-cable programming. They're starting to show penises now—it's only fair; they've been displaying women's nipples for the longest!

ALL BLACK WOMEN ARE NYMPHOMANIACS: FALSE. Well, I've been . . . Never mind.

SEX IS NO FUN UNLESS ORGASM IS ATTAINED: FALSE. Sometimes it takes a little longer for one mate to achieve orgasm, which means if the other mate can't wait, someone is going to be left without. There's nothing wrong with that. If you allow yourself to become engrossed in the physicality of it all—the sweat, the heartbeats, the sounds, the muscles, the heat—you will still have a very pleasurable experience. Intercourse reminds me of what someone once said about success, "It's not a destination; it's a journey." Just because there weren't any fireworks at the end doesn't mean the picnic was no fun.

ALL WOMEN HAVE SENSITIVE BREASTS AND NIPPLES: FALSE. The only time mine get sensitive is right before my period starts. And even then, it's a painful sensation, not a sensual one. Yet, there are some women who can experience orgasms if someone just plays with their breasts and nipples. We're all different. If your honey enjoys fondling your glands, but it does nothing for you, just make sure this is communicated. Allow them their pleasure, and they will allow you yours.

FELLATIO AND CUNNILINGUS ARE KINKY AND NASTY: FALSE. Not getting enough fellatio (oral sex performed on the male genitalia) is one of the largest complaints brothers have. Likewise, there are many sisters who won't cooperate if a brother doesn't perform cunnilingus (which is oral sexual pleasure given to the female genitalia, a.k.a. "taking the southern route.") Don't knock what you haven't tried. And if you have tried it and found it distasteful, I've been told that it can become an acquired taste. And remember, you've got to give in order to receive.

HIV IS AIDS: FALSE. HIV, human immunodeficiency virus, is the virus that causes AIDS. The virus acts by attacking certain white blood cells, called T-helpers, which are the key orchestrators of the immune system. According to the Center for Disease Control, as of 1995, it was estimated that there were more than nineteen million people worldwide infected with HIV and 231,000 of these people reside in the United States.

Early signs of AIDS are called AIDS-related complex, or ARC. These symptoms include night sweats, prolonged fever, extreme weight loss, chronic diarrhea, skin rash, chronic cough, and shortness of breath. ARC becomes AIDS when the immune system is overpowered and the body becomes vulnerable to unusual cancers and opportunistic infections, such as herpes viruses, fungus infection, protozoan intestinal infection, PCP (Pneumocystis carinii pneumonia, a common AIDS lung infection), and Kaposi's sarcoma (a malignant skin cancer, identified by blue-red lumps on the body and in the gastrointestinal and respiratory tracts, where the growths cause severe internal bleeding). More than seventy-five percent of individuals diagnosed with AIDS die within two years of the diagnosis.

The only known way to prevent the spread of AIDS, other

than abstinence, is through the use of condoms during sexual intercourse, the discontinued use of shared needles among drug addicts, and the continual screening and monitoring of all blood products introduced into health care facilities.

Myths can be a result of ignorance, a lack of understanding, and misinterpretation. Therefore, they can be harmful, if not downright dangerous. The stories surrounding the sexuality of the black race have been passed around since the first European returned from Africa. Nevertheless, these falsehoods must be dispelled.

The untruths encompassing the sexuality of African-Americans have brought us nothing but harm. The mythical proportions of the black man's penis and the imaginary voraciousness of the black woman's sexual appetite have objectified us, making us appear like playthings to some and satanic animals to others. And sisters who claim that they "can't do nothin' with a man who has a small [penis]" are only helping to perpetuate this antiquated, fraudulent, stereotyping. It's time for sisters, really all black folks, to put a halt to this nonsense.

Furthermore, any unproven information regarding sexual activity is dangerous because it fosters risky behavior. If you think having sexual intercourse automatically results in your partner falling in love or becoming infatuated with you, when it actually does not, you are in for an enormous shock. If you believe that it's okay to slip once and have sexual intercourse without using a condom, you might be in for a *fatal* blow.

Likewise, the fabrications that sex is always great, that it should always end in orgasm, and that it always relieves tension are simply that—ego-generated, locker-room lies. If you want to know what's up when it comes to sexuality and sexual intercourse, consult your doctor, read books written by physicians and psychologists, and don't believe anyone else because they very well may know less than you.

12

Ripe Bananas and Switch Flippin'

SAFE SEX IS NOT BAD. SAFE SEX IS GOOD. Sex gets its bad reputation when individuals prematurely participate in sexual activity and have to pay the penalties, or when it is used, like so many other instruments of pleasure, to manipulate and control others.

salmonella and pimples

At the least, you should be into the second or third year of having menstrual cycles before you have intercourse, unless you began your menses during mid to late adolescence (sixteen years of age or older). Why? Because our bodies must be mature to engage in sexual intercourse and a human female's body is generally not mature until she has been menstruating for a couple of years. Although menstruation can begin anytime between the ages of twelve and nineteen, and sometimes as early as eight years of age, personally, I think a fourteen-year-old, although she may be two years into her menses, is not ready for sex. This does not mean we need to have stopped growing before we have sex. No, our bodies are forever changing. However, the reproductive organs, which are most affected by sexual intercourse, should be mature. Menstruation is a signal of only the beginning of that maturation process.

Participating in sexual intercourse prior to the maturation of the body is like eating half-cooked chicken or a very, very green banana. It can make one very ill.

Young sisters with bodies that are not yet fully developed who participate in sexual intercourse may be exposing themselves to unnecessary pain. Their vaginal cavities may not be fully developed and thus penetration may be painful. In virgins, the hymen is often still in place, and breaking this membrane is usually a painful experience. Additionally, the sheer force of a male's body upon a female's body when it comes to intercourse can feel like a grizzly bear pouncing on a deer to young girls.

Besides physical maturity, another important factor, especially for adolescents, is emotional maturity. Adolescent sisters are a breed unto themselves, dealing with so many changes at once in what is, compared to the rest of their lives, such a short span of time. This is a time during which they are awakening to the sexual feelings caused by initial hormonal secretions. Many are beginning to deal with premenstrual syndrome and the physical and emotional anxieties that it sometimes triggers; they are trying to harness the desire to become a woman while Moms and Dads are still trying to hold on to their little girls; they are dealing with enormous peer pressure; additionally, there is pressure from advertisers, who know the dollar potential of the teenage market, advertisers who tell our teens what they should look like, what they should be wearing, and what they should be listening to. (And much of this instruction is detrimental to their self-esteem. How many young Sista-Girls do you know can look like supermodel Tyra Banks or superstar Iman?)

And these same young sisters are trying to maintain good grades on top of all of this. Now let's add the pressures of sexual relationships to it! Heaven forbid if the young sister is, like so many of her friends, being raised in a single-parent household where the single parent is Mom! This means that more than likely, if she's not properly guided, subconsciously she will be searching for Daddy and using sex as a divining rod. What happens when a child who isn't mature enough to handle pimples and the fact that she doesn't look like the hottest top model has to deal with the consequences stemming from an impetuous sexual encounter? Such as:

- The breakup with a boyfriend after he's gotten what he wanted: *What's wrong with me, I gave him what he wanted?*
- An infuriated parent: *She/He/They never understand me anyway. I just won't let them know what I'm doing from now on. My best friend will cover for me.*
- A sexually transmitted disease: *I can't tell my parent(s). Maybe it will just go away.*
- An unwanted pregnancy: *My baby will love me if nobody else will. . . . Or: My best friend will know where I can get an abortion. . . . Or: How could this happen to me? I thought we were doin' it right so that I couldn't get pregnant. I want to die.*

These are just a few of the repercussions confronting our young women when they enter sexual relationships ill-prepared. After these kinds of ordeals, not only do they begin to question their own decision-making, but they begin to question their value as human beings. We can't let them do this. Our girls are too precious for us to allow them to fall into the noxious void of low self-esteem.

Unfortunately I remember how I lost my virginity (falling for the "If you love me . . ." ploy). Because of this experience, I refuse to remain silent when it comes to educating our young Sista-Girls on the dos and don'ts and the wait and wait and wait some more regarding sexual intercourse. "If he loves you like he says he does, he'll wait until you're ready," I tell them, "And if he can't wait, then you move on." There's another bus right around the corner, remember.

Eventually, yes, it is going to happen and probably a lot sooner than we would like it to. The emotional maturation process tends to last long into adulthood before being fully completed, despite what our young ladies or we would like to think, and especially despite what young, hot-hipped gentlemen tell these young women. (One of the oldest hooks in the world is telling a young lady she's "so mature for her age.") So let's get our little sisters prepared, first by preparing them to say no (a lot). Tell them the lines they are going to hear and how not to fall for them. Let's educate our little sisters on how *they* should determine when and how sexual activity should happen for them. This will help them to realize that sexual relationships are circumstances they can and should always control.

Queen Mother Kathy was the first college graduate of her family. She attributes this achievement to her grandmother, who was willing to walk away from an abusive relationship and travel north from the south with absolutely nothing but seven children in tow. And it was in the north, in the land of opportunity at that time, where some of her family were able to flourish and provide Kathy with the strength and guidance she needed growing up. Now, while working full-time in social services as a caseworker for the homeless, working part-time as a producer and manager of cable programs and as a staff writer for a local newspaper, Kathy has also raised a daughter alone and is continually providing the wisdom and knowledge gained through family and experience.

Over pizza, we were discussing how young girls today are too free with their affections and how she is educating her daughter to be stingy. But also, she is willing to provide this eighteen-year-old with anything and everything she needs to know. Ms. Kathy quite frankly told her daughter that if she wanted to know anything about how to handle men, Mom was the best source because Mom was a *vet. Here! Here! As older, experienced vets, we must teach them that even young Ms. Thangs are always in control of the circumstances involving sexual relationships.* We can't afford to bury our heads in the sand today. Back in our mothers' and grandmothers' days, folks weren't dropping dead by the thousands from having careless sex, but they are today. So it's not only a matter of teen pregnancy, venereal diseases, and bad reputations, it's also a matter of life and death.

workin' out

Now, all of our bodies should be in good physical shape. We should not be overweight by more than ten pounds. Ms. Thangs rarely are, anyway. Strength training, stretching, and frequent aerobic exercise should be a regular regimen in our lives. Sex is a physical activity, sometimes, depending on the partner, a very physical one. Obesity can endanger a participant because of the fat surrounding the heart. Sexual activity often takes the blood pressure through speedy fluctuations which, if one is obese, may result in cardiac problems. Also, obesity may lessen the enjoyment because the number of sexual positions possible may be limited, thus making sexual intercourse monotonous and tedious. And I don't know about you, but this lady hates the same ol' same ol'.

In terms of hygiene, our bodies should be clear and clean, free from open sores, lesions, and soil. Daily bathing addresses this issue for the most part. But, due to the easy transmission of viruses and diseases, sisters should take extreme care when open sores or lesions exist near or on the genitalia or any bodily orifices.

I now am aware that close to the beginning of my menstrual period sometimes my tendency to bite the inside of my mouth increases. Whether this is due to increased irritability or anxiousness because of PMS is unclear. But, because I do this, I sometimes have an open sore in my mouth. When this happens, there is no way anybody's anything will be allowed near my mouth—uh-uh, not even with a condom, because the friction will aggravate the sore, slowing the healing process. Even now, though my husband and I both tested negative for HIV and AIDS in our most recent examinations, we still refrain from sexual activity involving orifices that have open sores.

Since herpes can be contracted via a cold sore, taking every precaution is advisable, including abstinence if necessary, when open sores or lesions are on either partner's body. Because the HIV virus can be contracted via the ingestion of bodily fluids, and bodily fluids include saliva, pus, and blood, also stay away from open cuts and the like. During your first sexual encounter with an individual, it is very important that Ms. Thang comes out and Miss Bashful goes away. Turn on all the lights and examine (in a most subtle way, but thoroughly) every inch of this prospect's body. If done creatively, this can also be a most arousing section of foreplay. It is unfortunate that many virgins as well as "experienced" sisters, because of their "shyness" and/or ignorance, find themselves suffering from an irritating venereal disease, infection, or worse after a first encounter.

Don't be afraid to look. By doing so, you are protecting your body, your life. If there are open sores or lesions around the genitalia of your prospect, ask, listen to the reply, and take a rain check. Don't actually plan to cash it in though. People who are willing to become intimately involved with someone when they have open sores on or near their genitalia probably care little about whom they sleep with and, thus, are dangerous people to be intimately involved with. Look, look, look, and then look again. *In this day and age, being shy is being foolish, and Queen Mothers will tell you that being foolish can be fatal.*

Joanne and I were having dinner after work at one of our favorite restaurants when she recounted the first time she and her fiancé made love. We've been friends for more than ten years, and sharing anecdotes about our love life is one of those Sista-Girl things we do. Anyway, we were giggling so mischievously, our server was simmering with curiosity regarding our conversation. Of course, we didn't tell him what we were really talking about; we told him a dirty joke instead. But I will tell you . . .

Joanne had finally decided to spend the night at the apartment of her then boyfriend, Richard. He had prepared a romantic dinner, and they shared a good wine. The moment of truth finally arrived, and Joanne went into the bathroom to disrobe and insert her diaphragm. When she came out, all the lights in the apartment were turned out, making it pitch black. "What happened to the lights, honey?" she asked sweetly.

"I like the dark," Richard replied.

"Uh-huh. Well, I like to see all the goodies I'm gettin'. So if you don't mind, would you please flip the switch?"

A little stunned by this comment, Richard replied, "We've been going out for more than six months now, Joanne. You should know if I say the goodies are good, I ain't lyin'."

She told me she then cuddled up next to him and touched his genitalia slightly to build up the anticipation. She blew a couple of kisses in his ear and then whispered, "Look, you're a med student, and when you examine a patient, you don't do it in the dark. So, turn on the lights so we can play doctor, and I can examine every inch of your gorgeous black body."

The switch was flipped without further ado.

circumcision and showers

The genitalia of your male partner should be clean and free from infection. Don't be shy when it comes to ensuring this, as I said. Turn on the lights if they are off, and examine this area closely. If he is not circumcised, gently pull back and forth on the foreskin and make sure the penis is clear of lesions and scars. A few Sista-Girls I know turn their noses up at men who are uncircumcised, saying it's unclean and/or unsafe to have sex with men like this. NOT TRUE. If the area underneath the foreskin of his penis is unclean, it has nothing to do with the process of circumcision; this just happens to be a nasty man who should be left to fend for himself, if you get my drift. However, if it's clean, it is not unsafe. Remember, there are a lot of brothers out there from different cultures, some circumcised, some not.

If there is evidence of past scars, don't be afraid to ask about them. Examining your partner may cause him to become slightly aroused, at which point a small amount of fluid may seep from his penis. If the color of this fluid is yellowish, greenish, or puslike in odor or consistency, say "thanks, but no thanks." This is an indication of infection or disease.

Some men, especially active men, perspire a great deal near their genitals. If the odor of your partner is somewhat offensive due to their perspiration, don't hesitate to gently suggest a shower together. In some cultures the female always cleanses the male prior to intercourse, promoting the purity of the act.

doctor's orders and mother's advice

Being sexually literate is imperative prior to engaging in intercourse, and sexual literacy cannot be obtained via "on-the-job-training" or through hearsay from peers. Sisters in high school, instead of giggling and making eyes at the guys, you should be listening and paying close attention during your sex education classes. Beyond learning in school, you should read every nonfictional article or book you can find on the topic, and ask no one but your doctor any questions you may have. Make sure you ask a gynecologist and not a general practitioner. Although good as family doctors, general practitioners are usually not as learned about the female's anatomy and/or the most up-to-date birth control as a gynecologist.

Also, if you have a good, open relationship with an older female, take advantage of it; talk to her and then *use your common sense.*

While I believe a great deal of wisdom and knowledge can be acquired by listening to our matriarchs, sometimes the messages they send are incorrect and ultimately cause more harm than good. For example, Judy, a Sista-Girlfriend of mine, Clark University graduate, and just an all-around beautiful, freckled, black woman, found herself in a quandary when she wed a man who had told her in no uncertain terms before they married that he did not want any children. She married him anyway, thinking perhaps he would change his mind in time or perhaps she could eventually persuade him into wanting a family. Several years and tear-filled episodes later, they divorced because Mr. Man was not changing his mind and Sista-Girl couldn't change it, either. Her mom and grandmother advised her that she didn't have to change his mind—just stop taking birth control pills and go ahead and get pregnant anyway. Fortunately, she didn't take their advice and feels much better for it. And I praise her decision.

Sometimes Queen Mothers, unintentionally, look at the world through lenses of times gone by, drawing upon those times and experiences for answers to today's difficulties. The challenges sisters have today, although comparable to our mothers' and grandmothers', require a different set of solutions because the nature of the problems may not have changed but their degree and their victims are different. It's like playing chess on a three-tiered board instead of the single-tiered board; it's the same game but needs to viewed from a different perspective in order to be played wisely.

Also, because they are older, there may be information relating to sexual physiology or technological advances that Mama or Grandmama may not be informed of. Imagine someone thirty years ago believing three small filaments placed underneath the skin would be able to prevent women from becoming pregnant.

Yes, many individuals say they don't want children, but weaken and even retract statements implying this once they are looking into the soft, gray-brown eyes of a gentle new life. However, many individuals mean what they say and don't weaken, sometimes even becoming as cold and hard as granite toward the life they planted, walking away from the situation entirely.

Thus, to avoid circumstances like Judy's, don't chance it. If a prospective mate holds an opposite position from yours on a fundamental relationship issue such as children, spirituality, or lifestyle, the best solution is to dissolve the romantic component of your relationship (if it has developed). Remain friends and allow for someone who is more compatible to come into the picture. If you don't, the entire relationship will probably end in a stew of anguish and resentment.

I suppose the only way to judge the advice Mama and Grandmama give when it doesn't feel quite right is to remember the Golden Rule. Treat your prospective partner the way you would want to be treated. When *you* tell someone how you feel, you want those feelings believed and respected, correct?

I was very surprised one day when I found myself describing to a gentleman friend almost old enough to be my grandfather how a man can tell if a woman is having an orgasm. We were standing in the kitchen of his home during a holiday gathering and discussing my book, and he asked me, "Just how can you tell when a woman is having an orgasm?"

(I find it interesting that most men think they know this but really don't and even more interesting that most women don't even know themselves the physiological events that take place.) Well, I described the ballooning and collapsing movements of the vagina, which can rarely be felt by a man's penis while inside the cavity and is better experienced during finger foreplay.

"Does she tremble and grip the sheets really tight, too?" he asked.

"Sometimes, it depends on the woman," I explained.

"Well, then I must have hit it," he remarked sticking his chest out ever so slightly.

"Well, you must have," I agreed, patting him on the back.

Family medical encyclopedias (which every household should have) and sexual guides from the library or bookstore are very helpful, and don't be afraid to read *Playboy* and *Penthouse* (if you are of age) or "Between Us," the advice column of *Essence* magazine written by Dr. Gwendolyn Goldsby Grant. "Between Us" provides very insightful and realistic answers to sexual or health-related questions. College sisters, parents, and grandparents could benefit from taking a college sex-education course, too. These suggestions may seem unorthodox, but nothing is more disheartening and more dangerous than sexual illiteracy.

My sisters, once you realize there's going to be a sexual encounter, even if you have to pull over onto the shoulder of the highway, go get a cup of coffee or a soda, or stop in the hotel lobby, **STOP—STOP AND TALK.** Remember, every time you sleep with someone you are pulling the trigger on a gun pointed at your head, which may be loaded, not necessarily because of AIDS but because you cannot completely know anyone except yourself.

You cannot know if the person you are about to have sex with just lost his/her job and is on the brink of a homicidal rampage. You cannot know if the person you are about to have sex with is into sadomasochism. You cannot know if the person you are about to have sexual intercourse with is bisexual or likes to cross-dress. You cannot know if he is married or involved emotionally with someone else; *you cannot know anything unless you talk to her/him.* Ergo, if you feel like doing an in-depth "Barbara Walters" interview, feel absolutely free and justified in doing so.

Discuss what it is you want. Be honest. Again I say, lay all the cards on the table. It may dampen the heat of the moment, but it may prevent you from burning between your legs later. Find out if your expectations are the same: casual or serious; utilitarian or emotional, or both. You may find the two of you are just right for the moment, and then again, you may find that you and Mr. Man have completely different expectations and though you still want to have sex, he is not the leading candidate right now. So what do you do? *Sista-Girls who want to have sex either have it with an agreeable mate or they masturbate.*

13

Orgasms and Exercises

Without going into detail as would Masters and Johnson, I need to relay some information on self-pleasure at this point. Some of us, I know, reach for the telephone to make that late-night booty call simply because we think the only organ that can bring us complete sexual gratification is the phallic member belonging to someone else. Other Ms. Thangs just aren't going to give it to just any ol' body—despite what this Sista-Girl says about booty calls. So, sisters, keep your self-respect and your precious jewel boxes closed, and note the following.

easy does it and squeeze

There is no better, easier, safer way of learning what pleases oneself sexually than by masturbating. Genuine self-knowledge is more important than any other attribute an individual can have. It allows you to share yourself and creates in others an interest to share with you, expanding the worlds of both you and those you encounter.

On my way to a party one night, I went to pick up a Sista-Girlfriend. She lived with her mother, who was recently widowed. This was the second time this lovely woman had lost a husband to a terminal illness, her first husband having been my friend's biological father. While waiting for Angie to come downstairs, the noise from the plastic slipcovers on the ice-blue sofa just called attention to the awkward silence hanging in the air as Angie's mom and I sat in the living room. She didn't care for television, so had been sitting quietly, knitting, when I rang the doorbell. Wanting to rid myself of the uncomfortable silence, I asked how she was feeling and if she needed anything.

"No, honey, but thank you," this black-haired, bespectacled woman responded. "We had been expecting Tommy to pass for some time now. I admit it's sometimes real lonely around here, with Angie constantly workin' or enjoyin' her youth. But I'm makin' it okay."

Angie came from her bedroom just at the right moment to rescue me from my need to silence the squeaking plastic covers once again. As we rode north along Lake Shore Drive in my beat-up, rusty, canary yellow sports car, I remarked on how strong her mom was and how at peace she seemed. I was very impressed, I told her, being one who handled death so poorly.

"If anything, you should be impressed by her long-lasting batteries and her thespian abilities," Angie replied.

"Excuse me?"

"Girlfriend, this is the second go-round for my mom. Now, don't get me wrong. She loved both of her husbands faithfully and to the end. But she also made sure her insurance was paid on time, that she kept up with catalogs from Frederick's of Hollywood, and that she always had a fresh supply of batteries."

"My Girl," was all I could say.

Angie continued, "No shit. You should see the size of her toys."

Now, I was truly amazed. My mother and I never discussed sex, let alone masturbation, sex toys, or anything of that nature. "She showed them to you?" I asked.

"Yep, and told me where to get one of my own, too. I couldn't borrow hers, wouldn't be right. I don't think I'd want to use hers anyway, the damn thing takes *three D batteries!*"

I was laughing so hard, I pulled over to keep from putting another dent in the car.

The only major problem with masturbation is that our high-handed, self-aggrandizing American society believes there is a problem, when actually many reputable therapists use masturbation as a way of treating sexually dysfunctional individuals. Often men who suffer from erection problems are advised to use techniques of masturbation to help solve their problems.[13] (Sometimes masturbating too often can lead to sexual dysfunction, but overindulgence in anything is likely to have some kind of negative effect.)

Sista-Girls can use many methods of masturbation, whether they are virgins, single and celibate, single and sexually active, or married. Masturbating for us, as it is for males, can be therapeutic, and, as in other forms of sex, an orgasm is not always required to enjoy it. However, if you have never achieved an orgasm, or "climax," as it is often called, or if you are not sure you have, masturbation should be used as a way to introduce you to the wonderful sexual workings of the female body and the glorious experience of orgasm. Once you're sure you have achieved orgasm and can recognize it, achieving it with a mate will be easier for you.

How do we achieve and recognize orgasms? Most ladies achieve orgasm easily by stimulation of the clitoris. Sometimes the clitoris is so sensitive to the touch an orgasm can be obtained by stimulating the area surrounding it.

So begin by stimulating the soft fleshy area surrounding your clitoris, using the index and second fingers in a circular or back-and-forth motion. The pleasure derived from this will be evidenced by the appearance of vaginal secretions or the feeling of wetness within your vaginal area. If you don't feel "excited" and if no secretions or "wet" feelings are present, try directly stimulating your clitoris. Sometimes, if you are not used to masturbating, it takes a few tries to reach orgasm.

Sometimes it requires another form of stimulation as well, such as touching your breasts or fantasizing; reading erotic material may help, too. If you are voyeuristic, perhaps a good adult movie from your local video store can help. (Although it takes a pretty sexually secure woman to rent adult movies from the local video store, don't sweat it. Men do it all the time. All you have to do Ms. Thang is walk right in. There's usually an Adult Only section. Flip through the video index if one is provided or look on the boxes, reading the little captions. Then, just select something that sounds good and looks interesting.)

Just be sure you are in a quiet, comfortable, private place where you have time to experience and explore all your body has to offer you.

Experienced sisters who masturbate use many different methods to enhance their pleasure. Adult toys, magazines, movies, pillows, feathers, shower massages, etc. Once a sister has learned to sexually please herself freely, she can share this knowledge with her mate and build upon their lovemaking repertoire.

There's a helpful little exercise one can perform, and if done regularly, it could not only increase orgasm frequency but also lengthen the orgasm itself, thus increasing the pleasure of masturbation as well as intercourse. This exercise is called the Kegel exercise, named for the late Dr. Arnold Kegel, who first prescribed the exercise for elderly patients who experienced difficulty retaining their urine.

The muscles used to "hold your water" are the same muscles that create the pelvic contractions of orgasm. If you exercise these little wonders frequently—simply by squeezing your buttocks and contracting your pelvis until you feel the muscles engaged, tightened, and then hold the squeeze for five seconds at first, working up to thirty seconds—it's quite possible to have multiple orgasms. It is also advised that pregnant Sista-Girls use this exercise during their pregnancy so that their vaginal muscles don't weaken and lose their elasticity during childbirth.

So, remember, Ms. Thang, if you're doing a two-step and "squeeze" is gently whispered in your ear, your partner is not talking about orange juice or an embrace.

crimps and complexes

Some individuals have serious difficulty reaching orgasm. With ladies it's often because of either a lack of stimulation or a psychological problem that prevents us from releasing mentally to enjoy ourselves physically.

Sisters who have this problem or have never experienced orgasm may be suffering from guilt and thereby psychologically blocking their ability to receive physical, sexual pleasure. Although on a larger scale this guilt can be attributed to the general attitude of the populace toward sex, there may also be underlying circumstances unique to the individual causing the anxiety. Physiological reasons that result in painful intercourse—endometriosis (the growth of uterine tissue outside of the uterus), for example—can also contribute to orgasmic difficulty for women.

With brothers, often, it is not the orgasm they have trouble reaching but sustaining the erection. As mentioned earlier, sometimes too much masturbation can cause the body to "turn off" to any other stimuli and therefore result in an inability to climax.

When a lover does experience this difficulty, you must show him you are his compassionate Sista-Girl. Often, if the guy is young (in his twenties, for example), he is quite embarrassed and feels miserable. Even a man in his forties, who is no stranger to these episodes, may find himself suffering pangs of anxiety and inadequacy during bouts of flaccidity. Cuddle up close behind him, explain to him these things happen and that the two of you can try again later. Whatever you do, don't laugh, giggle, or be harsh. This kind of attitude can put a serious "crimp" in a man's performance and perhaps lead to a psychological complex.

Some guys, especially if with a sister for the first time, are so excited they suffer from "performance anxiety," in which case they will either prematurely ejaculate or prematurely lose their erection. Be flattered, be sympathetic, and be patient. These gentlemen generally prove to be worth the wait. On the other hand, I find most studmuffins who can always get it up at first glance can do so because that is where their brains lie.

Sexual health is as vital a part of a sister's physical well-being as respiratory health or digestive health. It not only affects us, but it also affects our interaction with others. If you, Ms. Thang, couldn't move your bowels for months, I think and hope you would seek help; you should apply the same rationale to your sexual health. If moderate masturbation does not improve your ability to climax or if sustaining an erection is a problem for your mate, I suggest you and your mate, together, consult a licensed physician who specializes in such problems. There are some things that just can't be found in those big books Queen Mothers often refer to—you know, the ones they keep in the kitchen with the hundreds of yellowing pages and the dog-eared covers. But then again . . . they're always worth a try; you never know what kind of recipe or remedy you might find.

14

Foreplay, Fetishes, Fantasies, and Faking It

Sex is an experience that provides a multitude of pleasures and sensations. There are very few "abnormal" sexual practices, and we all should know by now that sexual activity has no age limit either, regardless of what some of you Ms. Thangs think. Once a girlfriend phoned me at work. She was terribly upset. When I finally convinced her to relax so she could tell me what was wrong and she did, I had to restrain myself from chuckling so I wouldn't hurt her feelings. The poor child was on the verge of tears because during a snooping episode she found a French tickler in her divorced fifty-year-old father's underwear drawer. I wondered what she was doing snooping in her Dad's underwear drawer, but didn't bother asking. I simply told her to chill and reminded her that just because men may (and that's a big *may)* slow down a bit after they reach a certain age doesn't mean the party stops altogether.

My late grandmother assured me of this when she showed me my late grandfather's "secret hiding place" for his girlie magazines, which were filled with pages of photographs of nudist colonies and nude pinup models. I was searching for extra doilies for the table when she warned me about what I might find if I opened up one of the drawers in the old armoire on the back porch. Gran snickered defiantly at the thought of him thinking the magazines were hidden. "Shoot, I know lookin' at the same ol' sack of potatoes can get a little dull after more 'n twenty years. A man's gonna wanna see some young spuds every once in a while even if he can't do nothin' with 'em," she remarked, putting the final touch on her famous corn puddin'. "Your Paw ain't foolin' nobody but himself. 'Cause ain't nothin' comin' in or goin' out of this house I don't know about, includin' them magazines." (Come to think of it, Gran was always good at finding things that were supposedly hidden. I suddenly remember now the time she found that bottle of peppermint schnapps in my drawer . . . Never mind.)

Anyway, like I said, there are very few abnormalities or limits when it comes to sex. Some folks like leather; some folks like satin; some folks like lace. Some brothers dig sisters wearing high heels while in bed; other brothers want to wear the heels themselves. There are individuals who are into bondage and being dominant and others who enjoy bondage but prefer being submissive. Some ladies and gentlemen just like to watch, while others like to swing. There are all sorts of different-colored showers and sex sports and toys for adults.

The phrase "different strokes for different folks" can be no more apropos than when applied to sexual relations. So the more Sista-Girls discover the various ways sex is experienced in and outside our Western culture, the more comfortable we can be with our own sexuality and the more we can enjoy our mates.

"not yet, dear"

When it comes to sexual relations, the complaint most heterosexual females have about their mates is that there is not enough foreplay. Even I have to occasionally remind my darling of the fact that although penetration is quite enjoyable, other parts of my body also like being touched and caressed. And unfortunately, if you are involved with a man, unless he has reached the stage of sexual sophistication and maturity (say forty-something), this is what you have to do. Gently tell Mr. Man by verbally or physically expressing, "Not yet, dear, let's continue playing." Explain to him, if you have to, stimulation before insertion makes the experience that much more enjoyable and makes him that more desirable to you. You should have already discussed the basic modes of foreplay: fellatio, cunnilingus, fondling, kissing. And hopefully, both of you understand that to receive, you should be willing to give.

One thing about foreplay is it can be so much fun, it can sometimes compensate for shortcomings in other areas (no pun intended). Foreplay is not a be-all and end-all to sexual intercourse, so, ladies, you cannot and should not expect it every time you lie down with your mate. Remember the times you skipped the main course and just had dessert?

Still, foreplay, and consequently intercourse, can be a momentary ride to heaven on earth, in several ways.

Location. Sex doesn't always have to take place in the bed or the bedroom. A different locale can add special flavor to your sex life. Try the floor (careful of possible rug burns), the shower (careful of loose towel racks), the kitchen counter (careful of overhead cabinets), the living room, the dining room table (how appropriately termed). Try outside the home (if privacy can be secured)—the beach (careful of the sand), the mountains (careful of sliding and falling rocks), the backyard, a picnic area (careful of the ants—I'm serious). If you and yours can spare the time and money, try a weekend at some hot spot or a quaint suburban hotel or a country bed 'n' breakfast.

Toyland. Adult toys can be quite stimulating (vibrators, ben-wa balls, etc.). Many household widgets can be used as toys, also. If you're unfamiliar with this particular genre of amusement, just visit your local adult fantasy store and browse through the many products available. If you have any questions, feel free to ask one of the store clerks; they are usually very friendly and helpful. When you make your purchase, be sure you are fully instructed on its intended use. While using certain items, make sure you also have plenty of lubricant and tissue around. If this is a little much for you yet, Ms. Thang, the *9½ Weeks* items can suffice—ice, fruits, vegetables, and certain kitchen utensils.

At the Show, etc. To break the ice, rent adult movies from a local video store, as I mentioned. I know one Sista-Girl who regularly contributes to her man's adult film library, and he loves it. From the adult fantasy store, you can also purchase videos or adult games. Or there are adult games that can be played at home such as strip poker or strip gin rummy or a verbal game such as explicitly naming the number of ways to physically fondle someone from the neck up, waist to neck, hip to knee, and so on.

Methods of Madness. Mutual bubble baths. Touching, fondling, caressing until one or both of you cannot take it anymore. Massaging each other using various scented and/or flavored oils and lotions. (Peppermint is very warm and relaxing.) You can purchase lingerie and give a "fashion show" and perhaps a "taste test" if you bought some "edibles." Read erotica to each other (a favorite pastime in our household—talk about bedtime stories . . . *hmm),* or watch each other masturbate. Sexually mature couples can attend an X-rated movie together or go to an adult dance club or something of that nature.

A word about aphrodisiacs for all you Ms. Thangs: the *brain*. I don't know about the rest of you sisters, but dumb men—I mean beefcake with no meat between the ears—make me want to run in the opposite direction. When I was dating casually, I always checked my toy batteries before I went out because the no-brainer conversations I would be drawn into by some of the finest men in the world would just leave me hot and bothered. However, I didn't want to be bothered with them. Dear Lord! The lines some of these guys would throw, and some of the women, too:

"Hey, you're not like most of the other women I date. You're more sophisticated. Wanna go to my place after this and listen to some jazz?"

"No, I just met you."

"That's okay. I just met you, too. You can still come over."

Was that supposed to be funny?

"Hey, that suit is sure fittin' you fine. Do you know you're the sexiest woman in this room?"

"Am I?"

"Yep, and I'm the sexiest man. So why don't you give me your number so we can get together and be the sexiest couple in town."

I think I told that man I preferred women.

And then there's the one who pulls out all of the stops:

"You know, you are a good conversationalist; let me get you another glass of wine."

"Thank you."

"Well, why don't we continue this good conversation at my place. I see you like cabernets. [And he pronounced the plural correctly—have to give the brother his kudos.] I have a great collection I think you would enjoy. We could sit by the fireplace, drink a little wine, and then have a nice breakfast later."

"I'm sorry, but I don't go home with anyone on the same night I meet them, let alone stay for breakfast."

"Well, I'm sure you could make an exception in this case. I am a reputable businessman—owning my own business and so forth."

"That has nothing to do with it."

"Why not?" he asks as he pulls a three-inch wad of money from his pocket with the top bill, a C-note, showing (it could have been Monopoly paper underneath for all that meant). "I forgot to make my bank deposit today."

Next . . .

But then, these were all folks at bars, and Ms. Thangs never become romantically involved with people they meet at bars, anyway. Why did I go? For the attention and the laughs, of course.

big toes and rubber suits

A "fetish" is defined in this context as the deriving of sexual pleasure from an object that is not necessarily of a sexual nature. Some brothers (and sisters, too, I would imagine) have what is termed a foot fetish—meaning they are sexually aroused and can even reach climax by massaging, fondling, kissing, and/or sucking someone's feet and/or toes. Other folks have lingerie fetishes; some have uniform fetishes (like cheerleader or nurse uniforms, for example); and others have device or texture fetishes (such as rubber, leather, and/or chain-link combos). These guys and gals usually have this voyeurism thing workin' on 'em, too.

One of my besta Sista-Girls, Tee, was telling me over a couple of cappuccinos and cranberry muffins about this guy she was seeing who appeared to have it all. They had been dating for about eight months and had been going to dinner, the movies, the theater, dancing, and so forth. Finally, he invited Tee over for a quiet candle-lit dinner. He was going to cook, and all she had to do was show up looking her "usual gorgeous self." So she did. He prepared a scrumptious Italian meal, which they shared over a bottle of sparkling wine. Smooth jazz music was playing and the soft candlelight was glowing; the ambience was perfect. He then disappeared momentarily and returned with a beautifully wrapped gift box.

"I want you to go into the bathroom and put these on for me," he whispered in her ear.

Tee was so geeked, she said she was (well, let's just say no lubricant would be necessary). She played it off though, telling him how sweet he was while she was moving slowly into the bathroom. She wanted to rip the paper off, but in the event he could hear her, she slowly removed the wrapping and opened the box. The first thing she did when she saw what was in it was close her eyes and reopen them to make sure she wasn't seeing things. And she wasn't. Inside the box was a pair of panty hose. Not silky, black sheer stockings; not frisky fishnets; not sexy seams; not down 'n' dirty crotchless. But, you know, the kind that some of our great-grandmothers wear, with that chalky brown "flesh-toned" color and thick, with an opaque waist and hipline and opaque reinforced toes? Like I told you, Tee was one of my besta Sista-Girls, but I howled with laughter.

"What did you do after that?" I asked her.

"Hell, I put 'em on, what do you think? And that was some of the best [let's say lovin'] I ever had, once he did the toe and foot thing and finally tore 'em off of me."

There is really nothing wrong with fetishism unless you or your mate ceases to be able to function within normal parameters without the fetish object. If you or your mate has great difficulty reaching or cannot reach orgasm without the aid of the fetish—a problem known as "paraphilia"—professional help should probably be sought.

centerfolds and rag-a-muffins

Almost everyone has sexual fantasies. Whether or not you desire to share these fantasies with your mate is strictly personal. Some fantasies Sista-Girls may feel comfortable sharing, and others we may want to keep to ourselves. This is absolutely acceptable. And the fact that you fantasize about another male or female, even while having sex with your mate, doesn't mean you are not enjoying your mate or are being unfaithful. The same holds true for your mate.

The one problem that can arise with fantasies, I believe, is if we find ourselves desiring the fantasy more than reality, or continually comparing fantasy to reality. Sisters, feel free to tell your mates that those *Playboy* centerfold photographs are taken in professional studios with a professional team of photographers (who use filters, airbrushing, and other techniques to enhance the photographs) as well as hair stylists and makeup artists. You may also tell your mates (if they are male) that many "gentlemens' club" dancers are lesbians. However, ladies, also be advised that a bunch of those "beefcake boys" are gay and have no desire whatsoever for female company after the show.

Fantasies are normal, but candidly speaking, we *all* wake up ugly sometimes, looking like leftover rag-a-muffins. There are also times when we just want to screw—no candles, no music, no ruffles, just a plain ten- or fifteen-minute buck; you know, a booty call. Don't sweat it; it's cool. *C'est la vie.*

Fantasy can be fun, but Sista-Girls know when to leave fantasy alone, because sometimes dealing realistically leaves fewer scars.

"sorry, I lied"

Faking an orgasm is not cool unless you're performing in some sort of professional capacity. If you fake orgasm for too long, you may eventually and unwittingly become sexually dysfunctional. Not only does faking orgasm hurt you, but it also damages relationships. This type of behavior prevents individuals who sincerely want to from providing you with pleasure. Faking orgasm is very masochistic in the sense that you are completely aware of your preventing someone from pleasing you or learning how to please you. So if Boyfriend has to ask and you didn't climax, be sweet but be honest and tell him that orgasm isn't always necessary and you had a great time.

Another bit about a problem some Sista-Girls have: stamina. Active females have a great deal of sexual energy and can often outlast males, especially because the average male, once penetration occurs, can last only two to three minutes. If your energy level is higher than Boyfriend's, foreplay, "stopping and starting," and masturbation can help make it just as rewarding for you.

15

Jokers Are Wild

As with any human endeavor, sex too has its consequences, some favorable, some not. Like the famed Dr. Jekyll, sweet and generous, sex can turn into a Mr. Hyde affair, monstrous and destructive. What we must do is protect ourselves as much as possible from the unfavorable consequences. The surest way of doing this is through abstinence. However, in today's society expecting the average individual to abstain from sexual activity is unrealistic. Even the French Catholic Church has proclaimed its advocacy of the use of condoms, because it now believes condom usage is the only way to prevent the spread of AIDS.

We may hope and pray our adolescent children grow to adulthood with the mind-set of the teenagers portrayed in *The Brady Bunch* and *The Partridge Family.* We want them to remain innocent, playing cute pranks, "dying" when afflicted with the onset of acne or a bad hair day, and never leaving Mom or Dad to face serious issues such as teenage pregnancy, dropping out of high school, or joining neighborhood gangs. However, we have to realize that progress (?) has destroyed this possibility.

Yet, before dealing with the prevention of negative consequences, let's look at the positive rewards of sexual activity . . .

Sexual intercourse can give one an exhilarating release of physical energy. Sometimes, even after exercising, working, and running errands, I still have a restlessness that only sex seems to satiate. Frequently during those times my spouse will matter-of-factly ask me why I am so fidgety or restless. I'll respond that I don't know (at the time I really don't); then he will pointedly ask, "Do you wanna do it?" At which point I'll pointedly reply, "Sure," and then we're off to cure my restlessness.

Intercourse also provides us a very practical comprehension of our body and the body of our mate if we are really tuned into what's going on. We will learn various ways of pleasing ourselves, enabling us to develop a deeper physical relationship with our mates. We'll discover our sexual clock, the times for us that are more conducive than others for sexual intercourse.

For example, some Ms. Thangs have voracious sexual appetites after a day's work and finishing a full meal; others are uncomfortable having sex right after eating. Many sisters, like myself, with heavy first-day menstrual flows and excruciating cramps hand their honeys a magazine, a tube of lubricant, and direct their mates to the bathroom. Other ladies, whose menses are light and almost completely nonimposing from the first day through the last, race their lovers to the bed. And still other girlfriends spend the entire week of their cycle absolutely inert and refuse to have anyone, especially a man, in their space.

Simple observation teaches us a lot. If a mate is a bear in the morning, we will eventually discover whether morning is a good time to "tame" the wild animal or if simply waiting until our mate becomes a pussycat in the evening is a better tactic. If we watch how our mates smile or frown at the way we touch them in a particular area, we learn directly how to provide them with pleasure.

Couples who are already mentally intimate benefit greatly from the physical intimacy of sexual intercourse. Often these couples describe some of their interludes as absolute releases, where they simply allow themselves to "get lost" within one another and, momentarily, become one. They sense what pleases and stimulates each other and apply this awareness to their sexual relationship. Couples like this often achieve orgasm simultaneously and find sex to be a most cleansing and ethereal ritual. In *Sisters of the Yam,* bell hooks affirms this particular wonder of eroticism. She explains the pleasure derived from using the senses sexually to heal our spiritual and physical pain as one of the most sensual moments between two people. In these moments our bodies are sacred and are places of recovery for us and our deserving mates.

The positive consequences of sexual intercourse can be magnificent. And as magnificent as the positive consequences can be, the negative consequences can be terrifying.

Imagine meeting for the first time someone who is just so damned sexy that words cannot describe how badly you want to get horizontal with this person. Forget the mental aspects; you're not interested in emotional commitment at this time in your life, but if you could just get some sex from this Mr. Man once or maybe twice, this would satisfy your desire for at least a month or two. So you, being the Ms. Thang that you are, flirt successfully and your physical desires are acknowledged and agreed upon. Then after a couple of rolls in the hay, you smile to yourself, place the experience in your "pleasant memory" box, and go about your way. Soon you get a telephone call, and for the sake of common courtesy, you return the call; you're pleasant but distant and busy, very busy. *Ms. Thangs are never rude.* A couple of days later, you get another message, which you ignore. Suddenly, you are receiving a barrage of messages, telephone calls, maybe even letters. And now you have to spend the next two months ducking, dodging, and screening . . . or . . .

Imagine you've been out drinking with this brother you've been seeing for a few weeks. The conversation is good; he grooves well on the dance floor; his home is attractive; he earns a very decent income and drives a cute car. As you two stand there in the middle of the street at one o'clock in the morning, in an alcohol-induced haze flagging down a taxi because you were smart enough not to drive, you think to yourself, "Well, maybe tonight—it's late and there's no way I'm driving home." So in the taxi there's a little kiss here, a thigh-squeeze there, and once your destination has been reached, the decision has been made—tonight's the night. Now there's a trail of clothes, beginning with your handbag and ending with your G-string, from the front door to the bedroom. The sex is hot, and the buzz is a perfect amplifier. You spend the night, enjoy a cup of coffee together in the morning, and then you head home to shower, change clothes, and get to work.

A few days later you are pleased to hear your new Mr. Man's voice over the phone until he advises you to see your gynecologist immediately. Evidently, Mr. Boy had an interlude prior to sleeping with you and is now experiencing a slight burning and tingling sensation. And since you, Ms. Thang, were drunk the other night and your purse (with protection inside) and sense were left behind on the way to the bedroom, you begin to panic . . . or . . .

Imagine you have just met "Suavé Bola." Not Mr. Man but Thee Mann (or Thee Woman, as the case may be). Let us say Suavé is slender, brown, and *phine,* on a solid career path, and, having just relocated with their firm, situated in a beautiful apartment in a luxury high-rise. On your first date you are picked up in one of those lavish, imported sleek sedans, and you discover over great French cuisine that Suavé has never been committed to a relationship for very long, but there have been a couple of lovers. The "right" one just hasn't come along yet. You continue dating, and you're not pressed for a sexual relationship. He is quite content to hold hands, walk arm-in-arm, kiss you on the cheek or peck your lips, and supply you with soft, nonimposing embraces, and you wonder if this wonderful person isn't considering a religious career. The former Suavé, who has now graduated to The One, is definitely not confused about his sexual orientation and seems mature, with a relatively down-to-earth head.

Okay, this is it for you, Sista-Girl. You've been dating for about four or five months, and your hormones can take no more. You've been invited for a quiet moonlit supper on the terrace, which you accept on the condition that you are allowed to prepare breakfast the next morning. The One has quietly accepted these conditions. While sipping an after-dinner aperitif, you explain you don't want to seem forward, but you would like the relationship to progress to another level and you've been looking forward to this for some time now. You receive a sweet grin and are promptly led into the bedroom.

The next morning you pray it was all a nightmare until you try moving out of the bed and your sides are aching and one look in the mirror confirms it was very real. Blood is drying from your cracked lip, the skin around your eye is swollen and turning blue. The note on the mirror quaintly says, "If you say anything to anyone, I know where you live, I know where you work. Say anything and I'll kill you."

Incidents like these and other similar unfortunate situations are common occurrences. And this Sista-Girl is here to tell you they do not have to occur at all. Ask questions, listen to Queen Mothers about relationships, and follow a few, but very important, rules.

ALWAYS PUT YOUR CARDS ON THE TABLE and define the kind of relationship you are willing to get into. This allows the individual an "out" if they are not looking for the same thing you are.

NEVER LET YOUR GUARD DOWN WHEN IT COMES TO PROTECTION. Keep your purse with you at all times, and in it keep two or three fresh latex condoms. There's no excuse for not doing this if you are single and sexually active. Remember unprotected sex not only injures, but IT CAN KILL.

NEVER LISTEN TO FRIENDS WHEN IT COMES TO SEXUAL ADVICE. Ms. Thangs that they are, they still probably know less than you do.

It's difficult to ascertain what goes on behind closed doors until you are behind them. Then it might be too late. **ALWAYS DELVE INTO A PERSON'S SEXUAL PAST AND CURRENT PLEASURES,** and don't be satisfied and get into bed until you have bona fide information. One Sista-Girl of mine has her sister, the sheriff, do a background check first on any guy she considers dating. So go on and get that license-plate number.

As a young woman, during sex education class, my physical education teacher impressed on me and the other students the risks of premature sexual intercourse: unwanted pregnancy, STDs (sexually transmitted diseases—gonorrhea, syphilis, herpes, chlamydia, and so forth), and emotional self-devaluation (for example, when you have sex with someone because they told you this would prove to them you loved them and then they drop you, implying to you that your love isn't good enough), which can have some devastating psychological effects. To this day, I thank God for her frankness and courage. Sista-Girls, before you engage in sex, show your future family how much you love it and yourself by using protection and some form of birth control.

Several birth control products are available. I have already named a couple, birth control pills and condoms. I advise any young woman, if considering sexual activity or already involved in sexual activity, to seek the advice and knowledge of a reputable gynecologist. There are many types of birth control pills. Additionally, you might consider using a diaphragm, or having an IUD (intra-uterine device) or Norplant (a group of filaments which secrete hormones that is placed under the skin) inserted. The choice is personal and should be made by you and your doctor—not you and your friend, mother, father, or sibling. A doctor can give you a physical examination and prescribe a contraceptive based on your physiological ability to adapt to it. No one else can. Remember, Sista-Girls, we're talking about your life here. And yes, unwanted pregnancy, disease and death can all happen to you.

Like most things in life, the significance of sexual relationships is duplicitous at best. On one hand, they are important to human relating because sexual intercourse is an inherent and natural desire of human beings. On the other hand, the significance of sexual relationships is overrated and thus the cause of much frustration and malaise. So, it is this dichotomy that requires us to have a sound understanding of our sexuality. Without such understanding and a grounded philosophy, healthy, intimate, loving relationships are very difficult to develop.

When we were first brought to this land, our sexuality, like anything else that came along with our bodies, was viewed as a commodity, a vehicle for breeding, and thus as an investment in the industry of slavery. That industry is over. Our young women need to understand that their sexuality should not be treated like a service or product to be purchased by the highest bidder, whether it's for a pair of hundred-dollar sneakers or a designer purse or an automobile. We have got to teach them that a dollar value cannot be put on some things, like our sexuality and our relationships. Neither should sexuality be used for emotional blackmail; if the man loves you, he will wait until you are ready.

Understanding our sexuality, really comprehending the position we hold as individual, sexual, human beings, is paramount to relating to others. We must have a reasonable amount of self-awareness and self-assurance before we can begin to share anything worthwhile (such as ourselves) with others. We should be able to admit that we are all different, that there are very few actual abnormalities, just as there are very few absolutes. These qualities (understanding, self-awareness, self-confidence, the acceptance of differences) combined with the willingness to attempt to appreciate them, are primary keys required for initiating a relationship with anyone.

Sisters today have to approach sexual intercourse as they would skydiving.

1. Who would practice leaping from a plane without verifying the credentials of their instructor?
2. Who would leap from a plane without practicing on the ground, first?
3. Who would leap from a plane without using a parachute?

There's only one answer, and I needn't say what it is.

A lack of sexual knowledge and understanding leads to haphazard sexual intercourse. Haphazard sex can lead to death and/or dysfunctional relationships. Trying to build satisfying and beneficial relationships with our brothers is difficult enough without adding to it the strain caused by sexual immaturity.

PART 3

LOVING OUR MATES

From the moment the first human child was born and its parents realized that the efforts of both of them were required to ensure the infant's welfare, men and women have been uniting to create and sustain families. However, within the last four hundred years, due to dramatic societal evolution, the mating ritual needed for this uniting to take place has become more complex and more exacting for the individuals involved.

Our unions are no longer arranged by parents, community elders, or heads of state. Within the twentieth century, especially, women are no longer being told to "just lie there and take it" or "pretend to enjoy it"; men are no longer expected to carry the full financial burden of the household; couples are deciding *not* to have children; men are marrying men; women are wedding women.

And in America, there is not only the great divide between black and white races, but also a great divide between milk-chocolate skin colors and ecru skin colors, between African-Americans who *have* and African-Americans who *have not,* between African-Americans who desire to know more about their lost heritages and African-Americans who could not care less about the people of Africa or any other colored people for that matter.

Sisters are angry with successful brothers because once these brothers start earning large incomes, they appear to be interested in coupling only with women of other races; their taste for black women seems to dissolve. Brothers are disparaging about sisters, feeling black women have condemned brothers unjustly and are now only interested in men of other races. Loving, intimate relationships between African-American men and women today seem to be more difficult to attain than the forty acres and a mule black families were supposed to get a century ago.

Yet, the genuine concern about our unhappiness and inability to come together, solemnly expressed by both black men and black women, suggests that these relationships are still desirable. Indeed, to take it a step further, if we want the black race to continue, not only are loving and productive unions between brothers and sisters desirable, they are indispensable.

Brothers bellow about the white man's games (how once they get the education required, they need experience, and once they get the experience required, they need more education, for example). Sisters shriek about the brothers' games (how, because of the shortage myth, brothers exploit the fears of sisters who don't think they'll be able to find a "good man," for example). And nobody is learning how to play the games so they can win them and replace those old games with new games of their own. Oh, yeah, we start out learning, but then we take our eyes off the ball and end up thinking (incorrectly) we're all that, or that they changed the rules and aren't playing fair. NEWSFLASH: NOBODY IS ALL THAT, AND LIFE AIN'T FAIR!

Life is a journey. Life is learning. Life is loving. Life is taking all you can, giving all you can, and doing all you must. For me, life is my husband, my sister, my family (which includes parents, grandparents, grandaunts, granduncles, in-laws, in-laws' family, cousins, nephews, nieces, and a host of others), my Sista-Girlfriends, my Mista-Boyfriends, my colleagues, my work, my home, my cooking, my bathing, my response to all the mean and nasty 'isms of the world, my failures and flaws, my accolades and finer attributes, my dreams, my self, and my Spirit.

I got no time to be worryin' about petty things like a door bein' held for me or irrelevant things like what my honey does when he's out with the boys. I got no time to be worryin' about my man makin' a mistake 'cause I gotta help him correct it, if I can, so we can move on. He got no time to be worryin' about whether my hair is straight or curly 'cause when we're finished lovin', it's all messed up anyway. He got no time to be worryin' about my complainin' 'cause he knows I get just as tired and fed up as he does and the only thing to do is listen to me and then grab my hand so we can move on. We got no time to be worryin' about white folks 'cause we got to spend time makin' babies so there'll be plenty of black folks. We got no time to be worryin' about what other folks got 'cause they ain't gonna never give what belongs to them to us anyway, so we got to move on and get our own.

Brothers and sisters, that's living and loving. It's worry-free work because there just ain't no time for worryin' if you want to move on and really *be* in love.

16

Dates and Mates

Intimate sexual relationships between men and women are complex, dynamic entities unto themselves. The serious ones need refinement, work, oxygen, space, and time for cultivation. Casual relationships, although not very important, still require a certain common-sense perspective if they are not to be destructive. Sisters need to have a clear understanding of themselves to understand the role(s) they can play in relationships, whether homosexual, bisexual, or heterosexual. These roles are often defined as "masculine" and "feminine," the masculine role being the more dominant, aggressive role, and the feminine role being the more submissive, passive one. What role do you play in your relationship? What is the role of your mate? Some relationships can be considered "neuter," where both partners equally share "feminine/passive" and "masculine/dominant" responsibilities.

Neither role is better nor worse than the other. Both

are interdependent, and whether you want to label them in gender or nongender terms is of little relevance. What is important is, that again, differences should be recognized, respected, learned from, and cherished.

If we understand who we are sexually, we are ready to begin the process of mate selection. The most important thing to remember about selecting a mate is to never *look* for one. Somehow, when you go out looking for that "someone," you always end up with the wrong "someone" or maybe no one ever. Perhaps it has to do with the mental bias that plays a part in wishful thinking. We want so much to find that special person, we end up profusely expressing what we want. So anyone reading the signals, with enough ingenuity, can create an image of themselves to perfectly match the picture of the person we're looking for. So, perhaps instead of calling it the process of mate selection, we might call it the process of mate agreement, if we consider the mutual consent required in mating.

Scores of individuals I have spoken with agree that the best mates are never "prospected" for. Every positive relationship I have been involved in, including my present love, was with someone whom I met through a friend, a relative, or some other ingenuous route. The worst relationships came via a bar and a nightclub.

It's funny to me that whenever I speak to brothers and sisters outside the bar scene, they always agree that scene is the worst place in the world for beginning relationships. Yet, I can guarantee you on any given night (especially Thursday through Saturday) some nincompoop at some bar allows herself to be picked up or at least prospected (she gives the guy her number and he promises to phone). In the ladies' rooms at bars and clubs, I never fail to overhear conversations about whether or not the individual speaking should go home with this guy or not; whether or not he's just out for some sex ("but he seems real nice" she says); whether or not he's going to be good in bed ("because I'm really horny" she reveals); or whether or not she should go out with him again because she still doesn't now what he does for a living. These conversations demonstrate that some sisters out there are just breaking all of Ms. Thang's rules when it comes to dating, especially the platinum rule: ALWAYS LEAVE WITH WHOM YOU CAME WITH, UNLESS THEY DUMP YOU; AND IF THAT HAPPENS, TAKE A TAXI.

It's just like a Ms. Thang I know who complains because all the men she gets are "losers." I quickly point out to her the places where she is meeting these "losers" and ask her if she doesn't see the signs Meat Market and Sex Barn over the doors. Any sister who thinks she is going to meet a brother out for anything more than "a good time" at a bar is very naïve. I am not saying good black men cannot be found at bars, because most men frequent clubs and bars at one time or another, but to expect something other than casual fun (which is unemotional sexual or nonsexual involvement as opposed to an emotional, intimate involvement) from these encounters is unrealistic.

This is not true, however, when we are *not* searching for that special someone, when we are just out and kickin' it. We send no obvious signals and are therefore more inclined to meet *real* people, and maybe even that "someone." Concentrating on ourselves, being happy with who we are and where we are or are trying to get to, and enjoying the people around us brings out the best in us. We shine and rise to a level where we naturally attract people who are good for us.

Unfortunately, when most available sisters (though out and not thinking about prospects) are faced with relatively attractive, single individuals, they immediately switch to "prospect" mode and begin interviewing: "What do you do?" "Where do you live?" "Who do you live with?" "What kind of car do you drive?" This is automatically translated into, "I am looking for someone who must pass several tests in order for us to become even remotely involved."

A translation that most brothers either respond to as best they can or immediately flee from.

Ladies, allow me to offer a few tips that may help you in the mate "agreement" process:

In a social situation, when someone first signals an interest in you, *ninety-five percent of the time it is purely sexual,* so keep the tests to yourself; if they want the sex badly enough, a person will do whatever it takes to pass—lie or be truthful.

As Queen Mothers, *if we are interested in a serious relationship,* we should know *it should begin as friends* (whatever the individuals' obvious intentions), and friends do not begin friendships with an interview.

A gorgeous, generous individual with a nice car, gainful employment, active credit cards, and beautiful home *will not mean a damn thing to you if they put you in the hospital,* so leave your CPA "bottom line" attitude at home.

The importance of developing a friendship first can't be emphasized strongly enough, especially if you are interested in being involved seriously with someone. Lovers and spouses may come and go, but good friends last a lifetime. It may be difficult, particularly when you want to find that "someone." But don't even entertain the thought that this new friend might be that "someone," at least not until the idea presents itself to you in a surprising manner. This is challenging, I know, because females in most cultures have been traditionally socialized to seek and find "successful" mates. Our mothers and their mothers were encouraged to marry men who not only were able to provide comfortably for a family, but who were, if possible, a rung ahead of the woman's family on the social ladder. This way their children would be assured of having better opportunities than they had. So whenever they were introduced to members of the opposite sex, they automatically viewed these gentlemen as prospective husbands, not friends.

This was confirmed by Queen Mother Cyrus when she

told me in her time (she's seventy-five years old), young women attended colleges and universities to find a suitable husband. If you couldn't find one, your education was something you could fall back on. Getting an education and beginning a career were not the primary reasons young ladies went to school. Our mothers and grandmothers (if they were blessed with the good fortune to be able to attend colleges or universities) were looking at possible fathers of their children. Friendship was something that might be attained once the marriage was consummated, but the most important quality a partner possessed was the ability to provide financial stability and security for a family. Well, ladies, if you don't know it, things have changed. We can and should be friends first and entertain thoughts of romance later.

Think of it this way, if in the beginning of your relationship with every friend you were to think of them as a potential mate and for some reason or another they didn't "agree" with you, you would have no friends.

"that was fun . . . so long"

I can honestly say I have successfully reached this point (alive, disease-free, and able to tell about it), even with my "casual relationships," by following a few rules. Okay, I know *rules for casual sex* seems a little contradictory, but if you don't apply at least some kind of common sense to even the most casual of interactions, you can and undoubtedly will get hurt.

NEVER SLEEP WITH A "CASUAL DATE" (SOMEONE YOU'VE MET WITHIN A TWENTY-FOUR-HOUR PERIOD) ON THE SAME DAY; there should always be a twenty-four to forty-eight-hour wait. Talk so you can be sure the two of you are on the same sexual wavelength. It gives you enough time to "cool" off so you can use what is between your ears to make the sexual decision versus allowing other body parts decide.

NEVER HAVE "CASUAL" SEX WHILE INEBRIATED OR OTHERWISE STIMULATED. You are too vulnerable, physically and emotionally, during these times, which is not a state you should be in while having casual intercourse.

NEVER DISCUSS EMOTIONAL DETAILS OF YOUR PARTNER'S PREVIOUS RELATIONSHIPS if at all possible. Talking about emotions might suggest you care when you really don't.

Those few rules worked for me and can work for you, too, if you're only interested in casual sex. Besides the above rules, don't forget what I call "short play" bedroom etiquette:

✓ Always carry the following: a phone card, fresh condoms (purchased within the last week), tissue, breath mints, and the usual girlie things (if you are a girlie kind of girl)—lipstick, powder, comb or brush, fragrance, and taxi fare if you didn't drive.

✓ Never leave your personal belongings (money, keys, purse, etc.) unattended; he or she may seem like the perfect casual dream, but you never know. I know of more than one sister who has left her purse behind while going to the bathroom that night and found money or credit cards missing the next morning. One sister found nothing missing but was telephoned, visited, and stalked for nearly two months by a guy she just wanted to sleep with once. He obtained her address from her driver's license when she carelessly left her purse alone on the sofa during that one time. She finally got another guy she was seeing and a burly friend of his to convince the brother to step off.

✓ Be very careful if you plan a casual interlude at your home; be sure you have all of your partner's very important info (employer's name, address, and telephone number, and your partner's home address and telephone number); I rarely allowed casual interludes to take place in my home, but I'm a private kind of girl.

✓ Never agree to meet at a place that is unfamiliar to you. If you have friends or relatives in the neighborhood and are familiar with the area, going to "their place" is an option. However, for safety's sake, if you are unfamiliar with the neighborhood, suggest a place you are familiar with. (A first-time, casual rendezvous is no time to be venturin' across the tracks for the first time, either. Sex with homeboys may be good, but don't be stupid, especially if you ain't a homegirl.) In the unfortunate case that something goes awry and you have to leave abruptly, it's best to be able to walk out into territory you know and are comfortable with as opposed to walking out into a strange area, especially if you are harried or upset.

✓ Always be cordial; although the engagement may be only a one- or two-time event, don't cheapen it for either one of you. Sisters have a tendency of rollin' the big brown eyes when they haven't been sexually satisfied. But, ladies, it's not nice, nor is it necessary, especially when this was just a casual thing.

✓ If you think you have to mention "respect in the morning," you have the wrong partner and should cancel the date.

the "real" thang

Back to serious relationships. We will assume the person you are interested in is a friend. (Not the kind of friend some Ms. Thangs have—you know, the "friend" who pays the telephone bill, the beauty salon tabs, and purchases your groceries from time-to-time.) During the discussions friends always have, you should have shared information about past relationships, the reasons why some succeeded, why some failed, how they ended, why sexual ones became platonic, why platonic ones became sexual, and so forth. If you haven't talked about this already, make time to do so.

This is some of the most pertinent information you can learn about someone who may become a serious mate. How they relate to others and how they view past relationships will have considerable impact on their future relationships. Are they introverted when it comes to expressing their feelings or are they extroverted? In their view, were the failures of past relationships always the other person's fault or were both parties partially to blame? Were the relationships all pretty casual or were some of them serious but just didn't work out? How, if at all, will these past relationships affect you? Are children involved? Parents? (Yes, parents. Ever had a relationship with someone whose parent always wanted to accompany your mate when he or she was with you, not just once a week or once a month, but three or four times a week? I did. This parent confessed the guilt they felt about not being there enough when their child was an infant. So they chose the time their son decided to start dating to make up for it.) Are there other individuals who may find an intrusive way into your relationship? Is their previous lover a coworker, or do the two of them share the same health club, for example, or is he or she, by some strange coincidence, someone whom you also know? Likewise, you should share with them as much as you are able regarding your past.

Beware of the "mystery" person. Usually individuals who act or seem mysterious are behaving so for a reason. Perhaps they really do have something to hide or perhaps they enjoy holding back and playing games. Either reason calls for caution.

Now, since you and Mr. Man (or Ms. Thang) have decided to drive the relationship into more intimate waters, you need to experience the dating side of the relationship. If you have not done so already, arrange for dates for just you two in various settings—nightclubs, music bars, restaurants, movie theaters, shopping malls—anything you can think of. If your comfort level has stayed the same or increased, then you are on the right track. If you are friends, more than likely you already have mutual friends, but next try arranging a couple of outings, perhaps dinner, with two or three not-so-mutual friends. Why not-so-mutual friends? Because these people don't know you as a couple; they only know you or your mate as individuals and, therefore, can give either of you a very objective viewpoint of the other (if either of you wants it). Then go out with perhaps with a few close friends or siblings. If everything is still copacetic, then comes the big test—the parent(s). When you meet your mate's parent(s), of course, you are going to be on your best behavior, but do "let your hair down" a little. This way they get a peek at the "real" you and can provide your mate with a more realistic opinion; they are no different from your parents when it comes to caring about their children.

So don't be afraid to ask your friends and family what they think of your new mate. (In some African cultures, it is the *responsibility* of the female relatives to perform what basically amounts to background checks on intended male fiancés.) They have your best interests at heart, so they should be honest and present you with any reservations they may have. And if they have reservations, you should, too. We all want to believe we are wonderful judges of character, especially when it involves that "special someone." But Queen Mothers know that being able to listen to others when it is most difficult to do so often gives us the most valuable insights, preventing the most disastrous circumstances.

I'll never forget bickering with my grandmother over one guy I was dating while in high school. She did not like the fact that he lived in a not-so-nice neighborhood; she did not like the fact that he rarely came to visit me and I was always going to visit him; and she did not like the fact that his mother was a single parent and so was his nineteen-year-old sister. So one day when I told her I was on my way to visit Michael, she decided that she and my grandfather would drive me to his house. As we pulled up to Michael's home, knowing the southern belle my grandmother was and her affinity for the genteel manners of the southern gentleman, I wanted my grandfather, who was driving, to turn the car around and take us back home. Much to my chagrin, Michael was standing on the front porch with no shirt on, pants cut off at mid calf, belt hanging unbuckled, wearing no socks with unlaced high-top gym shoes, and sporting what looked to my grandmother like thousands of little braids sticking up all over his head. To add fuel to the fire, he was yelling at somebody down the street. It was too hot to be wearing a lot of clothes, I told my grandmother. "Well, if it's that hot, he shouldn't be spendin' all that energy yellin' down the street like a wild banshee, either, then," she quipped.

"Gran, he's not a wild banshee. Would you like to meet him?" I asked, hoping to give him a chance to charm Gran as he had charmed me. But I suppose it didn't help either that his younger, beautiful, boysenberry-black-skinned, similarly dressed (or undressed) brother with a very uncombed, large, ominous Afro was sitting on the porch drinking a beer.

She shook her head softly while smiling and waving at my boyfriend, "No. Don't tell that nasty-lookin', sweaty animal to come over here. It ain't necessary. Me and your Paw will see you later."

"Who was that?" Michael asked me as they drove off.

"My grandparents."

"Oh, your grandmother seems nice."

I just grunted and took a seat on the steps. Although based in unjustifiable prejudice, Gran's instincts were on target. The relationship didn't last the summer.

Through years of blunders (including my first marriage), I learned my lesson and didn't give serious thought to marrying my current husband until I discussed him with my mother.

Queen Mothers know that, sometimes, even they should listen to the wisdom of others.

All right, we've received the approval of everybody who is important to us. We get along wonderfully, and those arguments we have are reasonably short-lived and not based on fundamental issues. Also, we need not mention, if we don't release some of that locked-up energy soon, we are going to explode. But wait, before you pull out the satin sheets and light the scented candles, did you get the history, the sexual history?

17

Whispers and Giggles

Once a relationship has been established, the work is not anywhere near being completed. Actually, it has just begun. Like all living, growing things, relationships require nurturing, patience, understanding, and communication (in its various forms—talking, debating, laughing, guffawing, giggling, weeping, and whispering).

stopping the madness

Because black folks can be so expressive and because of the rage we have suppressed over the centuries, brothers and sisters need to really focus on developing *and using* effective communication skills in relating with one another. Here are a few trouble spots and effective ways of handling them:

Brotha-Man isn't pleasing you sexually. Instead of doing

the Sista-Girl eye-rollin' thing, the next time you're in the groove, say to him in a soft, sexy voice, "Would you like to know what would make just me feel *sooo* good?" I promise he'll pay attention, and you will literally feel much better.

A shouting match has developed. As soon as you hear something that makes you want to react by raising your voice another decibel, collapse into yourself. By *collapse,* I mean shut down everything and find a place to sit or lean on. Collapsing allows for breathing room and signals the end of the match, as far as you're concerned. Once the room has quieted, really think about your next sentence or question (why it is important to express, how effective it will be, and if it is emotionally charged). If the next thing you come forth with is sincere, expressed calmly, and not loaded (rhetorical, blameful, or unnecessarily painful, for example), it will more than likely begin to defuse the argument. Once emotions are removed from an argument, the real issues can be focused on and progress made.

Boyfriend simply isn't getting what you are trying to say. Perhaps you should try using words and phrases you hear him frequently use, or perhaps, metaphors that are applicable to him. Let's say, for example, you're trying to tell him how he has hurt your feelings. If your honey is a sports enthusiast, let's say a football fanatic, maybe you should say something like, "Look, it's like this. Say your team was playing a championship game, the score was tied, and there were only six seconds left on the clock. The quarterback passed the ball to your favorite, most dependable receiver, who fumbled it. Think about it. How would you feel?" He should get the picture, and you can proceed from there.

You have begun expressing your anger and frustration physically by throwing, slamming, or punching things (like pillows or the wall). Occasional door-slamming and even throwing things (like pillows or slippers) is normal. But if this behavior becomes habitual, you should take the following steps to stop it. Otherwise, it could escalate into even worse physical outbursts and destroy your relationship.

1. Collapse into yourself.
2. Look at the object you are about to hurl or punch.
3. Touch the object and imagine it is your favorite heirloom.
4. Take a deep breath, move away from it, and go grab a sponge.
5. Start talking quietly and begin cleaning the house (you don't have to finish, but cleaning is better than punching).

In their book, *Friends, Lovers and Soul Mates,* Doctors Darlene Powell Hopson and Derek S. Hopson offer valuable instruction on how to alter the current ineffective communication style of your relationship into a style that is more beneficial in relating. They provide excellent examples of the various communication styles brothers and sisters employ to express their emotions, and show how some of these expressions are often more antagonistic than we realize.

grunts, erotica, and space

Although we've heard it time and time and time again, communication is one of the most important bridges to successful relationships, relationships of all kinds (intimate, parental, sibling, platonic, coworker, and so forth). To build rewarding, satisfying, intimate relationships, the lines of communication must always be open. For this to be possible, sisters need to be able to interpret their mate's method of communication and the symbols unique to their individual communication style.

For example, sexual communication is often very awkward between mates at the beginning of their relationship. It can even be cumbersome between brothers and sisters who have been together for years. Examination of verbal communication can assist in this area.

Is your mate sexually verbal? If so, you should not have a difficult time learning what pleases him or her. I find that mates who are comfortable speaking openly and honestly about sex are some of the best partners, not only sexually but across-the-board. Sisters can approach the subject over a meal or while taking a walk together, almost anytime. This makes it easy to learn what pleases and displeases your mate sexually and subsequently allows for a wonderful physical relationship. You can bring toys and adult movies, books, and magazines into play with no fear of rejection or of creating consternation. Suggesting new moves and positions while having sex is not a problem either, and probably welcome.

Is your mate uncomfortable speaking about the subject of sex? Try bringing home a book or reading to him or her an article on the topic. (See Suggested Reading at the end of this book.) Ask your mate about it. Hopefully, you will receive some sort of feedback indicating a willingness to further explore the sexual side of your relationship. With moderate or passive lines of sexual communication, sisters can begin by first discussing books on erotica and adult movies. Next, try to make your mate proactive by bringing him or her with you when you purchase your "toys." Begin talking about different sexual positions or locales prior to your next session together. If the resistance diminishes, eventually the margins of communication will expand enough for you and your honey to enjoy great, uninhibited sex.

If the above does not work, try discussing an article or book while cuddling in front of the television during a commercial. If that doesn't work, try cooing your way into talking about it prior to the next time you two are about to have sex. If that doesn't work, try a physical sneak attack. (Sometimes this kind of surprise says you are open to the risk of rejection, which is what a person who is usually closed to communication is afraid of—being rejected.) Your mate may feel that since you can allow yourself to become vulnerable, they, too, can perhaps open up a bit. However remember, be careful not to actually impose. I hate using old clichés sometimes, but they can be so accurate: remember, you can lead a horse to water, but you can't make him drink it. I earlier discussed not allowing yourself to be coerced into doing something that made you uncomfortable. It should be likewise for your mate. While you can coax, trying to make your mate do something he or she may not be ready for is not cool.

Is your mate absolutely closed to the topic of sex? Talk about why you don't talk about it. If this opens things up some, you may be able to gradually move into the moderate communication mode and eventually have a completely open avenue. If the lines still remain closed, if your mate still doesn't want to talk, has difficulty responding or referring to the subject, bring home books and guides written or edited by physicians who specialize in sexual health.

If all else fails, try therapy. If therapy doesn't eventually help, try a new mate. Depending on the ages of you and your mate, you may just need to skip the therapy and try a new partner. I say this because in autumn-autumn relationships (relationships between couples in their middle age), one partner may be set like concrete in their ways—bound to the "hush-hush" sexual dictates of eras gone by. Whereas the other partner may be finding the new sexual openness of today's world intriguing and exciting. If this is the case, there is very little chance the concreted mate will change. Therefore the changing mate will have to look elsewhere for the sexual fulfillment he or she is craving.

In order for a relationship to actually be worth being called such, each partner must understand how their mate communicates. There must be free-flowing and sincere discourse, even sometimes in the midst of fear or anger. Relationships should be encouraged to grow through both positive and negative discussion, through praise, constructive criticism, and debate.

The unfortunate thing about heterosexual relationships is that while females enjoy verbal expression, males tend to find conversation with females difficult and therefore not as enjoyable as communicating with other males. This is because the way males express themselves is different from the way females express themselves. Therefore we Sista-Girls often have to cajole or pry simple phrases of acknowledgment from the mouths of our male mates; it's positively unnerving.

Dr. Ronn Elmore discusses the various ways in which sisters can begin to effectively communicate with their men in his book, *How to Love a Black Man.* As he says, some of us Sista-Girls are just in love with the sound of our own voice and rarely allow our men, or anyone else for that matter, an opportunity to express their opinions or ideas. Some of us are excellent listeners, but when it comes time for us to take the floor, we cower away as if our feelings and thoughts were unimportant. Also men tend to begin with specific information and build upon it whereas women do just the opposite, present generalizations and narrow them down into specifics. Whatever the reason for the lack of communication in our relationship, we need to address the issue because it is one of the most important issues involved in human relating.

Maybe our mate doesn't enjoy much conversation. We should make sure that this is merely a personality trait and not reflective of feelings about us or the relationship. How?

Begin quietly but emphasize to your mate the importance of sharing feelings, experiences, and knowledge with loved ones. As some males will admit, many men do not have as many "deep" feelings and emotions as their female counterparts. If they do, they bury these feelings so deep within themselves that *they* don't even know they have them. Now, I'm not saying most men do not have complex, sensitive emotions, but some males place a different value on their emotions than females do. Although things are changing, traditionally men tended to view being emotional as a drawback (sensitivity and compassion were viewed as weaknesses, for example), whereas women view emotional expression as an advantage. This is a difference both men and women must acknowledge, appreciate, and work with continually.

As soon as communication lines seem to be breaking down, they should be checked. If you are serious about your relationship, stop whatever you are doing. Nothing short of self-preservation should take precedence over this. Tell your mate to stop what he or she is doing, because your relationship warrants the attention of you both. Then schedule a day and time when you won't be interrupted and can take as long as required to talk everything out. If you have to go beyond three days to schedule time together, your relationship is in severe trouble and one of you, if not both, is going to have to make a scheduling compromise if you want the relationship to succeed.

Sometimes communication is just not possible, and instead of relating to each other, there is a need for "space" or a break. A day or two or maybe a week is needed for you or your partner to resolve within yourself the issues you are confronting. Just be sure this is the reason the break is being taken, that the space is not being utilized as a form of procrastination or manipulation. Also, make sure this break does not become one in a continual miniseries of breaks. Often individuals who are ill-prepared for commitment can handle a serious relationship for three to six months at a time. But once that time frame is completed, they will sometimes go so far as to start subconsciously or consciously "pushing buttons" (behaving in a disagreeable manner or making disagreeable comments), fully aware the sparks to follow will escalate into a full-blown argument, giving them the opportunity to "take a break." If this happens more than once in your relationship, Sista-Girl, make sure you tell your mate the next "break" he or she takes from the relationship will be a permanent one and mentally prepare yourself for the inevitable.

There are times when I want and need to be just left alone, literally, for a few minutes or a few hours. In the beginning of our relationship, my current mate had trouble with this, unable to believe this is what I really wanted. "No one wants to be left alone when they're feeling blue," my honey contended, "or when there's a problem in the relationship." Wrong. I do, sometimes. I explained my need for time alone to think objectively, to allow for Spirit to come and talk to me, to allow me to breathe on my own because people, events, noises often distract and suffocate me. Eventually Mr. Man came to understand this need, and our relationship is better for it. Sometimes taking a few hours alone allows for a lifetime of togetherness.

funk, snorts, and the bump

Sex, involving a partner of relatively equal tastes and desires, can be a very pleasurable experience. Yet, there is much more involved for Sista-Girls wanting long-lasting, significant relationships. Intimacy, both physical and mental, plays a major part in sustaining meaningful relationships.

Many brothers practice an unspoken code of behavior: No PDA (public display of affection). Their reasons for doing this are they don't want to get "busted," or caught, in the event they are intimately dating more than one sister at the same time and/or they don't want to appear "whipped," like they have given control of the relationship to the sister. Holding hands or walking arm-in-arm, for a lot of black men, is a sign of a loss of power. Nonsensical, I know. However, if you're with a man who believes in this code of behavior, I suggest talking with him to determine the specific reason he practices it. And then *you* decide whether or not it's something you can tolerate over a long period of time.

I once was seriously involved with someone who was extremely averse to public displays of affection. Initially this aversion made me question my mate's sincerity toward me. Yet as months and years went by, I understood this was merely a part of my loved one's nature. So I told myself, convinced myself, that those public displays of affection were not a necessary element to our relationship, that the knowledge of our love and devotion for each other was all I required, all I wanted. And it was. I believed so.

But now, with someone who *asks me* for hugs and kisses on a daily basis, who is willing to hold my hand and embrace me publicly, I can't imagine how I survived in my previous relationship. Now if we don't touch daily, in public and in private, I feel like I'm starving. Touching is such a very critical part of human relating. I can see why people who dislike touching always appear so drawn and sallow physically and why their demeanor is so constricted and pitiful, and, on the other hand, why people who greet you with both hands or a warm embrace seem so large and vivacious!

Two other characteristics of physical intimacy (that some of us take for granted and others often find very difficult to display) are smiles and laughter. Nothing warms the heart, breaks the ice, or welcomes others into your space more than a big, good-natured smile or a hearty chuckle. During prolonged periods of what I call "artistic melancholy"—the blues you get when you're trying to make it by doing something you love (like writing)—my mate often brings me around by getting me to muster a smile, by saying something funny or loving me (mentally) to the point where a smile automatically blossoms between us. Have you ever been in the company of someone who had such a wonderful, infectious guffaw that you found yourself a little saddened by their departure? What a beautiful way to touch someone.

Loving people intimately includes the ability to share grins, giggles, wide-toothed smiles, and heartfelt laughter. Additional mental and nonsexual intimacies (some of which I discussed earlier) between lovers include long walks in the park, window shopping, quiet dinners by candlelight, long drives to the "country" (what us city folks sometimes call suburbia) while listening to our favorite tunes. Other ways to meld mentally can be achieved by dating again—going to movies, bookstores, coffeehouses; reading to each other; going to hot-tub spas; and working out together. Except for working out, these pleasures probably can't be enjoyed daily. But if done weekly or twice a month, they can help rejuvenate a relationship that is a little "too settled" or help a sparkling relationship remain so.

A brother I know reminds me that sharing the cultural nuances of being African-American is also a way in which brothers and sisters can be intimate. He explained, "You know, you're driving home from work and a tune like Parliament's "Flashlight" comes on and gets you movin' and groovin' because you haven't heard it in so long. By the time you get home, you're so excited you run in the house burstin' with joy about this song you and your honey can both relate to. And the two of you start singing the song and dancing together."

The author Leo Buscaglia discusses the importance of intimacy in today's society in the context of Western civilization's indulgent culture—how most of us are so well maintained via clothing, shelter, and food and yet, we are so inept at openly expressing sincere fondness without anxiety or trepidation. Indeed, we reach the outer edges of the solar system with spacecrafts, but embracing one another—the grandest of gestures—is so very difficult for us to do. In his wonderful book *Loving Each Other,* he offers some of the best advice on positive, loving, communication available. He describes the importance of showing how much we love each other, although we may deny that we need to have it demonstrated; the value of expressing all of our feelings, even the negative or depressing ones, to allow our mates to console us, because they need to know they can; how we should observe "nonbirthdays" and take time other than official holidays to express the happiness we feel; how we must acknowledge each other's feelings as genuine and important, although we may not understand or see their significance personally; and how we should honor the quiet time that each other needs for reflection and getting in touch with Spirit.

So go ahead. Touch your mate. Laugh together, even let out a rip-roaring snort. Step out into the sunshine and fresh air holding hands. Race to the end of the block. Sing together and do the *bump.* Remember when you and your best friend used to race to the mailbox? Enjoy your relationship in public as much as you do in private. The world needs to see happy faces more often. *Plus, Ms. Thangs, know that a healthy, happy relationship does more for the skin than any face cream ever can.*

18

Infidels and Monsters

If there are no whispers, no giggles, no passion, there is no need for continuing a relationship. It is time for the agreement to be dissolved.

And this dissolution, for two formerly intimate individuals, can be painful. It is sometimes so overwhelming that life no longer seems bearable. Most of us have had this gut-wrenching experience. *First, the heart starts rapidly beating. Breathing becomes erratic. Sometimes we hyperventilate. That awful tugging feeling in the chest begins. Lumpiness in the throat. Stinging eyes as we fight proudly but uselessly to hold back tears. And the throbbing from the mental sledgehammer pounding at the base of the skull.* This is what it feels like when we first realize that it is over.

How are we going to tell our friends and family? What about Christmas? We just shared Thanksgiving together. What about all the plans we made—moving into a two-bedroom place, marriage, kids? Everything, including our brain, goes into that big whirlpool of broken relationships.

But let's investigate the reasons why you should or should not let go:

infidelity

Although an unfaithful partner is certainly not a good thing, it is not the worst thing that can happen in a relationship, either. Infidelity simply undermines one of the most important foundations of a partnership, that of trust. What individuals sometimes fail to realize about infidelity is it not only diminishes faith in a relationship, but it often unravels several of the cords that initially bound the two individuals together. The discovery of unfaithfulness sometimes makes the partner who was cheated on question their own attractiveness and their worthiness of a good relationship, too. Simultaneously, the partner who was cheating may now have a difficult time trusting the mistreated mate because of the fear of revenge. And what comes into question more than anything else, once infidelity is confronted, is the validity of the relationship, itself. No, infidelity is not the worst thing that can happen, but it sure can cause some major damage. Confessing infidelity for the sake of relieving a guilty conscience is almost as bad as being unfaithful and is one of the most selfish and destructive things a mate can do.

Okay, so through some way (usually by being at the wrong place at the wrong time) you find out your mate's been playing around. After you contemplate abuse and revenge, you want to know why your partner was unfaithful. Did you ask? He or she may say they don't know why. Yes they do. They just haven't really thought about the reason for their infidelity or they don't want to talk about it because they are ashamed of the pain they have caused; or they don't want you to know the reason because they plan on cheating again and they really don't want you to fix it (brothers are good for this one). But, as the recipient of this injurious behavior, you have the right to know why. And if your mate is reasoning with either of the first two premises, communication is the key for you.

So, you eventually get to a point where you can talk about it and your mate reveals that he or she has felt unloved and/or unappreciated. Well, where have you been to make your mate feel neglected? What have you or haven't you been doing to incite these feelings of neglect? You've been working because you want your lifestyle to progress. What about your relationship? What's more important—the condominium or the relationship, the new car or the relationship? Who is going to remember you when you pass on, the condominium or the person whom you shared your little efficiency with? Brothers and sisters fortunate enough to become executives and professionals often find themselves in the grip of what I refer to as an "acquisition addiction." The Bible calls it *greed.* We work hard to get the condo or house; then once this is acquired, we have to work even harder because it's time for a luxury automobile, too; once this is acquired, it's time for real adult toys—like a boat, a full-length sable fur coat, a two- or three-carat diamond, a Rolex, an exotic three-week vacation, something. There's always something that's going to require more work, something that consequently prevents us from attending to the things that are really important in life . . . like relationships. It's something all of us workaholic Sista-Girls and Brotha-Men should reflect on.

Or maybe the reason was that your mate felt bored with your sexual relationship. Was it really the sexual relationship between you two? Reread chapters 13 ("Orgasms and Exercises") and 14 ("Foreplay, Fetishes, Fantasies, and Faking It") on sex. There are a few great how-to books listed in the bibliography at the end of this book. I also suggest you find some firewood and lighter fluid and get to work setting this relationship afire again. If there was only one instance or one affair, and boredom between you was the cause, start reading and go "goody" shopping now.

No, I am not saying it was all your fault, because lack of self-control and poor communication may have also played a role in your mate's unfaithfulness. Let me put it to you like a brother once told me, "If all a woman is going to do is lie there, expecting me to do all of the work, no matter how fine she is or she thinks she is, she's boring and eventually, I'm going to have to step out if she doesn't start moving to the groove." Anyway, no, it is not all your fault, but you should carry some of the blame. So if this relationship is important to you and you want it to continue, Ms. Thang, you've got to get busy. You may not be able to forget, but eventually you will most definitely get over it. Forgiving is not an issue, because I don't think anyone on this planet is so above reproach they cannot forgive the errors of another human being. If the relationship is not that important to you, or if infidelity is something you will not or cannot tolerate, even once, whatever the reason, call it quits. You'll still get over it, and someone else will eventually come along.

Or maybe your mate says they are bored with sex and it has nothing to do with you, saying something like, "It's not that you're not enough; I just wanted something different." Well, whether your mate wants to face facts or not, you had better. The fact is you are not enough. *Something different* means *something other than you.* You can color your hair, get a weave that hits the top of your butt, purchase sexy lingerie, buy new toys, "attack" your mate unexpectedly, surprise your mate with a "pick up" after work. You probably have done some if not all of the above already. But it didn't and it won't work. Your mate needs and/or wants another person or simply doesn't need a monogamous relationship at this time. However, what you must discuss and decide with your mate is whether this need or desire is permanent or just a stage (such as mid-life crisis).

Perhaps you can work through this period of your mate's maturation process together. Maybe you can tolerate your mate's behavior until he or she "grows out" of it. Perhaps you can't and thus must end the relationship. Seek professional help before making that decision, though. *Queen Mothers know that two heads are better than one, and sometimes three are even better than two.*

Well, no matter the reason, you've decided to work through this. It has happened only once, and he or she has promised it will never happen again, and let's assume this man or woman has never made a promise that wasn't kept. How to forget? How to continue? As I said, you will never forget, but continuing is possible. The pain will slowly and inevitably go away.

But the first step in mending your relationship is to make sure that all you felt is expressed—the injury, the anger, the frustration, the fear, the mistrust. Sisters may want to take a break before they proceed with step one, to allow time for the passionate anger to subside, so that when feelings are expressed, they are conveyed sternly but calmly.

When you do discuss the affair, make sure all of what transpired—before, during, and after the episode—is talked about. However, be careful not to ask about too many specific details. Often the offending party may feel this is a time when they can assuage their guilt and get it all off their chests. Don't let them. If Boyfriend (or Girlfriend) sounds like they are heading in this direction, put your hand up and tell them, "Freeze frame. I don't want to hear it. Tell it to your friends. This is about my pain, not yours." And like I said, be sure you find some solitude in which to deeply commune with yourself and the Creator so that you can be relatively assured it is possible to continue with this person after being so badly hurt.

Be sure your mate comprehends that it's going to take time for you to recover and that your anger is not going to totally dissipate in a twenty-four-hour period or even forty-eight or seventy-two. Explain that you will try your best not to "hit below the belt" during those times you experience painful flashbacks while recovering, *but make no promises.* Boyfriend also has to comprehend that a large block of the relationship—trust—will have to be rebuilt. And because this is one of the largest blocks upon which relationships are founded, it generally takes the longest to establish and even longer usually to reestablish. *Don't be afraid or ashamed to say, "You fucked up, big time." Because they did.*

Both of you should understand that while infidelity has ruined some relationships, it has also been the source of newfound strength and harmony in others. There is no reason why you and your mate cannot repair your relationship and let it become even more rewarding and satisfying than it had been prior to this incident. I urgently advise communicating and counseling. *Whatever you do, don't, and I repeat,* ***do not,*** *try to "get back at" your mate by committing an act of infidelity of your own. It will not solve the problem. Sista-Girls know that although it may make you feel better in the short-term, "two wrongs do not make a right."*

incompatibility

Certain couples have differences within the relationship that are *complementary,* and other couples have differences that are *incompatible.* For example, if your honey is very outgoing and loves socializing and you prefer staying at home reading or watching a movie, this may lead to a very uncomfortable relationship. If you grudgingly but lovingly accompany your mate to social functions occasionally, he or she may be willing to make apologies for your absence in other instances. However, if your mate *requires* your presence on all occasions, and you are constantly arguing about why you have to go, your relationship may be heading into very turbulent waters.

Or what if you find yourself on one path and your mate on another? You, for example, are going back to college to finish your degree or to do postgraduate work and are maintaining a full-time job, too. At the same time, your mate doesn't really like his or her job, doesn't really have the skills to move on, and/or doesn't really have a clue about where he or she would like to move on to if they acquired additional skills. Now, your mate can, on one hand, be very supportive, admiring, and even a little envious of you, which is fine as long as it is in that order. Yet, on the other hand, if your mate displays a nonsupportive, rebellious, even angry attitude, and you haven't done anything to spur him or her on, you are definitely growing apart instead of together.

Or perhaps you and your mate come from different "sides of the tracks." You, for example, were raised with a few brothers and sisters and had to share almost everything; you had to work during your entire educational career; you found happiness in thrift stores and the only manicures and pedicures you received were during slumber parties with your sisters and girlfriends. But your mate is an only child whose parents fed him or her from a silver platter since the day he or she was born; your mate never worked a day in his or her life (yes, it's difficult to imagine a black child experiencing this, but they're out there); they had an apartment of their own throughout their entire college education and a new car for high school graduation; and they can name designer garments on sight. He or she will buy you whatever you want, just don't touch their things. Opposites attract yes, but rarely do they stay together, especially after the novelty wears off.

The person you are interested in may be one of the

sexiest thangs you've met in quite a while. Still, sooner or later the differences between you will creep up and knock you over the head if you don't acknowledge them at the outset. This pate-thump usually happens after the initial "lustfest" (when the sex is hot because the body is new and so is the personality). It is at this time that you should determine if you have the same interests, hobbies, and taste in friends. If you are interested in physical fitness and good health, and he (or she) isn't, how are you going to cope? What if things you thought were cute initially, "Honey's a Republican, and I'm a Democrat," begin to burgeon into battle zones (for example, the right to life versus the right to choose)? What if most of your mate's friends are honestly into the retro style and way of living (the style dictated by the fashions and tastes of the fifties and sixties) and their belief system includes working for enjoyment, instead of a big home and a few children who eventually receive a private-school education? And most of your friends, and you, attended private schools and believe in working for the big home like the ones most of you grew up in?

When you come from different backgrounds, professional versus working-class, for example, you may not think that's a very large gap, but psychologically it is. If your parents are similar to the "Huxtables" or the "Tates" (doctors and attorneys—yes, there are several black households out there like this), and the brother you've been dating has parents who are like "Roc's" family (a nurse and a trash collector), what are they going to talk about during the initial family gathering? You may say, "Well, that's their problem," but, Sista-Girl, believe me, the problem will soon come home to roost on your doorstep. Why? Because your parents are going to want you to be with someone who is at least at a class level comparable to yours, and you're going to catch hell from them if Brotha-Man is not. You may even catch hell from your friends, too. Why do you think interracial coupling is so difficult?

Society is so determined to keep everything and everybody in their own nice little box, venturing out permanently is very disturbing to its psyche. We're (most heinously) taught, it's okay to go *slumming,* but you must marry and bear children with your own kind.

And when the two of you are exchanging gifts on birthdays or holidays, and you present Honey with a cashmere sweater and he presents you with a pair of gold-plated earrings, what's going to happen? "But that stuff's all material," you argue. Yes, I agree. But what about how this *man* feels? I can't count the number of times I've tried to play matchmaker only to have my friends, good black men, tell me, "I can't see anybody right now. I'm not financially secure enough to be in a relationship. And to have my woman do better than me is painful and not right. So thanks, but no thanks." Remember, sisters, the sociological conditioning that calls for the man to be able to provide more than the woman is still *mentally* a significant factor in relating for most black couples, whether it's felt by the man or the woman. Many good brothers are beginning to change this mentality because they can only do so much with the opportunities they are *allowed to have;* their mate earning more than they do is a nonissue for them, as it really should be. However, this attitude change is slow moving.

Furthermore, if the kind of entertainment your honey enjoys is partying, watching television, and going to the movies once a month or so, and if you prefer literature, art, theater, traveling, fine dining, etc., what your honey enjoys doing is quickly going to become monotonous for you and vice versa unless a fine, happy medium is attained. The reality is the more you've been exposed to culturally, the more it will take to entertain you (and it doesn't necessarily concern money, because the cost of museums, books, and philosophical conversations can be nominal). Different cultures, classes, and societies have different outlooks on life, and folks can be very narrow-minded and/or fixated when it comes to their perception of how life should be lived and enjoyed.

So though coupling with someone who is culturally different can and should be positive and successful, the work required to make it so can also be extensive and grueling. I wish it weren't that way because there is so much to be gained from playing and living on both sides of the tracks, but unfortunately it is still very difficult to bridge the gaps, be they racial, cultural, gender-based, or age-based. Maybe if we all just opened up a little . . .

green monsters

We all witness the arguments, face-offs, discussions, and side-glances between a couple when one member of the couple has been "caught" in a compromising situation—like when Brotha-Man damn near breaks his neck straining to follow a Ms. Thang that passed him and his lady on the street. And we say to ourselves, "How insecure she must be! I would never react like that!" Yet, when faced with the same or similar circumstance, we react in the very same way or even worse. I am still doing battle with this demon myself. Why? I'm not quite certain, yet. I'm successful, attractive, and intelligent, so I'm told. But let me see my mate get turned on by someone else, and part of me goes ballistic.

I rationalize by telling my spouse it's not him I worry about, but the women. That it's a matter of the women respecting me and respecting the relationship between me and my mate, like I would respect a relationship of theirs. Yet, I remember an occasion when my mate was masturbating while watching a lesbian scene in an adult video. Instantly, I let him and the neighbors hear how I felt—"going ballistic" is a euphemism in this case. After a while he explained to me how the girls in the video per se did not turn him on, it was more the act than the girls themselves that brought my spouse pleasure. "Yeah, right," I responded, as I always do when faced with an uncomfortable situation that is going to require some digestion on my part. I somewhat believed him, but I needed to let the matter settle within my brain first before I really gave it a closer look.

A few days later, after it had settled, I thought about it again and examined my own voyeurism. The attraction is the people to a certain extent—we all like watching beautiful people—but it is true that the act is the primary focal point. For example, watching Michael Jordan and Scottie Pippin walk down the street does nothing for me. I wouldn't give them a second glance, and no thought of screwing either one goes through my mind. But watching them perform together on the court, in the passionate heat of a fast and high-scoring game. The power, the intensity. Watching them perform, watching their act, puts me in a completely different mind-set. My eyes are glued to the television screen, to the sweat, to their muscles, to Jordan's tongue, to Pippin's arms. After thinking about this, I understood where my husband (boyfriend at the time) was coming from and could get over it. Besides, I thought about the times when I got turned on watching lesbian scenes, too, and had to place some of the blame for this particular jealousy torpedo action on ovulation.

Yet, videos are one thing and real life is another. At times I still have a little difficulty determining whether a "jealous" response of mine regarding a "live" woman was based on actual jealousy (therefore, insecurity—heaven forbid, *me* being insecure) or on my demand for respect from other women. But, I figure as long as Mr. Man understands it is still based on my feelings of love and not fear, I'm okay, right?

One aspect of relating sisters should note is that the closer we are to our mates, the more vulnerable we become. The more vulnerable we become, the more frightened we sometimes become, and thus we begin to feel those tiny twinges of insecurity. This is when we should trust in the fact that our mates won't use our vulnerabilities against us. Remember, this holds true for them, too. They become vulnerable (although men don't like to admit it) and have to trust us as well.

Sometimes jealousy is felt because we want to believe we are irreplaceable and the most special person in our mate's life. We give them little tests to see just how special we are to them. And they don't even know they are being tested. For example, we visit without phoning first. This is an old test of fidelity. Do it enough times and one will either get one's feelings crushed or become almost foolishly secure. Believe you are special, Ms. Thang, but that you *can* be substituted. Still, relish the fact that there is only a singular you and although they can probably substitute someone else for you, they can never exactly replace you. Do what you can to make the relationship between you and your mate happy and unique for both of you, and enjoy the day you have, not fretting about immature tests. If your relationship is strong, it will automatically triumph.

I think jealousy is caused not only by insecurity based on low self-esteem or by the fact that we want to believe we are the most special person in our honey's life, but also by our desire at times to protect our emotional selves. Those of us who have in the past been hurt by infidelity or disrespect will often ask or say things that sound jealous so that we can be assured that everyone's cards are on the table, face-up, and there's no double-dealing going on. Why not just accept the fact that we are all human, prone to loss of self-control and in need of ego boosters? Well, we do accept it, but we also try to protect ourselves as much as possible from the pain and suffering those human qualities can cause. For example, we ask "Who was that you were talking to on the telephone, your girlfriend?" We can be ninety-nine percent sure that the caller was a friend, relative, client, or someone else who is strictly platonically related. In fact, we can be one hundred percent sure that if the caller was not platonically related, our mates wouldn't admit it anyway.

There is only so much "protecting" of ourselves we can do. Then, the protecting becomes obsessive. And if it does, then either the very thing we're trying to protect ourselves against becomes self-fulfilling—that is, our mate has an unfaithful interlude—or our relationship fails because our overprotection becomes overwhelming.

Now, a certain amount of jealousy is normal, even healthy, in relationships. It validates the significance of the relationship. I admit I feel a little special when questioned by my husband about a particular phone call, neighbor, or colleague. Nonetheless, we don't go searching through each other's things regularly. We don't follow each other, nor do we know where the other lunches every day. Instead, we continually express our love and need for each other in more harmonious and reassuring ways.

Yes, a little jealousy is understandable. Quite naturally, we don't want someone we are emotionally involved with to be emotionally involved with someone else, at least not to the degree they are involved with us. And if someone comes along who can probably change their minds, we don't like it. This may be selfish, but it's normal and even flattering to a certain extent. *To a certain extent*—past that it becomes obsessive and dangerous.

I used to have this problem as a younger woman. Following people I was involved with. Checking the pockets and wallets of my mates almost daily without their knowledge. Calling and hanging up when they answered to make sure they were at home when they said they would be. All sorts of crazy things. I did this until I found myself on the receiving end of this kind of behavior. Then I saw how fanatical, disturbing, and wrong it was. I finally understood, when someone told me they couldn't live without me, how truly ludicrous I must have sounded when I told someone else that very thing. A big, bright light flicked on in my head when someone told me they would rather die than see me with someone else because I was the only one for them. Dear God, how very little self-worth this person had. And, oh, my God, how very low my own self-esteem must have been during the time I suffered through these kinds of jealous bends!

If your mate begins acting like I did or frequently starts arguments by making outrageous accusations, if he or she questions your every move and interrogates you after you return from being out or after you finish a telephone call, if you are continually being harassed about why you were looking at that person or why did that person look at you, these are warning signals.

Perhaps you learn your friends and family members don't enjoy being around you when your mate is present. Maybe your mate has offended them often enough to not enjoy being around you two. On the other hand, this could also be a warning of impending obsessive jealousy. A brother I know was once dating a sister who wouldn't let him out of her sight. If he and his sister-in-law were in the kitchen talking, Ms. Thang would go into the kitchen. If he and his brother were in the basement fooling around, wrestling, you would eventually find Girlfriend in the basement. If he and his father were talking in a bedroom of his dad's home, here she would come, looking for her honey. His father even remarked to me, "Damn! Can't I have a minute's peace with my own son? It's not like I get to see him every day with him being two thousand miles away. She lives with him for heaven's sake!"

We can prevent some of this unnecessary jealousy by immediately establishing a secure "trust fund" in our relationship. Saying beforehand what hurts and what feels good emotionally, not only as things happen, opens this fund and makes important deposits. We know where not to tread, and we can make sure we don't. Being independently accountable (not waiting for our mate to question our whereabouts and daily activities and so forth, but providing them with the information first) also feeds into our trust account. Above all else, emphasizing emotional fidelity will strengthen the relationship for the many tests it will undoubtedly face, as relationships are no more perfect than the humans who develop them.

Extreme jealousy can sometimes appear at first to be another one of those charming little traits. However, after a short while it can become very grotesque. Professional help should be sought if your mate, or even you, exhibit any of the above obsessive behaviors.

abuse

The tabloid newspapers, talk-show circuit, and soap opera programs are loaded with stories about abuse and domestic violence. Many psychologists (and I agree with them) find it difficult to discern or say that one form of abuse is worse than another. While physical abuse is horrible and damaging, psychological abuse (that is, emotional abuse, usually direct or indirect verbal slurs) can leave scars just as damaging and difficult to recover from. Maybe this, more than any other reason, is why I am sensitive to what I say to people and how I say it. *Being intentionally insensitive to the feelings and needs of loved ones is being emotionally abusive.*

We may live with our mates for years and think we know everything about their past, but there still may be things we are not privy to. If, in a moment of insensitive candor, we make a comment or say something that brings back for others negative memories, memories subconsciously forgotten because they were too painful to face, this may cause them emotional injury and may possibly result in an outburst directed at us. I believe the human mind has a defense mechanism that allows us to submerge things that are too painful, and unnecessary, for us to deal with.

Some therapists believe that bringing all painful memories to the forefront and dealing with them allows for a certain growth, that it somewhat desensitizes you to this kind of pain, which enables you to overcome some interpersonal conflicts. Well, personally, I can develop positively without having to dredge up horrifying childhood memories (such as witnessing the sexual molestation of a four-year-old friend by a thirteen-year-old boy and being Divinely spared, thanks to my mother's call for me). Bitter and painful memories can do nothing now but make me feel bad remembering them and make me feel good for just moving on. I'd rather just keep going, and I don't need anybody mentally abusing me by reminding me of these painful memories again. These therapists argue that this is why you need to face them, so that when you are reminded of the memory, you won't feel anything or you won't feel bad. A bad experience is just that. Your ability to move past it does not, in my opinion, diminish its negativity. And I, personally, cannot and will not be desensitized.

Emotions are powerful gauges of what is beneficial and what is detrimental to you as an individual. In my opinion, interfering with these gauges, shutting them off (which is what desensitization does) hampers one's ability to derive or contribute benefit or to prevent affliction. Therefore tampering with them, I believe, is ill-advised unless a severe psychological trauma is diagnosed.

If your mate is intentionally insensitive and frequently "pushes buttons" he or she knows will upset you despite the pain this button pushing is causing, beware. If your mate continually says things in a manner that you feel is mean or nasty, beware. If your mate endlessly professes his or her love for you and then finds ways to demean and belittle you more often than not, beware. And act quickly on this wariness. Psychological abuse can cause irreparable injury sometimes.

Most of us are cognizant of physical abuse—beating,

raping, slapping, pushing, shoving, and the like—because of its widespread media coverage. If your mate exhibits any of this behavior, even once, do not hesitate to leave. If you tolerate it once, you will be expected to tolerate it again and again and again.

People who take out their negative emotions on others via physical violence are uneducated, undisciplined, cowards. They are "uneducated" because they are ignorant of nonviolent constructive methods of dealing with anger and frustration; "undisciplined" because although they know violence isn't right (having been taught this no doubt as a child), they cannot or will not control themselves; and "cowards" because only insecure, frightened individuals try to control others by means of violence and force.

I have female friends who say that women who are physically abused once and remain with the abuser, deserve everything they get after they decide to stay. Didn't it hurt the first time? And if it hurt the first time, did they think it wasn't going to hurt as much the second time?

I argue these women didn't believe there would be a second time. When you love someone and they supposedly love you, you want to understand them, help them, and give them a second chance. However, I also understand where those sisters who think the second beating is deserved are coming from. Because unless therapy is obtained and continued, giving someone a second chance is futile; it's only going to be another opportunity for the next episode of abuse.

Some of our sisters are so low in self-esteem they allow themselves to be brutalized and dehumanized regularly; to them a good night's rest is a minor miracle. They can't believe the world they dreamed of, they boasted about, that they perfected the role of Ms. Thang for, became a crashing hell all about them. "Why me?" they ask. "This can't be happening to me," they deny. "How can this be happening to me?" these sisters wonder, so discombobulated that they see no way out. They can't leave; they won't leave. They ask you, the Sista-Girl whom they expected this sort of thing to happen to, what they should do, and you tell them to leave or make the abuser leave. But they aren't ready for the truth, so they get angry with you and decide not to speak to you for a couple of weeks. So you're wondering if they're dead or alive when they telephone you telling you they're working it out. But then it happens again, and this time it's over; they're thinking about getting a divorce or leaving. Still, this can't be happening to them. Not them. So they love the man, forgive the man, pray for the man, and pray for their children; and, finally, after their spirit and their bruised, battered bodies have been badly beaten down, some of them pray never to wake.

Sometimes sisters relegate themselves to abusive relationships because they have children and they, alone, cannot provide for their children the things their spouses or mates can provide. Bullshit. A study on domestic violence and its impact on children was done in late 1994 by the American Bar Association's Center on Children and the Law and the Hawaii Family Courts Divorce Education Project. Its conclusion, which many child psychologists agree with, was that children who witness domestic abuse (and this includes just hearing constant arguing from behind closed doors) suffer acute psychological trauma in the long-term, one of the more common results of which is an inability as adults to sustain a healthy, loving relationship.

Now, I don't know about you, but to me a child's ability to distinguish between healthy and unhealthy relationships is a hell of a lot more important than anything else a mate can provide. And if leaving is going to create a dramatic change in the lifestyle, one can infer the provider has a large asset base, something good divorce attorneys are always willing to fight for. The argument "I'm doing it for the child[ren]'s sake" just doesn't cut the mustard.

Get up off your ass and get two jobs if you have to, but show your child (or your children) that you're a Queen Mother who recognizes the importance of demonstrating real love versus having material wealth. Demonstrate that you love and respect yourself and will not tolerate anything less than love and respect from your mate. I don't care how much your daughter is "Daddy's little girl," when Daddy's abusing you, he's abusing her, too. Are you going to amplify the abuse by keeping your child in this environment? Do you want your sons growing up thinking this behavior is how a husband should be defined, that this is the definition of manhood? Do you want your little girl developing into a young woman who believes this is what loving men or husbands do? They will. More than likely, if you suffer abuse, you have come from an abusive environment. This is how the cycle starts, and this is how it will continue for them, our children.

One brother recounted to me how, as a very young man, shortly before his parents divorced, he would hear his mother and father constantly arguing—she continually accusing his father of infidelity and his father continually denying her accusations. He told me, "I thought then, why doesn't she just stop trying to make him confess to something he didn't do; why doesn't she just stop fighting him? Then, as I grew older and hung out with the brothers more and saw the games we brothers often run on sisters—our girlfriends, our wives—I understood where my mom was coming from and was glad that she decided not to stand for it after all."

If you aren't sure you can leave, there are Queen Mothers all around you, young and old alike, who have successfully left abusive relationships with nothing but children in hand. They find ways to provide shelter, food, clothing, and education for their children in environments that are stress-free and nurturing.

Sisters, if you're being abused physically, I beg of you, don't stay. If you do, you or your mate, or even your children, may not live to see the morning after the next confrontation. And then what?

There are so many strong sisters available for you to reach out to if you need to get away from this crap. Too many of us are willing and able to talk to you and tell you the truth. But instead, you want us to visit you at the hospital or attend your funeral and then see to *your* children, who are now perhaps in the custody of the monster who murdered you or, in the hands of the already overburdened State.

Fear is one of the strongest emotions in human nature. But it is surmountable. You can be half-out-of-your-wits afraid and still walk away. I've seen many women do it. You are not alone. Don't let the fact that an abuser charged with murder was able to walk out of court a free man intimidate you into staying put. He wasn't charged with abuse; he was charged with murder. If he had been charged with abuse, he would be serving time. Don't let the fact that the American workforce is undergoing dramatic changes frighten you into staying put for economic reasons. I plead with you not to be that materialistic. Put some faith in your Creator and some faith in the sisters who may not know your name but love you anyway, like I do, and walk away.

I fell into tears while writing this because I know some of you, personally, and I know you don't believe what I'm saying is honest because *you* cannot be forthright about it yet. In your dangerous state of denial, you project your deceptiveness onto what I am saying. But, to those of you who hear the reality this Sista-Girl is speaking, and before it is too late: Pack your bags, leave your bags, walk away, run away, to the nearest train station, bus depot, or airport. God is always walking, running, flying with you, wherever you go. You owe it to yourself, you owe it to your children, you owe it to all of us. And remember what I said about revenge. Don't think about it. Vengeance is not the answer. Simply get as far away as you can. Maybe you can find shelter with your family. If not, if your family can't understand why you've left an abuser, they're not your family; they are the family of the abuser, and let them love him.

Brothers, until you learn to properly channel the anger and frustration of four hundred years that we sisters know you've been feeling, you had better stop taking it out on us. No one wants to see any more of you in the prisons. They are wrongfully overcrowded with you now. But if you leave us no other alternative, if you continue to act just o.o.c. (out of control), you will be taking careful showers with several other large, black and Hispanic brothers, while we walk on. Brothers, listen to me. Sisters, tell your men. Somebody's got to survive, and I don't want our sons and daughters to have permanent pictures of you, their daddies, in the most unflattering light imprinted on their psyches. We may work with you because we understand the foot that's been crushing your neck, preventing you from breathing, crippling your brain. But you aren't going to keep putting your foot on our spines, uh-uh. We will seek the tender love and care we deserve elsewhere, from those who utilize their anguish constructively and acknowledge that love does not come behind a closed fist or a stinging slap or unnecessary verbal slurs. We will run to those who know that love comes with gentle embraces, kind phrases, and benevolent deeds. And mark my words, there are plenty of brothers and sisters capable of this kind of true, affirming, supporting, and Divine love.

All of the above relationship problems—incompatibility, infidelity, jealousy, even abuse—are difficulties that professional counseling, if sought earnestly and early enough, may very well help and thereby keep the relationship intact. On the flipside, with all of the above difficulties, professional counseling, if sought earnestly and early enough, may very well help dissolve what psychologists sometimes refer to as a "toxic" relationship.

Toxic relationships are those that we are more or less addicted to. You find that you would rather suffer through all of the indignities and pains inflicted upon you by this relationship than go through the hell of breaking up. Often friends and relatives see it before we do, and counseling can help us pinpoint this problem. Sometimes you attempt to break free, but you begin to suffer withdrawal symptoms and decide to try once more to make it work. But throughout the relationship, as an individual, you are losing. Your self-worth, your vigor, your self-respect, your enthusiasm are all being exhausted. The worst in you is being drawn out instead of the best in you. Your mate seems fine, but something just isn't right with you.

If you must dissolve your relationship, align yourself with friends and family members who are positive and supportive and won't let you slip into a deep depression, which can sometimes occur. If you are continually asked by friends and family to go out, find the strength eventually to say okay and go. You may have neglected them during this emotional upheaval. Let them entertain you, let them make you laugh, let them lure you into uncomfortable and awkward social conversations about relationships so that the healing process can begin.

Also, find quiet, peaceful, beautiful places where you can weep, laugh, think, and listen to Spirit. Read positive, affirming books on self-love and relationships, materials that confirm your decision, that move you to tears but also move you to smiles. Go for walks along the beach, along bright and busy main thoroughfares, in clean and bustling parks, along quiet treelined residential streets. Allow thoughts to run through your mind at night like water from a river running into a lake or sea. Listen to the thoughts coming forth as you look at the trees and watch the squirrels chase each other. You've never done that? It's about time you did. Hear what God is saying to you as the wind chases the leaves down the street and whips through the boughs of maple and oak. Understand what is being told to you by the heady waves splashing upon the shoreline. There's so much more to life and to living than the ups and downs we humans become so disheartened over.

Pour yourself into your work; sometimes this is when we do our best. Review your objectives for your career. How far have you gone in fulfilling them? How much further do you have to go? Is there anything else you can do on a daily basis to get you that much further along? Talk to your supervisor, your manager, your mentor. They'll be glad to see that you are still interested. Is this really the career for you? Perhaps it's time you started thinking about doing something you love, even if it's just part-time. Look into that. Ask friends and family members their opinions. Attend seminars and workshops on the topic; meet fun new people who are enthusiastic about what they're doing. It may not be for you after all, but you'll make new friends and the healing will continue.

Buy yourself pretty little things, like colorful floral bouquets, upbeat posters. Go window-shopping and make your wish list for the next twelve months. Okay, so you can't afford the latest Maserati, what about those Rollerblades or that bike you were thinking about? Maybe it's time for a new health club, or what about a personal trainer once a month for a few months to give someone else the responsibility of motivating you and your tired body? Bored with working out? Take a week or two off; it's okay, that is unless you're in training for the next Fitness America competition. Take a community course in wine tasting or learn a foreign language.

Treat yourself to warm bubble baths. Light a few fragranced candles and turn out the bathroom light. Put your headset on, careful though not to electrocute yourself, and sing along with some of your favorite tunes. Soak up the warmth and glow. Check out a good comedy at a neighborhood theater. Yes, Sista-Girls go to the movies by themselves all the time. It's very therapeutic. Or get a six-pack of brew, order a pizza, and watch some crazy horror flicks on late-night cable television. Be by yourself and get in touch with your best friend, YOU. If champagne is your thing, go for it, and don't forget to splurge on some caviar, if you can. Otherwise, champagne goes great with pizza, too. Love yourself and let the healing continue.

But, hey, Ms. Thang, be careful not to overindulge. After a breakup, it's easy to start smoking and drinking and *just looking* at but not eating food because the chocolate cake that once gave you so much pleasure isn't even considered an indulgence anymore. It's kind of weird. Things that once provided us with pleasure we may somehow relate to our former mates and therefore deny ourselves the pleasure. We don't want or can't have them now, so why have anything else pleasurable? We end up getting down to that size four or six that we always wanted to be, but we also end up looking just like we feel—sick and empty. It's really easy to anesthetize ourselves so that we don't feel a thing. Who wants to, after giving so much and getting a foot up the petooty in return? But eventually we've got to start feeling, because we have to start living again. So if that's the train you're on, get off at the next stop and phone a friend. Get some real lovin' from another Sista-Girl who's been there and can bring you back home.

See this as just one more experience you can share with someone who will need you to share it with them later on. Celebrate a new beginning and love yourself even more.

19

Dogs, Princes, and Other Strange Creatures

The best Sista-Girls can do in relationships is help to maintain them, nurture them, and allow for their natural development, as we would with anything we care about. We accomplish this by remaining true to ourselves, to our individual identities (thus ensuring the possibility for our growth); by acting responsibly and fairly toward the fruits of our relationships; and by allowing our mates to also be true to themselves and ensuring the possibility for their growth by not doing things to impede their maturity. A relationship between two individuals actually comprises three separate but interlocking entities: entity XY (that's you), entity YZ (that's your mate), and entity XYZ (that's the relationship itself). Each entity must be allowed to flourish apart from the others, but should also add to the value of the others. (And that is as far as I am going mathematically.)

the incredible shrinking sista-girl

If we remain true to ourselves, we will not lose sight of who we are as individuals and will not, therefore, permit ourselves to dissolve into the relationships. Yes, when we become seriously involved with someone, even if we marry him, we are helping to create a union of one. However, so many of us sisters become engrossed with the union, we forget about the individual personalities that led to the creation of this union. We (especially us married Sista-Girls) quite often forget that were it not for the singular traits both of us had before the alliance, there would have been no attraction and therefore no union.

"To thine own self be true" is so important within the dynamics of relationships and, yet, so easily forgotten. Did you go out to parties, movies, shopping with girlfriends prior to your relationship? If you did, don't stop. You may have to curtail those activities, but don't cut them out altogether. Your Sista-Girls deserve to know you still value their friendship. Did you exercise regularly? Did you sit at home sometimes, alone in front of the television watching a good movie or program while feeding your face? Did you go for long walks alone or hang out every so often at the local coffee shop, doing some random thinking and perhaps people watching?

Did you stay up past your bedtime sometimes with a good book or magazine article? When your best Sista-Girl had love troubles, did you change all of your plans after work to be with her? Continue doing so. All of these things created the independent, loving, respectful, kind, *attractive,* human being you are now. If you stop doing any of these things or refrain from them to the point that they are no longer fruitful, you are changing the person to whom your mate was initially attracted.

I realize the person we regularly sleep with is, excluding Spirit and ourselves, the most important entity with whom we are currently involved. While we lie next to them, while we eat with them, while we share a household, our lives are in their hands as well as ours. But if we change who we are too much to be with that person, we are changing the original source of our attraction, and the bond will eventually erode. It's like making bricks. If you make your first batch using clay, mud, and a little water, your bricks will be strong. But if to increase the amount of bricks you can make, you begin mixing sand in with the clay and using more water, now the bricks, though larger in number, will be weaker in strength and fall apart much sooner.

This is all too familiar to me. In former relationships, I would become so involved with my mate I would alienate all of my friends and most of my family. What my mate and I did, or what my mate wanted, took precedence over everything and everyone. It was the same each time I became seriously involved with someone until I realized, after a couple of breakups, I had no one to turn to and no one to comfort me while I was down. I had severely damaged the links I had with everyone who meant something to me before these relationships; the relationship sphere of my life fell out of balance. Not good.

When you are so in love and want to be with your honey almost twenty-four hours a day, often it is perplexing, to consider that other relationships have the same significance. It's confusing until those relationships are no longer there and you find yourself in the tar pits of guilt and quite alone.

When trying to determine how some people stayed together and why other folks broke up, I figured there were basically three stages involved in a loving, intimate relationship. In *stage one,* you are deeply infatuated with your prospective mate, thinking about them all the time and wanting to be with them 24-7. (It's usually in this stage that the initial "lustfest" occurs and the rose-colored glasses seem cemented to your face.) *Stage two* is, for some, the most difficult stage because it requires exposing imperfections and vulnerabilities; this is the time during a relationship when you determine if the things you *don't like* about your mate are tolerable and when your mate does the same; this is where the bridge of communication is developed and crossed by both parties; you determine if tolerance is possible, if change is possible, or if this is the end of the relationship. *Stage three* is generally the most difficult because at this stage couples have decided to stay together despite the personality differences they possess as individuals; this is the portion of the relationship where communication, compromise, more communication, and more compromise are used persistently; this is the stage of the relationship where married couples succeed or fail.

Anyway, the last time I was under the spell of *stage one* love and encountered one of those difficult "who to be with" decisions, I stopped and asked myself what I would do if my mate were just another platonic friend. How would I respond if I were not involved in an intimate relationship with this person? Suddenly the answer became clear, and I could act with a free conscience. I could be with whomever I wanted to be with, and if the persons whom I chose not to be with at this time loved me, they would understand my choice and I wouldn't feel guilty for neglecting them. (Often, in stage one, you neglect friends and family because of the natural lure of deep infatuation.)

At times you must also ask yourself, since the beginning of this intimate relationship, do our friends seem to see us in the same light, a better light, or a worse light? We should discuss this with our mates, our friends, and our family, especially when we get that "I'm being pulled in every direction" feeling. By our voicing this sentiment to friends and family members (who can often be very demanding of our time and energy), they may realize the undue pressure being placed on us and chill out.

With all the tugs from a significant other, friends, family, and coworkers, a girl can sometimes feel like one of those spinning wheels in the center of two strings, being pulled on both sides but just spinning and spinning and spinning. Make sure everyone knows they still hold a special place in your heart no one else can occupy. And if someone tries to make his or her space bigger, making it uncomfortable for you, just explain you're putting him or her in a "freeze frame" and stopping the madness right now.

Sisters, stay attractive, fun, nonjudgmental, and beholden to your own interests and previous friendships. Be dependable but slightly unpredictable. Love yourself as much as your relationship, and don't hesitate to put yourself first every once in a while. Your mate, if mature, will appreciate your individuality and your desire and need to maintain it.

the first national bank of ms. thang

Ladies, your pocketbooks and checkbooks (along with credit cards and all other financial assets) are yours and should remain so, always in your possession and shared when necessary, but not upon demand and not to answer a lien created by your mate.

This section is most applicable to individuals living with their mates or significant others. However, if you are not cohabiting, you are still sharing something with the person you are involved with, and what is applicable to money matters can usually be transferred to emotional matters.

Couples, unfortunately, often haggle over money and/or material issues. To circumvent these arguments at the beginning of your relationship (or, if you have already had these fights, to prevent them from recurring), ask yourself the following:

What did I come into the relationship with financially?

If you came into the relationship with substantially less than you have now because of your mate's generosity, your financial position is subordinate to that of your mate's. Therefore, although your opinion is important, your mate should be making the final decision in financial matters. If you came into the relationship with substantially more, then likewise, you probably hold the dominant financial position. When it comes to making major financial decisions, you should value your mate's opinions, but the final decision should rest with you and be agreeable to your mate. If both of you became involved as relative equals, this is how financial matters should be decided. Sometimes this calls for more compromise and even possibly arbitration (utilizing the objective observation of another family member or close friend, for example). However, both of you should be equally satisfied with all the decisions.

I realize that this is unpalatable medicine to swallow for some of my sisters out there, especially those of us in the traditional thinking mode: his money is my money, my money is my money, and financial decisions are *ours* to make. I have only one thing to say: if you earned three or four times more than your mate, would you be willing to share the bulk of the financial decision-making? If so, then look for a mate who believes as you do, and good luck in finding such a person.

Besides myself and my financial assets, did I have anything to offer (did I come into the relationship with anything else), and if so, have I been sharing it? It blows me away when I hear of couples living together who ask each other "may I borrow [this]" or "may I borrow [that]" when this or that is something like a hairbrush or a T-shirt. Now, we all have our special items, like a favorite mug or a favorite sweater, and asking permission to use an item like this is understandable. But when two people are intimately involved and cohabitating, it should be an all-or-nothing deal ("or nothing" means that you really shouldn't be living together). So whatever you came into the relationship with—clothes, jewelry, money, furniture, books, stereo equipment—you should be willing to share with the partner whom you are living with. Your partner should likewise be willing to share everything they have with you. Otherwise, you may as well not live together, because the significance of your material goods still outweighs the significance of your relationship. This may sound as if I'm contradicting what I said about finances; however, sharing what you have and making financial decisions about the resources you have are two different circumstances. Normally, if you and Brotha-Man share in the financial responsibilities of the household on a relatively equal level, sharing what you have includes financial decision making. However, in a more traditional relationship (which is quickly becoming the exception to the rule), where one party earns decidedly more, that individual usually has a more accurate picture of the household's entire financial outlook. Therefore, the final responsibility for making financial decisions, often, naturally rests with him or her.

Have I received anything in return, and if so, is it relatively equal to my needs and/or desires? You should be receiving the equivalent of whatever you came into the relationship with and are sharing. If you entered the relationship with a state-of-the-art sound system and your mate is free to use it, you should feel free and be free to ride his or her custom-fitted, $1200 bicycle. If your mate wants you to help pay the telephone bill every month and you comply, you are fully justified in asking and expecting your mate to contribute, financially or productively, something of relatively equal value to your telephone bill contribution. This all may sound very elementary, but you'd be surprised at the number of people in couples whose needs and expectations are being short-changed in their opinion, while their mates don't feel so at all. These things should be discussed and, if necessary, written down in some kind of informal agreement at the outset so that the partners are fully aware of what their obligations to each other are. It shouldn't be considered a premarital agreement; the relationship may not warrant such a serious tone. It should perhaps be referred to as a "roommate agreement" or a "shared-space agreement." And with African-American women earning on average more than their brothers, I believe it to be a very sound idea.

Is our relationship a utilitarian one, an emotional one, or a little of both? Think about this; it relates to the reason you are involved with your mate. If your relationship is utilitarian, then you and your mate fulfill each other's material needs. If it is an emotional one, the reason you are together is you share great emotion for each other. Most relationships are a little of both. Two incomes are better than one, but who is going to live with and contribute financially to a relationship with someone they don't care about?

As a black woman, if your relationship is an emotional one or established to meet both utilitarian and emotional needs, you may have this noble desire to "sacrifice" for the welfare of your mate. This is because many of us feel the need to support our downtrodden black men. And as I just stated, black women, on the whole, earn more than the average black man. Consequently, we, sisters, are forever sacrificing. This is no problem as long as you know that if the circumstance was reversed, there would be no hesitation on your mate's part to sacrifice for you. It's okay to sacrifice occasionally just as long as it is occasionally or understood to be for a certain period of time (for example, if your honey is in school) and not frequently or for an undefined period of time. Otherwise, I would sit down and have a heart-to-heart chat with Boyfriend (or Girlfriend) informing him you are not a sidewalk.

I realize this may sound like a difficult task, but, unfortunately, some of us tend to look at relationships too subjectively and end up getting our teeth kicked in for it. I've been on all sides of the board—earning more than the man I lived with or was married to, earning less, and earning about the same. The only equitable thing to do when it comes to finances is to treat the relationship as you would a business. You've got to negotiate on some points, relinquish some points, and overrule on others, and the outcome will depend on the strength of your position and how much you value your business associate. In relationships, where money is also involved, the decisions depend on the relative strengths of your and your mate's positions and how much the relationship means to both of you. *As I said, if material matters (including money) outweigh personal matters, there is no reason for you to be living together. Everything should be easily shared and the responsibilities, financial or otherwise, should be distributed fairly.*

I was once educated on the fact that women, black and white, will never gain equality with men as far as the workload is concerned, the total workload—career, family, and home. I was informed that the best to hope for is 60/40 (but the average is 70/30). Queen Mother Grandmommy White passed this knowledge on to her granddaughter, another good friend of mine, during one of their regular weekend telephone calls. She told her granddaughter a wife not only has to be a companion to her husband, but has about a half-dozen other careers going simultaneously—nurse, maid, cook, chauffeur, secretary, mother (if they have children), and psychologist. And heaven help her if she has an outside job she has to go to as well!

Judging from the roles men and women play now, I think Queen Mother White is still correct. Noting the amount of emotional strength found in women versus men (the "sensitive nineties man" is somewhat of a myth, by the way—I'll clue you in on that later), I am quite sure she is correct. So make sure you try to get your forty percent worth, but if you only get thirty percent, don't feel bad; it's just that you're stronger and capable of more than he is, anyway. If his workload share dips below thirty percent often, if you find you are always going down a one-way street—doing all of the sacrificing and giving—I think you should give a rest to this particular relationship.

cognac models and pagers

Frankly, lotsa men are dogs and black men are no exception. I am referring, here, to their instinct to "mate" with as many women as possible. Some men understand that because they are human beings and not actual canines or gorillas, they don't have to give in to these instincts, they can employ self-control. But some don't understand this, and others simply choose to ignore it. (And many brothers become exploitative because of the prevalent idea that most black males are either in the criminal justice system, gay, or illegal-substance abusers, which leaves about twenty-five percent of the black male population available for mating.) So, Sista-Girls, with the odds against us, there is little I can suggest to you about avoiding dogs except perhaps *beware.*

- Beware of the gentleman who wants all of your "411" but will only give you a pager number or a work telephone number.
- Beware of the gentleman who is so busy that he can meet with you only on a specified day at a specified time that only he can specify.
- Beware of the gentleman who has a tan line on his ring finger but no ring.
- Beware of the gentleman who is recently separated, divorced, or has broken up with his girlfriend and "needs a place to stay."
- Beware of the gentleman who whispers "I love you" only in the sack but professes a need for his "space" in the morning.

- Beware of the gentleman who models Remy Martin, hands you his business card, but cannot treat you and your girlfriend to a bottle of champagne or dinner.
- Beware of the gentleman who literally begs for you the first day or evening he meets you.
- Beware of the gentleman who invites you to dinner at a delightful bistro but, oops, forgets his wallet.
- Beware of the gentleman who can always make it over for a romper-room session but just can't seem to make his way to a nightclub or a movie.

Beware of these gentlemen unless, of course, you're looking for a "fuck buddy," which you might have to pay for, of course. And even if you are, I would still suggest a toy or movie from a good adult-fantasy store—it's cheaper and the orgasms are more reliable.

You have to admit there are some folks out there whom you have just got to stay away from. If he's modeling cognac, a thick mustache, and a body like "The Real Deal," but can't treat you and your girlfriend like the Ms. Thangs you are, leave him alone. Sista-Girl, I don't care if you're creamin' in your hosiery; if you must, go into the ladies' room, quietly and quickly take care of that hankerin' need, then go back to this man and tell him sweetly, "Thanks, but no thanks. I'm already taken care of." Take this from a magna cum laude graduate of the school of hard knocks.

Also, watch for the signs suggesting your mate is getting to close to "that line": Strangers start phoning the home and your mate never invites these individuals to meet you. Your mate goes out late at night and is unreachable (even in case of an emergency). Your mate often comes home late from work, and there's no reason given, even when asked. Stand your ground. Be considerate but maintain your self-respect. Don't tolerate behavior that you, yourself, wouldn't impose. *Ms. Thangs can be very obliging, but only to a point.*

ms. fix-it

Sisters should also be mindful of not falling into I call "the handywoman's special" trap. This is the tionship where sisters get saddled with prospective r because we believe that if we can fix the individual good relationship is feasible. Sisters, put those hamr drills, and nails down. If a mate needs repairing, it hooves you to let them do it themselves. Otherwise, toil you will expend will be for naught.

To put it plainly, you cannot fix another human bei You cannot make another individual see things the way y do, behave the way you want them to, or love you in t fashion you believe is best for you. If a person possess characteristics you feel the need to change or repair, th person is not someone with whom you should be involved Men (and women) whom we look to as mates, althoug we sometimes question it, are adults. If an adult enjoys partying three or four nights weekly, you do not have the right to try to make them stop. If they want to be in a relationship with you and are aware that this kind of behavior causes you discomfort, they will automatically stop out of respect and concern for the relationship. If they don't, there is nothing you should or can do. If you complain or discuss your objections, they may change their behavior for a week or two, out of sincerity or in an attempt to end your complaints. However, whatever their reason for stopping, if the conduct you objected to is a natural part of their personality at this juncture in their life, sooner than later they will return to it. I pointed out earlier that mates who argue viciously or abusively, unless they seek professional help to change their way of managing negative emotion, will continue to act abusively when facing disagreement because it is an inherent part of their being.

Sista-Girls, trying to be Ms. Fix-It is a waste of time and energy. If a prospective mate is looking for the

handywoman's special, give him or her your tool kit and tell them the job calls for a *do-it-yourselfer.*

the boys mama left behind

Whoever hath a daughter and doth not bury her alive[14] *or scold her or prefer his male children to her, may God bring him into Paradise.*

—Islamic Hadith

In his book *How to Love a Black Man,* Dr. Ronn Elmore also tells black women to stop mothering our men. I agree one hundred and ten percent. While supporting, loving, and assisting are necessary components of relationships (black men require these components a lot), sisters have to be careful not to become surrogate mothers for their mates. There is a difference between mothering and supporting.

Our men are really no different from other men in terms of how society initially views them. Male offspring have always been valued more than female offspring in Western as well as many Eastern cultures. African-American parents are no different from European-American parents or Asian parents or South American parents, often giving preferential and more lenient treatment to their sons while being very strict and overtly critical with their daughters. Thus, many of our men today expect this treatment from the women they become involved with. Oh, well . . .

How can we tell, though, if we are dealing with a "Mama's Boy"? I'll give you a few examples:

- ➪ He often behaves immaturely.
- ➪ Boyfriend acts irresponsibly, acknowledges it, and still doesn't care about his behavior.
- ➪ He thinks his irresponsible behavior is funny or explains it away by saying, "It's just the way I am."

- ➪ Mista-Man comes and goes as he pleases, offering little or no account of himself, giving vague answers to questions regarding his whereabouts (even if he's just been out with the fellas watching a football game or something like that).
- ➪ He refuses to answer questions about his whereabouts on the grounds that "My time is my time, and I'm the man, answerable to no one."
- ➪ He becomes angry and throws what are seemingly temper tantrums when he doesn't get his way or when you back him into a corner of responsibility or accountability.
- ➪ He goes away for a few days, without telephoning or letting you know where he's staying, after an argument has gone "too far," completely aware of how this unnerves you and makes you concede (against your better judgment) to his point in the argument.

If this behavior pattern is present, there's a very good chance Mama left her Boy with you.

One of the most indicative signs is that your man compares you to his mother and she always comes out more favorably. For example, "Mama didn't let my laundry pile up like this." Or, "My mother cooked, cleaned, worked, and took care of us kids." Or, "I didn't have to do anything but take out the garbage for my mom." Or, "Mom said that she told you peach-colored towels would look better in the bathroom than the white ones you liked."

If one or any combination of the above sounds familiar, I will tell you how to handle these overgrown children with facial hair and deep voices: Introduce them to a Daddy's Little Girl, if you know of a sister who fits the bill; tell them you hope they make each other very happy, and then YOU RUN AWAY FROM THEM, FAR FAR AWAY.

Mama's Boys are draining to the psyche and to the spirit. They take, take, take, and seldom replenish. They require professional help, so don't waste your time unless you're doing a case study.

Sisters can prevent themselves from becoming involved with these creatures by setting brothers straight from the outset, once you decide to start dating. Make sure your man knows if he makes any financial mistakes, he should be prepared to pay for them. Not that you won't help, but the instances requiring your assistance should be, oh, so few and far between. Brotha-Man must understand that just because you can balance your checkbook, and he can't balance his, doesn't mean you're the bank. Do not hesitate to inform him, in earnest, that if he does anything to jeopardize what you have built as an individual or what the two of you have built together as a couple, he had better be equipped to rebuild it, properly, quickly, and without your help, or the relationship will most likely cease. Let him know the only behinds you wipe are yours and those belonging to real infants. Adults wipe their own behinds, clean up their own messes, and do their own dishes. A brother might be put off by this in the beginning of a relationship, but assure him that because you are an adult willing to carry your portion of the load, you just want to make sure that load is fair, equally rationed out between the two of you. He should understand this and, as an adult, appreciate it.

20

Knights of the Black Table

Sisters are facing an ordeal of monstrous proportion today regarding our relationships with our brothers. It's a painful dilemma of such magnitude that if brothers *and* sisters don't overcome this impasse *together,* there is little hope for our future as a people. The ironic aspect of this problem is that brothers seem more concerned about its long-term effect on our people than sisters. Perhaps this is because brothers are still holding on to the ideal of a strong black people, whereas sisters have all but forsaken the concept.

Many black men work just as hard if not harder than most people to make ends meet and to provide for their families and, in the long run, to meet that ideal. They suffer the indignities of taking work below their skill and intelligence levels because they know they have to start somewhere. They dream about owning large homes and nice cars and work diligently toward the attainment of those dreams amidst a barrage of criticism from black women and negative images portrayed by the media. Many are legitimate entrepreneurs, engrossed with the pioneer spirit, working extra-long hours, because they realize nothing is guaranteed to anyone and, more important, if they fail, they have no one to blame but themselves.

Most African-American men cherish and respect African-American women. I know brothers who empty their pockets and hearts to women, leaving themselves with nothing but the bare necessities, because they want their women to enjoy life. African-American men can be found daily going to the store for tampons, setting up stereo systems, repairing cars, building decks, painting and paneling—anything we need them to do, there they are doing it. No, they are not saints, but they are trying to improve themselves, just as we sisters are trying to improve ourselves. They hate the part of them that does wrong and continually work inside themselves to better this part.

There are few black men who do not love and desire children. I know brothers who are more than willing to baby-sit brothers, sisters, nieces, nephews, and, of course, their own children, and watch these kids like the soldiers at Fort Knox watch over the gold bullion. They feed them, bathe them, change their diapers, and rock them to sleep. They want to teach our children the valuable lessons they learned, and they want to provide our children with examples of good black *men*.

However, sisters, for some reason, don't see this. All we manage to do, brothers say, is complain about what they don't do. This misunderstanding, along with the other obstacles, is not making things better. Unfortunately, the situation between black men and black women seems to be getting worse.

However, before we examine these obstacles and before I bring you messages from some of our brothers, let me tell you about some princes whom I have the pleasure of knowing or being acquainted with:

There's Sir Elliott, who saw to his sick mother for five years, quitting a very lucrative job to do so; when she passed, he was forced to take a dramatic cut in pay and status to reenter the workforce.

There's Sir Robert, who was offered but didn't accept an out-of-state, full, four-year college scholarship; he wanted to remain close to his family and assist with his sister, who is permanently disabled.

There's Sir Frank, who is doing the right thing by his infant and going to school during the day and working at night to provide both for physical needs and an example of a good father, a good black man, and a good human being.

Knight Rodney had a baby on the way and worked two jobs during his wife's pregnancy and maternity leave.

Sir Lanoris refused to idly stand by and watch fellow neighbors hurt themselves while jumping from a burning building; so he ignored the firemen and scrambled on top of the fire truck to try and "just catch anyone" who was jumping.

There's Knight Simon, who also works two jobs; one (full-time computer analyst) is his meat and potatoes, and the other (rehabbing real estate) his dream. In his spare time he moves around town in a sports car; but don't think about hitchin' a ride, because the passenger seat is always occupied, if he can see to it, with his five-year-old daughter.

There's a knight who saw pain in one of my Sista-Girls' faces one evening at church and commented on it, saying he could see she wasn't feeling well, and asked if he could pray with her, and there was no come-on to follow.

There's Sir Vernon, who drives in from the suburbs daily (a total commute of about two hours) as a volunteer for young black boys at a YMCA. He teaches and coaches them in basketball, baseball, and other sports. He also buys meals and equipment for those who can't afford them (and since most of these kids are poverty-stricken, residing in housing projects, lunch money is a luxury), provides transportation for them to and from the Y facilities to the parks and home, and triumphantly dissuades gang members trying to recruit or disturb the peace of his kids. He's never late, never ill, and always there for these boys with whatever they need.

Sir Ricky was so truly in love, he did as his fiancée requested and waited three years until his education was completed, waited another year after he was able to find a good job, and waited all of this time in complete abstinence. He became a member of her church and eventually director of the choir before marrying her as well. During the ceremony, he was so overtaken with emotion, he couldn't perform his part of the duo they were to sing together as part of their vows!

Just as my sister and I say to each other, "Give me the bad news first," I'll give it to you straight off. The bad news, Sista-Girls (like anyone needs to tell you, right?), is there are dogs, cognac models, beeper boys, mama's boys, leeches, and the like. But the good news is there are also knights, kings, and plain ol' good brothers out there. I realize many of my sisters are skeptical and believe in the shortage theory, but read further as I discuss why the shortage theory is bunk. Realizing, also, that sisters are very skeptical when listening to other sisters about men, I decided to obtain some of the brothers' reflections on black women and the shortage theory. A few of these brothers had spoken with me before and blamed some of what's happening in black relationships on black women. So I presented them with the opportunity to explain here why they believe sisters are contributing to the erosion of black love. I also wanted them to answer questions we sisters wonder about all the time; for example, Why are men unfaithful? and What kind of women are "good" black men interested in? I was surprised at some of the answers I got; I am sure you will be, too.

So first check out a portion of some rap between me and some heavy-thinkin' sisters. Then listen to these African-American brothers who are determined, hardworking, self-sufficient individuals with positive things to say about sisters, constructive criticisms for brothers and sisters, and a heartfelt concern for the condition of the black male-female relationship and community. And I bring this chapter to you, my sisters, because there is no shortage. Good black men are available—there is just a damned mountain of obstacles we Sista-Girls and Mista-Men must overcome before we can meet. And meet we must.

As we do about once every couple of months or so, my sister, a group of our female friends, and I gathered one evening for dinner, wine, and conversation. During our after-dinner Sista-Girl rap, settled on the floor, sofa, and chairs in Sis' living room, we began by discussing racism and religious intolerance and their effects with respect to the Bosnian war, and as usual, we digressed. One point of digression was the issue of the source of strength in the black community. Now, joining in this discussion was a Japanese-German-American Sista-Girl who said, "To me it's always been the black woman who has been the strong one in the black community."

Another Sista-Girl replied, "Yes, but that's because the black man has always been the target of white fear."

"Black women have been targeted, too, but we've just been able to fare better because we are stronger, stronger because they concentrated so much on getting the black male they left black women alone to grow," another sister responded.

I suggested perhaps it wasn't necessarily a male or female thing, because people are targeted all the time, that maybe it's a weak versus strong thing.

Another one of our dear sisters, who looks like a platinum blonde, silver-eyed, porcelain-skinned Betty Boop asked, "Does that mean that black men are weak?"

"No, because I know a lot of black men who are strong," one friend replied.

"Yes, I know a lot of strong black brothers, too. So what is it?" Sista-Legs, a tall, honey-brown-skinned sister with pretty, saucer-shaped eyes agreed with me, putting the question out again.

"Again, it's targeting the weak links, the ones who have been down, and you kick them and kick them again to keep them down," Sista-Multi-Multi-National affirmed.

And my sister added, it depended on how you responded to it, though, because it doesn't have to be a male or female thing, a masculine or feminine thing.

Another sister said, "Well, I've always been very masculine all my life."

But I reminded her that not allowing the so-called feminine side to be expressed creates an imbalance, similar to the situation I was in at work at that time. The people in my department were mostly female; and there was so much feminine energy the department was counterproductive, because there was so little masculine energy there to create a balance. (The concept of "feminine and masculine energies" as used here is synonymous with yin and yang in Chinese philosophy. Yin, or feminine energy, is passive; whereas yang, or masculine energy, is active. Unfortunately, societies, both Eastern and Western, have genderized these energies, ascribing the passive energy to women and the aggressive energy to males; whereas quite the opposite occurs frequently and naturally in the real world.)

Then Sista-Girl said something that deeply touched me. "Yeah, well, that's just it; people have to understand that it has nothing to do with black or white or any physical characteristics. We all are encompassed in one spiritual universe, in one spiritual entity, and it has nothing to do with color, or age, or sex, or any physical attribute. It has to do with the energy and the spiritual essence of each person, and if you address the spiritual essence of each person and communicate with that instead of with physical attributes, this world would be a lot better off. I communicate using my spiritual essence, therefore I've transcended the immaturity of communicating with people based on the physical plane." *Deep, huh?*

Yes, this world would be much more pleasant if people could overcome their fear of the unknown and stop prejudging. Psychiatrists say racism and prejudice are learned behaviors. If this is true, one may assume hatred is also a learned behavior. However, if it were not for the bad, how could we appreciate the good? If it weren't for sadness, how would we discern happiness?

Human beings are imperfect and therefore challenged to become perfect. Most adults know what good relating is, how to make someone feel good about himself or herself versus how to make someone feel bad about himself or herself. Yet, because so few people out there actually take the time to intentionally make others feel good, the flow of positive energy wanes instead of rushes, and our world remains bleak for many individuals.

Well, we talked a little while longer, and when I mentally reviewed this discussion, I was amazed by the fact that there are so many sisters wailing about the scarcity of good, strong brothers, yet here I was sitting in a circle of women of virtually every nationality and sexual orientation one could think of, all defending brothers and discounting the shortage theory. At this point, I was ready to talk to the men.

I compiled a list of eleven brothers I knew who were single, employed, and individuals I would date were I not happily married.[15] None of these men are homosexual or bisexual, celebrities, entertainers, or professional athletes. All are personable, gainfully employed, free of substance-abuse problems and attractive in their own way. Now, if these eleven brothers were in my tiny circle of influence, it is impossible that there aren't eleven more, hundreds more, thousands more like them in our communities.

The interviewees were as follows: Kyle, a police officer in his early thirties; Tim, a screenplay writer and film director in his late twenties; Felix, a security guard in his late twenties; Andrew, a meeting coordinator in his late twenties; James, a purchasing manager in his late thirties; Jon, a psychiatrist in his early forties; Melvin, a teacher and professional photographer in his mid-thirties; Michael, a commodities broker in his mid-twenties; Sam, a commodities broker in his late thirties; Don, a member of the military and full-time electrical engineering student in his early thirties; and Edward, an administrator for the Chicago Transit Authority. The median average length of long-term relationships the brothers had was a little over four years, with the longest relationship lasting ten years, and the shortest relationship lasting one year.

Now, I promised I wouldn't use their real names, but names aren't important here, anyway. What is notable are the insights and concerns they have regarding relationships between black men and women.

Contrary to what many sisters believe, most brothers are relatively flexible when it comes to physical attributes that attract them. For example, Tim stated the ideal physical description for his mate as simply *"black and over twenty-one."* Whereas Andrew, Don, and Edward were concerned with how the sister was proportioned: *"A woman weighing one hundred fifteen pounds and standing five-ten ain't goin' on,"* commented Andrew. Edward explained further, *"One minute you can see a chick in* Playboy *who has a perfect body and face and really turns you on, and then you can see someone walking down the street who doesn't look anything like the chick in* Playboy *but still has a slammin' body and a gorgeous face who also really turns you on. I guess ideally if her height and weight are proportioned, that's it. There are so many body types I'm attracted to, as long as the woman is proportional, she's fine with me."*

The brothers also seemed in agreement on preferring sisters who were intelligent and able to hold a conversation. Andrew said, *"The physical stuff gets old quick."* Felix appreciates common sense in addition to "book intelligence," and Michael enjoys women who can have meaningful conversations. When asked to define "meaningful," he replied, *"Something other than sports and entertainment."*

Another common denominator these men shared was their preference for coupling with women of color as opposed to dating women of other races. As reasons, they cited the emotional strength and devotion of sisters and the cultural nuances that can be shared between black men and women. Boyfriend Tim explained, *"The cultural differences often inhibit the complete flow of emotions between individuals of differing races."* Yet, Kyle confessed that due to his age, he was willing to date anybody: *"As long as they are breathing and have a job, and I'm not too particular about the breathing."*

Brotha-Men also agreed unanimously on what they perceived as the strengths of black women. More than half chimed in about our emotional determination and power of will. As Sam and I talked, he described it as *"dealing with the hardships in being in a disadvantaged position in society, as compared to women of other races, and the abil-*

ity of sisters to deal with it well." And my friend Melvin talked about *"the sheer will to accomplish their ends."* They also had quite a number of interesting things to say and interesting points to make about the obstacles encountered by black men and women today, which will be covered shortly.

Actually, the barriers between them that brothers and sisters are facing are few in quantity but overwhelming in size. (I narrowed the number of problems down to primarily three, but the scope of these three problems is immense.) The first problem is the negative images of black men continually portrayed in the media and sisters' belief in these images. Next is the passion we feel as a people and how the lack of control of those passions eats at the fabric of our relationships. And finally, there is the negative conditioning of Western civilization and the havoc it has inflicted on our three abilities to accept, attempt to comprehend, and communicate effectively with ourselves and each other. Each of these problems and their possible solutions will be discussed, but first, as I said, I want you sisters to hear what some remarkably *good* available black men have to say.

I told you what Mr. Melvin and Sir Sam had to stay about the strengths of black women; here is some of what the other brothers said, verbatim:

- *Very strong and independent. [Sisters will] fight for you and themselves and what they want till the end.*
- *Their resilience, capacity to forgive.*
- *Determination, able to take on various tasks, independent, decisiveness, emotionally strong.*
- *Their commitment to their offspring. There would have been a lot more miscegenation if they weren't as strong as they were.*
- *An innate sense of pragmatism. An innate sexuality and comfortableness with those indefinable and ineffable qualities that make up the feminine persuasion—they*

may not understand them or know them but are comfortable with them. It's related to the deep spirituality found within the black woman.

- *Patience with men; when a man can't do it, a woman can always back him and make him stronger in the workforce as well as in the homelife; [success at being] single parents.*
- *The knowledge black women seem to have, especially as they get older.*
- *They are strong-willed, confident, [and] are very, very loyal.*

Seems to me these brothers recognize some of the most important qualities we sisters possess, garnered through our decades of supporting and primarily developing the African-American community. Our strength, compassion, and spirituality are apparently shining through. *Heyyy!*

Still, we all know what is most important is not the accolades one receives but the criticism, because only through constructive criticism can we improve. So naturally, I had to ask the fellas what they perceived as our weaknesses, and these were their answers:

- *Sometimes too insecure in the general sense—weight, other women, [their boyfriends, spouses, etc.] hanging out with friends, your career. Everybody is insecure, but with black women it overlaps into relationships a little more than it should.*
- *Sometimes their expectations of their mates are unrealistic; sisters don't seem to understand the position of brothers right now. Some need to focus more on supporting black men and doing things together more for the sake of unity. Stop comparing black men with white men.*
- *Some seem to be too materialistic; many are too quick to show hostility.*
- *Can be unduly harsh and sometimes too demanding;*

and I hate to hear black women complain so much about black men and then compare us to white men, who supposedly treat them so much better.

- *To be honest, taking shit off of men. It's a lot of men out here that run game on women and women fall for it.*
- *Having unrealistic expectations of black men.*
- *Black women need to learn how to support black men. I know that a lot of brothers are fucked up out there; black women know a lot of brothers are fucked up. Instead of complaining about it, they should support the black man. But they use it as an excuse for the minute a brother fucks up, saying things like, "You're just like the rest of them. Ain't none of y'all any good." Deep down black men do have aspirations, but with all the negative shit floatin' around that we have to deal with, if you can't get support from your woman, from your home, what's the sense in doing anything? What is life all about—doing everything for myself so I can become big and wealthy and drop dead in the ground so that everything I built is left to the state and [siblings]? No, you want a family, children of your own. With black women, the minute a relationship hits a speed bump they start complaining and calling brothers stupid. Most women from other cultures aren't like this; they will support a brother. Most women of other races subscribe to the old saying, "If you don't have anything positive to say, keep your mouth shut." Black women end up being toxic individuals when they keep complaining and saying negative things.*
- *Their tenacity and toughness; it's a paradox—the very thing that makes them strong makes them think they can live without the man, particularly as black women become more successful and that disparity between black women and black men increases.*
- *Black women, more than females of any other race, tend to jump to conclusions too quickly. Seems like they're always waiting and ready to condemn a brother before*

they give him a chance to explain; situations that are really innocent are made to seem wrong.
- *Emotional baggage—they come into new relationships with stuff from the old ones.*

Hmm . . . One of the things other Queen Mothers and I agree with is that sisters have got to stop comparing brothers to white guys. It's unfair, unrealistic, and very divisive. Brothers can be good providers if allowed the opportunity and given the patience, time, and understanding. I know that some of you sisters out there are saying, *"We've given them that. How much longer is it going to take? How much more patience and understanding are we going to have to provide?"* The only answer I can find that sounds right to both my heart and my head is one I would want someone to give to me were I in the shoes of our brothers—*as much patience and understanding as necessary.*

We've got to get off of this status kick if we want to make it as a people. Large homes, imported luxury automobiles, and all of the other symbols of status and wealth are nice. But that is just what they are, *symbols* of wealth, not necessarily tokens of love and respect. I would much prefer to be involved with a man who respects me, loves me, supports me emotionally and spiritually, and provides materially what he can than to be involved with a big-money-makin' daddy who pays all the bills, buys me whatever I want, but disrespects me and/or disrespects the home. *Peace of mind is so much more important than pieces of jewelry, Sista-Girls.*

When it comes to dealing with brothers, it seems we no longer put the greatest value on the intrinsic characteristics of relationships. My friend Jon and I discussed this, and he made the following point: *"I suspect we've also lost our spiritualism and have become too materialistic. We've become way too entrenched in hedonistic, materialistic, Eurocentric philosophy. . . . A woman in slavery mated with a man because she loved him not because of what he had but because he was kind and gentle and a God-fearing man; black men had nothing back then but their love to offer their women, and this was enough."*

No, we are no longer in physical bondage (mental enslavement driven by our own emotions is another story), and since that time society has moved from the agricultural revolution through the industrial revolution and into the information revolution. Still, I wonder if the uneducated, unadorned, physically chained sisters of the eighteenth and nineteenth centuries understood more about love and building relationships and communities than her educated, sometimes overdone sisters of the twentieth and soon-to-be twenty-first centuries. Could it be they were really much freer than we are now? Masters couldn't prevent their spirits from taking flight, while our spirits seem sluggish and encumbered by enigmatic schemes for attaining that next symbol. We know back then our women often fought tooth and nail (if they could) to keep master and his sons out of their beds, regardless of the finery these men attempted to bribe them with. Now, it at times appears, we fight tooth and nail to get into them, to look like their women, act like their kind, because of the finery our men cannot afford. I wonder where our race would be now if back then most of the sisters had been more willing to succumb to master and his brothers, sons, and overseers and had been more spiteful toward their own black men, as many of us are now. How many of us would there be today?

Another repeated comment was that sisters tended to bring emotional baggage from previous relationships into new relationships. Consciously or subconsciously comparing the new man to the old one and waiting for the new brother to screw up the way the former one did is a most heinous no-no. If my current husband had entered our relationship expecting me to act like his ex-girlfriend, we wouldn't be married. Likewise, I refused to let the troubles from one marriage interfere with the possibility of marrying once again. Sisters, we have got to learn to let go. Learn from our past experiences, yes, but do not use them as exacting measurements for your future relationships. If you do, the relationships are doomed before they begin.

Some brothers also conceded that some of us are too patient, too loving, and too tolerant. So, on one hand, we have sisters who are too demanding, too materialistic, and too frantic for that carrot (or should I say carat?), and on the other hand, we have sisters who are too gullible. It sounds as if sisters need to start talking more with each other and sharing notes. There's a middle path in all of this that we are most definitely missing.

Ironically, before I could even ask the question "Do black women have unrealistic expectations of black men?" Some brothers repeatedly remarked sisters had unrealistic expectations of them. So this is how the men answered or expounded on this question:

- *No. There's nothing wrong with wanting a man to be a provider for his family.*
- *Not to my knowledge. I don't think it's a black thing; I think it's a man/woman thing. [Regarding the movie* Waiting to Exhale*] this relationship thing is very difficult; let's say all men are honest and faithful—if that were the case, ninety-five percent of your relationships still wouldn't work because there's only one ideal person for you.*
- *Yes. They don't seem to understand that brothers didn't come to this country as captains of the boat, we were in the same holds they were. And when [slave owners] saw how big and strong many of us were, that was it; brothers would never get the opportunities sisters would get because we were too intimidating. [Slave owners] probably thought they could always control a woman, but another man, especially a black man, you have to make sure he doesn't get too far. So now, with the op-*

portunities always given to sisters first, black men are the low man on the totem pole, and for some strange reason sisters are comparing us to the man who has made sure we weren't to get the opportunities, to the man who owns the totem pole. It doesn't make sense.

- *I think what I've noticed is that the younger ones do [have unrealistic expectations]. They pass up a lot of good men when they are in their early twenties, and after they deal with the world for a while and get knocked around by reality, they're more willing to deal with brothers from a realistic viewpoint. Women seem to think they have all these choices, so they would play around, not being serious, and some I see years later are looking at things differently.*
- *[It] probably speaks to problems on both sides: black women's unrealistic expectations of black men, and our inability to evolve as a group of people.*
- *Yes. Because take white people [for example]; I see them every day with their kids. They are so lovable with each other and are so humble with each other, and that's the way black men and women should be with each other. It's like nowadays everybody is so uptight, trying to get over on each other. It shouldn't be that way.*
- *No. I expect that they want the same things every man wants—a family, children, a spouse. Unfortunately those are things that can only be gotten by economic stability, which many black men don't have.*
- *Yes. I think maybe they have a preconceived idea of what they want in a black man and won't deviate from that preconception, [which originates from] their need for financial security.*
- *I think that a lot of black women have, not unrealistic dreams, but a lot of things and goals they would like to achieve but don't always achieve them when it comes to black men and relationships. Sometimes brothers just can't afford it, that's all.*
- *Yes. Women have a tendency to want that Cinderella*

story to happen. A lot of good, ambitious men are looking for women who will grow with them, and a lot of women are looking for someone already established.

- *No, because I don't call being gainfully employed and having enough money to take care of your wife and your family unrealistic expectations.*

Frankly, when some of the brothers responded that they, in fact, did *not* think black women had unrealistic expectations of black men, I was a bit surprised. However, reviewing the explanations they provided, I now partially understand how they can come to this conclusion.

In today's American society, with one of the wealthiest, most industrious and dynamic economies in the world, it is not unrealistic to expect that a man should be able to at least share equally in the responsibility of taking care of a family. If we look in the Sunday newspapers of metropolitan cities, every week there are several pages completely filled with employment advertisements. There's a national weekly magazine devoted to helping unemployed individuals locate and secure jobs. There are magazines devoted to men and women who want to start their own businesses. There are job fairs for practically every industry designed to help people gain employment or further their careers, putting them directly in touch with recruiting personnel of major national and international corporations.

Yet, in every major urban city of this country, there is also a neighborhood for the wealthy, a neighborhood for the comfortable, a neighborhood for the uncomfortable, and gutters, railroad tracks, alleyways, underpasses, and dilapidated loading docks for the miserable. In a city where on one side of town individuals eat seven- and eight-dollar pieces of meat, one would not expect it to be difficult for a man to be able to afford a three-dollar meal let alone one of those pieces of meat. Yet, this is exactly what we find. We find a line that wraps around building corners, on the coldest days of the year, when a new hotel announces it is accepting job applications. We find heroes asking for employment as reward for their heroism. So perhaps it is not unreasonable to expect a man to afford a family if he comes from the wealthy or comfortable side of town, or if he is educated, or if he has seen hope and persistence work for someone he knows. However, I sincerely question how realistic it is to expect a man to be able to afford even himself if he has none of the aforementioned opportunities.

Then, I listen to women who are relaxing in their winter years and watching us. They remind me that sometimes *a man has got to do what a man has got to do,* and there aren't as many brothers out here today willing to do what is necessary as there used to be. Queen Mother Cyrus, whose grandmother was a slave, told me, "Frankly [brothers today] have it too bloody easy. We determined our children weren't going to go through what we did, so we give our children credit cards and wonder why we have three-hundred-dollar bills to pay. The men that come along now are pampered. . . . Thirty or forty years ago a man's priorities were to take care of his family—his attitude back then was, I have to support my family—today it's different."

Queen Mother Grandmommy White gives a telling example of the love-felt duty her husband had toward his wife and children, "My husband worked three jobs to take care of us at one point—while working for the postal service, he also drove a taxi and worked at a grocery store. Young men just aren't willing to do that these days." I concur. How many brothers do you see willing to bus restaurant tables for next to nothing like their Hispanic counterparts? Even some brothers themselves realize the lackadaisical attitudes of some of their peers. Edward bluntly stated, *"The mentality of the majority of black men in this country is fucked up. They would rather bust their asses on somebody's street corner or do anything but having a regular job because they've got some type of mentality that says working a job for 'the man' is like being a slave again. So they would rather struggle and hustle than go to a regular job every day, or they have a defeatist attitude. Not all brothers, mind you, but most. We're afraid of hard work; I really do believe that. If we could find a way, black men would accept a lower standard of living if they could just basically sit on their asses all day—as opposed to busting their asses for eight hours for a little higher standard. Now, they'll get up off their ass if they can go from not doing nothing and driving a Pinto [to] bustin' their asses and driving a Benz; but they won't move if it means [from] not doing nothing and driving a Pinto to bustin' their asses and driving a Taurus; they'll stick with the Pinto."*

Although Brotha-Man Edward has a point, I really want to be optimistic about our situation now, because as Queen Mother Dr. Shirley (the consultant friend of mine I mentioned earlier) points out, "The young black men I counsel tend to listen more than women and are more open to criticism and suggestions. They are willing to try and work with the suggestions I give them."

Indeed, Queen Mother Cyrus points out that although the pace is very slow, brothers do seem to be changing—a little. She still suggests that sisters step up to the plate, that the trouble cannot be attributed to the black man alone: "Most young black women are brought up to believe that the knight on the horse is coming to rescue them; it's not true. They should do what we did—take what they can and make the best of it." Mr. Man Melvin also agrees: *"I think that if you have a dynamic, well-employed woman, [the responsibility of maintaining a household] falls on their shoulders to do a little bit of what men have been doing all along; if a black woman who works in an office can marry a grease monkey, this helps."*

So, once again, we have a situation calling black men and women to compromise—brothers agreeing to take employment that may be "beneath" them and using it as a springboard for their ideal careers, and sisters willing to become involved with brothers who may not be in corporate attire, but are making a concerted effort to better themselves. Milady Cyrus concluded eloquently with a sad and truthful statement: *"The generations after me have forgotten how hard we worked together and have forgotten the greatness that we were able to achieve through that hard work, determination, and unity."*

The advancement of technologies used for the manufacturing and distribution of illegal narcotics, in addition to the downsizing of major corporations and the loss of high-wage-paying blue-collar work, could lead one to discount the opinions of Mrs. Cyrus and Edward. However, as I stated earlier, very little changes over time. Where today our people struggle with the damnation caused by crack-cocaine, during Queen Mother Cyrus's time black folks grappled with the demons manifested through the use of heroin and morphine. While we are now having to deal with layoffs, black men during the forties and fifties had to deal with getting "laid on" (that is, finding work other than sharecropping). We have gangs; so did they. We have housing projects; not only did our grandfolk have housing projects, but they had shanty towns, too.

And if any group of black people had the right to feel "lost" or stripped of culture, it was the generations of blacks who came before us. They lived closer to the time of slavery than we did, closest to the soul-ripping breaking of native bonds. For this very reason, blacks today have generations who went before us who have tried their best to create a culture for their children and grandchildren. They understood completely the implications of not having a history to learn from. So they began developing a culture with what they had, as best they could—*our African-American heritage.*

Racism was, of course, a daily part of their lives, as it still is for most of us. Perhaps, though, *overt* racism is easier to handle, somewhat less difficult to overcome, if not physically, at least mentally and spiritually. Overt acts are in front of you, challenging you eye-to-eye to address them. It is the *covert* racism of today, those hidden, loathing eyes and malicious grins, that is most difficult to overcome, because those who practice it are experts at espionage, so to speak. And not knowing your enemy from your true friend, not knowing when or where or how the bomb is going to drop (but certain it will be dropped), makes living a paranoic, anxiety-ridden nightmare. Add to that the ever-widening chasm between African-Americans who have and African-Americans who have not, and it is not difficult to understand why some brothers choose a more dangerous and odious route—it's easier. It's difficult to fight enemies you cannot see, but it's easy to prey on the weak who are in front of you. It's difficult to struggle in the mailroom knowing your company is downsizing, but it's easy to get paid for providing momentary, addictive escape. It's easy and the job is guaranteed, for now.

No, I am not quite sure if our black men have it easier now. Yes, they've had greater advantage due to changing social policy, but they've also had greater disadvantage due to the changing face of racism. During Queen Mother Cyrus's time, if a black man somehow became lost and wandered accidentally into a white neighborhood, he may not have made it back home. And today, while traveling in their own neighborhoods, familiar with every cornerstone and back alley, our black men aren't making it back home.

I think whether they have it easier now than then or whether they have been pampered are irrelevant issues. The relevant issue is the fact that our men are dying, that our black boys are killing each other because of drugs and hatred. The other relevant issue is the question of whether the inflictions are self-imposed or not, wherein lies the answer to the problem. If a boy knows and sees nothing of reality but hopelessness, where is his reason for ambition and integrity? If he is exposed to nothing but savage survival and despair, where does he learn about the joy of living? Where is his reason for expecting to live a full and happy life?

When asked what's most important to them in a mate, this is probably the reason the brothers give answers such as trust, friendship, honesty, someone accepting of their moods, not taking things personally, and a stable lifestyle. Peace of mind is very difficult for black men to attain outside the home; their mates are often the sole source of comfort.

Also, I find it interesting that one of the brothers mentioned soul as an important characteristic in a woman: *"Soul . . . given that women are primarily emotional creatures, soul would be that quality which allows one to reveal or conceal, and I am attracted to women who are emotive in the best sense of the word and who understand the ebb and flow of their spirit and their emotional levels."* (Deep, huh?)

It appears sisters and brothers feel the same when it comes to those relationship-defining qualities, doesn't it? Except when it comes to being faithful.

Infidelity sometimes leads to the break-up of relationships, so it is important we sisters understand why brothers do it and how they, themselves, handle it. Perhaps it's not as personal as we sisters sometimes take it to be. (Remember, sex cannot be equated with love, and yes, that still doesn't make infidelity right.) The brothers' answers to the question, "Why are men unfaithful?" most definitely allude to this notion of detachment:

- *You have to understand that it's not a natural state of men to be monogamous; the natural state of men is to be a predator, not in a pejorative sense, though. Monogamy is a discipline that you were socialized into for the construction of morality—not that it is bad. And factor in the things society teaches you as a man—it's not only your prerogative but your obligation to sleep around.*

- *[I] have no idea.* (At least Brotha-Man was frank.)
- *I think [men] want to be unfaithful because you may have a wife or girlfriend and you might truly love her and the relationship may be fine, but if you meet another woman, it's new and exciting; everybody is different, and everybody has different opinions and ideas that hold your interest. After a while it grows into a friendship, and then it grows into a relationship; then you start treating them as friends, and then when feelings are involved, they pique your interest as a possible lover.*
- *It's a [penis] thang.* (Boyfriend was really frank, wasn't he?) *It's just genetically encoded in men to try to get our genes in the next generation; it's hormonal.*
- *[It's] because [men] aren't receiving the love they should receive in their relationships, so they go outside the relationships; plus, it's in our genes, men are more sexually driven than women.*
- *[It's] because men seem to have a desire for variety; people I've talked to over the years said they have a need for variety. If something is available that's different, they'll want it; fooling around is just inborn for men.*
- *I would say it's fifty percent environment, [meaning] peer pressure and traveling a lot—travel is a great inducement—and personal beliefs.*
- *Well, part of it is a need to conquer, and the rest of it, the majority of it, is a lack of self-control.*
- *Boredom; [and] it is an outgrowth of power. There's no greater prize than to capture a woman, and as a guy, when you're emerging professionally, how do you want to spend that capital? A guy's sex appeal is his power.*

And when asked if they had ever been unfaithful, they all responded yes and that they had been for the reasons they stipulated above. So, "How would you deal with discovering your mate was unfaithful?" I asked, and some replied they would not be as much angry as curious as to why; others would be angry, not necessarily at her, but at the idea of some other man having intercourse with their woman; one guy said he understood, because what goes around comes around; and two other brothers confessed they would be furious. But none said they would end the relationship on the spot; they all said they would want to discuss the issue to determine if the relationship could be or should be salvaged.

Now, you know I had to ask my resident psychiatrist, Dr. Jon, about his thoughts on the subject of infidelity and this is what he said: *"I don't know why [men are unfaithful]; the evolutionary theory is based on other primate models, gorillas, for example, whose estrus period is dictated by pheromones, the olfactory sense. If we look at those primates who humans are closest to, chimpanzees, after the male mates with female after estrus, he usually stays with her to make sure no other male mates with her to make sure that the offspring are his. The difference between the chimpanzee and the human is that the human male doesn't stay around long enough for reproductive success; he doesn't care. The evolutionary theory is goal driven, i.e., the desire for successful reproduction; brothers aren't usually interested in the reproductive aspect and often don't stay around long enough to see if the reproduction (if applicable) is successful. The evolutionary theory is an easy out."*

I must admit I believed the evolutionary theory had some merit (trying to give the brothers a play, you understand). But when Dr. Jon broke it down for me, I was stumped until I looked once more at some of the other reasons brothers gave for being unfaithful, for example, the need to assert power and the need for conquest. Considering the number of incidents of infidelity, there must be a lot of brothers (hell, men, period) who are feeling quite powerless. *Hmm . . .*

One thing to note is that perhaps because brothers understand and accept that infidelity (especially for men) is almost inescapable, they seem to be more understanding and capable of handling it on the part of their mates.

Actually, one brother admitted that the fellas have no right to get too perturbed because, to paraphrase him, "What's good for the goose is good for the gander." Black men seem to realize their weaknesses, so they are not so hypocritical as to refuse to understand the same weaknesses in women.

Okay. On GP I would forgive Brotha-Man once. Yes, I know a second chance is a difficult thing to contemplate, let alone give, especially when you're in that "get back" mode. Yet, remember what I said about revenge? Not talking out of the side of my neck on this topic but speaking from personal experience, getting even leaves a very bad taste in one's mouth for a very long time, and it solves absolutely nothing. However, if it happened again—*next* . . .

As far as it being an obligation for men to sleep around due to socialization, that premise for infidelity is another one that cuts no mustard with this Sista-Girl. While it is the obligation of the human species to procreate, the requisite for males to have sex with as many females as possible, relegating sexual relationships to a type of sport, is barbaric and insulting to not only the female spirit but the human spirit as well.

On the subject of dating single parents, most of the guys surveyed felt this was a nonissue, that being a single parent does not diminish the attractiveness of a sister. Some said they loved being around kids and that if you want to date someone, you have to date the package, and if kids are in the package, that's fine. They also mentioned the fact that in the African-American community, there are a great deal of single mothers who are attractive and shouldn't be eliminated from the dating scene just because they have children.

Kyle, however, doesn't date single parents: *"I have dated single mothers in the past and decided that I wasn't going to do that anymore unless there's something very special about the particular woman. The main reason is I don't like their kids; I don't like the way they've gone about raising them and the little people they've turned out to be so far."*

And Sam also has reservations: *"I have dated single mothers. If I'm really attracted and it looks like they have the baby-sitting thing together, I will; but sometimes that gets in the way."*

Still, eight out of ten ain't bad, Sista-Moms. So in no way should you feel trepidation when meeting a brother who piques your interest. There's a chance your children aren't going to be a factor. And if they are, skip him; *next . . .*

I also believe that, as black women, if we want to have positive relationships with our men, we should also concentrate on behaving like adult women. This means we do not become pregnant until we are financially and psychologically able to handle the responsibility. However, we also need to educate the brothers who are so averse to dating single parents. Perhaps our single parenthood was intentional, perhaps not. But, like many brothers said, this circumstance should not devaluate our personhood in the eyes of another human being. So, sisters, when you hear brothers making wrongful comments about our single-parent Sista-Girls, pull those guys aside and start teachin'.

I find that if brothers meet their mates through friends, single parenthood often becomes a nonissue because of the value the brothers place on the judgement on the their friends.

This is probably why most of the guys meet the women they date through friends, their workplaces, social gatherings, and private parties. Meeting an individual through someone you are already acquainted with or at work automatically provides a bridge for relating.

Now, whether or not that bridge is there, most brothers are uncomfortable with the relationship until some kind of infrastructure has been developed. I asked them about sex on a first date, and these were the answers they gave:

- *[It] varies. [I] don't go into first dates thinking about that; can't say that I would think bad of the woman, because each case is individual; it would still have to be very extreme circumstances. We do the date thing first.*
- *Now, I don't really relish it.* (I asked, "Is that because of the fear of contracting AIDS?") *Yeah.*
- *Scares me—performance anxiety.*
- *I'm not comfortable with that; it says something about both people.*
- *I would not expect it. I would think that if it did happen, the woman must have been conditioned by other men to think that she needed to do that; I would wonder why a woman would want to on a first date.*
- *These days I've been kind of shying away from it. When I was younger, there was that notch-in-the-belt factor; these days it's not a really good idea. [I] would advise against sleeping together; if it happens I ain't gonna stress over it, though. Establishing a level of emotional comfort is important to relationships, so unless it's a purely physical thing, I suggest waiting as long as possible.*
- *I don't because sex will tend to change the relationship. If you're looking for a relationship, you've got to wait to establish a foundation.*
- *No problem.* (Wonder if the brother understands that lack of inhibition is sometimes deadly?)
- *[It's] not cool. I know sometimes it's like that, but I just don't like it.*

Earlier we touched on the subject of the supposed shortage of good available black men. Personally, I don't think there is a shortage. I do, however, believe it is a theory that some black men have used as a tool to manipulate black women through the insecurity that this theory generates. Yet, while some of the brothers agreed with me; about the shortage theory some also disagreed with me.

These are some of the comments they had when asked the question, Is there a shortage of good available black men?:

- *No, because I feel that all the guys I know are good black men. Women just haven't hooked up with their particular good black man yet; maybe emotional baggage comes into play, but it shouldn't have anything to do with relating to someone new.*
- *Yes, because society as a whole has dealt black men a very bad hand. It's a lot of young brothers out here my age, smart but listening to all this shit on TV and radio and want to be like gangsta rappers; the media plays a lot of this. They take other avenues and end up either dead or in jail. When these young brothers get out here and get killed, they're killing off our race, because most brothers are good for three or four children. That's why so many sisters are dating outside of their race; these men [of other races] may not be better, but they have goals and are working toward their goals and have a plan.*
- *Yes. I think there are a lot of societal problems that work against the black male, and hand in hand with that I think there's a lot of bullshit baggage that black men get caught up in that gets them into shit.*
- *Yes. A couple of times I've been asked by women if I knew of anyone available, and I had a hard time thinking of someone. Those who are involved in crazy lifestyles aren't desirable, and those who are good are often locked up in a relationship.*
- *No. They may not be the finest brothers or the cats with the most glamorous gigs, but there are still good, gainfully employed, single brothers out there. The media gives us fantasyland, and women believe this.*
- *Not really, but back to hypergamy* [the sociological theory suggesting that women are taught to marry above the class they were born into], *culturally we're trying to turn it around—to tell women to not marry up, to settle for blue-collar workers and guys like that, because*

for most women there's no other alternative. If they don't do that, many will marry out and up.

- *No. I believe the avenue for meeting people may not always present itself, and black women are just not connecting.*
- *No. Women just don't know where to look. Everybody's been so misused and are so worried about things that have happened in the past, we're all scared to trust one another.*

Because of the hundreds of black folks I have spoken with and speak with continually, I tend to agree with the brothers who think the notion of black male shortage is a matter of perception. That it's a problem of comparing brothers to white guys. That it concerns the circles sisters travel in and associate in, and that it concerns timing and patience. Yes, there are masses of brothers in prisons and in cemeteries, but there are thousands who are employed and available as well. It boils down to whether or not sisters feel empathetic enough to deal with the brothers who are available. We should. They really do love us and want to come together. Listen to what the brothers said about relationships between black men and women:

Andrew: *Black women are mistrusting for a reason. I've seen the games brothers run. So I believe in trying to be honest if confronted, and most importantly, I try not to get myself into situations that even call for any confrontations. Self-control is very important.*

Don: *I think that the perception that it's getting worse is just a perception, and you shouldn't be concerned about what happens in other people's relationships, what they've heard or [what they've] experienced.*

James: *A relationship between a brother and a sister can be a good thing if you work at it, but it takes two halves to* *make a whole; with one pushing and the other one pulling, it's not going to work. Brothers and sisters have got to start working together.*

Michael: *The only thing a brother wants to do is show his woman that he can do what the white man can if given the opportunity. But often the opportunity is not provided because it is controlled by the white man. So while a brother does what he is allowed to do by the white man and is thinking of how he can take the opportunity (if necessary), all the black woman sees is what he is not doing, what he is not providing, and it's unfair and frustrating.*

Felix: *When it comes to relationships, my mother always told me to "just be yourself, always be honest, you can't go into a relationship with a lie." So that's what I believe in doing—being open. That's what black men and women must do—keep the lines of communication [open]. We also need to concentrate more on long-lasting relationships, instead of short-term relationships, for the future of black kids.*

Melvin: *There's a political concept: society, as prejudicial as it is, gives a larger degree of access and opportunity for development to black women, and because of that, black women have developed a greater degree of status and empowerment than black men, which makes a smaller pool of black men to choose from logically. But if the black woman can find it in her heart to support the brother who hasn't had it like she has, maybe we can begin to come together. My mom lived with my dad in a basement for two years while he was getting his business off the ground. She said it was tough, but she stood by him nonetheless.*

Brother Melvin mentioned it before and so did Queen Mother Cyrus: *black women have got to deal with black men who have potential,* and who may be earning less than we are, who may have less status than we do, who may be younger than us. This is essential if we want to have a strong, viable culture. Position and wealth are not unattainable. However, the quest for these things should be performed together so that our community is one of influence and wealth—not because of the efforts of a few individuals, but because of the efforts of all.

So there you have it. Some of the answers to my questions were fascinating, some were appalling, and some were just downright unbelievable. But I learned something from each one, and I hope I helped some of my Sista-Girl readers, too.

Speaking for myself, I have long contended the real problem existing between black men and black women is not the differences between us as human beings, but the monkey wrench used by white male American society and, more important, *our reactions to it.*

In her book *The Isis Papers: The Keys to the Colors,* Dr. Francis Cress Welsing discusses her belief that it is the deeply rooted psychotic fear of the annihilation of their race that is the actual cause of the persecution by whites of black men and verily all peoples of color. Furthermore she commented that this fear has resulted in the castration, dehumanization, elimination, and brutalization of black men, as they are the most dominant producers of color, and therefore the most threatening to white, noncolor.

Dr. Welsing also believes the reason there are only approximately three out of ten black men available to create a strong, black people is because white society doesn't really want a black people. It will tolerate one and use it. But the actual desire for black people is nonexistent. Consequently, she concludes, the desire to be rid of black people, as our growth in productive and positive terms is considered a threat to the white population, remains strong and is becoming increasingly stronger.

I do know that racism still exists. Whether it is growing

or diminishing is something I am unsure of because of its extremely surreptitious nature today. However, I also think it is only an expression of human nature that the dominator does not want the dominated to rise. If you are in first place, would you want to relinquish your standing to the person holding second—or last—place? No, that would be foolish. So, to keep black people from becoming a viable threat, black men are continually harassed, attacked, and bludgeoned. Their spirits are on the brink of destruction and their manhood, verily their humanity, questioned at the least and dismissed at the worst.

Sisters, remember one of the objects of racism is to keep the black male and female apart, so as to keep black people weak and "inferior." So when hearing and witnessing negativism regarding the brothers, make sure you consider the sources. Realize that there are black men who are employed, good-hearted, and available, they may not be as fine as Tyson Beckford, action-packed as Wesley Snipes, or debonair as Denzel Washington, but this isn't movieland, sistas; this is earth. Working eight or nine hours, doing something beneath your level of intelligence and ability, not only diminishes one's earning capacity but also erodes the spirit. Think about that the next time you see Brotha-Man the mail clerk, the next time you encounter a billboard with a smiling white male dressed from head-to-toe in the latest Italian apparel.

Sista-Girls might also want to think about the drive and determination required to succeed outside of the corporate world the next time a starving entrepreneur, artist, or activist brother is encountered. Likewise, my friends with the motherland garb and names should take a moment to extend themselves to, at the least, acknowledge those brothers who decided to play the game regardless of how many times the rules change, the number of players increases, and the scorecard is altered. It takes fierce tenacity to succeed both inside and outside the arena, especially for black men. Give them their due, sisters.

And while admiring both types of brothers, we must also be cautious, expressing our admiration and love in ways that are beneficial to both of us and the community. Let's concentrate on learning who we are from the inside, on accepting those who may march to a different drummer, and on trying to understand the various legitimate ways in which our brothers try to succeed in this often unfriendly world. The knights are out there. Their armor may not be bright and shiny. Their faces may not be smooth like butter, but their hearts are gold and their wills are iron. We just need to get our asses out of the haystack and off the high horses to find them and keep them.

Maintaining relationships is not easy. It requires patience, understanding, sensitivity, sacrifice, assertiveness, passiveness, the ability to share, learn, and forgive, all at the appropriate times.

Queen Mothers know adult human relationships are the most difficult to maintain because we all think we have all the answers and know the right way to do everything. But once we begin listening with our hearts and our minds, instead of our egos and our mouths, getting along will be easier for both knights and princesses.

21

The Renaissance Blues

mailroom melancholy

When in a comparable job, which is a rare instance itself, the wages of the brother are twenty to thirty percent less than his white counterpart and sometimes more. In corporate America the general wage disparity is readily identifiable because most brothers are still in the mailroom. In hospitals, they're the orderlies. In schools and universities, where the average instructor's income is demeaning considering the significance of the task, brothers are the domestic engineers. It is an irrefutable fact that unless a brother has a degree from a leading university and directly related experience, he is going to find himself on the bottom rung of the professional ladder.

Is it his fault? Is it our brothers' fault that at the time when blacks were gaining a foothold in the American workforce, the largest employers in this nation began laying off tens of thousands of employees simultaneously, increasing the number of unemployed and underemployed American citizens of all ethnicities to alarming numbers? Is it their fault these layoffs were and are not temporary but permanent, due to the transforming environment of American industry? No, it is not.

So why are we sisters continually punishing and rejecting our men when the competition for decent employment in America is more ferocious than ever and, furthermore, on a playing field that has *never* been level? Why are we forever mentally assassinating our brothers when so few of them are empowered with the education, experience, and self-determination required to meet the competition, let alone rise above it? It has only been the last two generations of African-Americans who have had the opportunity to take advantage of the successes of the civil rights struggle. Perhaps you feel, as many Sista-Girls do, that brothers can at least take some kind of employment, regardless of what it is, if they can't find anything befitting their qualifications now. Some of them do.

What do you think a college graduate is doing when he is agreeing to work as a mail clerk? But you and I both know how sisters usually view mail clerks. I've heard too many sisters say, "Forget about potential; *potential* can't buy me a house." So, ladies, we won't go there. Let's not delude ourselves into thinking brothers who are willing to take menial jobs, even as temporary stepping-stones, will fare better on the dating scene and be treated by sisters with a little more compassion and respect, because it's simply not true.

Until about twenty-five years ago, higher education was a dream, *a far-reaching dream,* for most of our people. On the crest of the civil rights era, our girls were given tickets to that dream, but our boys were handed billets to Vietnam.

Brothers today are facing the same predicament I faced when rejected by an employer fifteen years ago. I felt obliged to ask this personnel manager how I could acquire the experience necessary to begin a career if no one was willing to give me a first chance. Is there a sister out there who can give me and the brothers a just reply to this inquiry?

Tim, the screenplay writer introduced earlier, pointed out another reason why sisters are so unwilling to give brothers a chance. He discussed the media bias we are often subjected to. I talked about this earlier in the context of black women, and the same holds true for black men. On television, we see a pungent dichotomy of black men—celebrities and criminals. On billboards, in our neighborhoods, we see brothers who are either famous athletes or attractive unknowns modeling in alcohol advertisements. Rarely do we even see brothers who are not of celebrity athlete status outside of our communities on billboards modeling men's apparel, almost insinuating black men don't wear fine designer apparel. Applause, applause to brother Tyson, the first black male supermodel, currently under contract with designer Ralph Lauren. (You go, Mr. Man, with your fine self!)

Yet, since sisters see more white men succeeding on a regular basis, instead of standing back and analyzing the situation objectively, we denounce our brothers. Instead of reading between the lines, we automatically accept what we see as being the gospel. If we took some time and thought about it, we would realize that we sisters really don't have it that much better (with many of us unable to move further than administrative positions).

Black women need to develop a more understanding attitude toward dating and mating selection involving our black men. White folks in America are *centuries* ahead of black folks in America in terms of education and influence. And sisters don't want to give brothers even fifty years?! C'mon! Give me and the brothers a break, please!

sins of expression

The effect of media hyperbole is just one obstacle we must overcome if we are to develop into a unified people. Another is our lack of control of the natural passions we have as an oppressed people of color and that we allow these unbridled passions to eat away at our relationships.

Black folks are expressive people. We always have been and always will be. We enjoy communicating verbally, we enjoy our music and swingin' with our rhythms, we love makin' love, and when we act in love, it is frequently awe-inspiring. I pray often for the relationship between my husband and me because we are both mixed with some super-passionate ancestral blood—African, Native American, Caribbean, French, and Irish! So you know when the anger kettle is on, it's boilin', and when the lovin' is cookin', it's on fire! And we are not unlike any of our fellow sisters and brothers. Therefore, what me and my husband, and countless other black couples I know of, practice (and what we as a people must continually strive for and practice) is restraint of those passions so that they do not continue to destroy our people's chance for a successful posterity.

Remember me discussing the hyper-sex-drive of our younger sisters? We've got to help them to learn to rein that in. We've got to get our younger brothers to understand the value of waiting and waiting and waiting some more, too. We cannot afford, as a people, the continuing escalation of teenage pregnancy. It is destroying the fabric of our families and thus our communities, both present and future. It is taking our young girls and boys, our promising doctors, attorneys, teachers, and scientists and snaring them in premature parenthood. It is denying them the opportunity to develop into the wondrous human beings they have the potential to be.

Likewise, careless brothers and sisters are generating young men and women who, if they attend school, often come home to an empty house or to parents too tired to express the love and concern that needs to be expressed. Sometimes our kids come home with friends, peers who have nothing but destruction up their sleeves because they were generated by these very same circumstances a few years earlier.

So while you're at work or in transit, your son and his friends are out servin' up crack-cocaine to perhaps your best friend's sister or your cousin or the neighbor's kids. Why? Because you and your man wouldn't use condoms *and* equally accessible birth control pills until you had the time, energy, and financial resources to devote to parenthood. So we now have hundreds of kids on the street servin' and gang-bangin' to protect the territory they're servin' in and to gain what they consider to be respect and family love. This isn't the white man's fault. He may have provided the narcotic product, but who told our kids to say yes?

Were we told to have more children than we could afford? Were we told to not communicate self-love to our children? No, we were not. By saying nothing, by focusing on status and wealth, by blinking at this behavior, we let our children go. Our community conveyed (and is still conveying) messages that say wealth and power is everything, do what you must to acquire or escape. No, we don't grow cocaine; nor do we pilot the ships and airplanes that bring it and marijuana into our cities. Once again though, I remember what I was taught about the horse and water. Therefore, I must contend, it's our fault. It's our cross to bear. It's our garbage that must be cleaned up.

are we still on the plantation?

Related to the issue of governing our passions is the equally large dilemma caused by the repression of our passion and cultural expressions as a people of color and the need to feel or be accepted as a part of the dominant society, which for us is white America. It is a historical fact that it is easier for a people to assimilate into the dominant culture than to maintain the culture indigenous to them. Since we African-Americans have lost most of our direct cultural links (native languages through which we learn our histories and genealogy) to Africa because of them being whipped out of us, there have been several movements after gaining freedom to find our culture, to "return" to Africa, so to speak.

At the turn of the century, brother Marcus Garvey tried relocating with fellow brothers and sisters to Africa. During the height of the civil rights era, wearing Afro hairstyles, which were akin to native African hairstyles, and dressing in dashikis patterned after native African cloth was a way to recapture some of our "lost" African heritage. Now, again, black couples are "jumping the broom" as part of their matrimonial tribute to the *motherland* and purchasing and donning African and Caribbean fabrics and art in celebration of our heritage. I celebrate the marriage of my African and Native American bloods by wearing braids or by wearing my hair just naturally and by adorning myself with silver and turquoise.

Yet, for the most part, when we turn on the television, sit in a movie theater, turn the pages of magazines, and shop in large, mainstream apparel stores and malls, brothers and sisters are hard-pressed to find anything that speaks of our cultural heritage, African-American heritage, while Western European civilization's ideals of beauty and art are everywhere because they are the dominant culture in America. By the way, thanks for Christie and the brown Cabbage patch dolls.

During slavery, we, a most passionate people, were forced into silence. Holding our tongues was necessary for self-preservation. Non-Western mannerisms and forms of expression have always been belittled and perceived as savage or uncivilized, and therefore our African expressivity was confined to our communities if we wanted to "get along" outside our communities. Christianity was thrust upon Africans and Native Americans for the purpose of domination and control. Our peoples didn't need it; we were already highly spiritual and deeply connected to the genuine Universe, as well as the soil, water, air, and fire of our earthly plane. But we either capitulated and became Christians or perished at the hands of government goons who were in cahoots with the missionaries.

So now, the struggle to maintain our blackness while maintaining and developing relationships within Caucasian society has caused very painful rifts within our communities. We are still fighting internally with the old doctrines of the "house nigger" versus the "field nigger." Some of our brothers and sisters completely renounce any part of their colorful ancestry, while others lash out at white society—and at those of us who work and socialize between the two—with such hatred and malice that they cause deep fear among not only white folks but among black folks, too. I still get snubbed sometimes, as I was in elementary school, because my hair isn't kinky enough, my skin isn't dark enough, and/or my frame isn't large enough to speak to my African ancestry for some brothers and sisters. I get snubbed because I don't attend church and seemingly live in an extremely secular manner. Hell, I even get snubbed because my appearance isn't conservative enough for those brothers and sisters who believe in the corporate way, who feel its uniform, politics, and sports (such as tennis and golf) embody the only credible way to live. Still, I try to bond with them, disregarding their petty rebuffs and internal prejudice, because I understand how frustrating it is to feel lost, to want and need someone with whom you can identify and share. However, I am only one, and we all know these haughty attitudes do nothing but cause larger and larger chasms between our folks, especially between brothers and sisters.

Brothers are sometimes afraid that because a Sista-Girl attends service every Sunday, she might be a screamin' Holy Roller. And Ms. Thangs are often aloof with brothers who leave the nine-to-five uniform in the closet after work, choosing T-shirts, chinos, and maybe a kente belt or cap instead. The histories of people of color are wondrous, and should be used to bring about a cohesiveness to our relating as opposed to the divisiveness it has been used for. Plantation owners knew if they kept the lighter slaves separated from the darker slaves, this would cause jealousy and therefore make it more difficult for slaves to revolt. Do we still, today, think it's necessary to help the masters? I don't know about you, but the only master I have is the One who created me.

My God, if we have nothing else in common, we have the customs and traditions of our ancestors who, if looking in on brothers and sisters now, are probably rollin' in their graves.

Blacks and Native Americans found each other in love from the mid-nineteenth century through the beginning of the twentieth century. Imagine that—Africans and Indians in love and marriage. Now blacks and blacks can't seem to find even each other in this, the most beautiful and simple of bonds. We prefer to cite remarkably senseless reasons like "He's too black" or "She's too white," using archaic arguments from the days of slavery to keep our people apart.

There is nothing wrong with wanting to be liked and accepted by anybody, including white people. However, the cultural differences between black America and white America make this difficult, in addition to the historical relationship between the two communities. So while there is nothing wrong with wanting to be accepted, denying your heritage in hopes of "fitting in" or being more readily acceptable is despicable; likewise is the rebuking of a brother or sister because master happened to find his way into this brother's or sister's great-great-grandmother's bed or because their parents found a love that bridged the racial gap of black and white. We talk about how white Americans still suffer from plantation-owning mentalities and how they need to address and change these attitudes;

our suffering from and continual usage of slave mentality should also be addressed and changed.

gravity and hair reversal

Clinical psychologists have said when males and females marry, there often are two distinct fantasies taking place. The male fantasy is that the female is perfect and will never change; and the female fantasy is that the male, while temporarily tolerable, can be changed to measure up to her standards. Perhaps this is part of the reason for the high divorce rate in this country. People say "I do" while fantasizing.

Sisters, if you get involved with someone with the idea that you can change him or her, you are in for a rough ride. If there is one experience most humans are averse to, it is change. So to become involved with someone based on how you think you can alter that person is self-defeating. If you don't like the way this individual is now, you won't like the way he or she will be later. Just leave him or her alone.

Some of us become involved with a man who really isn't quite up to snuff because we think our time is running out. The biological clock began ticking a few years ago, and now it sounds like atomic bombs going off. These can be very frustrating times, but don't 'settle for less just because you think you can change him and/or you feel "it's time to settle down." There are few things worse when relating than becoming involved with the wrong person at the wrong time simply for the sake of being involved. Respect yourself and respect him, and don't do it. Wait. The right one will come along if you allow him to.

And if the "right" man seems to have appeared, discuss a possible future together. Be sure to inform him that, although we don't like it, human beings are an ever-changing species, that there really is such a thing as gravity and although the health club is a good friend of yours now, the pull of gravity is a little stronger than stair-steppers. Explain to him that while black women don't do so as severely as white women, we do lose elasticity in our skin and don't all end up looking as good as Queen Mother Lena Horne, Queen Mother Tina Turner, or Queen Mother Nancy Wilson.

If his attitude becomes a little sullen upon receiving this special dose of "change is inevitable" reality, reassure him that you will be very supportive when he loses that twenty-something hour-long stamina. That it will be okay with you when that washboard tummy turns to a small innertube and when a forehead now covered with curls mysteriously grows *backward* toward the top of his head.

Brothers and sisters need to come together as mail clerks, attorneys, secretaries, CPAs, postal workers, doctors, bus drivers, teachers, executive managers, and so forth. We cannot, I repeat, we cannot afford as a people to ignore prospective mates because they don't meet our unrealistic expectations. Talk about discrimination! Sisters, do you want to know what was so wondrous about the Harlem Renaissance? Every person of color, whether the lightest vanilla or the darkest pumpernickel, whether bellhop or pianist, whether educated or illiterate, lived, loved, married, and had babies in Harlem. Sure, there was a little jealousy, but they knew that one ounce of native blood meant we were still all just the same.

We all want security, stability, and love. So let's stop discriminating against our own; there are enough folks outside our community who want that job for themselves. *Ain't no time like the present to start thinking, talking, and working rationally and together.*

22

From This Day Forward

Greg and I had our family [wedding] reception dinner at Mom's house yesterday. Everything was wonderful. Mom ordered a lovely cake for us and made a beautiful salad. Sis dressed the table, and I prepared chicken breasts stuffed with spinach, provolone, and pine nuts; angel hair pasta with a white wine, zucchini, tomato broth; and mini gourmet pizzas. Dad Elliott, Bea, Shirley-Mom, Deb, Bill, the kids—David and Daniel—Steph, Dad, Big Mama, Lily, Gene, Harold, and Maxine were there. Greg blessed the food, and, much to his ultimate delight, Dad Elliott conceded to try my chicken instead of fixing his own prime rib. Dad brought champagne, and at the evening's end everyone was full of good food, drink, and love.

I know we have a great deal in front of us, but if we can just remember how much love there is between us and around us, I believe we can last a pretty long time. God, we need you and love you, please help us always.

—Journal entry, June 16, 1994 (My husband and I had eloped on Friday, May 13, 1994.)

Earlier I remarked that monogamy is an unnatural state for human beings. Thus, the institution of marriage must also be unnatural. However, over the thousands of years of conditioning and socialization, human beings (on the whole) have not sought a different way of communing. So as unnatural as it may be, marriage is not necessarily wrong. People may argue this point, insisting marriage is natural because it is beneficial, but I must point out that simply because learned and continually practiced behavior (which is what monogamy is in human beings) is not natural does not mean it is harmful, nor does it mean that it is not beneficial. I wouldn't have married, had I believed it was not a mutually progressive endeavor.

It is true marriage was originated as an institution to acquire or enhance political and financial strengths. From the outset, families arranged unions for the purpose of increasing territorial wealth. Usually, the individual partners had no say whatsoever in their own mate selection process. Later, besides expanding estates, kingdoms, and empires, marriages were also arranged to maintain or overcome balances of power between regions.

Presently, Western civilization has evolved to a position where marriage is entered into, ideally, because two individuals have come together in love. They desire to create a life together, embellishing their love for each other with children and the setting and achievement of mutual aspirations. So there must be something positive to matrimony that keeps attracting people to it. Still, with the number of annual divorces practically equivalent to the number of marriages, there must be something also going awry. What can be so right to make couple after couple head to the altar day after day, year after year, and how can it turn so sour with nearly the same frequency?

Clearly women, along with men, are waiting longer to marry. The remarkable changes that have occurred within American culture have produced a new face for American couples.

Thanks to the "sexual revolution," single or divorced women past the age of twenty-five are no longer stigmatized. The spinster is now a creature of days gone past. Changing economic forces now also influence couples to wait until their late twenties, thirties, and even forties to marry so that they can be relatively assured of financial security for their new families. What is being observed, too, is postponement is not only an attempt to achieve financial security, but a result of allowing for emotional maturity as well. Young adults are finally realizing and admitting they are "just not ready, yet" to take on the huge responsibility that accompanies a large commitment like marriage. So the faces of American married couples are older and, therefore, so are parents. Fathers are staying at home now as much or sometimes even more than mothers. And sometimes, couples leave childbearing to others, preferring not to have children of their own.

Still, even with more couples having emotional and financial stability on their side, approximately half of all couples who say, "I do," end up saying, "We quit." Why?

wanna play house?

Perhaps these couples who quit should have tried it on for size before they jumped into the matrimony box. As a teenager, I promised myself two things: one, not to have a child until I could afford it on my own (and since affording myself is an expensive task, I could pretty much guarantee this promise), and two, to live with my mate before we married. Granted, living together did not prevent my first marriage from breaking up, but nonetheless, I still condone and promote cohabiting before saying, "I do." Why? Because, as one brother I know puts it, "All of those little things you just played past while dating suddenly multiply a thousand times when you live with someone." And once the multiplication is completed, you may be better off being friends instead of husband and wife.

A mutual friend of ours (my then boyfriend and I) was contemplating marrying his longtime girlfriend when we advised him to live with her first. They were still young (early twenties), and if they loved each other but living together didn't work out, perhaps it was just a matter of maturing, which time would take care of. They could always try it again. So our friend finally agreed to live with his girlfriend first and moved in with her. Within two months he moved back out. We were right, and his moving out didn't break up their relationship, either. It just confirmed that the relationship still had some ground to cover before embarking on the large voyage of matrimony.

Now, this isn't to say all couples who decide to stop living together can continue dating. For some, leaving a cohabitational relationship is not nearly as simple as just packing a few boxes and saying, "See ya." More often than not, it's a case of seriously reevaluating the relationship and sometimes determining who gets what because things have started to become "ours" instead of "yours" and "mine." On the other hand, many couples continue to live together and never marry. They don't need the matrimony insurance box. So what is the difference?

The answer is without marriage there are no papers that need signing upon breaking up, no divorce fees to be incurred, nor any money wasted on the pomp and circumstance of matrimonial ceremonies and parties (which can run into the tens of thousands of dollars). So there are some differences. Yet, because marriage is such a lofty commitment, we should do everything we can to be extra sure about our selection of spouses. Queen Mother Dr.

Shirley emphatically agrees with me on this: "I don't have a problem with [couples living together]. A lot of people think it's not morally correct, but I've been around so long and have seen it so much, it doesn't bother me at all. In fact, I have always been a firm believer that before people get married, they need to live together for at least six months so they can become aware of all those little habits that their partners have." *See, Boyfriend was right.*

When we decide on a business partner or a doctor or a church, what do we do? We give it or them a trial run and then make our decision. I know this concept may not sit well with some of you more conservative, morally chaste sisters, even as civilization approaches the year 2000. . . . *Shucks.*

adonis, gold diggers, and retro

In speaking with single sisters, girlfriends who have been married for eight years or more, and divorcées, I find it's evident that one of the main reasons many marriages fail is that the individuals about to be married have different perspectives. Oddly enough, some sisters are the partners who enter matrimony for pragmatic reasons, and some brothers are the partners who do so for emotional reasons. How can that be? Because from the time we Sista-Girls understood big boys married big girls, our mothers and fathers also made sure we, their daughters, understood the boys to marry were those who could provide for a family.

Therefore, unfortunately, the first thing single, never-been-married, sisters usually concern themselves with when thinking about marriage is the financial capability of their partner. The second factor is his personality and how well the two of them get along together. The third factor is whether or not he possesses the characteristics the sister thinks will make for a good father. Sisters who are single parents usually consider the financial abilities and good parenting characteristics first, not really wanting one without the other. Taking into consideration the social conditioning women have gone through, these perspectives are understandable. However, they are misleading.

Before I explain why, let me continue for a minute, because the perspective gets worse with younger sisters, especially those who are educated and have had a certain amount of exposure to the "finer things in life." These sisters, through some inexplicable reasoning, graduate college looking for the perfect man and are absolutely unwilling to settle for anything less because they believe they don't deserve anything less. Their expectations are far too high, and they are setting themselves up for numerous disappointments and heartaches. These Sista-Girls, living in worlds of disillusionment, searching for Mr. Adonis Rockefeller, confound me. I try to explain to them that, yes, you deserve the best of everything; we all do. Sometimes, however, it's just not possible to get, not at the outset. Sometimes you have to settle for what you perceive as second best (or third) because it is attainable, and then the two of you work for the best. Sure, go ahead, aim for stars, but if you happen to get a moon, don't spurn it. If you do, the next thing you might get may be *a whole lot of nothing,* as my granddaddy used to say. But, no. They say Brotha-Man has to be fine, has to have *a lot of money,* and has to be righteous in the personality department.

Ms. Thangs, fine brothers come a dime a dozen. There are so many handsome, pretty, gorgeous, black, heterosexual, and single, young men out there, it's frightening. But what are you going to do in ten years when their hair starts thinning? When their stomachs grow over their belts a little because of all that good living? When those high cheekbones droop a little due to the effects of gravity and age? Are you going to turn them in for somebody younger, after having built a life together? Is that what you would want them to do to you after your character lines start revealing themselves markedly when you smile? After your breasts begin sloping downward due to the effects of gravity? After your hips and thighs spread a few inches because of the birth of your children? Are you saying because many men can't seemingly tolerate aging in women, you aren't going to tolerate it in men? Are you saying beauty consists only of physical traits that are visible and touchable?

Is this what four-plus years of higher learning taught you? That beauty really is just skin deep? Do you mean the sisters who are trying to convince their daughters and girlfriends that breast implants, laser surgery, collagen treatments, lyposuction, a billion-dollar cosmetic bill, and working out so much they damn near become infertile are not all they're cracked up to be are deceiving themselves and their fellow women? Just what are you saying to the women who continually fight the media blitzkriegs of the beauty and fashion industries, which are trying to force us to accept their superficial definitions of beauty? If you're not willing to marry a man who isn't what you regard as "fine," are you saying men should not marry women whom they do not perceive as fine also? Aren't you taking the progress women have made over the last thirty years back about forty or fifty years? Do you imagine this attitude is really compatible with the attitude of your sensitive and holistic "nineties man"? NOT!

Brothers understand the dynamics of your thinking and in retaliation shout, *"Golddiggers! That's what most sisters are!"* Yet, I know too many sisters who are working just as hard as the brothers (if not harder), making just as much money (if not more). But, if you stipulate being wealthy (this is what most of you stipulate, and we know very few of you younger sisters acknowledge middle-class comfort as an acceptable financial level) as a necessity for a marriage partner, aren't you diggin' for gold? Yes. Okay, now let me just hip you up, *one more time:* If you're looking for gold from the average brother, I suggest you travel to San Francisco instead, dig up someone's yard, and pray there's still some left from the 1849 gold rush, because the average brother just ain't got it like that. I went over this earlier, and you now know how some of the good brothers feel. *Sisters? Knock, knock. Anybody home?* The average black man just does not make as much as the average white man, and you want to marry a brother who is wealthy?!

I agree that selecting a mate who is financially secure and can help provide for a family is important. Money problems are often the cause of many separations and divorces. Children have to be fed, and rent or a mortgage, tuition, utilities, insurances, automobile notes, and so on have to be handled. All this combined is a heavy burden. However, two people can share and manage the financial responsibilities of a household well if they use good advice from financial counselors and books on financial management. Yes, taking care of a home and children is hard work, but this is no longer the day of *Father Knows Best,* when one salary could cut it and Ms. Thang could stay at home. That situation is an exception to the rule in today's society. And a Queen Mother always taught me to prepare myself for the hardest row. That way, if things get easier, they will be much easier, or if circumstances become very difficult, they will not be as difficult as they could have been. Sounds like you girls have been watching *Father Knows Best* a bit too much, maybe taking retro style a tad too far.

unicorns, pegasus . . . and the nineties man

Now, there's a fascinating mythical creature that has been invented for women in the nineties. I casually mentioned him earlier. This fantasy has everything a woman could ever want and more. It is the *nineties man.* Like all myths, the descriptions of this creature are based on both true and false romantic ideals. However, Sista-Girls who believe the nineties man is an ideal marriage partner need to know the nineties man doesn't really exist. He is a figment of your imagination produced by advertisers wanting to lure females into purchasing men's products that at one time only men purchased for themselves, and touché for the brothers arguing with this point. The nineties man cares about his appearance, so he uses skin-care products manufactured especially for men by cosmetic companies that used to devote all of their product lines to women. Ergo, while you're picking up lip color, you can also buy your honey some astringent. The nineties man is open, honest, sensitive, and sharing, so sisters should feel free to purchase his-and-her boxers and that unisex fragrance that was just introduced.

So, very interested in this phenomenon, I asked several Sista-Girls to describe this wonderful creature, and I also asked those brothers I spoke with earlier about the reality behind the attributes of the nineties man. While I was surprised by some of their responses, knowing brothers like I do, I wasn't surprised at all by others. Check this out:

The nineties man is attracted to your brain and not your body and face, seeing you as a person first, a female second. All of the brothers thought this was unrealistic. Tim replied, *"This is unrealistic; it's simplistic and reductive. You never ever see a member of the opposite sex (if you're a heterosexual) as a person first. Men and women are attracted to each other because they are men and women—it's healthy. After the initial meeting, if you conduct the relationship in a timely manner and peel the layers away, eventually all the qualities of the personality come out."*

Sisters, this is another one of those "man" thangs. And, ironically, I find our younger women feel pretty much the same way the men do. The first thing that attracts young Ms. Thangs to another individual is not the individual's personality but his face or his body or, for unfortunate heaven's sake, the automobile he drives or the sneakers he wears. Fortunately, as we Ms. Thangs mature and have seen pretty faces, have had pretty bodies, and purchased our own vehicles, our values change and the physical appearance doesn't carry the weight it used to. Not true for men, sorry to say. They are very visual creatures.

The nineties man is sensitive to your feelings and tries to accommodate them almost always. Ladies, the good news is they realize we have feelings and are trying to be sensitive to them. Brothers realize this is important and are working on it. The bad news? "Always" or "almost always" is impossible.

The nineties man enjoys helping out with domestic chores—cooking, cleaning, etc. Guess what? He doesn't always enjoy it, but he is more than willing to do his part, especially if his mate is a working Sista-Girl.

The nineties man wants to stay home with the children as much as possible and enjoys taking care of them. With the exception of Kyle and Sam, the brothers were all for this one, too. Maybe the nineties man is a genuine creature after all?

The nineties man is not looking for nor is interested in corporate power or social status. *BUZZZ!* WRONG! Most of the brothers are interested in going as far as they can in their field of work. They asked, how can a man get a woman if he is not interested in attaining power or status? This is what sisters seem to want—someone who can provide those things symbolic of social status and wealth.

A nineties man does not need to do "manly" things (bachelor parties, football, and beer, etc.) to affirm his manhood. NOPE! WRONG AGAIN! Brothers still value their time with the fellas, maybe even more than ever, as one guy explained: *"The problem that we're having as a society is the qualities that define masculinity are coming to an end. This is because society has less and less use for those qualities due to the fading industrial society. So now, those traditional hunt-and-gather qualities are becoming more important to males to hold on to."*

The nineties man is all for women's rights. Yes, they

are. However, one brother needs to be thumped on the noggin, as my grandmother would say, for his reasoning that women's working and being able to earn as much money as men takes a big load off of their mates. *THUMP, THUMP!*

The nineties man doesn't think about sex first when he meets a beautiful woman. WRONG! This goes back to the first point, what individuals see when faced with someone attractive. Andrew says, *"That doesn't make you a bad person, and if you're a man and a thinking being, you move past that. If not, you're fucked up and won't get to anything positive, anyway."* I think he's got a valid point.

The nineties man is open, vulnerable, and freely admitting of his weaknesses. NOT! They all admit this is a fallacy, unreal due to the nature of the male species.

Here you have it, and if you think you've been dealing with a nineties man, before you say "I do," you had better put on your glasses or have your prescription double-checked. The brothers' answers suggest that while they understand the importance of treating sisters as human beings, there is no stopping the brothers from looking and thinking about sisters as the opposite sex, too. As one brother put it, *"A woman is a woman is a woman is sex."* I don't know about you, but while I'm walking to the grocery store or running on the treadmill or sitting on the toilet, I am not equating myself with sexual intercourse or my vagina. I wonder how Brotha-Man would feel if he was constantly referred to or thought of as a penis. Call it chauvinistic if you like, but the attitude is real and it hasn't changed in the thousands of years it's been around.

Why do you think I don't believe in discarding the use of *feminine wiles?* Because, as rudimentary as they are and whether we like it or not, with brothers as with most men, sometimes they're the only way to get things accomplished. Sad, I know, but as history has illustrated, it has been this way for thousands of years, and I don't see it changing anytime soon. Well, that's not actually true because six hundred years ago, we women weren't allowed to speak unless we were spoken to and that's certainly changed. Only two hundred years ago we had very little or no say about whom we were to marry, and that's changed. One hundred years ago it was a woman's duty to learn to cook and sew, and that's changed. And fifty years ago the only careers open to women were teaching or nursing. So, maybe there's hope somewhere on the horizon . . .

Irrespective of the true difficulties involved in relationships between brothers and sisters, successful marriages are possible. I think there are ten keys that unlock the door to matrimonial harmony:

1. Proper timing (i.e. deciding when it's the right time for you)
2. Communicating honestly and benevolently
3. Having mutual aspirations and interests
4. Respecting individuality
5. Accepting and understanding
6. Work (through compromise)
7. Work (through crisis)
8. Work (through conflict)
9. Work (through/with children)
10. Work (with compassion)

Many sisters and brothers may rightfully argue that the characteristics of a good marriage are those that they are currently enjoying with their live-in, their significant other. So why should they marry? What's the difference? In the hearts and minds of partners who genuinely love each other, there is no difference. However, because society has this need to label everything, to place things in nice neat little boxes made just for their particular labels, for the sake of not getting caught down the road in legal mumbo-jumbo bureaucratic red tape, there is the neat little box called "matrimony." In this box two individuals can get married by a state-recognized official and the legal bonds of their relationship protect the assets and the children produced by that union. If partners don't get into this box, there is always the likelihood, hanging like the sword of Damocles, that should anything happen to one partner, decisions usually made by the surviving marriage partner may be made by the State, despite the existence of a legal will and insurances. The marriage certificate provided by the stats is just a little box of added insurance, that's all, my friends. That's the difference between being married and living together.

Getting back to the ten items—once we successfully accomplish one through five, though they provide us worthwhile references and reasons for doing all the work associated with the last five points, six through ten are still not the easiest to perform, because they are continual. We can reflect on what we have done as a couple and use those positive instances to motivate us to continue. As the list suggests, making relationships last requires major effort, but it is a labor of love, one that should be looked forward to and not easily dismissed or relinquished. Often, individuals give up on being a couple because they feel they "can be miserable alone" or "can be happy alone." While both are true, it takes no effort to be alone, either. There is no one to be accountable to except yourself, and how challenging and fulfilling can that be 365 days a year? Never mind . . . Don't answer; I just put a double-edged sword over my head, I know.

No, I am not chiding any sister or brother who finds the single life happy and rewarding, because that often can be the case. Marriage or living together is not for everyone. I'm just questioning those who give up after the initial "lustfest," when the realities and imperfections of their mate begin to reveal themselves. Why even consider becoming a couple when all you seem to want is some sex with someone who *seems* perfect for a month or so?

This is one of the reasons why the timing of marriage—the ultimate social commitment—is so important.

time for devotion

Younger sisters, when talking with me about marriage, always ask me, when is the best time for marrying? My answer to them is always the same: Because blacks are so far behind on the socioeconomic ladder of American society we, African-American sisters, should be in our early thirties, versus the traditional early-to-mid-twenties, before we even consider marriage an option. (As with almost everything in life, there are exceptions to this rule.) Humans are living longer, so why not take some time to develop emotionally and professionally? I advise them to finish school (getting as much education as possible), establish their career paths, and then think about marriage. In their twenties, many sisters usually find themselves perpetually in the Ms. Thang mode: "I know and am everything, and that which I do not know, I don't need to, and that which I am not, I need not be." What brother—especially those in their twenties (in their Mr. Man phase, which parallels Ms. Thang)—wants to and can handle that kind of attitude for an extended period of time (say beyond the "lustfest")?

But in our thirties, *ahhh* . . . we sisters come back down to earth (a little) as we begin to face "catastrophic" issues: wrinkles, recurring cellulite, contempt for the careers we have been educated for, having outgrown our newest mate, sounding like our mothers as we give advice, discovering what genuine sex is all about, learning we can say "no" or "kiss my ass" to whomever and not feel guilty about it. Sista-Girls in that thirtyish range find themselves flawed and realize that *it's still all good.* We haven't done everything we set out to do in our teens and twenties, but we still have a lifetime ahead of us. Besides, some of those things aren't as significant to us now as they were then. We've discovered we have outgrown some of our ambitions. We're not mortified to go outside and face the world with rusty, dusty skin and chipped fingernail polish because we have learned the value of what is inside. Thus, we're not freaked out when our spouse sheepishly gawks at that five-foot-ten, slender, buxom Ms. Thang walking down the street. We simply pat our spouses on the behind saying, "Down, Rover. Down."

If we really do despise our work, we are mature enough not to do anything rash—for example, go to lunch and not return, ever—as we might have done a decade ago. And our behavior is due, not to a need for security, but to our having learned that acting before thinking is one of the worst things Sista-Girls can do. So we gather our contacts and network our way into a job or position that is more suitable. We take our time, knowing that to accept just anything for the sake of getting out of the place we're in now may be like taking the proverbial jump—you know, from the (all together now) frying pan into the fire.

Otherwise, my sisters in their thirties who are climbing that corporate ladder or painting that soon-to-be-world-renowned fresco or treating those grateful patients or teaching those will-be-grateful-later-in-life teenagers are on their respective paths to financial and career stability and can devote some of their spare time to positive, loving, intimate relationships. Hopefully, you sisters have had good and bad relationships, both long- and short-term, both serious and casual. In this case, you have also had opportunities to discover the many subtle essentials of intimate relationships that Sista-Girls just can't learn about via word of mouth. You've learned where the line in relationships must be drawn for you, where the gray area is and where prospective mates usually draw their line. I think Queen Mothers call this maturing.

honest and benevolent communication

Okay, communication has been hashed over pretty well, thus far. But honesty and benevolence have yet to be covered in depth and are essential to a good marriage. If communication in a relationship isn't honest, it's counterproductive, and if communication isn't benevolent again, it's counterproductive. Why?

Well, the necessity for honest communication is somewhat self-explanatory. The success of a relationship depends, in large part, on true and accurate information being exchanged between its partners. It is what spouses work with to help the marriage endure. Sisters, we know this stuff. So let me add to this point. For us thirty-somethings, honest information is minor league. The big-league problem occurs when our feelings have been injured and we have this incendiary need or desire to hurt in return, and we retaliate with a kind of honest but unnecessary communication. For example, if our spouse says something insensitive (unintentional, but nonetheless insensitive), we may reply with a remark alleging the lack of size and/or ability of his penis. (Personally, I have graduated from this level; I just call him an asshole—which, I know, is also not helping.) Sisters, we should just stay focused. The momentary lapse of our partner's sexual ability becomes an unnecessary focal point of this argument when the real focal point should be the insensitive remark. By stooping to irrational defense mechanisms, that is, name calling, often the other spouse in turn becomes defensive, for example, slamming doors. Then further communication efforts become useless, the incident escalates, and feelings are injured even more.

When spouses say something that is hurtful or inappropriate, Sista-Girls should practice a little self-restraint and foresight. And in response, be honest constructively. Ask, "Do you know that what you said just hurt the hell out of my feelings?" And go from there. Be truthful but not brutally so. What if there was no injury to feelings, just something important that needed discussion? Discuss it in a straightforward, truthful, and serious manner. Communicate using "we" phrases instead of "me" phrases. Use eye-to-eye language and keep togetherness-building in mind.

respecting individuality

One of my closer Sista-Girls is a gregarious, fun-loving, rambunctious woman. A gorgeous, almond-brown-colored lady of Caribbean descent, she doesn't believe in holding her tongue about anything. Yet, being ever the lady, she remains mindful of when and where she should speak her piece. Sista-Girl is lively, active, sexually bodacious, and fiercely independent. Her husband, whom she lived with for almost seven years prior to marrying, is a soft-spoken, gentlemanly, homebody accountant. They have been together as a couple for almost ten years now, and although they may sound like opposites, they share fundamental similarities. Both come from working-class families, were loved by strong parents, and have the same tastes. They also share another very important aspect of relating: self-respect and respect for the other's individuality.

He understands, accepts, and actually encourages her affinity for shopping, fine dining, and traveling. And though he seldom joins her when she goes out for an evening with friends, he always offers to pick both her and her friends up, offering to take her friends home, wherever they may live. In turn, she respects the fact that he likes a quiet home, that he often likes to work at home, and that he loves football.

There is nothing wrong with individuals within a marriage having different interests; it's normal and healthy. If your spouse likes listening to R & B, while you prefer rock 'n' roll, that's fine. If you enjoy sleeping in late, while your mate is an early riser, that's okay, too. Just roll over and go back to sleep. I do, almost every morning. Honestly, I find most happily married couples are twosomes doing individual things outside the relationship, coming together often, but enjoying life's amenities without each other, too. This way each spouse can bring new and interesting experiences into the relationship. Remember the math I did earlier (XY+ZY=XYZ)?

On the contrary, I find couples who feel the need to spend every waking hour together (after the "lustfest") and who feel the need to *constantly* publicly display their affection for each other are often covering up a lack of security felt within the relationship. Not only is their continual coo-cooing, "baby-caking," and lovey-doveying making others around them nauseous, but it reminds one of the famous quote from *Hamlet,* "The lady doth protest too much, methinks." Couples like this are screaming for others to acknowledge their relationship. Why? Because saying "I love you" twenty-five times in the company of family and friends helps them to convince the audience of the soundness of their relationship, which suggests that, perhaps, it is also a way for the partners to convince themselves. It's like forced conditioning.

For example, if you are working out on a treadmill in the health club, jogging next to someone who is also jogging, someone who is faster but seemingly less tired, you're more likely to push yourself to finish your goal. You may even go a little further or finish a little earlier than you normally would if there were no one beside you, if there were no perceived audience or competition. While this kind of conditioning can be somewhat healthy in circumstances such as the pursuit of physical fitness, I sincerely question its appropriateness in relationships. If what you feel for your spouse has to be affirmed publicly and frequently, something is wrong. You should be your only motivation when it comes to relating with others, not the public.

Secure, happy spouses respect each other's differences

because they know that these variations are not threatening to the marriage. Quite the opposite, these spouses enjoy the differences because they keep the relationships fresh and alive.

Sisters, let your spouses play if they want to. Then you go out and play, too. I'm not speaking of playing around or being unfaithful. I'm talking about playing for the sake of the child in you. In addition to Ms. Thang, there is a child in all of us who also should be allowed to have fun occasionally. So go jump some double-Dutch, play jacks or cards, and laugh. Take the little girl inside of you out for a while.

Sometimes we want to do one thing and our spouses want to do something else. What to do then? I call it Marriage 101, Lesson One: Compromise. For example, you enjoy one television program and your spouse enjoys a different program. The problem is they come on at the same time on the same night and the kids have the other television set or there's only one in the house. What's the solution? Easy—compromise by you watching your program one week and your spouse watching his program the next week. Another common problem, especially for newlyweds who just flew out of the "nest," is where to go on holidays. Both families are probably pulling the two lovebirds in opposite directions simultaneously, and one spouse, like mine, hates going from place to place to place to place. (The eating is all good, but the traveling is a pain.) Well, go to your family on one holiday, go to your spouse's family for the next holiday or the next year, and then have everyone over to your place for the next time. And if a family member decides to give you two grief, just tell them to lump it because your marriage is the most important relationship to you now and that should be respected by both families.

There is, however, one thing that should never happen in a marriage regarding social gatherings. There should never be a time when a spouse is uninvited or unwelcome to join his or her partner on an outing or gathering. Let's say it's

Friday-night-after-work-with-the-boys time and you're feeling frisky and although you usually let him go alone, you want to go this Friday. There should be no discussion, other than maybe warning you about how raucous the boys can get after a few drinks. He should simply welcome you along. Likewise, if you and the girls are getting together for dinner and wine and he wants to come, do not make him feel unwelcome to join you. Simply tell him, "Honey, you may be a little uncomfortable because it's going to be all women, but come on." I give you my word on this because both my husband and I have been in these situations. Once the conversation starts flowing, no one stays or gets uncomfortable because it is respected that we all have one thing in common—adulthood. Now, my sister and I will occasionally hold a "girlie girl night" (I described one earlier), of dinner, conversation, wine, and music and tell our spouses, "No guys invited." However, they know if they truly want to join us, they can. We'll still talk about Wesley Snipes, Dennis Rodman, Brad Pitt, Avery Brooks, interior decorating, cooking, sexist leftist racist fascist politics . . . oh, and menstruation, PMS, new sex toys, superfluous hair and waxing, the latest lip colors, the latest video studs (as opposed to video hos), the latest hot literature . . . oh, and David Schwimmer, Seal, Kadeem Hardison, Patrick Stewart, and . . . Never mind. Mr. Husbands usually, however, understand the girls want to bond, just like the fellas sometimes do, and don't force the issue.

Because marriage is the ultimate social commitment and especially because women have been conditioned to romanticize marriage and, additionally, because of the myth regarding the black male shortage, sisters must take extra caution so that we don't lose ourselves once inside the ribbons of matrimony. And this is very easy to do because we want so much for our marriage to succeed and prosper. We should realize, however, it can only do so when, as I said earlier, each partner still has a little bit of themselves left for themselves. So let's make sure we stay in touch with friends, relatives, and, most important, our singular selves.

mutual aspirations

The most successfully married Ms. Thangs will tell you that as vital to a marriage as individual projects are, mutual aspirations are just as important. Now, I did get this one right in my first marriage: we wanted to open a hair salon together . . . he eventually succeeded with my business plan without me. Anyway, goals you share give you something to work toward together. A shared project provides a way to spend time together, be it a business, purchasing a home, buying a new automobile, getting a boat, or finishing the basement of your home. One of the brothers I spoke with, Felix, mentioned this as one of the most important aspects of a relationship to him, *"A couple should have goals and a plan that they can work together on, something they can accomplish as a team and be proud of, something they can share because they built it."* Because no two people are alike, you and your spouse can bring unique and interesting perspectives to the same goal, making the achievement that much more unique to your relationship—often making it that much easier to solve the problems and overcome the obstacles that arise when you are working toward an aspiration.

It does not have to be an aspiration, though. It can be a hobby, an interest shared by the two of you. My husband and I are physical fitness buffs. We are always purchasing each other fitness magazines and body-building equipment. We have discussions and sometimes debates on how to sculpt the body or get the best out of a workout. Another married couple I know enjoy wine tasting and spend time dining and sampling different vintages and plan vacations to vineyards in such places as Napa Valley and Sonoma Valley. Find something that interests the two of you. It shouldn't be that difficult because if you married for the right reasons, you probably already have similar interests or a shared hobby. Perhaps you enjoy dancing and so go out club hopping once or twice a month. If you both enjoy reading, spend time browsing and sharing at one of the new monolithic bookstores that are rising up all over the place. You may be interested in photography. Get a camera, take classes, turn the bathroom into a part-time darkroom. History buffs? What about tracing the lineages of your families? It's a great way to get to know each other's kinfolk, learn some fascinating black history, and the stories older Queen Mothers can tell . . . (Well, you know how I feel about that.) One couple I know simply share political debate and discussions with each other; they have completely opposite political affiliations, but both are devout nonconformists. Do something together outside of the home at least once a month. Get some fresh air and share some fresh ideas *together.* Then again, sometimes it's nice to just lie in bed, side by side, reading silently while playing footsy.

acceptance and understanding

She snores. He leaves the toilet seat up. She leaves her funky panty hose in the middle of the floor. He lets the toothpaste get all gooey around the cap. Dinner is never on time. He never offers to cook. She is a neat freak. When he does the laundry, her white socks always end up pink or gray. She spends hours at the beauty shop, and then two days later he can't tell why. Whenever he goes out with the boys, he comes home drunk. She hates girlie magazines. He hates dining out at restaurants.

If these (or similar examples) are the only things you and your spouse have to argue or disagree about, congratulations, you have nothing to worry about. You should be married for the rest of your lives. Now, if there is another spouse in a different state who is also married to yours, then there might be a problem, but this stuff—peanuts.

Peanuts because nobody is perfect and Ms. Thangs can distinguish between petty differences and insurmountable conflicts and the areas between the two. Queen Mother Rae, who outlived one husband and at the ripe old age of seventy-three, has a couple of boyfriends, once told me about her husband and prospective husbands: "All I ever ask is that they don't beat, don't let me know or hear about them cheatin', is home for dinner a few nights a week, is there when I wake up in the mornin' every mornin'—unless he's in jail on a disorderly, and that he calls me if he does get arrested so I won't worry."

Anyway, I gave examples of some princes earlier, and if you've got a brother who exhibits compassion like these guys, here are a few answers to those grievances listed at the beginning:

- *There are earplugs for snoring; make him buy some, and you take responsibility for getting everybody up when the alarm goes off in the morning.*
- *Just put the toilet seat down and make sure you check the bathroom before company arrives.*
- *Because your spouse will pick your hosiery up from the middle of the floor, you wipe the gooey stuff from around the toothpaste cap if it bugs you that much.*
- *Let your spouse know dinner has to be late sometimes, especially the romantic, candlelight dinners.*
- *Be glad your spouse doesn't cook; ever had spaghetti sauce made from ketchup?*
- *Remember to tell your spouse the one good thing about us neat freaks—we always know where everything is.*
- *Just make sure your light-colored clothes aren't in the laundry when your spouse decides to do the wash—give him your old jeans and funky, stained sweats.*
- *Your hours at the beauty shop can mean hours for him with the boys on the basketball court, and explain you*

will never be able to tell the difference in his game either, unless your spouse becomes an MJ.

- *He comes home drunk after being with the fellas? Just make sure the driver isn't drunk, and in the event there's the smell of a distillery coming from your honey, always keep some linen near the sofa. You'll sleep better, and he won't have to far to fall.*
- *Most women hate girlie magazines. I'm sure he would be made a tad uncomfortable by gorgeous men with full erections staring out from the full-color pages of magazines belonging to you. So simply ask him for postage money so you can mail his girlie magazines to him at his job.*
- *He hates dining out at restaurants? That's what Sista-Girls are for. Phone a friend, kiss him good night, and tell him you'll try to be quiet when you come in. And if you want to be with your honey, order in.*

work, through compromise

I discussed this in the previous section and in an earlier chapter—the need for Sista-Girls to choose their battles wisely. In a good marriage, ideally there should be very few battles, because there should be very few situations where compromise should not be sought. (I mean, of course, verbal battles.) Matrimony is no place for war or egos. All of those positioning, ego-tripping tactics should be left outside if sisters want to enjoy marital relations for a decent length of time; let's say past the "four-year itch." (It used to be seven years, but with divorce being so easily attainable, the itch-time has been cut by almost fifty percent.)

One of the most critical factors to the success or failure of marriages is how quickly *both* spouses acknowledge the importance and need for compromise. I was speaking with a friend of my husband's about relationships, and it turned out his parents have been married for "decades."

I asked how they managed to stay married for so long, and he told me his mother said it all has to do with one word: *compromise.* (See, I told you, Marriage 101, Lesson One.) It is essential that you recognize your partner's need to hear you say, "My happiness is not as important as *our happiness.*" It is equally essential that your partner recognize your need to hear him say, "I care about this marriage *more* than I care about anything else." Not only do compromises ease sometimes awkward situations, but by making spouses express or imply sentiments like those above, compromise reinforces the loving foundation marriages are built upon.

So how do you go about compromising? By taking yourself out of the equation. By your spouse removing himself from the equation. Then the focal point becomes the marriage, and the compromise is one that is good for the relationship, for the marriage. And naturally, anything that benefits the marriage benefits the spouses. Sometimes I hear sisters remark that if too much compromising is going on, something is wrong. But, I explain to them, that is not necessarily the case.

Understand, that when dating, even if you are involved in a serious relationship, quite often individuals still consider their own welfare before that of the relationship or of their partner. They are involved with someone and may even live with them but still look at the relationship from a "me" perspective. When two individuals who think like this get married, there is going to have to be a lot of compromising until both spouses begin to habitually look at the relationship from a "we" perspective, almost as if the relationship is an entity in and of itself (and it actually is).

Sisters often complain that black women give and give until there is no more left of us to give and then brothers check out of the relationship, leaving us "high and dry." Well, if we thought about the relationship using a "we" viewpoint instead of a "them" viewpoint, we would realize a relationship cannot sustain itself indefinitely on the gifts of one spouse. We would see that once the only source of nourishment to the relationship was depleted, the relationship, itself, would eventually collapse. No one, neither a sister nor a brother, should ever give all she or he has, all she or he is to any relationship. The toll it takes on the individual spirit is just too much. (I once was a gin 'n' juice, one-hundred-fourteen-pound, anorexic-lookin' babe because of the sacrificing I did for my angry and frustrated black man; thank God for Queen Mother Aunt Lily who told me to leave the Seven-Up and *Bumpy Face* alone.) It's all right to be a little selfish. Marriages are living entities, just like you and me. They are fully capable of using up all of the available resources. So hold a little of yourself back for the sake of your self. (So you can be like the rest of us *healthy* married sisters and fight weight gain instead of weight loss.) Expect that of yourself, and hope your spouse would do the same. This way, there is always something left to create with for you, for your spouse, and for your marriage.

Brothers say sisters always argue, are always complaining about one thing or another, and we don't know how to shut up. It is true. Many of us do argue and complain frequently and don't know when to shut up. However, it's because we are tired. Most black women have been carrying the burden for some time now, a burden that black men should have been carrying a while back. But many brothers got caught up in negative situations, and sisters had to pick up the slack. So now, when we finally get a man who can take some of the slack back, we push and push and push on him some more, trying to get him to take all of the slack back as quickly as possible because *we are tired.* We want the world to see our brothers are men and should be treated as such because they can handle the weight. This is where compromise comes in. Explain this to your man. Tell him you're tired and the reason you bitch sometimes is because often he's so busy concentrating on how the black man is being negated, he is neglecting the heavy burden the black woman, his black woman in particular, has to carry.

work, through crisis

Marriages are living entities because of their primary components: two living human beings. Therefore, when the humans suffer, the marriage suffers as well. Ultimately, we all have to face the death of loved ones (too frequently in the black community, many of our young loved ones' lives are cut short); some of us must face financial ruin; some of us must face destruction of homes and loss of valuables; some of us must face horrible random acts of violence, leaving a loved one permanently disabled or disfigured.

Any crisis puts a heavy burden on a relationship. What must be remembered (in all cases except the death of a spouse) is that the foundation upon which the two of you built your marriage—of trust, communication, respect, and love—is the foundation you can use to support you through any crisis. Trust that your spouse will be by your side. Communicate your honest feelings with him—the despair, remorse, anxiety you may feel. Let him know all you are carrying in your heart because your spouse may be able to lighten the load. Respect the solutions and suggestions your spouse brings to you. If the crisis is impacting you more directly, your spouse may be able to look at things a little more objectively. And finally, love your spouse and allow your spouse to love you. You may not realize you need to be held, that you need a shoulder to cry on. You've faced things alone or with Sista-Girls before. But remind yourself that your husband is feeling everything you are, and he wants to be a place of refuge and solace for you, so let him.

If your man is the one on whom the crisis is impacting most, remember just because he is male doesn't automatically mean he can deal with crises better than you. Be his Sista-Girl, his wife, and take his head in your lap and rock him to a peaceful slumber. We are all infants when facing overwhelming loss or dire circumstances. We all need to be coddled, embraced, and led to safety. A good marriage provides the haven its partners need in times of trouble.

Crises sometimes act like magnets between spouses, too, pulling them closer than they thought possible. Queen Mothers call these *blessings in disguise.*

work, through conflict

Conflicting schedules, conflicting personalities, conflicting careers, conflicting this, conflicting that.

It is not the conflict that we should concern ourselves with so much as how we, husbands and wives, manage the conflict.

The most typical conflict between spouses is a simple personality disagreement. Often these disagreements begin simple but turn into volcanic, earth-quaking arguments. Why? Because we allow our emotions to become involved and take over. Being a passionate individual, I generally don't voice my disagreement with something unless I feel emotional about it, and my feeling emotional is enough fuel for any fire. So what do my husband and I do? Take deep breaths, count to ten (sometimes twenty, sometimes thirty), pace the floor, all at the same time of course, and then look at the disagreement as if it were a jigsaw puzzle. When considering purchasing a home, we had the following debate over the offer:

"Well, we can't offer nothing down," I argued.

"Why not?" he asked.

"Because ten percent down is the normal purchasing agreement, and they agreed to five percent. If we counter with nothing, it will look as though we're coming from a position of weakness."

"But if we counter with a higher price and I can do more with the ten percent because of the nature of my job, why let the money sit in the bank earning five percent interest when I can possibly increase the rate of return to fifteen percent?"

We examined the various pieces we had to work with, and we went from there. And so should you and your spouse.

I won't deny the fact that sometimes we need to put some time and space between recognizing the conflict and finding the solution. Sometimes sisters are just too angry and know this anger will not be contributing to the solution. We know that the next thing to come out of our mouths won't do anything but exacerbate the conflict. During those times, as calmly as possible, tell your spouse, "I really need to be left alone right now." Then go for a walk or put your headphones on and listen to some music. Retreat and clear your heart and your head. Let your feelings cool and meet your man on more peaceful ground. *Don't go there* just because of what you're feeling; it won't help.

work, through/with children

I discuss the significance of children in the following chapter. However, let me say that in a marriage, like any other time, the children must come first—not Mom, not Dad, not the marriage, but the children. Unfortunately children are used as excuses to keep failing or failed marriages legally together. (I say legally because emotionally the marriages have usually been dissolved long ago.) These helpless individuals are used as crutches.

"I don't want my daughter raised without a father present," or "If we get a divorce, the kids will be devastated emotionally, suffer severe heartache."

No, I repeat, the heartache is watching children attempt to develop into healthy, normal adults while living in a household filled with continual arguing, abuse, deceit, or bone-chilling disregard between parents who look through and act as if each other were invisible and/or insignificant.

Another issue that should be addressed is the need for African-American adoptive parents. Black couples need to understand our orphans, black babies given up for adoption, are at the bottom of the list when it comes to babies wanted. When white couples travel to China for the purpose of adopting Chinese babies before they consider all the little brown babies right here in the good ol' U.S. of A., we need to step into the ring. If we don't, as usual, no one else will. So if you and your spouse are financially and emotionally capable, for the sake of these little ones and for the sake of the future of the black community, I implore you to consider adoption when you consider raising a family.

work, through compassion and intimacy

Remember, keep the home fires burning. No true love relationship lasts without it. On her wedding anniversary, a friend of mine came home from work to find the children gone for the weekend and their refrigerator filled with every favorite food she had eaten during the year: two kinds of pizza, shrimp egg foo young, crab cakes, peach sorbet, strawberry cheesecake, and all kinds of additional delights. The next evening, her husband proceeded to prepare a romantic dinner of broiled salmon, steamed asparagus, and rice pilaf, served with a lovely sauvignon blanc, champagne, and frozen raspberries. Food for thought?

Funny, the things people consider romantic. For me, it is the three or four phone calls I receive during the course of the day from my husband every day. Just to say hello or just to ask what I'm doing or just to hear my voice again or just to find out what's for dinner. Even as I write this, I think once I am finished for the afternoon, I'll go and freshen up a little before he comes home. Brush my hair, put a little color on my face and change my clothes. Like I said, I don't care about showing the public a rusty-dusty face, but every once in a while, I think it's nice to give my husband a fresh-faced, sweet-smelling wife to come home to versus someone who has labored intensely all day and shows it.

Once you've been wined and dined and have woken up with each other day after day after day, after year after year, it's the little things that mean so much more and carry so much more weight in the relationship. Like waking up and finding your mate staring at you and smiling because they like watching you sleep. Or having your spouse wake you up, take you by the hand, and lead you to bed because you've fallen asleep on the couch and if you were left to sleep there, you would have a very stiff neck in the morning. Or asking you if you've taken your vitamins. Or your husband buying barrettes for your hair. Or after returning from going out for a newspaper, your spouse hands you one of your favorite convenience-store treats (chocolate-cake doughnuts, for example, yummy!). Sisters, don't discount these things. Cherish them as the treasures they are. And, incidentally, it won't hurt to return the kindness sometimes, either.

marriage and money

Hopefully, before you have married, you have lived together for a year or so and have had an opportunity to discuss and reach an understanding regarding the financial aspects of your relationship. If you have not lived together and are about to jump into that matrimony box, don't put the conversation off any longer; discuss finances—thoroughly. I'm just going to review some of the basics here.

As far as material goods and properties are concerned, prenuptial agreements may seem callous, but they can alleviate a great deal of turmoil during a marriage or upon its dissolution. I believe in them two hundred percent, even being the sensitive, romantic creature I am. Many people look upon them as a defeatist tool, asserting prenuptial agreements imply you're considering divorce even before you marry. No, they imply you've considered your situation realistically.

Suppose that when she died, Great-Grandmother Jessie left you a beautiful piece of jewelry as a family heirloom. In a divorce settlement, you might have to sell the jewelry and split the proceeds with your former spouse. Whereas with a prenuptial agreement, there would be a clause keeping the piece with you in case of divorce; the heirloom would in fact remain with your family as Great-Grandmother Jessie had wanted. Girlfriends, suppose your career makes you a millionaire and your spouse decides to continue pursuing a career in sculpting, not earning ten percent of your annual income. After a couple of years, for whatever reason, your relationship is nullified. Do you want to give half of your earnings to-date or your future earnings to your spouse because they have become accustomed to living a lifestyle your hard work laid out for them? I think not.

Often, a prenuptial agreement is only fair. It removes a lot of filth from what are often nasty circumstances.

In most marriages, each spouse works. Therefore, each partner should have their own bank account (in addition to the hidden "nest egg"). There should also be a joint account for household expenditures and a savings account.

One of the hardest things for black folks (actually, most American folk) to do is save money. We always find something to spend it on. But this is unwise and dangerous.

Think about it—when we're young sisters, living with our parents or roommates or spouses, other than paying our personal bills, our money is primarily for our enjoyment. However, as older adults, often the cost of living increases for us due to medical expenditures, increased life insurance premiums, and increased living expenses in general. Yet, simultaneously, because of our age, the ability and opportunity to earn as much as we did in our youth is no longer present.

Being an elderly Queen Mother is costly. Yet brothers and sisters don't discuss it. We procrastinate saying, "We'll catch up." But tragically many of us never do, and instead of spending our winter years in glory and warmth with our children and grandchildren, we spend them being bitter and cold and often lonely because no one wants to be around caustic, cranky, old folks.

One of the things my mother told me during my first marriage that I have remembered and carried over into my second marriage is, "Make sure you get good life insurance on him." By "good" she meant insurance with a reputable company known for paying out accurately and in a timely fashion when circumstances called for it. She also meant enough so that if my spouse died unexpectedly, my material lifestyle would not have to change dramatically.

In addition to more than adequate insurance, brothers and sisters need to be extra careful with the plastic—you know, credit cards. It can be like playing with a loaded gun. Most financial consultants will tell you one or two credit cards is all that a household or individual needs. And one of the most logical pieces of advice about using credit cards I ever heard was if you won't be able to see the item or use it by the time you get the bill, you should pay for it with cash. (A good source of information is a program called *Money Talk,* which airs on CNBC.)

Finally, set goals, develop a budget, and stick to it. Talk to financial advisers, read financial magazines like *Money,* and watch the financial news reports and programs that are televised. They can especially help when you're considering the purchase of your first home, by providing you and your spouse with current information about the real estate market and interest rates.

And listen to the Queen Mothers telling you to save

while you're young because it gets harder to do once the children come along and you buy the car and the house and your parents get older and require looking after.

the second time around

Sisters, do not believe that if you marry and divorce, you can't get married again because you're older or for any other erroneous reason you may have heard. Take it from a Sista-Girl who has been there, *the second time can be better than the first.*

A long while back (before the sexual revolution), divorced women were looked upon with great disfavor, and therefore married women remained in destructive relationships to avoid that stigma. Sisters are aware this is no longer the case. But we should also be aware that, contrary to what society seems to want us to believe, it is not heresy to be married more than once or twice or even three times throughout the course of one's life (as long as it's not simultaneously). Society has created this ideal according to which after getting your education and establishing your career, you should find one person and settle down—forever. We have been socialized to believe it and are willing to accept the challenge it presents, although for many individuals it is an unnatural state.

Sisters (all women, really), should understand that it's acceptable to have more than one marriage; that after ten or fifteen years of being with someone, there is nothing wrong with saying, "Aren't you tired of me . . . ?" ["Yes."] "Good, 'cause I'm tired of you, too. Let's quit now while we're still friends and there is still some semblance of compassion between us. Plus, we can go and find somebody else who may make us happier at this point in our lives." Or that if after a year or so of matrimony, you realize the timing and/or the partner was all wrong (like

I did, with some Queen Mother help, of course), correcting your mistake is acceptable.

People are so afraid of dying alone they're willing, for the sake of comfort, to live with someone (in or outside the ties of matrimony) whom they are no longer emotionally tied to and no longer have anything in common with. What sisters need to realize, as women, as human beings, is if we create that support network and establish that sisterhood, we won't have to live alone. You come into this world by yourself, and that's how you go out. The end. We've got to understand that while a loving, long-term relationship is a good thing, *long-term* doesn't necessarily mean for life; it means for however long the nurturing love between two individuals lasts.

And look at it this way. Once you've said "I quit," there will probably be a reasonable period of time before you say it again, a period when you get to know yourself a little better, when you get to understand the dynamics of relationships a little better, when you mature a little more, and when you learn a little more about the kind of partner that's most suitable for you. All this will make the next time you marry much more enjoyable, fulfilling, and rewarding.

Marriage, although an unnatural state, can be a very satisfying and enjoyable experience. It takes a lot of effort, time and understanding from both spouses. It should not be entered into cavalierly, as it is a legal and binding agreement. Nor, however, should it be constrained to the seriousness of a funeral home.

My husband and I did, of course, begin by living together so that all those annoying little habits could multiply, but they didn't, so we eventually married. With both of us being intensely driven, he a little more than I, we *make* time for each other. And if time begins to get a little short, I complain or he says to me, "Remember balance?" Our arguments are few and far between. We get testy at times, but this is due to our passionate natures, but we never hit below the belt and our communication always moves us forward. We have come to realize that if each spouse recognizes that the other is indeed human, imperfect, and forever in a state of change (whether he or she admits it or not), half of the work is done. I know what it is like to be hard on oneself, and my spouse occasionally has to remind me that it's okay for me to be human, that mistakes are allowed. I, likewise, have to tell him the same thing from time to time.

Each of us makes compromises almost daily, not only to please the other, but also to make time for our relationship. We've endured a couple of crises by hand-holding and embracing each other in the small morning hours.

When in need of solitude, we take a few hours here and there, but we always return. Conflicts are usually resolved the day they erupt, and we never go to bed angry with each other. If one awakes from a nightmare, the other is there to caress one into a calm slumber. We take drives and walks, go see movies, play blackjack, chase each other around the house, and tickle one another. Money is not an issue—we pay bills, we save, and we enjoy life. This second go-round is so much fun, the first time seems like a peculiar, diaphanous illusion. We are truly blessed.

23

Little People and Big People

I do a lot of beggin' in this chapter, you'll see. But it's for the children.

The decision to go forward with a pregnancy or terminate it is one of the most important decisions a black woman can make. We have to be optimistic in our view of procreation and careful in our mate selection and timing, or we will find ourselves with a much greater dilemma on our hands: pregnant at the wrong time or impregnated by the wrong man, or heaven forbid, both.

Although humans are living longer, blacks have a great deal of work to do in the name of our progress as a race. The last thing we need are children being born to those who are unprepared to be the Queen Mothers and King Fathers black parents should be. Don't rush. Waiting until you're thirty or even forty to have a child is perfectly appropriate and acceptable if that is the time it will take for you to be as prepared as possible. (Honestly, you will never be fully prepared—raising children is like that.) The frustration of waiting will be far outweighed by the wonderment and pleasure of the experience once it happens. Maya Angelou, in her book *Wouldn't Take Nothing for My Journey Now,* states profoundly the wonderful experience of not only childbirth but pregnancy, how we must be prepared for the changes that will take place and how we and our mates must utilize this time by loving and cherishing every inch of our bodies before and after the changes.

I know sometimes the "biological clock" resounds with the furious beat of a Congo drum. But nothing is worse than bringing a life forth when you are not ready. It can have a devastating effect on the lives of both you and your child. When that clock starts ticking, sisters, and you know you're not prepared yet, do what you have to do to quiet or silence the beat, but don't give in. It could be the worst mistake of your life.

I beseech you to understand that bringing forth a life when you are not fully prepared to parent it is doing the same thing as aborting it—except that your child will be a statistic of walking death instead of a statistic of officiated death. When you approach sex haphazardly and aren't ready for the full-time commitment parenting requires, you're killing the child before it is conceived.

It's sad enough that blacks still face a hostile world simply because of the color of our skin. So, for the life of me, I cannot comprehend bringing a child into an already antagonistic environment unless its immediate home and family is peaceful and strong.

Although I believe human life is precious, I believe the voluntary termination of pregnancy also has its place. Besides in such cases as the tragedies of rape and incest, abortion has its place when the mother cannot support herself let alone a child. It has its place when the mother has yet to complete her high school education let alone her college career. It has its place when the mother is on a career path and has not yet prepared herself mentally and physically for parenthood. It has its place when the mother is suffering from narcotic or alcohol addiction. It has its place when the mother is on welfare. In speaking with many younger sisters who have mistakenly gotten pregnant, I find they refuse to discuss abortion as a solution to their problem because it is against their religion (though more significantly, premarital sex is also against their religion.) I am not one to turn anyone away from spirituality.[16] Still, the ministry and clergy needs to understand that babies churning out babies is a most egregious sin and those who condone it are, respectively, most egregious sinners.

Individuals like this always point to alternatives such as giving the baby up for adoption. Yet, since the black babies in the adoption system now aren't all being picked up, aren't all wanted, how can they argue that additional babies placed in the system will be? They can't; it's irrational to think so. Persuading young women to abstain is another alternative they offer. To do this, we would have to persuade the entertainment and advertising industries to cease using sexually suggestive imagery to sell their products, or we would have to dissuade our young sisters from being influenced by these industries. These, too, are irrational expectations.

The only rational response is to face the music and love our children as they develop, teaching them that giving birth is something that must be left to adults because only true adults can handle it. During a meeting of a book club I am a member of, we began to do that Sista-Girl-Rap thing and talk about everything after the book discussion was over. The single members talked about how, when we were coming up, the one thing we feared more than anything else (and which made us behave responsibly sexually) was becoming pregnant. I don't see that same fear in girls today, and it is not because abortion is a legal option. *That fear doesn't exist because our girls are missing something we had, and in today's society getting pregnant will supposedly give it to them—someone who loves them back. And do you know what's more frightening than this? They aren't even taking HIV and AIDS into consideration. They're thinking sex minus protection equals baby and baby equals love. They aren't thinking that not only does sex minus protection equal pregnancy, but sex minus protection (protection equals a condom) may equal DEATH.* Now, go and tell that to your priest, minister, reverend, and, most important, mother, grandmother, sister, daughter, and antichoice congressman or congresswoman.

Queen Mothers must recognize the importance of pregnancy and therefore the gravity of preparation for conception. At a time when "good" black males are thought to be few and far between, birthing black infants is probably the most important task a black woman can undertake next to nurturing and raising them properly. So if you want to conceive, consider the timing, and I beg of you, do right by you and your baby.

conception

Contrary to popular belief, it takes longer than nine months to prepare for pregnancy. Queen Mothers understand that to nurture a life inside you, your internals must be clean, healthy, and ripe, free from the toxins like alcohol, caffeine, and nicotine that sometimes accompany the jovial, single life. They know their bodies must be strong and resilient, so they modify their regular exercise routines a bit before conception to allow for this wonderful change of life. They also know nothing is more important to the health of an unborn child than the spirit of its mother. So these Queen Mothers surround themselves with happy, secure people and majestic places, speaking to Spirit often, asking to be blessed with a healthy child and the wisdom and strength necessary to raise it properly in this not-so-proper world.

The mental and emotional state of a woman while she is pregnant directly relates to the health of her fetus. We know that if we are in poor spirits during any other time in our lives, individuals and circumstances around us suffer. During pregnancy the same holds true. Therefore, sisters, align yourselves with positive people and maintain good thoughts. Don't allow any boat-rockers in your space and if anyone does try to rock your boat, throw 'em overboard. Make sure everybody knows you're not havin' it. Love yourself. Take pleasurable, lukewarm baths, get relaxing full-body massages, have your feet pedicured, sleep as much as you can for as long as you can. Working mothers-to-be who are able to plan ahead can maybe take some long-weekend vacations throughout the first trimester to just rest. Start planning your life around the life that's growing inside of you. Take time to work on strengthening some weaknesses, purging some negatives, and reinforcing your strengths. Make a path for you and your family that's filled with knowledge, excitement, wisdom, and color. Enjoy and look forward to the changes that will be occurring over the next year and over your life.

The father's mentality is just as important as the mother's. After all, two of you made the life you're bringing forth, so he has to share in the responsibilities as well as the rewards. Get Mr. Man to visit the doctor with you, at least once if time is an issue or more frequently if he can. He is also a good source for those full-body massages, and make sure he works especially hard on your feet and legs, too. Sisters need to pay special attention to their circulation at this time, and massages in the lower part of the body help. It also helps a little with hypertension, another problem black women are prone to have. Tell him to make sure you stick to your diet, and make sure he is mindful of the goodies he brings home. The two of you should go for walks daily, which can be an excellent way to get exercise and develop that life's path I talked about.

Daddy-to-be should also realize the baby is now the primary concern, not "the boys." So his going out with the fellas should be curtailed quite considerably. Stress that you need him to be around because while you're working on this baby, you can't do everything quite the way you used to. (Truth is you probably can, but no sense in letting him know that.) Get your man to feel accountable from the outset. Relinquish some of the responsibilities you had and let him handle them. This way he'll be used to it when the baby comes and getting him to help will be a lot easier. I know it sounds as if we've got to train them. (Well . . .)

Planning to have a baby is probably an oxymoron for most women because the sisters who have it all together and are ready usually find something or someone won't cooperate, like their body or the body of their mate. Yet, if you are planning to conceive, you should be in the healthiest condition ever of your life. You know how Sista-Girls often diet and work out daily before heading for that Caribbean vacation? That's the ticket for conception if you include the cessation of smoking, drinking alcohol, and using drugs, even over-the-counter drugs. And as far as dieting is concerned, to get rid of the initial water gain and the first few five to ten pounds, a strict short-term diet is okay, but from then on just watch what you eat—your fat, caffeine, sugar, and salt intake—and make sure you drink eight to ten glasses of water daily and take your vitamins. Because once you have conceived, no dieting is allowed unless your physician suggests you do so, and probably like many women during their first trimester, you won't be able to diet anyway because your cravings won't allow you to. So lose those few extra pounds before conception if you are concerned about more than the usual weight gain. Yet, remember to increase your dietary intake enough for you and your growing baby—by about twenty percent, but maintain a good nutritional balance. Make sure you exercise regularly and have a program you can work with while pregnant. (*Shape* magazine publishes an issue dedicated to information on nutrition and physical fitness for pregnant women. It is published quarterly and is a valuable source of tips on how to make the most of your pregnancy.) There are dozens of programs approved by top hospitals that offer exercise and fitness classes for expecting moms.

I've known women who have gone through major changes in order to conceive and prepare for a child. Not only did they change their diet and exercise routines, but Ms. Thangs changed their lifestyles so dramatically they made everyone else around them miserable. One particular friend who used to go out with us Sista-Girls at least two or three times a week, barely came out once a month, and when she did, her man was not very far behind, either phoning her on her cell phone or meeting her at whatever haunt we were chillin' at. Her conversation turned superficial, and all she talked about was materialistic things and how she had to protect herself, her unconceived child, and her husband from wicked, jealous, conspiring women. By the time she decided to conceive, the bold vivacious Ms. Thang we knew had turned into a frustrated, old, married going-to-be-mother before her first anniversary! Sisters, it's serious, but it's not that serious. Some alterations are going to have to be made, of course. For example, you and your partner may consider moving into a larger place, or you may want to change doctors because you prefer a female doctor over a male doctor at this point or vice versa. But 180-degree turns are unnecessary because change will most assuredly happen anyway once conception occurs.

And once conception does happen, concern yourself with the health of your unborn child twenty-four hours a day so that you will properly maintain your health. Make sure you get the proper prenatal care to ensure everything that should be done is being done for your precious one while it is still in your womb. Talk to your doctors and nurses or midwives whenever you feel the need to. That's what they are there for. If they seem as if they don't want to be bothered or are too busy, inform them that if they truly are too busy to speak with you, changing doctors is always an alternative. And make sure you have another doctor's name and number just in case, too.

Think about all that should go into preparing to conceive: cleansing the body, cleansing the mind and spirit, cleaning house (figuratively and literally speaking). Then think about all that goes into being an expectant mom: maintaining proper eating and exercise habits, getting enough sleep, cutting out all toxins, visiting the doctor regularly, having the necessary prenatal examinations, learning to love a larger you, and dealing with the bodily fluctuations as well—nausea, cravings, discomfort, swelling, discoloration, and a host of other things sometimes. Being pregnant is a glorious state for Sista-Girls who have prepared themselves for the maintenance required.

However, if you cannot sustain the above, preparations prior to conception, do not conceive. You would be acting unfairly not only toward your unborn child, but also toward yourself and humanity. Above my concern for myself, family, friends, peers, and colleagues is my concern for black children. I urge you not to bring one forth if you do not possess the wherewithal to raise one as it should be raised—royally. If you have already conceived, are knowingly ill-prepared, and cannot see your way to preparation and maintenance, seek consultation regarding an alternative to parenting this child.

parenting and responsibility

The importance of parenting cannot be emphasized strongly enough.

Watch, listen, and guide. I'm not sure how my parents did it, but I believe it had to do with the way they learned to tend gardens. My sister and I were always their primary concern. Never secondary. Bringing a life into the world is a major responsibility, and whether you meant for it to happen or not, once that life has arrived and is staring you in the face, looking to you for all it needs to survive, it is up to you to provide the primary care, guidance, beneficial examples, and wisdom. Schools were meant to be institutions of learning, not day-care centers. Day-care centers were meant to provide care for your children during the day while you worked, nothing more. Grandparents are wonderful baby-sitters but should not replace you in the eyes of your child, which can easily happen if you allow it to. Your child is your child. No one else can replace a good parent.

Black children are products of black women and black men. Therefore, it is *our* responsibility to ensure that our offspring have the best opportunities available for their development. Just because a child may have come about as the result of your carelessness doesn't mean you should continue acting irresponsibly. Frankly, it means it's time for you to grow up.

Sex can be fun and wonderful, as any court jester can attest, but children are the responsibilities of kings and queens, not fools.

"Family values" has been a much touted theme of politicians during this decade. Nowhere is the erosion of such values more evident than in the black community. Drugs and violence have turned what used to be families into packs of wild dogs. It is time for us to get a grip. Nobody is going to do a damn thing for us, especially if we don't do anything for ourselves. I chastised myself for not doing all I could and using "lack of time" or "I'm only one person" and various other excuses until I realized I wouldn't be able to garner respect from my child if I had to tell him or her that I had turned my heart away from the suffering babies of this day. So, sisters, *ain't no time like the present* to start taking care of what is ours using those good ol' family values. I know folks say times have changed and our children are facing a greater evil than those who came before them. Yet, I try to determine what is a greater evil, a drug dealer's gang or a lynch mob. *Blacks have dealt proudly, defiantly, and triumphantly with the most backbreaking, heart-stopping, bloodcurdling of ad-*

versities. Ain't no time like the present to start proving those who overcame in the past did not do it for naught. Ain't no time like the present to overcome the present-day adversities facing our children, whatever they may be. Even if they *be us.*

Everyone acknowledges the fact that children are the seeds to the future. However, in today's frantic and hedonistic America, it seems there is more planting than caretaking being done. People are more than willing to drop the seed, but as time draws near for the actual farming—fertilizing the fruit with goodness, love, wisdom, experience, forbearance, time, and energy—no one wants to farm. They would rather label the crop Generation X and either let the children "express their individual freedom" or participate in some kind of *Thirtysomething* family psychotherapeutic drama to determine what went wrong.

One does not need to be a psychotherapist to recognize what went wrong. Any farmer could tell you. What do you think can go wrong when a young, tender seedling is treated like an old, strong tree? What do you think can go wrong when a seed is planted simply because planting is fun? What do you think can go wrong when a crop is planted but the fertilizer used isn't compatible with it? What do you think can go wrong when a seed is planted among poisonous weeds?

We ship our babies off to homes for delinquent children. We kick them out of the house, let them return, kick them out again, and let them return again. We rent apartments for them, buy homes for them, send them money, buy them cars, send them to therapists, and take them to group counseling. We expect to be able to find a remedy out there somewhere for whatever is ailing them, and we send them to it or we try to buy it for them. But the true remedy, the real potion cannot be bought. It is not something we can send them to, nor is it something they can join. It is something that is already a part of human existence and simply needs our attention, focus, and efforts. It's called loving another human being responsibly. It's something a lot of parents who blame current socioeconomic conditions aren't doing with their children.

Raising kids is not easy. Honestly, it's sometimes hell. But if we do it responsibly, it's worth it. All we have to do is remember. Times were tough for Frederick Douglass. Times were tough for Richard Wright. Times were tough for Lena Horne. Times were tough for Eldridge Cleaver. Times were tough for Alice Walker. Shit, times were tough for Whoopi Goldberg. Guess what that tells me? Times are always going to be tough, in one way or another, so we better stop doin' the stupid and passin' the buck and get real with our kids, or times are going to get a lot tougher than necessary for the African-American community at large. *And ain't no time like the present.*

I am doggonit confounded knowing some of us are willing to risk the welfare of our children. It's as though we've given up on the future. Or as if we'd been taught our children are capable of raising themselves and dealing with whatever comes their way. And if they can't . . . oh, well? No, no, no. Children are fragile little people, resilient in some ways, yes, but more than delicate in others; requiring cautious and nimble, nurturing and attentive fingers; requiring hope; requiring a tomorrow to live for.

Thinking about the importance of our children reminds me of the tragedy in Chicago, discovered during February 1994, that befell twenty-one babies. It was so appalling it made national headlines: nineteen children were found in a two-bedroom apartment on Chicago's West Side. They were found living, eating, and playing in conditions not fit for a dog (whom they literally shared food with). Cockroaches scrambling everywhere, fecal matter on the floor, paint chipping from cracked walls and ceilings, a stove that didn't work, and not enough groceries in the cupboard for two children, let alone nineteen.

These babies were discovered by police officers during a drug raid. The officers would probably have felt better that night had they found drugs instead of these children and their parents. These parents were in such a drug-induced state they were barely conscious of the circumstances surrounding the taking of their children and their own subsequent arrest.

The number of children increased to twenty: one mother was in the hospital giving birth as her other children were being liberated from the hellhole they were forced to live in. Upon the child's arrival into the world, this newborn was promptly made a ward of the state. The twenty-first child was found with a grandmother and also taken into the state's custody.

One of the fathers, who didn't live in this human casket and had allegedly petitioned for custody of his children, arrived immediately at the apartment upon hearing the news. He reported that since he was only allowed visitation rights, when he came to see his babies, he saw the filth and thus would never go past the living room. One wonders how a father would let his children remain in such conditions. Even if they wouldn't be given to him, certainly a clean, loving, home could be found somewhere? I wonder what was going through his mind when he left, time after time, after visiting his children; why didn't he report the madness that was taking place then?

There was also a neighbor with children of her own living upstairs. When interviewed, she said she had no idea this kind of household was being kept underneath her. Why not? It wasn't as though she lived in a towering high-rise or massive apartment complex; it was a two-flat, for God's sake, one that shared ventilation and the accompanying stench, I'm sure. Why didn't she, as a mother, know about the welfare of the children downstairs? Or was it that she knew, but didn't want to risk getting involved? Now it appears more people are willing to become involved, ironically thanks to the media this time. *But damn!* It took television cameras, nationwide, to do what real neighbors used to do when we took responsibility for *all* of the children and the community, ourselves.

I often ponder the irony of the fact that there are sisters I know who are emotionally and financially capable of having children and would make wonderful mothers but have resigned themselves to waiting until they become involved with someone who would make an equally wonderful father, while there are other sisters who are so obviously *not ready* to receive these blessings because their newborns are found in garbage bags in wastebins behind apartment buildings or in duffel bags on the doorsteps of neighbors' homes or in the backseats of abandoned cars. It's peculiar indeed that there are individuals who are responsible and fondly anticipate the ability to nurture creation, and while they wait, there are other individuals, reckless and oblivious to life, who are damn near destroying creation. The least these women could do is find their way to the emergency room of a hospital and drop the baby off there. But then again, they probably think so little of their own lives, how can we expect them to consider the life of someone else, even if the life did grow inside of them for eight or nine months?

To my sisters living in a dense, foggy, world, trying to escape the realities of daily survival: Your baby does not have to suffer with you. To make them do so because you've given up is heartless and unforgivable. I beg you not to murder your baby because of your inability to live.

parenting and guidance

As parents and prospective parents, you have the responsibility to think before you plant the seed of life. And if it is too late, you must work even harder, think even more about the garden that will soon grow before you. Children are children. They cannot be treated like adults. They do not have the emotional maturity adults should possess because they have no life experience upon which to draw. So they look to you, and you *have* to be there.

Those of us who are parents must set strong, yet flexible guidelines. We must pay the closest attention to our young. Once they are here, they come first, we come second. If we are not ready to place their needs above ours, our children will suffer, and then, so will we.

We must watch and listen carefully for signs of genius, high aptitude, and also for signs of the opposite where they may require special attention in order to grasp certain concepts more clearly. Genius can be easily stolen from the young and weaknesses can be used just as easily to crush them. If our children enjoy reading as opposed to playing, let them read. If they can be hypnotized by the television, don't use the T.V. as a surrogate parent or babysitter, and make them read instead. Children don't readily know what makes them weak or strong, adults do.

We should expose them to as much positive culture as possible so that they may experiment with music, art, dance, sports, literature, science, math, and history. Everything that is available for them to learn from and enjoy, we should try our very best to see they sample. Everything from computer chips to wildflowers. Show them that learning, though at times cumbersome and even difficult, can also be fascinating and fun and lifesaving. We must also take an interest in what they find intriguing and amusing. And though these things may not be at our level of entertainment, we may find this is the time when we get to be children again, by reliving what it's like through the activities of our children. Enthusiastically participate in things they enjoy and activities they initiate. We owe it to our children to fill their minds with as much positive, creative, industrious, thought-provoking material as possible. And at the same time, allow them to be children, gently guiding them from innocence to maturity, praying that some innocence and childlike qualities remain steadfast, not pushing them too fast, nor allowing complacency and slothfulness to set in.

Children are bright enough to test adults, so we must

be equally alert and attentive and recognize these tests for what they really are—expressions of need. Their peers know no more about the world than they do. Yet, impressionable children can easily be swayed by another child's feigned bravado. Remember, another seedling cannot be the staff that stands next to your seedling. It is your responsibility to provide the support your child needs. You must be there so he or she can grow straight, strong, and tall and have something to lean on when the heavy winds blow in their direction.

Children should get their required sleep even when they're not sleepy, eat properly balanced meals at regular intervals, exercise regularly, and receive plenty of affection. Moments when they are cranky and anxious must be respected. Trying to uncover what is wrong, without condescending by acting as child psychologists, is okay sometimes, too. We must discipline our young, being consistent but diplomatic. If there is a two-parent household or if others are left to care for your child, all rules must be understood by everyone involved so there is no contradiction. Contradictory household rules terribly confuse children and can cause severe problems later.

Our offspring need to know that though they are our primary concern and we value and love them, they are still children. Parents are adults, and the relationship will remain that way until the children become adults. Then the relationship will change somewhat, but the parental caretaking will last forever. We must effectively communicate that although they come first, there are other relationships we have that are important and require our attention as well. Our children have to accept that they cannot challenge or ignore the respect that we are due as parents and individuals. If they do not respect us, we will dispense some form of disciplinary action. It should be explained to them this punishment is not meant to express dislike for the child nor does it mean the child is a "bad" person. Punishment simply means the behavior that warranted the discipline is unacceptable and will not be tolerated.

As with determining punishment, it is also difficult to discern how much praise and how much criticism we should give our children. It is especially difficult given that it is critical that they strengthen their weaknesses and are encouraged to do better. They may incorrectly conclude that their strengths are not good enough, so we must be careful, ensuring that criticism, even when constructive, does not outweigh praise. We must also remember each child is unique, with different talents and abilities, and so, comparing children to each other is wrong and hurtful.

We can prevent sisters from falling into the throes of abuse and domestic violence if we both teach little brothers to love little sisters, to detest violence, and to use their anger and frustration constructively, so they don't take it out on their loved ones later, and teach little girls violence is unacceptable behavior and must not be tolerated at any age. We can protect the little ones from calamitous external forces if we teach them that the momentary happiness that comes in a bottle always has a higher than suggested retail price and shouldn't be bought. What happened to the "this is your brain on drugs" commercials? More of our youth are experimenting and using drugs now than ten years ago. Why? I fear we've perhaps become too lazy, too complacent, too selfish.

If we teach our young girls correctly and provide them with examples of men working—our fathers, grandfathers, community servants, teachers, dentists, and so on—as they get older, they won't be so quick to jump at men who are playing. One evening as we sat in her apartment overlooking Chicago's breathtaking northern city-lights view, a dear, dear woman I know recounted, "When I was growing up, we had examples and role models of good black men and women living together on the same block. There was a doctor, a teacher, a preacher, a lawyer, a policy [numbers] man, and a woman who dressed better and smelled prettier than any other woman around. Big fancy cars would come and pick her up every night. All of these people resided in the same area, so us little ones could see for ourselves that black folks could be successful. It's not like that today. Our children took from the community and left. Individuals have raped the black community of its most precious resources—its successful posterity."

She, of course, is correct. Not only have many of us left the community to live among other races, but most of us who do succeed seldom look back, leaving our neighbors' children to learn from the streets. Unlike a generation ago when black folks from all walks of life lived in the same neighborhoods, black communities are not as nearly diverse as they were before. So we must return for the sake of educating our youth and providing them with positive, legitimate examples of success. These are the children that ours will have to contend with, one way or another. The choice is ours.

If our young women understand that the ladies who go out at night looking (or willing) to be rescued by the men they meet are often discarded by those very men who go to bars to play, they won't go out hoping to be rescued. They will comprehend the irrationality of thinking that someone will take you seriously while you are in their playground. They will know that in order to develop meaningful and respectful relationships, they must display themselves in a meaningful and self-respecting manner. Now, while high heels and the funkiest outfits may guarantee fun in the evening, respect is usually garnered during the day over coffee, not at night over beer or vodka.

Most important, if we teach them not to belittle those who are suffering or who are different, they will be more receptive to all kinds of love from all kinds of people. We should teach our girls that no sister should malign another, regardless of the circumstance, that they should respect their elders, and that no human being has the right to besmirch another human being because we are all worth something to the Universe. As they see more women like themselves working in corporate offices, entertaining on the stage and screen, rising to the top of their desired professions, our girls will love themselves more because it will have been demonstrated that we are mirror images of whatever is out there, and what is out there can be found only because of us.

parenting and teenagers

Adolescents, regardless of what they may think, are children, growing children, but nonetheless children. Ironically, because of the rapid fluctuations in hormonal levels during puberty and adolescence, preteens and teenagers must be observed sometimes more carefully than infants and toddlers. These years are just as formative and important as the infant years, and now is when the relationship between child and parent sometimes runs amuck.

I hated my teenage years because I couldn't decide who or what I was to be. Of course, I was a beautiful, young black woman, but what did that mean? What was I supposed to do as a beautiful young, black woman? All these terms were being thrown at me at once: "feminist," "liberal," "entrepreneur," "professional," "superwoman." I was so confused by the time I was a freshman in high school, my teachers could do little more than just shake their heads in disbelief when they saw me at times. One day I had beads all over my head and was wearing a denim vest with feathers applied to it trying to look like Chaka Khan. The next day I had on corked platform shoes with glittering stars on the sides and checkered blue and black socks, trying to look like Jody Watley, who was a *Soul Train* dancer at the time. Sometimes I had on what I now call "ownership" T-shirts, announcing who I belonged to (was dating) at the time. Sometimes, I think, I may have even looked normal.

Yet, in the midst of all this, I had the audacity to be an

exceptional honor student at one of the top high schools in Chicago! *What to do? What to do? What to do?* My parents had few ideas. I was the firstborn, unbelievably smart, had relatively little or no common sense. I had become rather promiscuous and began going to nightclubs, although I was quite underage. I devised a way to beat the system in order to legitimately skip classes. I sang lead in a rock band (a very short-lived career) and lead in the church choir. I displayed remarkable acting abilities, discussed being an entrepreneur (at the age of sixteen), and spoke conversational French fluently. I contemplated being a ballerina and perhaps having my own troupe while studying dance at the Fine Arts School. Then I was barred from trying out for cheerleading or pom-pom squad (due to my suspension after they discovered my class-skipping scam), so I created a track-cheerleading squad (my school didn't have one). Actually my boyfriend at the time was a college track star and his former high school had a track cheerleading squad; moreover, I had a crush on one of my school's track stars. Mama said I just wanted to be in a short skirt in front of boys—looking back, I believe she was partially right. Let's see . . . I tried to start my own magazine for black teens, made *Who's Who in American High School Students* a couple of years in a row, and had an annual GPA of B+ or better. There was frequent making out in the backseat of a purple-and-white '67 caddy, and I could shoot pool with the best of hustlers. I also regularly helped look after a little girl stricken with cerebral palsy.

I could continue for another hundred pages or so. Sounds confusing? Try living it. Still, this might be the kind of child you or I have, and what would we do? I believe my parents were as perplexed as I was—a monster on one hand, an existentialist on the other, and a "genius" on yet another. (But . . . that calls for three hands). Thank God for Queen Mothers Reenie and Ginger. When my parents had taken all they could, these beautiful ladies would march in and just love me back into my "right" sense, at least for a little while. Instead of hitting the streets, like so many of our young do now, I could always find more unconditional love and security with my grandmothers. If I needed to, I could spend the night or weekend or stay as long as I (or my parents) needed me to. I was blessed that the validation these kids today seek from gangs I was able to attain within my family.

parenting and support

Unfortunately, for many black women, the job of parenting is performed single-handedly, and with us usually having full-time employment outside of the home, there isn't a great deal of time left over for taking care of ourselves, let alone seeing to community spirit. But you are not the only caretaker of your child; you must simply maintain the primary caretaker role.

Years ago, as I was growing up, not only was I responsible for my sister, but so was the neighbor next door and the neighbor across the street. Both of whom had children of their own and had earned my mother's trust and confidence—especially Queen Mother Reverend Pratt, directly across the street, whose curtains always seemed to know my comings and goings. A friend and I laughed about this recently when we were talking over old times in the old 'hood. And though we found it a source of humor, we also held it in great admiration.

In addition to being watched over by neighbors, my sister and I were sometimes placed in the care of aunts, grandparents, and nannies, all of whom were to be respected as though they were our parents.

Like our mothers and grandmothers, we have to make an effort to construct those types of kindred bonds so that the responsibility of parenting is not overwhelming and, more important, so our children's welfare is guarded by everyone. Fathers, unfortunately, may be absent, but if we have brothers, sisters, cousins, and neighbors with values like our own, we are not alone. Close, loving relationships with other family members and neighbors create a community where neighbors and family trust each other enough to know that the most important community members, the children, are properly cared for. With community harmony and security, our children can grow with the strength of a people behind them. Utopian ideology, I know. But this is what we, black women, must strive for—the best, the ideal. Striving for anything less, working toward second, is illogical, ill-serving, and disrespectful to the self, the people, the children—our gardens, the future.

parenting within our community

To my sisters struggling within the community to make a way for their children: Get to know your neighbors. Learn abut the children because they are what it's really all about. Without them, without taking care to see they are fed, clothed, sheltered, and loved, our people are doomed and so is humanity. If your neighbor's child is suffering, that suffering may spread to your child, to the neighborhood. By not acting on the wrongs you see, especially wrongs you see being imposed on our little ones, you are facilitating the problem, not the solution.

I know what it's like to not be able to walk a neighborhood at night, to live in panic while coming home from work during the day. This is an inescapable fear in many of our areas. But it will never change unless we do something about it, because this is where we live. This is where our children live. The mayor doesn't live in Englewood. The governor doesn't live in South Central. The Vice-President doesn't live in Harlem. And we all know where the President resides. Queen Mother Lady once told me the only way my house is going to be taken care of is if I take care of it myself. And is that not what our neighborhoods are, our houses? Isn't it time our neighborhoods began to deserve to be called that—neighborhoods—and not just "areas," where people of the same color live in different dwellings? We have got to begin taking care of ours—our homes, our areas, our children. We also have to see to our homeless, our addicts, our alcoholics. We might even have to fight our gangs. Indeed, there will be high prices to pay. But pay we will. We must. If we don't, the higher price that we are already paying will continue to increase, which is always the price of neglect. We'll pay with more of our children's and grandchildren's blood.

parenting and role models

It is indeed up to regular folk like you and me to be daily examples of our young and to sisters and brothers who are lost, yet it's ironic that the very African-American celebrities toward whom I feel almost idolatrous awe say they do not want to be considered role models. Oh, well . . . they are. We all are—to any child watching us. Big-money-making drug dealers, basketball players, movie stars, rappers are the ones they want to be like. But teachers, doctors, grocery store clerks, janitors, secretaries, paramedics, police officers, Mom, and Dad are the models they see every day.

As role models who play roles in the daily lives of our children, we owe it to them to earn an Academy Award—to be larger than the beemer-drivin' beeper boy, to exude more energy than the slam-dunkin' backboard crasher, to have a larger intellect and a larger-than-life presence than the latest teen idol. Our roles may not be that big to us personally. We very well may have fallen short of the dreams of our youth. But to our children the parts we play can mean the difference between life on the streets or a life in science, law, finance, or civil service. Are you going to play your role so that you one day see your child in his or her office? Or are you going to play your role so that you one day see your child on his or her very own slab in the morgue?

It is somewhat comprehendible that one would not want to assume the persona of a role model because of the great responsibility involved. But it's a responsibility worth having. Okay, so we're not perfect, and role models are often placed high on that pedestal, near perfection. However, isn't it about time that instead of hearing that tired excuse "Well, I'm not perfect," or "Nobody's perfect," our children hear and see someone striving toward perfection?

It is not as if some perfection is not attainable. Aren't Olympic champions perfectionists? Aren't magna cum laude graduates perfectionists? Aren't cardiologists, professors, certified public accountants, engineers, scientists, and nutritionists perfectionists? How does one obtain a full scholarship to Howard University or Hampton Institute? How does one get accepted into the naval academy at Annapolis? Into West Point?

Isn't there also perfection of the spirit? Mahatma Gandhi, Jesus, Dr. Martin Luther King, Jr., Buddha, Malcolm X all attained that essence. Think of all those individuals you know who make you feel good or special whenever you are in their presence, who make you feel that somebody cares. Perhaps one of them is your grandfather, your aunt, your cousin, your uncle, your neighbor—somebody who always has something good to say about everyone or they don't say anything at all, who always sees the silver lining.

With all the naysayers and doomsdayers in the world, our children need something positive to strive for and someone positive to look up to. As a role model, you can give them that something and that someone. You can show them the world is not the complete travesty it is so often portrayed as. You can show them that the world extends far beyond their own backyard and that moving in that larger world is realistically within their capability. One thing I continually thank God for is that my parents emblazoned in my mind I could do anything I wanted to do, and both went about their own way of providing a living example.

"Well, what about the drive-bys that are happening *now?*" you ask. "Your providing a good example won't stop them," some argue.

All I can tell you is that these may be the most difficult times yet because we are killing each other, but no problem created by humankind is insurmountable and that is what these problems are: *man-made* creations. Crack-cocaine is *man-made,* so its effects can be nullified by man as well. The damning effects of poverty are also man-made and therefore can be eliminated, too. *It's just going to take a hellacious amount of effort and love.* Remember, these are the lethal agents killing our babies—drugs and poverty. So I believe these are the enemies worth fighting.

Perhaps some of the good old-fashioned solutions that some cities are implementing need to be supported by us, for example, earlier curfews and punishing parents for the actions of their children. Perhaps garnering support from neighbors to tear down the crack houses and keep them torn down. If the city won't lend us the wrecking ball, let's take up a collection and hire a private enterprise to do it for us. Then let's build a shelter on that site for homeless families. If the mind can create a question or a problem, the mind can devise an answer or solution.

Let's be role models inside of our homes and communities. Let's show our children that loud quarreling and unabashed swearing are not the methods by which love can be expressed; that discussions can be quiet and adults can agree to disagree and embrace afterward. Let's show them television isn't the only enjoyable form of entertainment available, that reading and exercising can be entertaining and enjoyable also. Let's give them more than a kiss and a key in the morning to see them off to school; let's take them there or plan to see them somehow at lunch. Maybe not everyday, maybe only once a month, but it can be done. Let's show them and their teachers we didn't give birth to impenetrable stones, that we gave birth to future achievers and that is the reason why we visit and phone the school unannounced. Let's show the children down the street that people don't have to be strangers, that food from neighbors doesn't have to be poison.

Yep, that basketball player can really jump, but will he be equally skillful at loving your child? I don't think so. You're the role model, and as such, you get what you give. If you give love, it will come back to you; our children will remember our birthdays and the words to the songs we taught them and the verses to the prayers we read to them. They will still have their commercial icons, all children do, but the individual who will hold the number one spot for the longest time will be the one who loves them the longest and works with them the most. So when celebrities unthinkingly proclaim they aren't role models, don't sweat it. Remember what athletes often say immediately after scoring, with perspiration dripping from their brows, breathing heavily, while looking into the television cameras? "Hi, Mom." That gesture often speaks more to our children than a tapeful of sound bites written by image-making PR people.

24

A Final Note on Living

we've come too far to die

Too many of our African-American ancestors suffered through hell on earth—lynchings, burnings, beatings—for us and our young to ignore their legacy. We and the generations to follow have the advantages our predecessors only dreamed of. Yet, somehow our young, the posterity our ancestors dreamed for, are murdering, raping, plundering, and destroying each other mentally, physically, and spiritually on a daily basis.

Is this why Harriet Tubman risked her life? Frederick Douglass? Sojourner Truth? Dr. Martin Luther King, Jr.? Malcolm X? Is this the legacy they fought and sacrificed for? A legacy of self-hatred, violence, and fear?

We have allowed the anger and frustration we have felt over the centuries to become like spoiled milk churning in the belly of our community. Instead of mischievous little children playing on the streets who eventually grow up to be proud African-American citizens, worthy of honor and distinction, our community is now spitting up mischievous little children who eventually grow to be monsters, rightfully repudiated and detested by everyone. In the city of Chicago, it is estimated that approximately ninety percent of the crime committed in the black community is committed by black males from fifteen to thirty-five years old.[17] These are our children, our products, our young men who are committing these heinous acts. No one else's.

Black people have the inalienable right as human beings to enjoy the fruits produced by the blood, sinew, and labor of our folks and their folks before them. But somehow we are turning away from that right, forgetting the glory of our forefathers, and writhing in a smelly and stifling sea of self-destruction, blame, and self-pity instead of constructively using this country's history and our history to our best advantage.

We just don't seem to like each other, let alone love each other and want to help each other and our community flourish. On the contrary, many of us seem hell-bent on ensuring the failure of the black community. It was only twenty or thirty years ago when African-Americans were rising to meet the demands and promises of our heritage, when we were using the lessons of the past to build a bountiful and powerful future. Now look at us. Young black women have the highest rate of childbirth and the highest rate of below-average basic skill level among young parents. Single, young, black mothers have the highest rate of impoverished households in the nation—56.7 percent. Of black students thirteen to eighteen years of age, 47 percent have seen stabbings, 61 percent have seen shootings, 45 percent have witnessed murders, and 25 percent have been witnesses to all three. And the percentage of black-male-teen arrests has tripled since the mid-eighties.[18]

It is a grim fact that black men have been physically and psychologically victimized to the point that there are presumably a small few who are not in or a product of the criminal justice system and who are not addicted to drugs or alcohol. In response to this, many black women are considering giving up on being with the black man; many sisters already have. But that is no answer. Not when there are good black men available who want to love us if we would only allow them to. Not when these men can help us rid our streets of the monsters spawned by generations of demoralizing dependency (on drugs, alcohol, welfare, etc.) and expediency (through drug selling and other illegal businesses). Not when together we can begin rebuilding a community a people to be proud of.

I realize that the imbalance caused by the perception (whether genuine or not) of there not being enough candidates for mating creates an anxious state of being. But if all we've got, my sisters, is some flour, some water, some salt, and some heat, we just better make sure the biscuits we bake are filling, and we'll work on getting some vegetables tomorrow. And maybe the day after that, we'll find some meat. Black women are so distraught because we can't seem to find any brothers worth our time and energy that through this inaccurate focus, we're losing ourselves. We're working so intensely on captivating men who are deserving of us, the loving and protecting grasp we had on ourselves is slipping. In exasperated searching and/or longing for that knight in shining silver armor, that haystack needle, we're slowly being drawn into a sinkhole of devaluation and disrespect. Brothers are starting to ask what makes *us* worth it? They are asking *who are sisters* to be deserving of the needle in the haystack? Many justifiably feel we've given up on them, so why should quitters deserve the proverbial needle?

I realize loving an individual who is predisposed to rage and frustration is often an irritating and frustrating task. Many times I, observing the often distasteful behavior of some of my brothers, swear if a breakup occurs between me and my husband, the next and only men I will become involved with are those outside of my race. But as I said earlier, that is not the answer to the problem; running away rarely solves anything. If I refuse to try to love my brothers, what am I saying about the love I feel for my people as a whole? What am I saying about the love I feel for myself as an African-American? Yes, I know it can be challenging (to say the least) because our brothers are challenging individuals. Yet, as I learned a while back, usually that which is most valuable is most difficult to attain, requiring a stick-to-it–iveness that can sometimes be very painful.

Even now, I still find there are difficulties I face in our relationship simply because my husband, as a black man, is conditioned with a certain amount of hostility and anxiety. Fortunately, for us, we came across each other's paths at a time when both of us had become comfortable with our individual selves, had come to love our individual selves, and, therefore, were able to extend that love and the necessary patience and understanding to each other. So whenever one of us is down, the other one has enough love in their own emotional bank to offer to the other, to help lift the other out of whatever funk we may be in.

That is the first key to worthwhile relating: you have to love yourself and be comfortable with who you are as an individual in order to be able to love others.

Loving is a wonderful act, but it is also a complex act, asking that we be not-so-pleasant at times and that we be downright difficult at other times. When you love someone, one of your responsibilities is to help him or her if necessary, and sometimes that ain't easy (for either party). Likewise, learning to love ourselves is, at times also unpleasant. For in order to love ourselves wholly, not only do we have to acknowledge our strengths and accomplishments, but we must confront our personal weaknesses, the destructive conditioning we've been exposed to (via family, peers, and environment), our failures, and our fears. This is a lot for one person to contend with while walking the earth, let alone to ask someone else to contend with. Yet, to be able to fully love and appreciate another human being, we have got to be in touch, positively and constructively, with *all* of our own personality traits. *I cannot love you and help you, if first I cannot love me, love all of me, and be willing to help myself with all that I know about me.*

This is where black women can use those three dimensions of our soul I often talk about—Queen Mother, Ms. Thang, and Sista-Girl. Once in touch with our Queen Mother self, we are in touch with the Universe, listening to that First Mind, and observing the big picture; we are concentrating on the nuances of life's creation and paying little heed to the petty things that often destroy life's energy. Ms. Thang helps us exude the confidence we need to attain the goals we set for ourselves; this assuredness also helps to inspire self-confidence in others, which is a part of loving. And in knowing our Sista-Girl self, we are able to work with our strengths and weaknesses, forever in the giving and improving mode, which is also a part of loving.

Each of these dimensions—Queen Mother, Ms. Thang, Sista-Girl—is in all of us. The demand is to determine which dimension should be called upon in answer to the daily situations life confronts us with. The next demand is to strike a balance, an inner harmony among the dimensions, so there is not one which is continually subordinated or superior. It is once this inner accord is acquired that we are our strongest and most dynamic.

Using intelligence, aplomb, and fortitude, we can determine fiction from fact when it comes to the manner in which other people interact with us and choose to portray us. We can assuredly and justly dispute false and misleading images of African-Americans and the African-American community.

Putting our three-dimensional consciousness to work, we can also relax and be comfortable with our physical characteristics, however different or not they may be from those of other races. When we love ourselves, we don't compare ourselves to others, because we realize we are all unique, individuals. Cosmetics are adornment, and skin colors mean nothing. Physical attributes are interesting, but they no more determine or define who we are as individuals, a people, or a community than does the jewelry we choose to wear or not to wear.

Once we comprehend this, we can understand that what we are (almond-skinned or black-olive-skinned, short or tall, small-boned or big-boned, brown-eyed or green-eyed) is of little consequence in comparison to who we are and what we do. When other individuals begin discussing the less important characteristics we possess (such as physical traits), we let it go in one ear and out the other, and then direct them to the content of our character and our manners, as opposed to how we choose to wear our hair.

Focusing on who we are leads us to focus on that in others as well. When we concentrate on the "who," we tend to treat our other Sista-Girls, relatives, and acquaintances with the love, consideration, and interest we feel inside ourselves. Our conversations are more worthwhile because we are no longer fixated on superficialities and are concentrating on substance instead. We want to know what folks think about the latest book, how their children are doing; we want to know how Grandma compares the people in the south with the people in the north and how to prepare the fantastic Jamaican dish we had at our girlfriend's home the other evening. We want to learn about current events and history, as opposed to the latest nail-art design. And that love and substantive concern is returned to us a thousandfold.

When you go out into the world, your relationships become more engaging and purposeful because you bring the world back with you into those relationships.

A part of who we are as human beings is sensual and reproductive, being someone's lover. Loving ourselves means we must learn about and love that sensuality within ourselves as well. We must develop a healthy and realistic approach to sexuality that will allow it to be a delicious and, if wanted, fruitful life experience.

Our expectations must be tempered with reality, and to do that we must read and converse with those who are genuinely knowledgeable, refraining from relying on hear-say and peers, who may be as lacking in knowledge as we are. This way, when we come to experience sex initially, we are not terribly disappointed nor are we swept up in a wave of falsely interpreted emotion.

Also, when we learn from sincere and unbiased sources, we gain information about the sexuality of others and the alternative lifestyles available to human beings. We should be open to learning about homosexuality, bisexuality, asexuality, all of the *alities* there are involving sexual relationships. We are not God, so we are not to judge. We don't want others instructing us on how we should express ourselves sexually, in our own home; we don't want others passing judgment on how we behave sexually in the privacy of our residences, so we cannot tell others how to express themselves nor can we pass judgment on their behavior. Publicly we hold hands with our mates and give each other quick little kisses, expecting neither disapproval nor disdain. We must behave likewise when seeing the public expression of others who may not share in our sexual lifestyle. The more open we are to expressions, the more open we are to the joys of life.

In being open to romantic sentiments and constructive information about sexuality, we must also be open to certain truths. Sex is not love. All sex isn't great. Homosexuality is not a disease. AIDS is not a homosexual disease. Condoms are a must and so are regular gynecological visits if you are sexually active. If you love someone who has not conveyed the same sentiment toward you, having sex is not going to make them love you. Sex cannot fix anything; it can't really break anything either. It is a physical act, meant for enjoyment and procreation, that's all. And like anything else we humans do, we can perform it dangerously or cautiously. Our great truth in sexual relationships is that the choice is always ours, as women.

Understanding our sexuality is part of loving our selves. Our sexuality, our sensuality, and our decision to reproduce are important components of our lives. Logically, the knowledge and understanding of these components should be a prerequisite for becoming seriously involved with anyone. *If we cannot understand, appreciate, and love our sexual selves, how can we understand, appreciate, and love the sexuality of our mates?*

Speaking of mates, okay, loving black men is difficult. But black women have dealt with difficult circumstances ever since we came to this country, and even before then. So this is not a convincing reason for not loving our men. Black men say loving black women can be difficult also. I offer that neither is as difficult as escaping slave-catchers. Come on y'all, *all y'all.* Time to get about the business of bridging the gap instead of doing and saying things that only make it wider.

Now, when we Sista-Girls go about the business of bridging that gap, the first thing we must determine is whether or not we are interested in and ready for serious relationships or whether we are interested in casual relationships. In casual relationships, there is an understanding that both parties are dating other people, that there is no commitment, and when one party desires to stop dating the other, no protracted explanation is necessary. There is nothing wrong or illicit about casual relationships (including casual sex). They can actually help in recovering from the breakup of a serious relationship; they are helpful if you are trying to establish a career; they are helpful if you are still in school. But once the decision has been made, it should be stuck with. If the casual feelings become serious, we owe it to the other party to let them know ASAP, and if the seriousness is not reciprocated, we cannot blame the other party for our pain. We must take it like the strong Sista-Girls we can be and say thanks and walk away with our heads high, remembering a serious relationship with someone else who is better suited for us is probably right around the corner.

Serious relationships are based on a commitment, defined and agreed upon by both partners. The commitment can be just an agreement not to date anyone else or it can be the decision to marry. What distinguishes serious relationships from casual relationships is serious relationships require work, work, and more work. They are usually formed because the parties involved are interested in each other as possible lifetime mates. So great pains are taken to design, build, and sustain these relationships that encompass respect, honesty, and intimacy.

Expressing our feelings is one of the many forms intimacy takes in relationships. Other forms of intimacy are laughing with your mate, walking, caressing, embracing, sharing interests, and sharing glances. Many individuals get bogged down in conveying intimacy in only one or two ways. The relationships grow stale and eventually sour. Remember, it's the little things that count and make your relationship special. So go ahead and tickle his toes.

Whereas intimacy is vital to a loving relationship, lack of intimacy is not the only thing that can cause it to sour. Extreme jealousy, blatant and insensitive infidelity, physical and emotional abuse, and just plain ol' incompatibility are also causes of relationship breakups. These are all valid reasons for letting go. In casual relationships there is really no need to try to work things out or to seek counsel. However, in serious relationships, there is every reason to try to work things out through counseling and whatever other alternatives you may have. Remember, serious relationships are based on commitment, usually a commitment to a lifetime together.

In our individual worlds, we continually experience peaks and valleys. Relationships are no different. We climb a peak and are together on top of the world, only to be pulled back down into the valley by something neither one of us anticipated. Then we see a peak that sits higher than the one we were previously on, and we are motivated once again to begin another climb. Sometimes we need mountain-climbing gear; sometimes we just need a good pair of hiking boots. Sometimes we need wading pants, and then other times we need hip boots and a heavy-duty fishing pole. *This is what serious relationships are about, working and enjoying the work as well as the rewards, working and hating the work but loving the rewards. Then sometimes, it's just not worth the personal pain, suffering, and embarrassment to the self, which is when we have to muster up that wisdom, courage, and strength to just let go.*

Letting go of the bad guys is not so easy as holding on to the good guys. Sometimes the bad guys resemble the good guys so much we're fooled until the very end, when we've lost everything except the hair on our heads and are wondering what the hell happened. Just remember, good brothers want you to have friends of your own; they rarely need financial assistance unless they are entrepreneurial and even then often find ways to sacrifice and take care of their own needs without asking you to sacrifice or provide assistance; they aren't *pro bono* booze models and are willing to give you all the information you need from them to make you feel comfortable and secure; they aren't mechanically or emotionally broke, so you don't have to fix them, and although they love their mothers they do not allow their mom to act as chaperone on your dates, nor is mom provided to you as a yardstick for you to measure up to. *Unlike those other brothers, good brothers are mature and loving, just like good sisters. They may be apprehensive about commitment; most mature people are. One of my favorite sayings is, "I rarely make promises I don't keep because I rarely make promises." And that is what a commitment is, a promise.*

Yet, when a good brother is ready to make a commitment, especially that of marriage, like I said, it is still going to require a lot of effort, time, patience, and understanding from both of you. *When you marry a black man, you double the incidents of racism that you may experience (if you marry a white man, the incidents are usually quadrupled), you marry their partners (the guys usually referred to as buddies), you marry four hundred years of bottled-up anxiety, you marry his family, and you marry his success or failure. Likewise across the board for him. So how does a marriage with all of these heavy components succeed? Through communication, devotion, respect, mutual interests, intimacy, realistic thinking, and adult behavior.* Give all that and share all that with somebody and you are loving them.

Often, a product of that love is children. As black women we must, I emphasize must, prepare ourselves for conception. Parenting is a large responsibility, the greatest responsibility one may have, so you have to be equipped for it. Most of the preparation can be done by eating properly, getting regular exercise and plenty of rest, keeping peace about you and inside of you, and ridding your body and your space of any and all toxins. Daddy has to do the same, as much as possible, because half of the responsibility belongs to him.

Once baby comes along, the work really begins and, from what I've been told, never stops. It slows down after thirty years or so, but it never stops. Not only do we have to guide these little beings through all of the steps we took, but we have to do it gently and try to remember the steps we took that we don't want them to take. With our teenagers, we have to remember there is a lot working on their nerves, and their anxiety is transferred to us because of the important role we play in their lives, although as teenagers they can't admit this, which works on their nerves even more.

We have to seek support from other parents and our

kin. Two eyes or four eyes on one child is just not enough. Like our parents and grandparents, we must ensure that neighbors, teachers, aunts, uncles, and grandparents know the rules of the house and allow them the necessary authority to enforce the rules and issue discipline when rules are broken. We must be willing to do the same for other parents in the community also, realizing this strengthens our community and bridges the fjords.

As parents and part of that community support system, we must also take on our roles as models of behavior for the children. We have got to provide them with examples of loving, positive, dynamic black folk. *Our examples have got to be so strong that our children are not overwhelmed when confronting what can be tremendous peer pressure; examples so strong they do not succumb to the expedient, life-threatening mentality of the street; but examples so grounded they are also streetwise. It is a fine line we must walk, because we cannot become peerlike to them and thereby risk losing their respect and the weight of authority we have in their lives, undermining our very support for them. They must know that we understand their eagerness, curiosity, and mischievousness and sometimes are amused by it, but that we are the adults, the parents, the examples, not their peers, who make the same mistakes and lack experience.*

In loving ourselves and our mates properly, we have some of the tools necessary for loving our children properly, and after that, life is just a journey of love.

instructions from a spider

To you twenty-something, thirty-something, and older Sista-Girls, please explore before you criticize or rebuke. Research. Ask. Be careful, but get out there. Get into sex; get into life.

Get out; go with a friend, someone you trust, if you are

afraid; but step out into the world. It may or may not bite, but you can always bite back. Some of you may ask why firsthand experience is so vital when you can take someone's word for it instead. Well, at times, you should take the word of someone trustworthy. Then there are other times when you should find out for yourself.

Because experience has shown me what crack-cocaine does to my people. Brothers and sisters selling their souls, stealing from their mothers, killing their own. So, after seeing this, I can swear on Queen Mother Ginger's grave that the stuff will never touch my lips.

Because experience has taught me sex on the beach, with the waves crashing in, was something the imagination couldn't faithfully re-create, regardless of how descriptive the paperback romance novel was. So now I can tell you to always carry a blanket when going to those beach excursions—sand burns can be twice as irritating as rug burns.

Because unfortunate experience allows me to explain to my children how drinking excessively, even if you're not driving, is not worth the stomachaches and backaches you will have after "praying to the porcelain god."

Because questionable experience allows me to tell all the Sista-Girls out there about how a casual interlude can help you over a bad breakup and, yes, some "older" men are fantastic lovers and can be very generous. But watch out for the strings attached or lack thereof, depending on what you're looking for.

Sexually, I am sure there are things I do that some folks would not participate in, and likewise, there are things that some folks do that I don't. But for me the choices were made after sampling the pudding, not beforehand, and I feel the better for it.

Life experiences enable us to share and supportively guide others. Without tasting some of life's fares yourself, you cannot validate judgments you may be called upon to make. You may not be able to answer "Why?" Life's most-often asked question.

Again, it's all about yin and yang—balance. Some things you hear and you heed, and some things you simply must experience for yourself. Sometimes the experience will be fortunate, and sometimes it will be unfortunate, but find your symmetry, and enjoy and learn about what life has to offer.

Life is frightening, yes. But if we—Sista-Girls, Ms. Thangs, and Queen Mothers—are to serve on the thrones that are rightfully ours, we must rise to the occasion and look life straight in the eye, going toe-to-toe and head-to-head. You're frightened? Fine, be afraid, but don't let that stop you.

> *A Chinese proverb says,*
> *"The silkworm weaves its cocoon and stays inside,*
> *therefore it is imprisoned;*
> *the spider weaves its web and stays outside,*
> *therefore it is free."*

Notes

1. From *The Sacred Pipe: Black Elk's Account of the Seven Rites of the Oglala Sioux,* recorded and edited by Joseph Brown. Copyright © 1953, 1989, by the University of Oklahoma Press.
2. Philip Novak, *The World's Wisdom: Sacred Texts of the World's Religions* (New York: Harper Collins, 1994), p. 372.
3. Deirdre Mullane, *Crossing The Danger Water: Three Hundred Years of African-American Writing* (New York: Bantam Doubleday Dell, 1993), p. 185.
4. Chaka Khan and Rufus, "I'm Every Woman," © 1978 by Nick-O-Val Music Co, Inc.
5. A study performed by Phyllis A. Katz (discussed in her paper, "Perception of Racial Cues in Preschool Children," 1973).
6. David Ritz, "Janet," *Rolling Stone,* September 16, 1993, p. 38.
7. "Baby Got Back" written by Anthony L. Ray © 1992 Songs of Polygram International, Inc. and Mix-A-Lot Publishing, Inc.
8. The screenplay writers were Edith Sommer and Mann Rubin; the screenplay was based on a novel written by Rona Jaffe.

9. William H. Masters, M.D., Virginia R. Johnson, and Robert C. Kolodny, M.D., *Masters and Johnson on Sex and Human Loving* (New York: Little, Brown, 1988); p. 385.
10. Lynn Witt, Sherry Thomas, and Eric Marcus, *Out in All Directions: The Almanac of Gay and Lesbian America* (New York: Warner Books, 1995). Neil Miller, *Out of the Past: Gay and Lesbian History from 1869 to the Present* (New York: Vintage, 1995). Paul Russell, *The Gay 100: A Ranking of the Most Influential Gay Men and Lesbians Past and Present* (New York: Citadel Press, 1994).
11. Mullane, op. cit., p. 205.
12. Masters, op. cit., p. 333.
13. Information in this section was gathered from, among other sources, (1) *The Kinsey Institute New Report on Sex: What You Must Know to be Sexually Literate* (New York: St. Martin's Press, 1990); and (2) Masters, op. cit.
14. Masters, op. cit., p. 498.
15. This is a reference to the pre-Islamic practice of infanticide, which was abolished by Muhammad.
16. Please note that this was an unscientific sampling.
17. Christiane Klapisch-Zuber, *A History of Women: Silences of the Middle Ages* (Belknap Harvard, 1992). This book provides insightful information regarding the abominable practices organized religion has inflicted on women.
18. Estimated figure provided by a member of the Chicago Police Department.
19. Ted Gest, "Democrats Chance to Attack Crime," *U.S. News & World Report,* February 22, 1993, p. 28. Thomas Toch, "Violence in Schools," *U.S. News & World Report,* November 8, 1993, p. 30. Scott Minerbrook, "A Generation of Stone Killers: Why Cold Blooded Kids Do What They Do," *U.S. News & World Report,* January 17, 1994, p. 33.

Suggested Reading

The American Heritage Dictionary, third edition. Houghton Mifflin, New York: Dell Publishing, 1994.

Angelou, Maya. *Wouldn't Take Nothing for My Journey Now.* New York: Random House, 1993.

Berer, Marge. *Women and HIV/AIDS.* San Francisco: Harper Collins, 1993.

Buscaglia, Leo. *Loving Each Other.* New Jersey: Slack Inc., 1984.

Comfort, Alex, M.D. The New Joy of Sex: A Gourmet Guide to Lovemaking for the Nineties. New York: Pocket Books, 1991.

Cosby, Bill. *Love and Marriage.* New York: Doubleday, 1989.

Cowan, Thomas. *Gay Men and Women Who Enriched the World.* Los Angeles: Alyson Publications, 1992.

DeCotis, Sue, M.D. *A Woman's Guide to Sexual Health.* New York: Simon and Schuster, 1989.

Elmore, Ronn. *How to Love a Black Man.* New York: Warner Books, 1996.

Giddings, Paula. *When and Where I Enter: The Impact of Black Women on Race and Sex in America.* New York: William Morrow, 1984; New York, Bantam Books, 1985.

Giovanni, Nikki. *Racism 101.* New York: William Morrow, 1994.

SUGGESTED READING

Haley, Alex and Malcolm X. *The Autobiography of Malcom X.* New York: Grove Press, 1964.

Heimel, Cynthia. *Sex Tips for Girls.* New York: Fireside, 1983.

hooks, bell. *Killing Rage: Ending Racism.* New York: Henry Holt, 1995.

———. *Sisters of the Yam: Black Women and Self Recovery.* Boston: South End Press, 1993.

Hopson, Darlene Powell, Ph.D., and Derek S. Hopson, Ph.D. *Friends, Lovers and Soul Mates: A Guide to Better Relationships Between Black Men and Women.* New York: Fireside, 1994.

Klapisch-Zubar, Christiane. *A History of Women: Silences of the Middle Ages.* Boston: Belknap Harvard, 1992.

Masters, William H., M.D., Virginia E. Johnson, and Robert C. Kolodny. *Masters and Johnson on Sex and Human Loving.* New York: Little, Brown, 1988.

McCall, Nathan. *Makes Me Wanna Holler: A Young Black Man in America.* New York: Vintage Books, 1994.

Miller, Neil. *Out of the Past: Gay and Lesbian History from 1869 to the Present.* New York: Vintage Books, 1995.

Mullane, Deirdre. *Crossing the Danger Water: Three Hundred Years of African-American Writing.* New York: Bantam, Doubleday, Dell, 1993.

Reinisch, June M., Ph.D., with Ruth Beasley, M.L.S. *The Kinsey Institute New Report on Sex: What You Must Know to be Sexually Literate.* New York: St. Martin's Press, 1990.

Sterling, Dorothy. *We Are Your Sisters: Black Women in the Nineteenth Century.* New York: W.W. Norton, 1984.

Subotnik, Rona, M.F.C.C., and Gloria Harris. *Surviving Infidelity—Making Decisions, Recovering from the Pain.* Holbrook, MA: Adams Media Corp., 1994.

Taylor, Susan L. *Lessons in Living.* New York: Anchor Books, 1995.

Vanzant, Iyanla. *Acts of Faith.* New York: Fireside, 1994.

———. *Tapping the Power Within: A Path to Self-Empowerment for Black Women.* New York: Harlem River Press, 1992.

West, Cornel. *Race Matters.* New York: Vintage Books, 1993.

Williamson, Marianne. *A Woman's Worth.* New York: Random House, 1993.

Witt, Lynn, Sherry Thomas, and Eric Marcus. *Out in All Directions: The Almanac of Gay and Lesbian America.* New York: Warner Books, 1995.

Yaffe, Maurice, and Elizabeth Fenwick. *Sexual Happiness: A Practical Approach.* Consultant editor, Raymond C. Rosen, Ph.D., New York: Henry Holt, 1988.